W9-BZB-221

FORGED IN HONOR

ALSO BY THE AUTHOR

Charlie Mike
*The Iron Men**
The Hill
The Last Run
The Expendables

*Published by Ballantine Books

FORGED
IN
HONOR

Leonard B. Scott

BALLANTINE BOOKS • NEW YORK

DISCARD

PUBLIC LIBRARY
EAST ORANGE, NEW JERSEY

Cop1

Copyright © 1995 by Leonard B. Scott

All rights reserved under International and Pan-American Copyright Conventions. Published in the United States by Ballantine Books, a division of Random House, Inc., New York, and simultaneously in Canada by Random House of Canada Limited, Toronto.

Maps by Mapping Specialists, Ltd.

Library of Congress Cataloging-in-Publication Data

Scott, Leonard B.
Forged in honor / Leonard B. Scott.
p.   cm.
ISBN 0-345-39009-1
I.   Title
PS3569.C647F67   1995
813'.54—dc20   95-2004
CIP

Manufactured in the United States of America

First Edition: June 1995

10   9   8   7   6   5   4   3   2   1

*To the people of Burma
who keep alive the hope of freedom
in their country.*

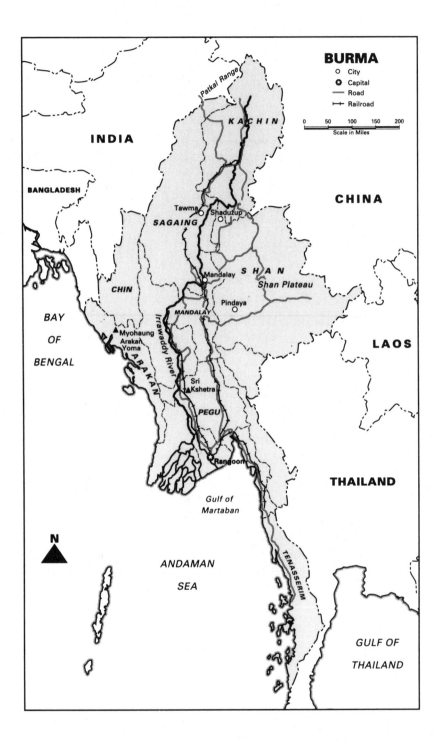

BURMA

○ City
◎ Capital
— Road
⊢−⊢ Railroad

0   50   100 150 200
Scale in Miles

INDIA

BANGLADESH

CHINA

Patkai Range

K A C H I N

Tawma   Shaduzup

SAGAING

CHIN

Mandalay   S H A N

Shan Plateau

Pindaya

MANDALAY

BAY

OF

BENGAL

Myohaung
Arakan
Yoma

ARAKAN

Irrawaddy River

Sri
Kshetra

PEGU

LAOS

Rangoon

THAILAND

Gulf of
Martaban

N

ANDAMAN

SEA

TENASSERIM

GULF OF

THAILAND

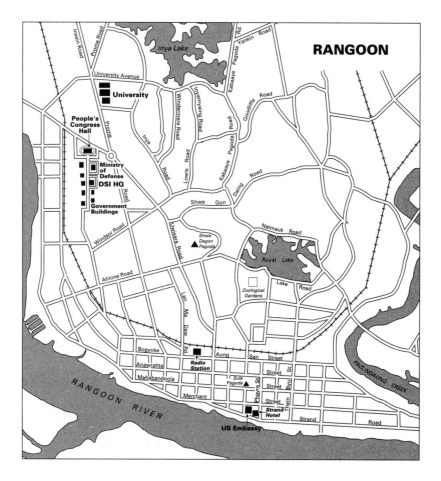

RANGOON

Inya Lake

Insein Road
Prome Road
Yankin Road
Kabaaye Pagoda Rd.

University Avenue

University

Windermere Road
Inyamyaing Road
Goodliffe Road

People's
Congress
Hall

Prome

Inya

Kabaaye Pagoda Road

Lowis Road

Ministry
of
Defense

DSI HQ

Government
Buildings

Daing Road

Road

Shwe Gon

Natmauk Road

Windsor Road

Uwisara Road

Shwe
Dagon
Pagoda

Royal Lake

Ahlone Road

Lake Road

Zoological
Gardens

Lan Ma Daw Rd.

Bogyoke

Aung San Street

Anawrahta

Radio
Station

Street

Street

Byu St.

Mahabandoola

Sule
Pagoda

Street

Thein St.

Phayre St.

Merchant

Street

Strand
Hotel

Strand Road

US Embassy

RANGOON RIVER

PAZUNDAUNG CREEK

FORGED IN HONOR

PROLOGUE

PRESENT DAY

June, Rangoon, Burma

With a groan the heavy chain tightened and slowly began winding around the wrecker's winch. Feeling sick to his stomach, Gilbert Halley, chief of the Drug Enforcement Administration's Country Team, watched the recovery operation with dread. He had received a call only thirty minutes before from the Rangoon chief of police, who told him that one of his agents had been involved in an accident and was believed dead.

Halley's gut tightened as the light blue Toyota emerged from the muddy canal and was pulled onto the bank. He moved closer as the stinking water rushed out of the open windows. A Rangoon police officer opened the car door. Halley looked inside, praying his agent had somehow lived. But the body was not in the car.

Another embassy car skidded to a halt in front of the taped police barrier. The CIA chief of station, Alex Manning, got out of the vehicle along with the military defense attaché colonel. Manning motioned for the colonel to check the DEA agent's car, then looked over his shoulder to see where their tail had parked. The Burmese junta's secret police, or DDSI, team that had followed them from the embassy had pulled their white Mazda to the curb a block away. Manning patted his driver's shoulder. "Keep your eyes on them."

As Manning approached the DEA chief, Gilbert Halley said, "It's Drisco's car, but his body isn't in it. I think we should talk to witnesses who saw his car go into—"

Manning raised his hand to cut Halley off and nodded toward the nearby local police. "Don't talk here."

The colonel strode back from the car and pinned Manning with a worried stare. "There's no body and no manifests . . . nothing. Are you thinking what I'm thinking?"

Manning visibly tightened as he surveyed the police and crowd behind the barrier for warning signs. "Yeah, it could be a setup. Everybody get in my car *now*."

Halley didn't move. "But what about the witnesses? Aren't we—"

The colonel took hold of the DEA chief's arm. "Move it, goddamn it! Have your driver follow us, and tell him to stay right on our ass."

Only a few blocks from the American compound, the two embassy cars came to a stop in traffic. In the lead vehicle, the CIA driver impatiently drummed his fingers on the steering wheel as he kept his eyes in constant motion, checking the people on the busy sidewalks and the occupants of the cars stopped beside him.

In the backseat, Gilbert Halley glared at the CIA chief of station, seated beside him. "What the hell is going on?"

Manning took a cassette tape from his shirt pocket and handed it to the colonel in the front seat.

Manning sat back and looked at the DEA chief. "Gil, as you know, all incoming calls into the embassy are taped. This one came in at zero-nine-forty-three hours to my office."

The colonel put the cassette into the car's tape player and pushed the Play button. Immediately the excited words of the missing DEA agent filled the car.

"Mr. Manning, this is Pete Drisco. I'm at the airport. I got it. Please listen and don't interrupt me. I don't have much time. I think they saw me checking the manifests. I've got the proof with me now; I've made copies of all their manifests with the names and destinations in the U.S. where they went. They've been using phony visas and infiltrating into . . . oh shit, I see them coming. I'm leaving now."

Halley closed his eyes and lowered his head. "Jesus, the bastards got to him first."

Manning nodded dejectedly. "The secret police probably took him to Dinto prison and tortured him to see what else he knew. They'll get rid of the body. It would be too incriminating."

Halley gazed out the car window and clenched his fists. "A year's work gone. Damn those DDSI bastards!"

The colonel shifted his body around and looked over the seat toward the two men. "General Swei must be real worried to order a hit on one of our men. Something has to be going down."

Manning showed agreement by wrinkling his brow. "They've got to be making a move. As soon as we get back to the office, order a satellite photo run over the probable drug labs to see if there's an increase in activity. I'll talk to my Brit and French counterparts and see what they've turned up."

The car began moving again and passed the cause of the traffic jam. Two wrecked cars were being pushed to the curb. The driver sighed in relief and sped down Merchant Street toward the small American Embassy compound.

Feeling his stomach twisting into knots, Halley asked, "What are we going to tell Drisco's wife?"

The driver stopped in front of the iron gate of the American Embassy. The Marine guard inside the small guardhouse recognized the driver and vehicle and pushed a large button on the control panel. As the gate began sliding back on heavy rollers, the guard stepped out of the shack and leaned over to speak to the passengers. "Gentlemen, the ambassador wants to see you as soon as—" He heard the sound first, then caught movement out of his right eye. He pivoted to look at a large truck speeding down Merchant Street. "What the hell is that fool—"

The young Marine suddenly jerked backward and sank from view as bullets tore into the left side of the car. Showered with shards of glass, Gilbert Halley fell forward in his seat and felt as if he had been hit in the side with a red-hot sledgehammer. The colonel screamed, "GET OUT OF—" He never finished the sentence for he was splattered with hot blood and brain tissue when a bullet blew through the driver's head. Unhurt, Alex Manning reached for a door handle, but it was too late. The fast-moving truck suddenly turned, jumped the curb, and plowed into the right side of the car. The heavy extended bumper smashed through the car's window and frame, severing both Manning's and the colonel's upper torsos.

Halley was thrown out of vehicle by the impact and landed beside the dead Marine guard, who lay in a pool of blood. Writhing in excruciating pain, he heard the roaring engine and the screech of bending metal as the truck shoved the wreckage through the open gate toward the chancery entrance. Screaming, the DEA chief rolled over onto his stomach and faced the embassy just as the truck crashed into the glassed-in entrance and disappeared in a blinding explosion. The searing blast cloud, traveling at twenty-two thousand feet per second, abruptly ended Halley's screams and his pain.

5 June, Washington, D.C.

An accident at the Chain Bridge exit had ground the four-thirty westbound traffic on the George Washington Parkway to a halt. Trapped in the metal logjam, a computer programmer who had left his office in Foggy Bottom thirty-five minutes before, sat in his old Ford station wagon telling himself to remain calm. The traffic had to start moving again soon. The unseasonably warm temperature had already caused his shirt to stick to his back, and perspiration was dripping down his forehead. He was telling himself for the third time that they would soon begin moving when he saw the temperature-gauge panel light flash on. Dammit! He slapped the steering wheel, knowing he couldn't stay in the bumper-to-bumper traffic and chance burning up his engine. He saw a scenic turnout just ahead and eased the Ford onto the shoulder, praying the wagon would make it that far before seizing up. On the exit ramp he breathed easier and took his foot off the accelerator, letting the wagon roll into a parking place.

Getting out of the car, he walked to the edge of the tree-lined embankment that overlooked the Potomac River and took in a deep breath. The panoramic view before him was breathtakingly beautiful. Far below him the slow-moving, dark green river flowed eastward toward the Chesapeake. Stately oaks, sugar gums, and maples of every shade of green covered the high banks. The finishing touch was the crystal-clear, light blue sky that held not a wisp of a cloud.

Then a man rowing a scull upriver came into view. The small craft was causing a V wake that rippled and expanded in perfect symmetry toward the banks. The sculler was wearing only shorts and a faded blue baseball cap. His body was lean and hard, glistening with sweat. He was in perfect rhythm, digging the oars in and pulling back, shooting the craft forward over the dark green water as if it were on ice. The computer programmer stood and watched the man's efforts. He was out there all alone, doing what he wanted, while the rest of them grew fat and tried to pay the bills. The programmer watched until the scull was out of sight.

His chest feeling as if it were about to burst, Joshua Hawkins rested his oars and threw back his head for a breath. Sweat stung his eyes. He reached down and threw water up into his face and took several more deep breaths to recover. Not feeling dizzy anymore, he grasped the oars again and began a slow turn for the long crawl back to the boathouse. He felt the high coming on and accepted it as the reward for his efforts. Maybe, he thought, he might even have a chance in the fall race.

For the first time since beginning the workout, he looked around him to take in the beauty and serenity of the part of the river he loved the best. The land past the Francis Scott Key Bridge to the west always seemed like another world. Unlike the wider lower river, where the park-lined banks could not conceal the city's hustle and bustle, the narrow upper river was enclosed and protected by high, tree-covered enbankments.

Josh took it all in, refreshing his soul and rebuilding his strength. Then he slid forward on the rolling seat, extended the oars out, brought his legs up almost to his chest, and then scooted back, digging the oars in and pulling with his arms and shoulders while pushing back with his legs. After only two strokes he had the rhythm again, and his body and years of practice took over without the need for conscious thought.

The sweltering heat and the sound of the water rippling off the prow reminded him of another time and another river, long ago. He shook his head. It had been more than thirty years since his great adventure had begun and ended in the country that had been front-page news the past two days. When he'd first seen the television report on the embassy bombing in Burma, he had felt a chill. The memories of his childhood and young manhood there had flooded over him, and he'd been unable to think of anything else.

PART I

CHAPTER 1

Burma, June 1960

"Joshua, don't get so close to the side. You might fall in."

"Aw Mom, I'm not gonna fall in."

"Do as I say, young man!"

Blond-haired, eleven-year-old Joshua Hawkins moved his feet back a few inches but still kept his grip on the wood rail of the old paddle-wheeler. He listened to the chugging of the ancient diesel engine as he took in the strangeness of the world to which his mother had brought him. Six feet below, Burma's Irrawaddy River swirled and boiled like thick, reddish-brown mud soup, staining everything it touched. The far jungle-covered banks were impenetrable walls of vines entangled with huge trees in every shade of green, yellow, and brown. Monkeys occasionally screamed in the treetops. Siapans glided by going downstream, piled high with colorful fruits, vegetables, and bamboo-caged animals that Joshua had never seen before. He marveled at the delicious smells of strange foods cooking in pots on the paddle wheeler's two decks. It sure ain't Kansas, he thought to himself. It already seemed like a month instead of just a week since he had left Leavenworth, where he had been born. His mother had been a grade-school teacher in the small town but had come to Burma to join her new husband. Sarah Brown was determined to save the heathen mountain people who were without benefit of God's word. If anybody could do it, Joshua knew, his mother would be the one. Joshua often likened his mother, only a little over five feet tall and no more than one hundred pounds, to the cartoon character the Tasmanian Devil, who was

11

always leveling everything in his path. Sarah was like that—once she adopted a cause, she was relentless. No Leavenworth store owner could refuse to give her a contribution for the Church Homeless Fund or Christian Veterans in need of a Thanksgiving dinner.

Joshua glanced back at his mother and smiled to himself, knowing she had been too confined in the small town. Henry Lamar Brown had truly given her a chance to unleash her god-given talent. Pastor Brown had come to Leavenworth four months earlier to speak at the church and show color slides of his missionary work in Burma. That night Sarah swore God had spoken to her and told her the mission was the way to his glory. Henry Brown was hopelessly smitten, and two weeks after meeting they were married. Henry returned to Burma a few weeks later, and Sarah began to prepare for her and Joshua's departure as soon as the Baptist Fellowship in New York approved their travel.

Joshua shifted his gaze back to the muddy river and wondered what it would be like to have a dad. He'd asked about his real father years ago, when he'd become old enough to understand he was different from other boys in not having a daddy. His mother had sat him down and told him Benjamin Hawkins had been a soldier and died only a day after Joshua was born. Benjamin was a good Christian man, she'd said, and the Lord had seen fit to call him to heaven since he needed soldiers in heaven. Sarah never spoke of him again until just after she and Henry were married. Then she had taken Joshua's hand and told him he would always be a Hawkins and that he should be proud of his family name. "Benjamin wanted a son more than anything in this world," she'd said. "He got you, Joshua, and he's looking down from heaven watching you grow. I know he's real proud."

Joshua lifted his eyes toward the cloudless sky, hoping his mother was right and that his real father could see all the way to Burma.

Pastor Brown, a mountain of a man with a full, dark brown beard, met the boat at Namti with a kiss for his new wife and a handshake for Joshua. He had porters load the baggage into two relics—World War II American ammunition carriers—and the great adventure continued. In two days they traveled just ninety miles, over the worst roads Joshua had ever seen. At least ten times they had to ford streams because bridges were washed out; on the second day they had to stop to dig out a mud slide that covered the rutted dirt road. Constantly climbing, they finally left the oppressive heat of the jungle river country and lowlands and entered the pine- and teak-covered mountains of northern Burma. They saw no other motorized vehicles, only mule- and bullock-drawn wagons filled with brown, gnarled people wearing turbans, who chattered and waved, some with smiles and

some with hostile glares. On the third day, after negotiating a twisting mountain road barely big enough for their carriers, they arrived at
the mission in the village of Shaduzup.

Joshua had expected grass-covered huts, but there were none.
Henry Brown was a builder of more than faith, and he had done miracles in the five years he'd been the pastor of Shaduzup. He had constructed a church, a school, a dormitory, and a residence on the
outskirts of the village. And he had also helped rebuild the village
houses with clay bricks and pine boards. It wasn't the town of Leavenworth, but it wasn't a heathen camp with naked natives running
around either. All the villagers were dressed in too-big Western clothing from the missionary barrels sent from the States, and most spoke
broken English except for words like "Jesus Christ" and "salvation,"
which were pronounced flawlessly.

That first night, Henry explained that Joshua and Sarah would have
to learn a new way of life. There was no electricity or phones, televisions, radios, or even indoor toilets. All drinking water had to be
boiled, and vegetables could not be eaten raw unless scrubbed and
soaked in chlorine-treated water for a full day. All major supplies had
to be ordered from Rangoon and shipped up the Irawaddy, then
trucked over the horrible road they had traveled to the mission. Supplies often didn't arrive for months. Some canned goods were included among the supplies, but they were expensive so the mission
ate mostly local food. Mail came about every two weeks, depending
on the weather and the condition of the road.

Henry explained that the Burmese who lived in the lowlands and
major cities considered themselves the true Burmese. Most were Buddhist and were not open to God's word. The rest of the population
was made up of mountain tribes. Here in the northern mountains, the
most predominent tribe was the Shan.

Henry led his new family out onto the covered front porch and
waved his huge hand toward the mountains. "The Shan are like the
Mayans of Mexico," he said. "Centuries ago the Shan kingdom was a
great nation ruling all of Burma. But like the Mayans, for unknown
reasons their nation crumbled. Today, the Shan live here in small villages in the northern mountains they call the Shan State. Most of
them are animistic, believing in forest gods, myths, and superstition.
They have many heathen customs—they take more than one wife,
and they will not bury their loved ones until enough wealth is ob-
tained for a proper funeral party. In many of the villages petrified bodies have sat in corners of huts for years. Also, a woman cannot marry
until a large dowry is raised by her family. In several of the villages I
have visited, there have been no marriages for three years.

"The mountain Shan have disgusting personal habits. They smoke huge, rolled-up leaves filled with horrid-smelling tobacco and chew something called betel nut, which turns their mouths red. Another vice is their love of zu, an alcoholic drink made from rice. Any event such as a birth or a death or a stranger's visit—or even a trivial thing like a change in the weather—calls for a drinking celebration. Drunkenness is very common."

Henry shifted his intense eyes back to his family. "This country is very dangerous, filled with evil men. Bandits roam in packs. There are no police or government soldiers here, so you must be careful when outside Shaduzup and always have elders of the church with you when traveling. We do have a Sawbaw, a warlord of sorts who is supposed to protect us, but I have found him to be nothing more than a bandit himself."

Seeing Joshua's wide eyes expand even more on hearing about the bandits, Sarah tried to change the subject. "Tell Joshua about the politics of the country."

Henry leaned against the porch rail. "Since Britain gave up its Burma colony at the end of World War II, the Shan have wanted independence from the Burmese government, but it has never been granted. The Burmese government is ruled by the army, which has spent years trying to bring the rebellious Shan under control. The army has sent units into the north to stamp out the resistance, but they have always met with defeat. It has been a standoff for years now, and we must thank God for this. It gives us time to show these people the only way to true peace is through God's word."

Henry broke into a smile and again waved his arm toward the darkened mountains. "The devil has corrupted their hearts and souls with ignorance, but we will deliver them. It is a fertile land awaiting only God's word, and we are the chosen ones to show these wretched souls the light."

"Amen," Sarah said, staring at the mountains with determination.

Joshua nodded to show his support but didn't really understand everything. The part about the fierce Shan rebels, however, did get his attention, and he hoped he would be able to see some. It would be neat.

They used the first days in their new home to get settled and learn their duties. Sarah would be a teacher and nurse and Joshua would be a student, a wood and egg gatherer, and a helper for the native cook and gardener. Although Henry had a Shan assistant pastor and four other native church helpers, it was evident to both newcomers that the mission revolved around Henry. And to him, the mission school was the key, for the Shan people's young, not as biased as their elders by the old customs and traditions, were more open to God's word. It was the young whom Henry expected to become God's disciples and to go out in the wilderness and convert more of their own. The mission taught just over fifty children. Most were from Shaduzup, but twenty were from outlying villages and lived at the school dormitory.

It was the young age of the children that was a problem for Joshua. Most of the boys were nine or younger, so he found himself the oldest boy in the school. He had no one to play with or talk to except the schoolgirls. Henry explained that Shan families needed all boys over ten to work. Joshua learned to do his chores quickly after his classes so that he could take off and explore and get away from his inquisitive female classmates. Within days he learned his way around the village and met some boys his age, but as Henry had said, they were working—gathering wood, tending the crops and bullocks. Despite Henry's warnings, Joshua ventured a little farther each day and soon found that the whitewashed Christian world Henry had built was only a very small island surrounded by a sea of green.

Beyond the whitewashed village and cultivated fields, Joshua learned, the real northern mountain Shan lived in the protective darkness and majesty of the forest. These people were alive, laughing, crying, praying to stones and to gods of the forest. None wore the Western clothes from the mission barrels but rather long ankle-length, homespun skirts, loose-fitting shirts, and the traditional blue turban of the Shan. They were small people, almost delicate looking, but they were the strongest people Joshua had ever seen. Their lives revolved around working and hunting to provide food for the family, yet they lived within a web of customs and traditions that affected all that they did. Joshua sometimes pitied them for their hardships, but more often he envied them, for they were proud of who they were.

A month after arriving in Shaduzup, Joshua was playing on the bank of a small river that ran five hundred yards below the village. He and the younger boys from the school were trying to spear fish like the elder fishermen but were having no luck, so they soon began jumping off the huge boulders into the cool, inviting water. Joshua was poised to leap when the boys' laughter was drowned out by the loud clanging of the mission church bell. Every head turned toward the distant steeple, the radiant smiles replaced with looks of terror. Joshua froze when he saw the other boys' reaction. The bell wasn't ringing as it did on Sunday with three-second intervals between clangs. Instead it was clanging rapidly. Joshua turned to ask what the ringing meant, but the other boys were all running toward the village as if their lives depended on it.

Scared, Joshua joined in the flight to Shaduzup as fast as he could
run. His fear doubled when he got within a hundred yards of the first
buildings, for he could see screaming villagers running hysterically
toward the church. Some carried chickens and small pigs, others
pieces of furniture, and all were pushing their terrified children ahead
of them. As Joshua got closer he saw two of the village men carrying
antique-looking rifles. Unlike the other people, they weren't running,
but they did have the same look of terror on their faces. Joshua slowed
and yelled to one of the men. "U Wat, what is happening?"

"Bandits! Run to the mission!"

Joshua came to an abrupt halt and looked in the direction the two
men were facing. There were three men on small, shaggy ponies,
stopped on a rise just out of rifle range. They were bearded and wore
filthy white turbans and light green uniform shirts and pants. They
had bandoleers strapped to their chests and rifles slung over their
shoulders. Joshua's heart felt as if it were going to pound through his
chest, but at the same time he was strangely thrilled to see actual
bandits. Then the center horseman turned in his saddle and waved toward the forest behind him.

Joshua stopped breathing as at least thirty more horsemen rode out
of the trees in a perfect line. Unlike the first three riders, the larger
formation was all dressed in dark blue turbans, jackets, and pants.
Swords hung from the men's belts, and bandoleers crisscrossed their
chests. With stiff backs, heads and eyes set to the front, they advanced
with their rifles resting menacingly across the front of the saddles.

The two village men lowered their old guns and slowly backed up,
one of them gasping, "The Chindit."

Joshua was frozen in place, unable to take his eyes off the approaching men. One of the horsemen raised a hand and barked a command. The mounted formation came to a halt, and a single rider
galloped from the tree line on a sleek, jet-black horse. His turban was
cobalt blue but his billowing clothes were raven black. A huge curved
sword hung from his belt and glistened in the sun as the line of horsemen made a gap for him to pass.

Joshua finally took a breath, looked behind him, and saw that the
village men had abandoned him. The village had fallen oppressively
silent. Then he heard the dull thuds of the fast-approaching hoofbeats.
The sound became louder and louder until Joshua could feel the
ground vibrate beneath his feet. He slowly turned back to face the
lone rider who was bearing down on him. Everything within Joshua's
being was screaming for him to run, but the approaching rider's mag-
netic eyes held him in place.

The rider reined back and brought the snorting animal to a dusty halt only a few feet away. After keeping his stare on the boy for a full ten seconds, the rider finally spoke. "So—you alone challenge me?"

Joshua tried to speak, but he had no saliva. All he could think to do was nod. The rider burst out laughing and waved his men forward. He was still laughing as he leaned over and offered his hand. "Little Sao, a brave soldier such as you must ride."

Joshua was mesmerized by the regal bearing of the man before him. The rider was not Shan; he was big and his face was long and angular as if chiseled from stone. His piercing eyes were hazelnut brown and seemed to look right through Joshua. The boy's gaze slowly lowered to the leader's offered hand. On his wrist was a thin silver band that gleamed in the hot sun.

Taking a breath for strength, Joshua raised his arm.

In a single movement the leader grasped the boy's hand and swung him up on the saddle behind him. The spell broken as the rider prodded the horse forward, Joshua asked excitedly, "Are you really a bandit?"

The rider bellowed with laughter and translated for the other riders what the boy had asked. They all laughed and smiled but none spoke. The leader patted Joshua's leg. "I have killed men for calling me such things, but you are a brave lad and I will answer you true. I am many things, little Sao, but a bandit I am not. I am your Protector."

The leader and his horsemen rode through the deserted village and halted in front of the church, where the people of Shaduzup had gathered. Over two hundred villagers stood behind their pastor, whose bearded face was set in stone. The villagers all bowed their heads toward the lead rider, but Henry only lowered his eyes for an instant before speaking coldly. "You put fear into the hearts of us all, Chindit. We thought your men were bandits."

The leader's eyes lost their gleam and his face tightened. "Greetings and blessings *to you too*, Pastor Brown. I see you still have not learned your manners." The rider then smiled and dipped his chin. "I am truly sorry for the mistake. My lead scouts dress as bandits because we are on the hunt for three gangs that have been reported in this area. Even you, a godly man, can see the tactical advantage of this deception."

"Joshua!" Sarah cried out, seeing her son. She broke out of the crowd and ran toward the leader.

The tall rider grasped Joshua's arm and gently lowered the boy to his frightened mother. He bowed his head and touched his turban in a theatrical way. "I have heard of your beauty, Mrs. Brown, but the stories pale in your presence. It is a pleasure to finally meet you." Sitting back erect in the saddle, he spoke in a deeper voice. "I am Sawbaw Xu

Rei Kang, Horseman and Protector of the Ri and Chindit of the Forest
. . . at your service, kind lady."

Frightened, Sarah backed up until alongside Henry. "Who is this
man?" she whispered.

Henry, not hiding his disdain, kept his cold stare on the leader as
he spoke. "This is our warlord who says he protects us from the bandits, but for a price. He calls himself the Protector of the Ri—which is
the land and people that encompass the northern region of which we
are a part. He is better known as 'Chindit,' which means 'the lion.' He
has fought for years against the government—"

"They fight *me*!" bellowed Xu Kang. "We are a free people! We will
never be puppets to the junta."

"You cause death and destruction with your fighting!" Henry fired
back. "You blackmail these people with this pretense of bandits!"

U Do, the Shan assistant pastor of the church, quickly stepped in
front of Henry and bowed his head up and down. "I apologize for our
pastor, Chindit. He does not know of the bandits that plundered our
village before you came. We gladly pay for your protection."

Xu Kang ignored the small assistant pastor as his cold glare bored
holes into Henry's forehead. "You must learn manners, Pastor Brown.
I am hunting bandits and have fought two battles with them in the
past two days. They are more brazen and come farther south, but they
are not the biggest problem. The Wa are returning."

The villagers gasped when they heard the word *Wa* and pressed
closer together.

"The Wa were civilized years ago," Henry snapped back.

Xu Kang shook his head as if dealing with a child. "Ah, but many
are returning to their old ways and are collecting heads. Several packs
have come back to the mountains to reclaim their land. The junta has
allowed them to return and has even given them arms. The junta believes the Wa will make war on us as they did before." The saddle
creaked as Xu Kang leaned forward and pinned Henry with his eyes.
"You see, Pastor, as I've told you before, the junta wants all Shan
dead. We mean nothing to them. One day, perhaps, you will come to
understand."

Henry rolled his shoulders back. "You endanger us all by your presence here. If the government learns of your coming and of our people
paying you, they will close the mission. Please, leave and take nothing. In God's name I beg you to leave us."

Xu Kang's chiseled features broke into a cruel smile. "Pastor, you
have been my guest here for years and still you know so little. The
government will never know. Your flock knows that if they speak of
me I will know of it and the offender will be nailed by the tongue to a

tree. The Chindit has spies everywhere and knows everything within the Ri. Calm yourself, for I have not come for payment. I have come to deal with the bandits and the Wa . . . and to give you my son."

Raising his hand, Xu Kang made a circling motion. The horsemen behind their leader reined their ponies out of the way to make room for two riders. An old, barrel-chested man with a huge white moustache rode forward leading another horse with a small, black-haired boy perched in the saddle.

Joshua stepped closer in awe of the old rider's moustache, for it was the strangest and most beautiful one he had ever seen. The snow-white whiskers flowed downward from beneath the old man's brown nose but split just above his lip and flowed upward again to be swept back almost to his ears.

As if feeling Joshua's gaze, the old rider looked at the boy and gave him a wink. Closing his open mouth, Joshua saw a glint coming from the old rider's right wrist. He was wearing a silver bracelet identical to that of the leader.

Xu Kang motioned to the thin, dark-haired boy without looking at him. "This is my son. He is twelve and his name is Stephen, named so by his Christian mother who has joined her ancestors. I promised his mother the boy would be educated and not be a Sawbaw like his father. Take him, Pastor Brown, and teach him your ways. He speaks English as I do but needs your school words and thoughts."

Henry quickly stepped forward, took hold of Xu Kang's horse's bridle, and spoke in a harsh whisper. "You can't leave him here, Chindit. The government will find out—"

Xu Kang cut him off with a wave of his hand and motioned toward the old man. "I leave Master Horseman Bo Bak here to teach your village men how to protect themselves. He will also ensure silence." Xu Kang raised his chin but kept his penetrating stare on Henry. "Pastor, my son stays. I made a vow to his mother. If you know anything of Shan honor you know I must fulfill my promise."

Henry held the Sawbaw's gaze for several moments before lowering his head with a reluctant nod.

Xu Kang's hard expression softened, and he bowed toward Sarah. "It was indeed a pleasure, Mrs. Brown." Turning his attention to Joshua, the Sawbaw smiled. "You have a Shan Horseman's heart, little Sao. I shall always remember your challenge to me."

The leader glanced only a moment at his son, and his face showed excruciating pain. He reached out to touch the boy's shoulder but suddenly withdrew his hand and reined his black stallion around. Kicking the horse's flanks, he was in a full gallop in seconds and his troop with him. In a moment all that remained was a cloud of dust.

The old rider's creaking saddle broke the silence as he climbed down from his pony. "Greetings and blessings, Sao. I am Master Horseman Bo Bak, the teacher."

Henry eyed the old man coldly. "Never call me Sao—there is only one Lord. That is the first lesson of your stay in Shaduzup."

The Horseman's leather face cracked into a disarming smile. "And you have many lessons to learn as well. The Shan custom of greeting is always 'greetings and blessings.' You insulted my Sawbaw by not giving the proper greeting. I will learn from you, Pastor Brown, but I ask that you too learn and respect our customs."

Sarah nudged her husband. "Henry, the people."

Henry broke his glare from the old man and turned to face the villagers. Raising his hands, he bellowed, "Return to your homes, the danger is over. I will have a special prayer service tonight for deliverance from the evildoers the Chindit has warned us about. Go to your homes knowing Jesus is with you."

As Henry was speaking Sarah walked up to the mounted boy, who was staring at the vanishing dust cloud. She reached up to touch his hand and spoke softly. "Come with me, Stephen. I'm happy to have you as a new student."

The boy didn't move. He sat staring toward the north with tears running down his cheeks.

CHAPTER 2

"How's Stephen doing?" Sarah asked Joshua as he came up the front porch steps.

"He's in the dorm but won't talk to anybody."

Sarah turned to give the man across the table an icy glare. "Your Sawbaw is a heartless man."

Horseman Bo Bak leaned back in a wooden porch chair. "Many think so, Mrs. Brown, but I have known the Chindit for fifteen years. You are correct only because today he lost his heart when he left his son. No man loves his son more."

Sarah's glare dissolved as she saw the sincerity in the old man's eyes. "Tell us about your Sawbaw," she asked. "Where did he learn to speak English so well?"

Seated beside his wife at the table, Henry pushed his chair back and stood up. "I've heard all this before. I'm going to the church and prepare for tonight's prayer service." He nodded to Bak and strode down the steps.

Joshua took Henry's place at the table as the old man began speaking.

"Mrs. Brown, the Chindit is Chinese, Cantonese Chinese. He was a lieutenant in the Chinese National Army and came to Burma with his unit to help force out the Japanese during the war. His unit fought alongside the mountain Shan in the Ri region. It was then I first met him. He was a very brave man in battle and earned the respect of the Shan. For his courage we gave him the name 'Chindit, The Lion.' " After the war the Chindit returned to China, but things turned very bad when the communists took over.

"What was left of the National Army was forced to retreat across the border into our country. The Chindit was then a captain. The Shan welcomed him and his men and helped build their camps. Your country's secret intelligence, I think you call it CIA, provided the Chindit with weapons and money to go back to China to foster a rebellion. The Chindit's army marched into China six months later, but the communists already had their stranglehold on the people. The Chindit was again forced to retreat to our country and wait for another day. That day never came, Mrs. Brown, for he fell in love with this country and our people. He married Stephen's mother and became a colonel in the Shan Army. His successes against the government forces could not be counted on two hands, the people thought of him as their protector and he was made a general in charge of the defense of the Ri.

"Some ten years ago the Shan government leaders were assassinated by the junta and the Shan resistance crumbled except for a few regions like the Ri. The Burmese government has been trying to catch the Chindit ever since. They have failed, Mrs. Brown, because he is truly a lion, who has more cunning and courage than any man I know. But sadly the price has been very high. Shea, Stephen's Shan mother, bore the Chindit three sons. The first was killed by the Wa when he was Stephen's age, and the second was killed by a government artillery round. Shea blamed the Chindit for the deaths of her sons since he had been away fighting. The losses caused a sickness within her. A month ago, knowing she was dying, she made the Chindit promise her last son would not follow in the ways of the Chindit. A devout Christian, she wanted Stephen to become a pastor and help her people."

Sarah lowered her eyes. "It must have been very hard for your Sawbaw to give up Stephen. But as a mother I can understand his mother's feelings."

Bak shifted in his seat and spoke while gazing at the northern mountains. "You asked me before about the Chindit's English. His family was Christian and sent him to the English missionary school in Canton."

"The Chindit is a Christian?" Sarah asked with hope in her voice.

Bak motioned toward the distant mountains. "He worships the Ri and its people, Mrs. Brown. Your god and the gods of the Shan and even Buddha are respected by him, but his church, Mrs. Brown, is those mountains."

Sarah leaned back in her chair and looked at the old man. "And you, Bo Bak. What does it mean to be a Master Horseman?"

"You see, Mrs. Brown, the title 'Horseman' goes back in our history for centuries. The Shan ruled Burma many years ago, and the Horsemen were the Shan king's knights. Our Shan Army brought back the old tradition and selected the best one hundred fighters in the army to be trained as Horsemen. I was fortunate enough to be selected for the training as well as the Chindit. The one hundred Horsemen were given assignments to the Shan villages with the duty of protecting the people and the land."

Bak's eyes became distant and his voice became more reflective. "When our Shan government leaders were assassinated by the junta, our army and government crumbled—but not the Horsemen. They would not surrender to the junta. The Horsemen joined with the Chindit. You saw them today. We, the Horsemen, are sworn to protect the Chindit and the Ri with our lives. The Ri is everything to us, for it is all that remains of what was. It is our last hope. The cost for us has been high; there are only thirty-one of us left. Many Horsemen have died in battle, or have grown too old, like me. And the young men don't care about the old ways. They are impatient and want to learn only about the modern weapons."

"The Chindit has only thirty men in his army?" asked Sarah incredulously.

"Oh no, Mrs. Brown," Bak said with a smile. "The Chindit has more than six thousand soldiers, but they are in outposts throughout the Ri protecting the mountain passes and roads. The Chindit also has hundreds of spies. He knows everything, Mrs. Brown. He knows beforehand when and where the junta plans to attack, and more important, he knows who are his enemies and who are his true friends."

Bak looked deeply into Sarah's eyes. "Mrs. Brown, talk to your husband. The Chindit's warning about the Wa was true. I will train ten of your parish men as a militia for the protection of the village. Trained men properly armed will persuade the Wa and any bandits not to attack Shaduzup. Without the militia you will be at their mercy."

Reaching out, Sarah patted the old man's hand. "I will talk to him, Bo Bak, but I can't promise anything."

Bak held Sarah's gaze as if reading her thoughts before slowly nodding. He then stood and pushed back his chair. "I will be camped on the plateau above the river, Mrs. Brown. If the pastor decides to give me men, I will train them there."

Sarah motioned toward the dormitory. "And Stephen? What do you suggest we do?"

Bak walked down the porch steps toward his pony. Grasping the reins, he looked over his shoulder at Sarah. "Time, Mrs. Brown. It takes time for the wounds of the heart to heal." He put his foot in the stirrup and swung easily up into the saddle. Bowing his head toward Sarah and giving Joshua a wink, he headed his shaggy horse toward the river.

Joshua stood and took his mother's hand. "I like the Horseman, Mom; he's really neat. And so is Stephen's father. You should have seen him gallop his horse toward me. He was like—like a king."

Sarah squeezed her son's hand as she gazed toward the northern mountains. "He is a king, a warrior-king like David, with great power." Her voice softened to almost a whisper as she looked into her son's eyes. "But right now I believe he wishes he were me, holding his son's hand."

CHAPTER 3

"Greetings and blessings, Master Horseman," Joshua said as he approached the old man.

"No!" Bak looked up from the rifle he was cleaning. "You wait until I acknowledge your presence, and look me in the eyes as you offer the greeting. It is a sign to a Shan that you are sincere and honest. Now back up and do it again."

After three days of visiting the old man at his camp, Joshua was used to his ways. Joshua backed up several steps before walking forward again. He came to a halt and waited until Bak slowly raised his eyes toward him. "Greetings and blessings, Master Horseman," Joshua said tentatively.

"Greetings and blessings, little Sao," Bak responded kindly. "How is Stephen today?"

"He's still sad," Joshua said, "and won't talk to anybody. He just sits up there in his room looking out the window."

"The sadness will pass," Bak said, setting down the rifle. "Go back and tell him I need his assistance in the training of the militia."

"Bu . . . but you don't have any men to train!"

The old man brushed back his moustache with a gnarled finger. "Aren't I teaching you how to ride the ponies?"

Joshua beamed. "I'm in the militia?"

"You are until the pastor gives me men. Now go, fetch Stephen. He has mourned enough. It is time for learning."

•   •   •

Joshua walked into the room without knocking, knowing that Stephen would not answer. The dark-haired boy was at the window looking toward the northern mountains, waiting. Joining Stephen, Joshua reached out and patted the other boy's shoulder. "I don't care whether you talk. It's okay. Some of the other kids talk too much. I understand why ya don't wanna talk. My dad left me too. 'Course, I never saw my dad; he died in a war somewhere but I sometimes blame him for dyin'. I guess that don't make much sense, but—"

Stephen interrupted, "Why did you not run like the others when my father and his Horsemen rode toward the village?"

Joshua shrugged. "I dunno. I think I knew he wouldn't hurt me."

Stephen pushed Joshua's hand off his shoulder. "If my father *had* been a bandit, you would be dead and your body would be food for worms."

Again Joshua shrugged. "But he's not a bandit and I'm here."

"Fool," Stephen said.

Joshua turned around and walked for the door. "I came to tell you the Horseman wants you," he said, speaking over his shoulder. "He said it was time for you to stop mourning." Joshua slowed at the doorway. "I think the Horseman is wrong. You *like* to be sad." He closed the door and strode down the hall.

"The pony has a mind! Yank back on the reins and show him *you* have one!" Bo Bak bellowed.

Joshua pulled the reins back but the obstinate pony kept heading for the lettuce field.

"*Yank back* on the reins!"

Joshua yanked back hard. The pony reared back on its hind legs and tumbled the young rider to the ground.

Bak slowly shook his head and sighed.

"Greetings and blessings, Teacher."

Bak turned to face the dark-haired boy who had walked up behind him. "Greetings and blessings, Sao. It is good to gaze upon you again."

"And I am happy to see you," said Stephen as he took the reins from Bak's hand and swung up on the Horseman's pony. "Is the white Sao your only 'militia'?"

"Until the pastor gives me men. The boy has heart, but he doesn't understand the ponies."

Stephen motioned toward the distant boy, who was picking himself up from the dirt. "It appears you need some help."

Joshua was mumbling to himself as he walked with a slight limp toward the pony, which was munching lettuce in the middle of the field.

Stephen frowned as he rode up beside the blond boy. "I see that you are not a cowboy. I thought all Americans were cowboys."

Joshua kept walking, not showing his surprise at Stephen's presence. "Nope, I'm not a cowboy. I'd never been on a horse before yesterday, but I'm gonna ride that devil before the day is through. He *will* go where I wanna go."

Stephen reined his pony to a halt. "Then you have learned the first lesson. You must have a stronger will than the beast. These are Yunnan ponies from China. My father says they are the best mountain ponies in the world because they are so mean and strong. They don't understand kindness, little Sao, but they do understand a good kick."

Joshua mumbled a sarcastic "thanks" as he plodded on.

Stephen watched as Joshua took the reins of his pony and swung himself up into the saddle.

"Keep your feet in the stirrups," instructed Stephen, "and press your knees against him tightly. Keep a good grip on the reins. . . . Now rein him around. Good. Now a little kick in the flanks . . . Very good. You see, a kick works with him. He will respect you for it."

An elated smile covered Joshua's face as he headed the pony toward Stephen. "I'm doing it! Look! I'm doing—" The pony suddenly reared back on its hind legs, pawing the air with its front hooves. Joshua was still in the saddle, but his smile had turned into a terror-stricken grimace. He dropped the reins and grabbed the saddle horn for a better hold. The pony reared again and came down in a dead run.

Stephen sighed as he watched the horse head for the tree line with its bouncing rider. Giving his own horse a kick, Stephen headed the animal after them.

It was like twilight under the canopy of trees as Stephen reined his pony to a halt, and listened. It took only a moment within the quiet before he heard crashing and hoofbeats off to his right. Sighing again, Stephen reined his horse toward the sound. He had traveled only twenty yards when directly in front of him the runaway broke through a green wall of vines and headed toward him. Still holding on, Joshua looked as if he had been flayed with a whip. His shirt was in tatters and his face, chest, and arms were covered in bloody scratches.

Stephen had no time to do anything but shut his eyes and cringe before the impact. The collision bowled Stephen and his horse over. Stunned by the blow, the runaway horse collapsed to its front knees, and its bloody rider leapt to the ground.

Lying on the moss-covered forest floor, Stephen slowly raised his aching head and blinked to try and clear his double vision. His eyes focused and he saw a hand in front of his face.

Joshua smirked as he held his hand out to help Stephen up. "I see you're no cowboy either."

"Fool!" Stephen yelled angrily, slapping Joshua's hand away. He tried to get to his feet, but Joshua put his foot on the boy's chest and pushed him back to the ground.

Leaning over, dripping blood into Stephen's face, Joshua spoke menacingly. "Looky here. You've called me that twice and it ain't nice. I'm standin' up and you're layin' on the ground, so who's the fool?"

Stephen glared up at the boy. "You were stupid to stay on the pony when he ran for the trees. The ponies are smart and know the branches will knock you off."

"He didn't knock me off. He tried, but he didn't. I beat him."

"Beat him?"

"Yeah, at his own game. I won"—Joshua backed up and motioned to the still stunned horse—"and he lost."

Stephen got up, and slowly the corners of his lips turned upward. "You *are* a fool, Joshua Hawkins, but a likable one. My father was right—you have a Horseman's heart."

Joshua grinned as he saw Stephen smile for the first time, and he stepped closer, offering his hand. "Friends, then?"

Stephen slapped his hand on Joshua's right shoulder. "We Shan do this, not shake hands. It is a sign of trust and comradeship."

Joshua slapped his hand on Stephen's shoulder. "Good. Now you get to explain to my mom how I got all scratched up and tore my good shirt."

Stephen laughed and shook his head. "Not even my father could help you with your mother. She is what we call a *futaa*—a little storm. You must face her wrath on your own, my new friend."

Joshua shrugged and turned to face his horse, which had just got back up to its feet. Taking a step forward, Joshua slapped the animal's forehead and barked, "Remember, you devil, I won!" Taking the reins, he swung himself up into the saddle and gave Stephen a wink. "He respects me now."

Worried and out of breath, Bo Bak leaned against a tree to rest and allow his racing heart to stop its pounding. He had begun running as soon as he had seen Joshua and the horse disappear into the trees.

He heard something coming from deeper in the forest and froze. For a split second he felt a sinking sensation, for he thought it was the sound of a boy crying out. But then a wave of relief rushed through his body. The sound was two boys laughing.

After a dinner of vegetables and roasted goat, the small Shan cook took the plates away. Henry placed his napkin on the table and leaned back in his chair, looking at his dinner guest. "Stephen, I'm pleased you could join us tonight." He shifted his narrowing eyes to Joshua's badly scratched face. "I'm happy that Joshua persuaded you to come. I apologize for his appearance, but it seems he had an accident today while trying to learn to ride horses. But I understand you know all about it. Please, if you two are to be friends, for my sake and Sarah's, keep an eye out for him. He is a rather persistent boy. 'Hard-headed' and 'prideful' would better describe him, but Sarah is partial to 'persistent.' "

Sarah's brow wrinkled upward. "Henry, I have already talked to Joshua and Stephen, and they have promised to be more careful. We should all be thanking our Savior that neither of them was hurt badly. I don't think any of Joshua's scratches are deep enough to cause scars."

Turning his attention back to Stephen, Henry pursed his lips.

"Stephen, in an hour I'm going to be talking to the church and village elders about volunteers for a militia. My faith in God is absolute, but my faith in evil men makes me fear for my people. But first, I would like to know more about Bo Bak. Sarah has told me how he got his title of Horseman, but he also called himself a teacher. What is it that he teaches?"

Stephen's eyes widened in disbelief that the pastor didn't know. "Pastor, the Teacher is not just a Horseman. He is the *Master* Horseman. He trains Horsemen for the test, and—"

"Test?" Henry interrupted.

"To become Horsemen all candidates must be tested," Stephen said. "A soldier is nominated to be a Horseman because of his bravery, but it is the Teacher who decides if the candidate is worthy. The Teacher is the last of the line of Horsemen who protected the king hundreds of years ago. He alone can bestow the Horseman's bracelet of honor."

Henry leaned back in his chair. "So that is the significance of the bracelet. I noticed it on the Chindit."

"It is a very special band," Stephen said. "It is made from silver taken from the mines in the Ri and metal taken from a bridle and sword of a Horseman who served the king a long time ago. The Teacher says the silver is like the Horseman—it must be made pure by fire, then strengthened and formed. Old metals from our ancestors and new ones from our Ri are joined. The Teacher says the band and the man are forged in honor. To wear the Horseman's band is a symbol of truth, commitment, and courage. It is the highest honor a Shan can have."

"And doesn't it mean the wearer must pledge his life to the Chindit?" asked Henry, not hiding his contempt for the Sawbaw.

Stephen's eyes narrowed. "Yes, the Horsemen have pledged their lives to my father, but only because he has pledged his life to the Ri. He is the Protector, Pastor Brown. He has been wounded many times fighting for the people and the Ri."

Henry raised his hand. "Stephen, I apologize for my comment, but please understand I believe fighting is not the way of our Lord. Jesus taught nonviolence, and we all must do the same."

Stephen kept his eyes locked on Henry's. "I have seen what the bandits and Wa do. They give no mercy."

"The Master Horseman will have his men to train," Henry said softly. "But it is God's word that will eventually win over evil men's hearts."

Stephen turned his head to hide his misting eyes. "My father isn't coming back for me, is he, Pastor Brown?"

Henry reached out and put his hand on the boy's shoulder. "I do not like what your father stands for, Stephen. But I do respect him as a man of honor. He will not come back for you because he made a promise that he knows in his heart is right. He wants you to be what he is not . . . a man who can truly help his people. In his heart he knows his way of helping also hurts his people. Through knowledge and God's love you can be what your mother wanted . . . and what your father wants—a man who can make a difference in this country."

Tears rolled down Stephen's cheeks as he lowered his head and spoke in a whisper. "I will try, Pastor."

CHAPTER 4

Henry stood with head bowed in front of the ten-man militia unit. ". . . and I pray the training you have received over the past two weeks from the Master Horseman will never be called upon, but if the day comes, know Jesus is with the righteous and will give you strength."

The formation of men responded as one. "Amen."

Henry lifted his head and Bak strode up to address the formation. "Remember to have your rifle and ammunition clean and ready at all times, and keep it in a secure place where your children cannot get to it. That's all, you're dismissed until drill next week."

Very pleased, Henry smiled as he watched the men walk to the village. "You truly are a gifted teacher, Horseman Bak. I was very impressed with their shooting. Every man could hit the targets at two hundred yards. Where did you get the weapons?"

Bak held out the rifle that was slung over his shoulder for Henry to see. "The Chindit sent a mule train with the rifles and supplies. These are old British Enfields, but they are very accurate and easy to use."

Henry nodded without taking the proffered rifle. "Tell me again, Horseman Bak, what else we must do."

Bak motioned toward the village. "You must tell the villagers that when the warning bell is sounded they must not run to the church, but rather stay in their homes and lock all doors and windows. Bandits and the Wa must attack swiftly to be successful. Their tactic is to strike and take what they want before resistance can be formed. If the villagers deny access by locking their doors, the attackers will be easy targets for the militia, which will be on the dormitory and school roofs."

Henry dipped his chin. "I will have a village meeting tonight." He turned to go, but Bak lifted his hand. "One more request, Pastor. The boys helped me during the training. They fetched ammunition and put up the targets. I would like to have them continue to help me with the others. I will see to it that they go to classes and do all their chores before helping me."

Henry canted his head and stared into the old man's eyes. "That is not the real reason you want them, is it?"

Bak shook his head. "No, Pastor. The truth is I want to be with Stephen all I can, I must teach him his heritage. My Sawbaw gave you his son to teach, but he also left me to teach him to be a Shan. You and I want the same thing. We want the boys to grow up and be respected men. In the Ri to be a man means many things, things I must pass on to Stephen."

"What kind of 'things' will you teach?" Henry asked suspiciously.

"A Shan must learn the forest, how to track, hunt, and care for what our ancestors have left us. These things must sound trivial to you, Pastor, but to a Shan they are everything. The mountains and the forest are a part of us."

"And your gods? Do you teach Stephen about them as well?" pressed Henry.

"I teach him to respect all things people believe in."

Henry lowered his head and thought for a moment before speaking. "What about Joshua? The boys have become inseparable."

"If he stays in Shaduzup he must know and understand the Shan. You know this to be true, Pastor. You see how the village people take to him; he already can speak our language. They see he has a big heart and cares for them. I want to teach both boys—where one is weak the other is strong. Together they have no weaknesses and will be able to learn even more."

Henry took a deep breath. "Horseman Bak, you and the Chindit believe me to be a religious fanatic with no understanding of the Shan. I know far more than you think, and for this reason I will allow you to instruct the boys."

"And Mrs. Brown?" Bak asked with a twinkle in his eye.

Henry sighed. "It will take time for her to understand, but she will."

Joshua and Stephen waited until Henry had left for the village before coming out of Bak's new hut. "What did he say?" Joshua asked excitedly.

Bak put one hand on each boy's shoulder. "Today begins the many lessons you will learn from this old one. From this day on you will address me as 'Teacher,' for that is who I am. When a lesson is complete you will say, 'Knowledge will give us strength.' Both of you are to be my students, and I will teach you the ways of the Shan and the Ri. One is incomplete without the other, as you will see. Now go home, study the books for Mrs. Brown's classes, then sleep well. Tomorrow you begin learning how to ride the ponies a new way, the Horseman way. Go and remember, knowledge will give you strength."

Both boys turned to go, but Bak grabbed them by the hair. "Have you already forgot my instructions? What are you supposed to say after my lessons?"

Stephen began the line, and Joshua joined in. "Knowledge will give us strength."

"Now go!" Bak bellowed and waved them off as if shooing away pests. Only when they had their backs turned did his leathery face crack into a smile.

The weeks passed and dark clouds began gathering in the north, foretelling the coming monsoon season. With the clouds came the hunting season and the closing of the mission school. The wild boar and *gyi*, or small deer, born in the spring were now big enough to be hunted. They would provide meat for the Shan throughout the wet season.

"Pig dogs? They really are pig dogs?" Joshua asked. He had looked forward to this first hunt for weeks.

Stephen motioned toward the skinny mongrels scampering ahead of his pony. "Of course. How else do you think you hunt boar?"

"They just look like normal dogs to me. How can you tell they're pig dogs?"

"Because they aren't fat and lazy like pye dogs."

"Pye dogs? What is a pye dog? Are there any in Shaduzup?"

Leading the hunting party, Bak twisted himself around in the saddle with a scowl. "You two have been talking instead of looking for signs. Joshua, tell me what trees these are to the right."

Joshua glanced at the trees and shrugged. "Teak, Teacher. And the ones ahead are sayo with water vine climbing up their branches."

Bak pointed to his left. "Stephen, what ferns are those and what use are they?"

"Teacher, those are giant fiddlehead. The young shoots are good eating, as are the roots if boiled. The hair on the fiddlehead can be used to stop the bleeding of wounds."

Bak grunted and nodded. "Good, you two *have* learned something in the past weeks after all. During the war with the Japanese, many of us in the Burma Rifles lived off the forest for months. Everything you need to survive is here—food, water, weapons, and medicine. The forest is your friend if you know and respect her. If you are ignorant and don't respect her, she will kill you. Now, Stephen, explain to Joshua how the pig dogs hunt and—"

The lead dog abruptly spun to its right and bolted into a full run heading down the side of the ridge. Bak chuckled as he broke his horse into a trot. "Never mind, he will see for himself. Keep the dogs in sight but watch out for low branches."

As he followed Bak down the steep ridge, Joshua was beside himself with excitement. Ducking branches and trying to keep the dogs in sight while negotiating the incline required all the horsemanship skills he had learned, and more. The excitement he felt came not just from his first pig hunt, but also from the realization that he was riding as well as Bak and Stephen. They did not have to watch out for him or give instructions as they had before. He was on his own and loving it.

At the bottom of the ridge Bak reined to a halt and pointed ahead to a stand of bamboo. "See how the dogs surround the thicket. The pig is in there. Joshua, watch now. We will see which dog is the bravest."

Joshua and Stephen came up alongside the old man just as a thin, yellow dog lowered its growling head and dashed into the bamboo. Immediately a loud squeal came from the clump, followed by a yelp and a sickening whine that seemed to infuriate the other dogs. The five other mongrels dashed into the clump. Joshua cringed as he heard the combined squealing and yelping of the ongoing hidden battle. Suddenly out of the bamboo came a bristle-haired boar in a dead run with five dogs biting at its back legs.

The mammoth boar suddenly spun around to take on its attackers. The pig's huge curved tusks flashed as it lowered its massive shoulders and slashed by jerking its head side to side.

Motioning toward the pig only twenty feet away, Bak leaned over to Joshua. "She is making her stand early. She is very smart not to be tricked into running. The dogs can run all day, but she would become very tired and unable to fight."

The boar spun left and then right at the growling dogs that circled her like hungry wolves. Sickened at the sight, Joshua swung his eyes back to the bamboo but felt worse as he guessed the fate of the yellow dog. The boar's squealing caused him to look back at the fight. One of the dogs had attacked and latched onto the maddened pig's right ear. The boar flung its head, but the tenacious dog's jaws were clamped tight. Another dog grabbed the other ear. Both mongrels were lifted from the ground and swung like rags each time the squealing boar shook its head, but they held on. Distracted with the pain of the two dogs biting her tender ears the other three dogs attacked her vulnerable underbelly.

Unable to take it anymore, Joshua yelled at Bak, "Shoot her! Don't let her die like that! Shoot her! Please!"

The Horseman stared at Joshua for a long moment before speaking above the squealing and growling. "This is the truth of the forest. If she is strong enough she will fight and live. Killing her with a gun gives her no chance."

With tears in his eyes Joshua was drawn back to the struggle. One of the dogs that had an ear lost his grip and was flung through the air into a tree. Forgetting its other attackers, the boar charged the stunned dog and tore into its flank with its tusks. The wounded dog yelped and tried to run but the boar attacked again, catching the mongrel under its belly and ripping him open all the way to the throat. Then the other dogs were on her.

Joshua sat watching the struggle without making a sound or moving a muscle for the entire ten minutes it took for the boar to finally breathe her last. In the end she had become so weak she could not even lift her head to fight. All she could do was grunt as the dogs tore open her stomach.

Bak leaned over and put his arm over Joshua's shoulder. "It is not a pretty thing to see, but she was an old sow with only a few seasons left. The tigers would have killed her easily within the year. Today the gods have given her a proud death. A part of life is death, and this old one died as I should want to die, fighting. To die feeble and used up is not a warrior's way and all the forest animals are warriors."

Feeling as if he were going to be sick, Josh looked away from the bloody-faced dogs. "Is the yellow dog dead too?"

Bak's brow wrinkled. "Yes, he died for his courage. Life is very strange, Joshua. We do not understand why but pig dogs live only for the hunt. They are born with the knowledge that the ears of the boar are the only vulnerable place besides the underbelly. They know that once they latch on to an ear the boar can't slash them, but they know there is a price for holding on. I have seen dogs die, smashed against rocks and trees as the boar thrashes its head about but yet the dog still holds on even in death. The yellow dog attacked alone knowing it would die, but yet it attacked. It was driven by the hunt . . . by something in its being that needed to kill the boar."

Bak sighed and patted the boy's back. "Do not mourn for the dogs or pig. Such is life for death comes to us all. Today the dogs and the pig met death and did so bravely. It was a good death and that is all any of us could ask for."

Joshua looked into the old man's eyes. "Teacher, why do you want to die fighting?"

Bak knitted his brow. "I am a Horseman, little Sao. It is a Horseman's death to be like the pig and make a last stand to face the enemy a final time. To join my ancestors with sword or rifle in hand gives me eternal glory and honor. My name would be spoken over every hunter's campfire in the telling of stories of brave men. I would live forever, little Sao . . . forever in the hearts of the Shan."

Joshua bowed his head in understanding. "Knowledge will give me strength, Teacher."

Night gave way to morning, leaving a whispy white mist that floated along the dank forest floor. Joshua and Stephen rode in single file up a switchbacking trail. Both boys were silent as they listened to the morning birds high above in the green canopy. Joshua suddenly checked his horse and narrowed his eyes.

Stephen reined up and looked where Joshua was focusing his attention but didn't see anything. He whispered, "Did you see something?"

Joshua's eyes didn't move as he slowly pulled the old British Enfield from the saddle boot and whispered back, "There are two *gyi* just beyond the bend behind the bamboo stand. We'll dismount here and wait for them. . . . They're moving toward us."

Stephen looked again toward the bend in the trail. "Are you certain? I do not see them."

"They're there," said Joshua, climbing down from the saddle. He took several steps, halted, thumbed off the safety, and slowly raised his rifle.

Stephen joined his friend seconds later and kneeled. Still keeping his eyes on the track, Joshua whispered, "You take the first when they come into view again. I'll take the second."

Stephen began to smile, thinking it was another of Joshua's jokes, when to his astonishment two *gyi* stepped out from behind the clump of bamboo just fifty yards away. The one in the lead was larger and darker in color, its head erect and alert as it looked and smelled for danger. Sensing a threat, the lead *gyi* abruptly stopped, swinging its head right and left, its large brown eyes searching. Stephen raised his rifle, but seeing his sudden movement, the animal bolted.

Joshua fired, and the second *gyi* toppled over. Running forward, Joshua worked the bolt while keeping his eyes on the escaping leader. It was bounding down the ridge, having to zig and zag around the monstrous teaks. Joshua stopped, raised the weapon, and fired again.

He stood with the rifle held to his shoulder, not moving a muscle.

He was waiting for everything to come back into focus. He had not heard his two shots nor had he seen the trees, mist, or vegetation. All he had seen were the two *gyi;* everything else had blurred. He had seen the first one quiver just before it bolted. He had seen indecision in the second animal's eyes just before the bullet struck. The escaping *gyi*'s eyes had been at first full of fear, but the look had changed to hope when it thought it would live. Its huge brown eyes had dulled in that instant the bullet tore into its flesh.

"Joshua? Joshua, are you alright?" asked Stephen, worried by the fact that his friend had not moved.

As if in slow motion, Joshua lowered his rifle and turned to face his friend. "I . . . I'm fine."

"Did you kill the big one?"

Joshua nodded as his eyes came back into focus. He strode to his pony and placed the rifle back into the saddle boot.

"By the gods, you shot both of them! It is true you Americans are all cowboys."

Shrugging his shoulders, Joshua grasped the reins of his horse. "Beginner's luck, I guess. Come on, let's get 'em and find some more. The next are yours."

The sun was setting as Joshua and Stephen stood by the water pump behind the dormitory cleaning themselves. Joshua put on his shirt and felt for his sheath knife. "Darn, I left my knife in Teacher's hut. I'm gonna run back and get it."

"I will go with you," Stephen said, buttoning his shirt.

"Naw, you'll miss the dorm supper. I'll see you in your room after I've had dinner at the house."

Stephen dipped his chin in reluctant agreement, and Joshua broke into a slow jog. It was dark by the time he slowed to a walk just short of the hut. When he heard voices and laughter, he froze. Who could it be? he wondered. Bandits, Wa, or— Something hard poked him in the back and a harsh Shan voice said, "Move and you die. Raise your hands."

Gulping, Joshua raised his arms as the voice had commanded. "Who are you?" the voice continued.

"Joshua, student of the Teacher."

The pressure against his back was removed and a man stepped around in front of Joshua and took his arm. "Come, little Sao."

As soon as Bak's door opened, Joshua stepped in and his mouth fell open. Xu Kang turned from the small cooking fire with a smile. "Have you come to challenge me again, little Sao?"

Bak chuckled and set down the cup of zu he was drinking. "I fear your secret is no longer one, Chindit."

Xu Kang motioned Joshua to a bench and said, "Your teacher is correct, but the question is, what should I do about it?"

Joshua stammered, "I won't tell anybody."

"Of course not," said Xu Kang as he sat down beside the boy. "You know the power of the Chindit. I suppose I should explain. I came to watch the hunt. To shoot your first *gyi* is a first step toward manhood, and I was very impressed with your shot today. The *gyi* was at least fifty yards away."

"One hundred," Joshua corrected, knowing he was in no danger.

Xu Kang laughed and tossed his arm over the boy's shoulder. "Yes, one hundred, and next year at the hunter's campfire it will be two hundred. You are truly becoming a Shan." The Sawbaw's smile slowly dissolved as he looked into the boy's eyes. "How is my son, little Sao? Is he doing well in school?"

"He is the smartest in our class in arithmetic and writing," said Joshua. "My mother says he is her best student."

Xu Kang's face beamed. "Do you hear this, Bak? My son is first in his class!"

The old man sipped his zu and nodded. "He is far more intelligent than his father."

Xu Kang laughed and patted Joshua's back. "You must return home, little Sao, before your family worries. This is our secret. Tell no one you saw me, not even Stephen. He would not understand."

Joshua stood to face the Sawbaw and waited for the shoulder clap. Xu Kang nodded to Bak. "You have taught him well. He knows our customs and shows respect." He placed his hand on Joshua's shoulder. "I am proud of you, little Sao. You and my son ride and shoot like Horsemen. You both lifted my heart. I thank you for being my son's friend. He is honored."

Joshua clapped his small hand on the Xu Kang's shoulder. "I am the one honored, Chindit. Stephen is my best friend."

Bak guided Joshua to the door and walked out into the darkness with him. "Be careful on the walk home, and remember to say nothing of what you saw."

Joshua stopped and looked up at the old man. "The Chindit misses his son, doesn't he?"

Bak patted the boy's back. "Yes, very much. He will be back often, for he cannot stay away, but Stephen must never know the Sawbaw watches him."

Joshua turned away in silence and began the long walk home. He knew that his father was watching him, too . . . from afar.

CHAPTER 5

1964

Shaduzup, Burma

"Don't be distracted!" Bak bellowed. "Stephen, you are first. Watch your front and remember what I taught you."

Both boys turned back to face the meadow. Stephen took a step forward and raised an old British pistol. From the opposite side of the meadow's tree line, six militiamen stepped out and began running toward the boys. Stephen aimed and fired the pistol, which held only blank ammunition.

Bak stood directly behind Stephen, watching his every move and sight alignment. "Hit!" he barked after Stephen fired at his first target. Stephen aimed at another oncoming attacker and pulled the trigger. The militia were closing in fast, shooting rifles loaded with blanks as they ran.

Bak kept his eyes on Stephen. "Hit . . . miss . . . hit . . . miss . . . miss."

The militiamen ran past the boys and Stephen turned to his teacher, who was shaking his head. "You are dead. Yes, you fought bravely, but not wisely. Remember what I taught you. You must pick your targets based on their threat to you, and once you select a target you can see or hear nothing else."

Stephen dejectedly handed the pistol to Bak. "But Teacher, they came so fast. There isn't time to determine which targets are most dangerous, let alone shoot them all."

Bak reloaded the old revolver with more blanks. "You blinked when they shot at you. Blinking demonstrates a lack of concentration. It is a difficult test, my students. I have never had a student shoot all the targets the first time. You will get better with practice and concentration." Bak handed the weapon to Joshua. "Now it is time for your first attempt. Remember, the weapon is an extension of your mind. Point, aim, and shoot. When under attack the victor is the man who keeps his senses and is not distracted. Fear is your enemy, more so than the attacker. Fear causes blinking, and fear causes you to jerk the trigger instead of squeezing. Shooting a man is difficult to teach, but a man who can accept death will always be the victor in a fight over a man who fears for his life. When facing an enemy with weapons it is a truth that someone will die. Accepting death is like a shield because you no longer have the fear of dying. There is an inner peace with this acceptance, a peace that steadies the hand and prepares the mind and body to kill."

Joshua took the weapon and faced the meadow. Letting his arms hang at his sides, he took a breath and let it out slowly. Six more militiamen burst out of the trees. Standing perfectly still for a full two seconds, he finally raised the pistol.

"Hit," said Bak, watching Joshua's movements and his sighting of the weapon. "Hit . . . hit . . . hit . . . hit . . . hit! By the gods!"

Joshua stood with the empty pistol in his hand, still pulling the trigger. Only when Stephen reached out and touched his shoulders did Joshua lower the pistol and face the Teacher with a distant gaze.

Bak stared into his student's eyes for a long moment before stepping up and taking the weapon from his hand. "What did you feel?"

Joshua spoke as if in a trance. "At peace."

"Did you hear the rifles shooting at you?"

"I don't think so, Teacher. I don't remember hearing anything."

Bak nodded. "The gods have blessed you. I have seen it before but never in one so young."

Stephen slapped Joshua's back excitedly. "You got them all! And you did it so fast!"

Joshua's eyes came into focus and he looked down at his hands. "It—it felt so strange."

Bak handed the pistol to Stephen. "Go to the range and practice. I want you to hit the target at twenty paces with all six shots. Take a box of ammunition and use it all."

"What about Joshua?"

"Can you two not be separated even for an hour? Go on, I will be working here with him. Now go."

Bak waited until Stephen had walked over the ridge before facing Joshua with an intense stare. "How long have you known you were blessed with this gift?"

Joshua lowered his head and looked at his feet. "Four years, Teacher. I felt it when I shot my first *gyi*—I had complete focus."

Bak took Joshua's arm and led him to the shade of a gnarled banyan tree. "The blessing the gods have given you makes you different. Those I have seen with the gift fear themselves, for they know the gift is there, wanting to be released. Do not fear what the gods have given to you, my student. Understand it is a gift given to few and that you were chosen. Accept this gift, use it when necessary, but never look for a reason to use it."

Bak smiled and patted the boy's shoulder. "I will help you to understand the gift. It is the first time I have had this opportunity in all my years of teaching Horsemen. I am honored."

Joshua bowed his head. "No, Teacher, I am honored."

The mission church bell clanged three times to signal the approach of a supply convoy. As always, the arrival of the trucks from Namti was cause for all work to cease and for everyone in the village to come to the mission compound. Henry and Sarah were just as excited as the villagers.

The first large, Japanese-made truck topped the rise followed by two more and a surprise: a new white Land Rover. Henry stepped off the porch as the Land Rover came to a stop in front of the house. A large white man wearing khaki clothes stepped out of the vehicle and removed his slouch hat. Smiling, the stranger offered his hand to Henry.

"You must be Pastor Brown. I've heard a lot about you. It's a real pleasure."

Henry grinned and shook the stranger's hand. "An American! We don't see many up here. Please come and have tea with us and tell us what has brought you to Shaduzup."

The tall stranger offered his hand to Sarah as he stepped up onto the porch. "And you must be Mrs. Brown. I'm John Swift from the American Embassy in Rangoon. It sure is a pleasure to meet you."

"Please sit down, Mr. Swift," said Sarah, shaking his hand and motioning to a chair.

Swift took a seat and looked out at the compound, his smile replaced by a frown. "Pastor, I'm afraid I've come here with some bad news."

Sarah and Henry held their breath as the tall American sipped his tea before speaking. "Pastor, the Burmese government leaders have ordered all foreigners out of the country. But for the time being, the order does not include missionaries. A new general has taken over the military leadership of the government, and he blames foreigners and minorities for the country's horrible economic state. He is making foreigners and the various mountain tribes the scapegoats—and the people are believing him. I'm afraid it will be just a matter of time before the missions will also be closed."

"What has happened to turn the government against foreigners and minorities?" Sarah asked. "A truce was signed between the rebels and the army four years ago."

Swift forced a small smile. "Mrs. Brown, you live in another world here in the mountains. In the lowlands and especially in Rangoon, the Burmese live in horrible poverty. Their economic system is in shambles. The government is corrupt. Vietnam and Laos are close to all-out war because of the communists. The junta doesn't want the same thing to happen to them, so it is clamping down, and it has convinced the people that their enemy is us, the foreigners."

Swift shifted his eyes to Henry. "I don't think the truce will stay in effect. The new general is talking of waging a campaign to once and for all rid the country of rebels and communists. The Shan are included."

Henry lowered his head. "So much good has come in the past four years . . . and now this. Since the truce, our Sawbaw has been able to concentrate on the bandits and the Wa. He has eliminated them as a threat to the Ri. It will be all for nothing if the army comes to the Shan state. It will mean war again."

Swift stood. "I'm sorry to have brought the bad news. Now, I must ask a favor of you. I need to get in contact with a warlord named Xu Kang. I understand his camp is in this area."

Henry studied the taller man's face a moment. "Why would you need to contact him?"

Swift furrowed his brow as if not used to being questioned. "Pastor, Xu Kang is one of the best-known and most respected rebel leaders of the minorities. We are trying to mediate a meeting of the rebel leaders and the junta. None of us want another war. It is not in Burma's best interests, nor our country's."

"You will not find Xu Kang, Mr. Swift. He will find you," said Henry, motioning toward the village. "Take the new road that travels north just outside the village. Somewhere along it you will be stopped. Xu Kang's men patrol all the roads in the region."

"I'd best be off, then. I'll stop here again on the way back to Namti. It was a pleasure meeting you both, and I hope everything turns out all right."

Sarah shook the American's hand. "Don't hope, Mr. Swift. Prayer is the answer."

Henry walked down the steps with Swift and spoke in a harsh whisper once the two men had reached the vehicle. "I think I know what you do in the embassy, Mr. Swift. I warn you, don't use these people. It can only come to ruin."

Swift gave Henry a deadpan stare. "I don't know what you're talking about, Pastor."

Henry lifted an eyebrow. "You know . . . and our Savior knows you have ulterior motives for coming here. I'm not a fool. I am aware of your CIA working with Xu Kang. I know you send your secret teams into China from Kang's camps to gather information. I have seen your planes and some of your people when I travel to the northern villages. Just remember my warning. Using these people for whatever you're planning will cause their ruination. Let them be. In God's name, don't involve them."

Standing alone on the porch, Sarah watched the sun set behind the distant purple mountains. She closed her eyes to pray for more strength but heard the gentle plod of hoofbeats and creaking leather. Turning, she smiled at the old Horseman climbing down from his saddle.

"Greetings and blessings, Master Horseman. I am pleased to see you."

The old man bowed his head as he walked up the steps. "Greetings and blessings, Mrs. Brown. I am always made to feel younger in your presence."

"Sit down, Master Horseman. Join me in a cup of tea. Henry has gone to Namti and then on to Rangoon. It will be nice to have your company and wisdom."

Sarah walked into the house and moments later came out with a tray. After pouring Bak a cup of tea, she sat down with a smile. "I haven't seen you since school ended two weeks ago. How are the boys doing?"

Bak took a sip of tea and put down the cup. "That is why I am here. They are ready for the last tests. I have come to seek your approval."

Sarah shrugged her shoulders. "I'm afraid I don't understand. What are these tests?"

Bak leaned closer to the small woman. "Mrs. Brown, your son and Stephen have been very dedicated and have learned far more than I expected. They have challenged me."

Sarah chuckled. "If Joshua has challenged you, then you have gotten a lot more out of him than I have. Stephen, I can understand. He's an excellent student and makes me work harder than I have ever had to in all my years of teaching."

Bak did not change his serious expression. "Mrs. Brown, Joshua is my best student. I'm not speaking of my teaching here at Shaduzup. He is the best student I have ever taught."

Sarah's mouth dropped open a fraction and her eyes locked on the old man's. "You are serious, aren't you? I . . . I had no idea. I know he's loved your teaching, but he never talks about it with me. He's—he's really your best?"

Bak nodded in silence as he leaned back in his chair. "Mrs. Brown, I ask permission to test the boys as Horsemen. They are ready. Please understand, and do not worry. They cannot be given the title of Horseman or bestowed the silver band of honor, for there is a final test they cannot perform, the test of real combat. What I am asking for is an opportunity for my students to take the tests and see for themselves what they have learned. It is a passage into manhood which both students are prepared to make."

"Are these tests dangerous?" Sarah asked with concern.

"There are two phases. The first is to travel north to a distant river and live from the forest for a week before returning. The second is a demonstration of horsemanship and weapons skills that you may attend on the plateau below the village. Dangerous? No, not to my students. They are too well trained, as you will see."

"But I haven't given you permission yet," said Sarah, eyeing the old man.

Bak brushed back his moustache ends. "Would you keep your honor students from demonstrating their ability? I think not, Mrs. Brown. I am asking, one teacher to another, for such an opportunity. I have two honor students who have attained all that this teacher can teach. It is time for graduation. It is time for our boys to become men."

Sarah sighed and slowly nodded her head. "You are a very wise man, Master Horseman. I have learned much from you over the past four years. I know you have worked very hard with the boys and I appreciate all you have done. Joshua has changed. He has always been a good boy, but you have given him what Henry and I could not: an appreciation of this land and its people. I approve of the tests and will be happy to see the demonstration."

Bak smiled and reached out to take Sarah's hand. "Thank you, Mrs. Brown. I believe you will be very pleased with the results."

Sarah squeezed the old Horseman's hand. "I need your wise counsel on another matter. You know as well as I that Joshua and Stephen have become like brothers. And as you probably know, Stephen has become like a son to me. It pains me . . . it breaks my heart to think of his leaving the mission, but as you said, it is time for graduation. Stephen is a gifted student, very gifted. He needs to go to college next year. A good school, so that he can use his gift. I thought at first, when Stephen first came, that he might become a man of God . . . but it is not to be. His gift is in math. I'm saying this to you because I know you stay in contact with the Chindit. Many times I've heard that our people have seen him watching the training. I ask of you, Master Horseman, talk to the Chindit and tell him what Stephen needs to better himself."

Bak dipped his chin. "Stephen's heart has grown cold for his father. I do not think he would accept anything from him, even if it was an opportunity to go to a university."

Sarah's lips curled upward. "There are scholarships granted to gifted students. If the Chindit would provide a 'scholarship,' Stephen would not have to know where it came from."

The old Horseman smiled. "Ah, Mrs. Brown, you are a very clever woman. I can assure you a scholarship can be made available whenever you desire."

It was the second day of the test, and both Joshua and Stephen were sweat-soaked as they made their way up a steep, twisting trail. Stephen led and stopped for a moment, glancing over his shoulder at the sun that was just beginning to sink behind the mountains. "We'd better camp once we reach the top."

Stephen began to step off, but Joshua grabbed his arm and pulled him back.

"What are you doing?" Stephen protested.

Joshua pointed at the bamboo viper coiled among fallen leaves on the trail just three steps in front of them. "I'm keeping you alive. You'd better let me lead."

Stephen rolled his eyes. "I saw him. I was just seeing if you did."

Joshua took the lead and knocked the green snake off the trail with his walking stick. "Yeah, sure. Just like you saw the boar's lair in the valley."

Stephen sighed. "Okay, so you know the forest better than I—I give you that. And I give that you are a better rider and shooter. But who helped you with your studies, and who is helping you become friends with Su?"

Joshua abruptly stopped and turned around. "Yeah, big help you are. She won't even speak to me. Stephen, I think you're after Su yourself and just messing with me."

"Su? Never. The only woman I can see is beautiful Chi. She is my dream and the one for me."

"Wait a minute. Last week it was Sak See and the week before that, Daa. Since when is Chi the one?"

Stephen grinned like a Cheshire cat. "Since she asked me to take her riding after the tests. She loves me. She said so in a note."

Joshua sighed and again began walking up the trail. "You may be a brain in school, but with women you're as dumb as they come. Maybe we should ask Teacher to help us with girls instead of making us fetch black stones."

Stephen laughed and motioned ahead. "There's the top. Let's get there, start a fire, and discuss how we will approach Teacher on this delicate subject—" Stephen froze as he saw Joshua suddenly raise his hand.

Joshua lowered himself slowly to the ground and whispered, "Do you smell it?"

Stephen sniffed the air and immediately recognized the putrid odor of saddle sores that he and Joshua had smelled during other treks in the forest. He nodded. "A mule train."

Both boys scrambled off the trail toward a huge sayo tree's aboveground root, which stood like a winding wall. Joshua climbed over, then slithered on his belly to a spot where he could see without being seen. He had to wait only a few minutes before the lead scout of the train appeared. It was a Wa guide, easily identified by his flat nose and greased hair. Short and powerfully built, the scout was obviously in a hurry, for his face was glistening with sweat. Behind him came the first mule, loaded with large woven sacks that formed a huge mound on the small animal's back. Waiting, Joshua counted ten mules—and more were coming. He also counted the drivers, all lowlanders, identified by their dirty Western clothing and shaggy, unkempt beards.

Stephen had crawled up beside Joshua. He whispered, "What kind of train is it?"

Joshua backed up. "It's a *lai* train, an opium train. The drivers are carrying new rifles."

Stephen pulled at Joshua's arm. "They will shoot first and ask questions later. Let's just stay here and wait for them to pass."

Joshua leaned against the root wall with Stephen to wait. Suddenly a shot rang out, then another. The mules brayed and struggled to break their ropes. Men shouted and more shooting broke out, louder and closer, the sound like a wave of thunder rolling over the ridge. Joshua and Stephen lay balled up on the ground as bullets cracked overhead. They heard a man grunt as if he'd been hit with a bat; another screamed like a child.

Finally there was a long, oppressive silence in which not a leaf rustled or a bird chirped. A bray from a wounded mule finally ended the eerie quiet.

Joshua began to rise slowly and then froze. The Wa scout was standing only a foot away on the other side of the root wall, pressing his bloody hands against his stomach. The wounded man raised his eyes to Joshua as if pleading. A loud report behind Joshua caused him to jump. The bullet cracked over his ear and hit the Wa in the forehead, making a dull noise like a stone hitting an overripe melon. The Wa dropped like a rag doll and lay looking up at the canopy with unseeing eyes.

Joshua pulled his pistol and spun, but Stephen grabbed his arm. A blue-turbaned Horseman holding a rifle stepped forward and stared at the two boys for a long moment before lifting his chin and barking a command. In seconds both boys heard the hoofbeats of approaching riders.

Walking past Joshua and Stephen, the Horseman approached the Wa's body cautiously until he saw where the bullet had struck. He smiled and looked at Stephen. "I was worried about you, Sao. It is good to gaze upon you again."

Stephen bowed his head. "Greetings and blessings, Horseman Lante. It is good to gaze upon you as well."

The Horseman walked up to Joshua and took the old pistol from his hand to inspect it. "I have heard much about you, white Sao. It is said you are a true Shan and one to behold when riding and shooting. I am fortunate my Sao stopped you from shooting me."

"Did you have to kill them all?" asked Joshua, still in shock at seeing the Wa shot dead before his eyes.

"Of course," retorted the Horseman levelly. "They were warned five days ago and told to pay the tax before crossing the Ri. They stole away during the night thinking they could cross without our knowledge." The Horseman motioned toward the dead body. "It is the law to pay the Chindit for crossing his land. This one and the others knew this law and insulted us by breaking it. They knew the penalty was death." He pinned Joshua with his eyes.

"Sao, this bandit is a killer. The black tar he carries will kill many people and cause nothing but ruin. Farther north the people are cutting down the mountain forests and growing more and more poppies to make into this black tar. The Chindit cannot stop the people from doing this. The *lai* is worth more than rice or teak. The fields are spreading like storm clouds and soon will devour our Ri."

Joshua nodded in silence, having seen the white and pink flowers in fields of other villages.

The Horseman stepped forward and slapped his hand on Joshua's right shoulder. "I must go, white Sao. I have wanted to meet you for many monsoons. The Chindit speaks of you with a smile. I will pray to the gods that you and the Chindit's son have a good journey to the river. It was long ago that I made the journey, and I remember well the Master Horseman's praise upon my return with the stones."

The pup pig dog growled at the hut door. Bak rose up from bed holding a pistol and shouted, "Identify yourself!"

"Teacher, it's us," Joshua said, pushing the door open.

Bak lay back down and mumbled, "I should have known you two would be back early and try to impress me."

Stephen walked in from the darkness with a beaming smile and held up a small bag filled with the black river stones. "We have traveled all night. Here are the stones for you, Teacher, a full day early."

Bak waved his hand as if shooing them away. "Good, good, now lie down and rest. I'm an old man who needs the darkness to sleep."

Joshua exchanged smiles with Stephen as they lay down by the coals of the fire in the corner of the hut. Joshua whispered, "I think he's impressed."

Stephen shook his head. "I told you we shouldn't walk all night just to return early by a day. Teacher does not impress easily."

"Naw, he's impressed, I can tell. He'll say so tomor—"

"QUIET! You two sound like whimpering pye dogs!" growled Bak.

"I told you he was impressed," Joshua whispered in Stephen's ear.

Sarah walked over the rise and abruptly halted. Below her, on the plateau, were two mounted men. Goose bumps ran up her arms and neck and she suddenly felt a warm rush of pride course through her body. The two riders were sitting erect with their heads and eyes set to the front. They wore the traditional blue mountain Shan turban and loose-fitting white shirt and pants. Around their waists were crimson sashes; both wore swords stuck in their sashes and had rifles slung over their shoulders.

Bak stepped up beside the small woman and bowed his head. "Mrs. Brown, I am honored for you to witness the last test of the two candidates. They returned from the river two days ago and have been resting and practicing for this last event."

Sarah kept her gaze on the two riders. "You've worked very hard with them, Horseman Bak, and it shows." She turned and looked into the old man's eyes before bowing her head. "I'm very proud of what they've become, test or not. Thank you."

Bak returned the bow. "And I thank you for your understanding. I am sorry the pastor could not be here to witness the test. I ask your permission to begin."

Sarah looked back at her son and Stephen, thinking of how much they had grown in the past four years. Stephen was no longer a thin, gangly boy—now a half-foot taller than Joshua, he was rawboned and had the look of a slick racehorse, all muscle and sinew. Joshua too had grown and filled out. He had become broad-shouldered and thick-chested like his father. His bronzed face contrasted sharply with his sun-bleached blond eyebrows. She thought both young men had the look of the Horsemen she had seen, confident men who knew no fear.

Sarah nodded. "Please begin."

Bak raised his hand, then dropped it to his side. Immediately both riders spun their ponies in opposite directions and took off at a full gallop.

Although his pony was galloping, Joshua's body seemed perfectly still. There was no bounce or movement of his head or shoulders, as if he were floating just above the horse. Suddenly both ponies stopped abruptly at opposite ends of the field. Both horses reared up on their hind legs and pawed the air as the two young men pulled their swords from their sashes. A chill ran up Sarah's spine hearing the swords' distinctive singing sound as the blades were pulled from their metal sheaths. The horses came down in a full run and headed directly for each other. The riders lifted their swords in the attack position. As the distance between them closed, each rider raised his blade higher, as if to make a slashing attack, but as they passed within inches of each other each rider twisted in the saddle and plunged his blade into the grass field. Both swords swayed on their glinting shafts but remained perfectly perpendicular to the ground.

Bak nodded in approval and leaned closer to his guest. "The placement of the swords was well done. Notice they are parallel to each other, which shows good timing. Now they must recover their blades. It is very difficult at a full gallop."

Both riders had reached opposite ends of the field, had made their turns, and were barreling back toward each other. Each rider leaned over the side of his pony, plucked his sword from the ground, and swung it over his head.

Sarah let out her held breath and clapped. "They're wonderful!" she cried out excitedly.

"Watch now, Mrs. Brown. They will perform without their reins, using only the pressure of their legs to direct the ponies."

The young men were now in the center of the field, facing Sarah. At the same moment both horses began sidestepping in opposite directions as both riders held their arms across their chests. The ponies halted and backed up, stopped, and came forward at a trot. At the same time each peeled away and made a wide loop before coming back to their original positions and halting.

Bak leaned toward Sarah. "Now you will see the final phase of the test, combining horsemanship and weapons skills. Notice the melons at the far end of the field."

As Bak was speaking, Joshua spun his horse around and lined up behind Stephen. All at once both ponies sank to their knees and rolled onto their sides. Both young men took their rifles from their shoulders, lay over the ponies' flanks, and fired at the melons. Stephen hit a melon, as did Joshua. Stephen fired again, followed by Joshua. Two more melons exploded in succession. Jerking their horses back up, both boys remounted and reslung their rifles. Grasping their sword hilts, they smiled broadly at each other and together made the blades sing as the shafts were pulled from their sheaths. Holding the glistening blades

high, they kicked their ponies. "Ayeeeee!" they screamed as they galloped full speed toward two remaining melons on barrels. With swords
held high they closed within striking distance and slashed downward.

On a distant hill overlooking the plateau, Sawbaw Xu Kang lowered his field glasses but kept his stare on the field. A single tear trickled down his cheek and fell into the dust.

Horseman Lante stepped up to his leader and nodded his head.
"Stephen performed as a true Horseman, Chindit. You can be very
proud."

Xu Kang rolled his shoulders back and took a breath. "Yes, I am
very proud. Of both of them." He faced the Horseman and canted his
head. "Were we ever as graceful as they?"

The Horseman smiled and handed the reins of the Sawbaw's horse
to him. "We were, Chindit . . . many, many monsoons ago."

Xu Kang bellowed in laughter and swung into the saddle. Reining
his raven horse around to face the other mounted Horseman, he stood
in the stirrups and shouted, "My brothers, the gods are smiling on me
this day! My son has become a man!"

Sarah was trying to smile as Joshua rode toward her, but her tears
wouldn't stop.

Joshua climbed down from the saddle, lifted his mother off the
ground, and gave her a kiss on the chin. Lowering her slowly to the
ground, he winked. "How was I?"

"Wonderful, really wonder— I'm sorry for crying. It's just that you
were both so good. I still can't believe it."

Stephen rode up and bowed his head to the small woman. "Your
son is an insufferable showoff." He pinned Joshua with an angry stare
before breaking into a grin. "But I love him anyway. We were good,
weren't we?"

Sarah bobbed her head, still trying to stop her tears. "I'm so proud
of you two. I'll fix whatever you want for dinner to celebrate."

The young men exchanged worried glances before Joshua sighed
and faced his mother. "Mom, it's kind of traditional for those who pass
the tests to have a little party. The Teacher and the militia are giving
us one at the Horsemen's camp. I—we won't be home tonight."

Sarah's smile dissolved. "Is there drinking involved?"

Joshua lowered his chin. "A little zu. But we know to be careful."

Sarah stepped closer. "And will there be girls at this party?"

Joshua's head dropped further. "Yes, some were invited," he said
meekly.

Sarah was about to speak but stopped herself and took a deep
breath instead. Then she spun around and headed back toward the village. After ten steps, she yelled back over her shoulder. "At least you
two be at breakfast on time."

Joshua sighed in relief and winked at Stephen as he climbed back up on his pony. He began to direct his mount toward the Horseman's hut but glanced over his shoulder at his mother walking back to the village. He looked pleadingly at Stephen, who nodded and said, "If you don't, I will. Go on, I'll explain your tardiness to Teacher."

Joshua kicked the pony's flanks and galloped toward his mother.

Sarah heard the hoofbeats approaching and turned. Joshua reined in the lathered horse and grinned as he offered her his hand. "A pretty lady should always ride. Will you allow me the honor, Mrs. Brown?"

Tears began trickling down Sarah's cheeks again as she bowed her head. "It would be an honor to ride with you, Josuha Hawkins."

Stephen took a sip of zu and tried not to make a face. Seated beside him in a white cotton dress, Chi leaned over and touched his shoulder with hers. "Will you take me riding tomorrow after our choir practice?" she asked.

Stephen felt suddenly hot and flushed. Taking a breath for strength he shrugged. "If you like."

"Oh yes, I would like it very much," she said and glanced back to the campfire where the militiamen were gathered listening to Bak tell his stories. "When will your Teacher give you the silver band of the Horsemen?"

Stephen shook his head. "He cannot. Joshua and I can never be Horsemen."

Chi's eyes darted back to him. "But you passed the test today."

"Yes, but there is another test, one that we can't take. It is the test of combat, real fighting."

"It's not fair. You have worked so hard," pouted the young woman.

Stephen leaned forward and lifted Chi's chin. "Joshua and I have always known we could not be Horsemen. The Master Horseman has taught us the old ways so that the traditions of the Shan will never be forgotten. It was an honor for us."

Chi glanced again at Bak. "Why are there so few Horsemen? It is said you and Joshua were the first to be taught by the old Horseman in many years."

Stephen began to answer but Joshua walked up behind him and answered, "Because it takes years to be trained in all the skills. The Teacher says young men who join the rebels don't have the time or care about the old ways anymore. They don't think it's necessary to learn to ride the ponies like the old Horsemen and use a sword. They want to learn about the new weapons and modern fighting." Joshua leaned forward to touch Stephen's shoulder. "Excuse us Chi, the Teacher wants to talk to Stephen and me."

Bak stood as the two young men approached. He rolled his shoulders back and filled his lungs. "My students, you have exceeded all requirements. Today it is my honor to proclaim you true Shan. As a symbol of your accomplishment I bestow these."

The old Horseman held out two brass bracelets. "The metal was taken from bullet casings and made pure by fire," he said. "Soil of the Ri and blood from this Horseman were added to the molten metal, as was the hair of a boar and water from the river. The soil represents the land we hold so dear. The blood represents the people and their toil. The hair of the boar represents the courage and cunning of the forest dwellers you have come to know and respect. The water represents purity and truth. Cooled and shaped, these bands were truly forged in honor, just as you have been over the past four years."

Bak held a bracelet up and motioned for Stephen to raise his arm. Placing the band around Stephen's right wrist, Bak squeezed it tightly until the ends touched. "This is a symbol of truth and your commitment to the Ri and your people. Wear it proudly."

Facing Joshua, he placed the other bracelet on the young man's wrist and squeezed it as he had done Stephen's. "You are not the first foreign-born to wear the symbol of commitment to our land. The Chindit was the first. Like him I have seen your love grow for my homeland and I see in your heart you are a true Shan. This band is a symbol to all that you are committed to truth, the Ri, and the people. Wear it proudly."

Bak placed his hands on the young men's shoulders and stared into the darkness. "I am proud to be called your Teacher. You have made this old man's heart sing this day." Shifting his eyes to Stephen and then to Joshua, he squeezed their shoulders and broke into a wry grin. "Tomorrow you begin new lessons. I have much more to teach. But tonight drink zu and talk to the ladies who have come to honor you. This night is yours. But remember, tomorrow you are again mine."

CHAPTER 6

1966

Shaduzup, Burma

Sarah couldn't bear to wait on the porch, so she ran out to meet the old bus that had stopped in the mission courtyard. As Stephen stepped down from the bus Sarah wrapped her arms around him. "I've missed you so much!"

Stephen returned the hug and kissed Sarah's forehead. "You are as lovely as ever, Second Mother."

Sarah pushed him away but still held his arms. "Let me have a look at you! My, aren't you handsome. Oh Stephen, I'm so proud of you." She hugged him again as Henry stepped forward and patted Stephen's back. "You do look awfully good, Stephen. We were worried that you wouldn't be able to catch a boat upriver. There have been so many rumors—"

"It was no problem, Pastor," Stephen replied, extending his hand.

Henry pumped his arm. "We have prayed for you every day. The university must be feeding you well—you look fit as a fiddle."

Stephen smiled, but he was looking past the pastor for the person he most wanted to see.

Sarah saw his searching eyes and shrugged. "He said he would be here. I don't understand where he could—"

"AYEEE!"

Stephen turned toward the sound and the approaching rider who galloped full speed into the compound. Joshua yanked the horse to an abrupt halt and jumped from the saddle in a dead run.

The two young men collided in a jolting embrace, then Joshua roughly pushed Stephen away. "By the gods, you stink of the city and civilization!"

Stephen's face contorted. "And you stink of pony and campfires!"

Joshua grinned. "I've missed you, brother. The Teacher and I have—"

"The Teacher is still—"

"Alive? What and who could kill the Master Horseman, except maybe Mother. She is killing him with her meals—he's growing fat."

Henry laughed, put his arms around both young men, and led them toward the house. "It's true. If the Horseman weren't seventy years old I'd be a very jealous man. Sarah invites him over for dinner almost every night."

"You men are terrible!" scolded Sarah. "The Horseman appreciates my food. Henry and Joshua just gobble it up and don't say a single nice word."

"Where is the Teacher?" Stephen asked.

"Up north," Joshua said. "There's been a lot of trouble with the bandits again. Since the army broke the truce the Chindit has had his hands full. The Teacher is training more militia to help the northern villages. I was helping him, but he sent me to see you."

Reaching the porch, Sarah pulled back a chair for Stephen. "Sit. I've got some roasted goat and potatoes. I'll get the food, and then I want you to tell us all about the University of Hong Kong."

Stephen waited until the small woman had disappeared into the house before pinning Henry with a worried stare. "What is going on? I saw hundreds of people on the road. They were all heading for Namti."

Henry exchanged glances with Joshua. "It's not a good time for the Shan, Stephen. The military has been attacking other minority groups in the south. The army has only sent small units to the north thus far, but the rumor is that a large force is coming to find the Chindit and his army. The Shan you saw are seeking refuge in the lowlands."

Stephen's face became a cold mask. "So the great Chindit leads an army. He won't stop until the Ri is destroyed by his foolishness."

"Foolishness?" blurted Joshua. "Don't dare say that! He's fighting for what we trained together for, the Ri and the people. The army has driven the Mon, Karen, and Kachin people off their lands, and now they're in refugee camps dying of hunger."

Stephen raised his hands, and his expression changed to one of submission. "I'm sorry. I shouldn't have said that. I apologize."

Henry shook his head. "You're both right. It's terrible what's happening to the other minorities, but fighting causes all to suffer. I would have said prayer was the answer a few years ago, but now . . . I just don't know anymore."

"I'm going to have to go back tomorrow," Joshua said. "The Teacher needs me."

"Then I will go, too," Stephen said. "Tomorrow we'll ride north together, as we used to."

Sarah came back to the porch with food and an infectious smile. "Now tell me all about the university. What classes are you taking? Have you made friends? Have you found a church?"

"Ah, Mom, let him eat a bite first."

"Hush your face, young man. Come on, Stephen, tell me everything!"

Stephen couldn't help but laugh. He stood up and surprised Sarah by giving her a big hug. "I'd almost forgotten how full of energy you are. I've missed you, Second Mother." He gave her a second hug, then released her and pulled back a chair. "Please sit down. I have so much to tell. The university is magnificent, but Hong Kong is beyond description."

Joshua slipped into the darkened room trying to be as quiet as possible and tiptoed toward the bed.

Stephen rose up and chuckled. "You never were any good at surprising me . . . until today. You've grown up, brother. When I saw you galloping toward me I thought for a moment it was a Horseman."

Joshua shrugged and sat down on the end of bed. "You're the one that's grown—new haircut, shoes, pressed shirt. You look like those pictures we used to look at in magazines. Stephen, is college really okay? I mean do you think I can handle it? Mom is sending me back to the States next month to start classes and . . ."

"You will love it, brother. It is not like anything you've experienced. The colors, sounds, people . . . so many things you can't imagine . . . And the women, by the gods, the women! They all smell like the sweetest flowers you've ever smelled and they wear so little you can see all we used to dream about."

Joshua grinned. "Really? They're really that different?"

"Different? Is black different from white? Our Shan women are beautiful but the educated women I speak of will drive you mad with lust."

Joshua's grin slowly faded. "But I'm not smart like you Stephen . . . do you really think I can make it in college?"

Stephen smiled. "A man who can ride and shoot like you can do anything he wants. College is nothing compared to the lessons of our Teacher. No professor I have had is as tough or as strict as the Master Horseman. He prepared us well. You will find the classes child's play after what we have gone through. Your only difficulty will be in getting used to the other world outside of the Ri. Your mind will be overcome by so many things to see, touch and hear. Cars, buildings, machines, music, movies, television are all things that will attack your senses and leave you shaking and breathless. The smells alone will give you a headache, there are so many. The cities will scare you as you've never been scared before, and the people . . . they are so different . . . so weak. They complain about the smallest things, it's too cold or too hot for them. And they are always in such a hurry to do everything. You will find yourself walking fast everywhere as they do. They are so spoiled, food is bought at stores or eaten at restaurants. They wear different clothes everyday and they take baths nightly. Your fellow students know everything, they think, but it is book learning. One day they are for democracy then next, after reading an article or listening to a professor they are for communism. They have no mind of their own, they are like pye dogs, whimpering and barking but never taking a stand."

"And you love all that?" asked Joshua, trying to imagine such a world.

"Yes! It is difficult to explain, but yes a hundred times. There is so much to learn and everything is there for me to learn it. Believe me Joshua, it is hard to leave the Ri but there is another world out there for you. I have seen it . . . and I want to go back and experience it all."

Joshua stood and walked to the window. "I've missed you Stephen . . . it's not the same here without you. I was kidding when I said the Teacher was growing fat . . . he's growing old. I see him and it breaks my heart. He can barely ride now . . . it's why I went with him, to help him. He forgets what he's saying. I'm going to have to go back tomorrow . . . he needs me."

Stephen pursed his lips and nodded. "Then I will go too. I have come back to see you, Joshua . . . the things I said about the university and other world are true . . . but there is not a day that goes by that I don't think of you and the times we had. I often think that together in Hong Kong we could become anything we wanted. Nothing could stop us."

Joshua looked up at the stars. "I'm going to miss the Ri . . . I love it." He turned slowly and began walking for the door. "Go to sleep Big Brother. Tomorrow we'll ride together up north like we used to. Good night."

Stephen waited until Joshua was at the door. "Have you seen him?" he asked in a whisper.

Joshua spoke with his back still turned. "Yes, just two weeks ago. Your father is looking well . . . he always asks about you. You should go and see him."

Stephen laid back on the pillow and shut his eyes. "Good night, Joshua."

•   •   •

Bak squinted and slowly a smile came to his face as he recognized the approaching riders. Stephen kicked his pony and galloped ahead. "Greetings and blessings, Teacher. It has been many months."

"Greetings and blessings my student. This old one's heart is lifted this day by gazing upon you. I see you have not forgotten how to ride."

Stephen laughed, "But I had forgotten the smell of these beasts. How goes your training?"

Bak's face seemed to droop and his eyes lost their twinkle. "The men I was to train have left me. They said I was an old fool. I think perhaps they are right. I'm too old to teach."

Stephen rode closer and hugged the old man to him. "They are fools for leaving you. Joshua and I will talk to the village elders and get them back. I have missed you."

Bak's eyes misted as he hugged the young man. "And I have missed you."

Joshua walked down the line of militiamen shaking his head. "No, no, no. You must gently squeeze the trigger after letting out a half-breath. Most of you are jerking the trigger. Now try it again, and this time concentrate on the trigger squeeze."

The men turned around and lay down on their stomachs facing posts that were serving as targets.

"Load!" commanded Joshua. "Concentrate on your target. Now take aim and take a breath. . . . Let it out slowly and fire when ready."

Standing behind the firing line, Bak leaned over to Stephen, who was watching for those not following instructions. "Joshua is an excellent teacher. He reminds me of myself, when I was younger."

Stephen grinned but kept his eyes on the shooters. "He speaks Shan better than I. He has grown up, hasn't he? He truly is a man."

Bak smiled and gave Stephen a quick glance. "You both are. I must have been a good teacher, eh?"

"You still are a good teacher, Master Horseman. I have watched you the past week, and you still have all of your skills. These men will be ready in just a few more days."

Bak straightened his back and lifted his head higher. "The gods are smiling on us. I have been made young again with my finest students at my side. Come, we have work to do." Bak strode toward the firing line and bellowed, "Concentrate! Take a normal breath and quit panting like pye dogs!"

•   •   •

The campfire crackled and popped when Joshua tossed on another log. Bak smoothed back his moustache and shifted his gaze from the coals to Stephen. "So, the university pleases you?"

Stephen leaned back on his saddle savoring the smell of the burning wood. "It is beyond my dreams."

"Tell the Teacher about the women," said Joshua, poking Stephen in the ribs.

Bak chuckled. "Ah . . . women? Yes tell me about these creatures. Perhaps you will teach Joshua something. He is like a rutting boar, sniffing and hunting but finds nothing to satisfy his lust for female companionship."

Joshua rolled his eyes and was about to respond when a branch snapped somewhere in the darkness behind him.

"Identify yourself or die!" barked Stephen, raising his rifle.

"Jesus has blessed me! I have found you!" cried out a man still hidden in darkness. "It is me, U Wat. The bandits have attacked the village! The pastor sent me to find you! They took the schoolgirls and Dau Brown—" A little gnarled man staggered forward into the fire's light and collapsed to his knees.

Joshua ran to the militiaman and jerked him to his feet. "My mother was taken?"

Bak touched Joshua's shoulder. "Let him get his breath. We need a full report. Stephen, saddle the ponies."

Bak stepped closer to the small man. "U Wat, it is important to tell us everything. Start from the beginning and leave out no details. Take another breath and begin."

Wat's chest was still heaving and his eyes were wide with terror. "They—they came without warning, just as the sun was setting. We never saw them. They attacked the church, while—while Dau Brown was teaching the young women to sing. They took them all! Oh, where is Jesus? They took my daughter and shot the pastor and—"

Bak raised his hand. "Calm yourself. Breathe and tell us about the pastor."

"He—he heard the screaming and ran to the church. They shot him in the leg and foot."

"How many bandits?"

"Tam Cuu saw them from the dormitory window. He said fifteen or twenty."

"Weapons?"

"Tam Cuu said they looked like lowlanders plus a few Karen. He saw rifles and short swords."

"How many women did they take?"

"Nine, and Dau Brown."

"Which way did they leave the village?" Bak pressed.

"East into the forest, Horseman. I sent three of our best hunters after them to mark their trail. The pastor sent me for you. I have run for hours—"

Bak patted the man's shoulder. "You have done well."

Joshua's eyes had become burning coals. He spun and faced Bak. "They have at least four hours on us."

Bak walked back to the campfire, picked up his rifle, and slung it over his shoulder. "The lowlanders can't travel far at night with ten women. We will catch them on the plain above the Yak River."

"But tonight they'll—"

Bak shook his head. "No, they won't touch the women tonight. They took them to sell to the Wa. The Karen are probably leading the pack. They will control the lowlanders. We'll stop them on the plain."

Stephen came up to the fire with the saddled ponies. "Stop them? I heard U Wat say there were at least fifteen men."

Bak took the reins of his horse and climbed up into the saddle. "We will stop them. Hand me my rifle and sword and leave the rest. We have much ground to cover before daylight. U Wat, when you are rested go back to the village and have the militia go to the plain. The bandits will have to cross the ford at the twin rocks of the Yak River."

"Take me with you!" the small man begged. "They have my daughter. You need me."

"You will slow us down," Joshua said as he mounted his horse. "But you can help. Go back as fast as you can. We will delay them until you and the others arrive."

Bak spurred his horse forward. "Follow me closely, my students. It will be a hard ride."

"How many do you count?" Bak said, unable to see that far.

Stephen kept his eyes on the distant grass field. "Nineteen men plus the women."

Joshua bit his lip, seeing his mother and the other women tied together and being led like a mule train. The men before them were spread out as they crossed the open ground. His mother and the young women were stripped from the waist up, and their dresses had been cut off above the knees so that they could walk more quickly.

Bak looked over his shoulder, then back to the field. "The sun will be in their eyes. Take your positions and do what I said. Shoot to kill if they don't follow my instructions." The old Horseman took the rifle from his shoulder and chambered a round. He set his eyes to the front again and stiffened his back. "You have been trained for this day, my students. I have prayed to the gods you would never have to face an enemy, but that day is here. If the plan fails, delay them as long as possible, then fall back across the ford and delay their crossing. They will not be able to get away by the time our militia arrives. We have defeated them." He spurred his horse forward and left the protection of the trees along the riverbank.

The Karen leader saw a movement to his front and held up his hand. The men behind him halted except for a Karen who was second in command. He came forward to his leader, put his hand to his forehead to shield the sun, and asked, "Who is it?"

The leader shook his head. "Too far to see. He is on a pony. . . . It is not a Wa."

The leader waved his men forward and stepped off to close the distance. He covered a hundred yards before he halted again and turned to his sergeant with a cruel smile. "It is a lone Horseman."

The sergeant shielded his eyes again. "They don't travel alone. There must be—"

Bak stood in his stirrups and bellowed across the field. "You are dead men if you do not drop your rifles and release the women! Do this and we will let you cross the ford and go your way unharmed!"

The Karen leader chuckled. "He is alone and yet challenges us. He is a fool."

"But he said 'we,' " said the sergeant, searching the distant tree line.

"They would have killed us if there were more. You know the Chindit's law. Shoot him."

"But—"

The leader turned with a scorching stare and hissed, "You have a rifle. Shoot him."

The sergeant stepped forward and raised his rifle to take aim.

Joshua squeezed his rifle trigger. The sergeant never heard the report. His head snapped back and he sank to the ground just as the rifle's report echoed across the field. Another man raised his rifle but he too was flung back, his throat ripped open by Stephen's shot.

Bak hollered, "Those were warning shots! Throw your rifles down *now* or we kill you all like pye dogs! Drop the guns and walk forward! Leave the women and you can cross the ford without harm! It is the truth, on my Horseman's honor!"

The leader spun around and barked, "Throw your rifles down." He lowered his voice. "But keep your knives." Turning back to Bak, he yelled, "We are following your orders, Horseman! May the gods curse you for eternity if you lie!"

Throwing his short sword down, the leader stepped forward and turned as if checking his men, but he slid his pistol from his belt into his shirt. "Throw them down and follow me." He turned about and strode toward the Horseman with his men following.

Joshua and Stephen waited until the men were twenty paces from their dropped weapons before breaking out of the trees at a full gallop. They flanked the bandit formation and headed for the women who were left behind.

Sarah had already untied the rope around her neck and was helping the younger women when Joshua reined his horse to an abrupt halt beside her. "Mother, gather the girls and run to the other side of the plain."

Trembling, Sarah began to speak but Joshua yelled, "Hurry, Mother," and spun his horse around. He kicked the animal's flanks to join Stephen, who had positioned himself behind the formation of bandits to cover them.

Bak had remained in the same spot and spurred his pony into a trot only when he saw that the women were running back across the field to safety. He came to a halt twenty paces from the Karen leader. "I have made a promise to you, pye dog, but I will remember your face. You will see me again one day, and you will die for your insult to the Chindit."

The leader gave the Horseman a cold glare. "You are an old goat and I spit on your threat. Two riders and one old goat are no threat to us. I will come looking for *you* and cut your heart out."

Bak kicked his horse forward, holding his rifle in the ready position. He passed the leader and spat toward his feet. "That is my vow to kill you. Keep walking and remember, I, the Master Horseman, will be coming."

The leader ignored the old man and kept walking. He took five more steps and spun around with his pistol in his hand. He fired.

Bak was thrown forward in the saddle by the impact of the bullet that hit him in the upper back. Spooked by the report, Bak's horse leaped forward, galloping toward Joshua. Still in the saddle, Bak righted himself just as the leader fired again but missed.

"No!" screamed Stephen as he kicked his horse's flanks. Joshua had already raised his rifle but Bak was heading toward him, blocking his view of the bandit leader. Stephen closed the distance in seconds, firing his rifle from the hip.

The leader smirked as he raised his pistol and fired. Stephen's horse's front legs buckled, and it tumbled headfirst, throwing its rider to the ground. The dead horse's body continued its forward roll and slammed onto Stephen's back, pinning him to the ground.

The leader ran forward, yelling at his men. "Kill them! There are only two left!" The bandits pulled their knives and ran screaming, joining their leader who was sprinting toward Joshua and Bak.

Joshua yelled in defiance and kicked his horse forward to meet the attack, but Bak blocked him with his pony and commanded, "Protect the women!"

The old man spun his horse around and reined the animal hard right and back. The animal collapsed to its front knees and rolled on its side. Bak lifted his rifle but the bandit leader fired first. The bullet tore through Bak's side, throwing him back. He tried to lift the rifle again but the pain was too much, and he fell to his knees. Joshua spun his horse around and galloped forward. He jumped off, pulled his pistol, and took up a position in front of his Teacher to make his stand.

The leader stopped running and fired at the young rider. He saw the rider's head jerk back, but the man didn't fall. Seeing he had only grazed the rider's cheek, he lifted the pistol again but saw something that froze his blood. The white rider's strange, penetrating eyes were locked on him, as he raised an old revolver.

Joshua blocked out the other screaming men who were running headlong toward him. He saw only the leader as he gently squeezed the trigger to seek revenge for Stephen and the old Horseman. The pistol kicked with the recoil and the Karen leader's arms windmilled as he fell back with a bullet between the eyes.

Joshua aligned his sights on the next running man. He was dark-skinned and wild-eyed, and his neck veins stood out like blue cords as he screamed. Joshua fired and the dark-skinned bandit's words abruptly ended as he spun and fell, tripping two others. Moving only a fraction, Joshua brought his sights to bear on the next man, who was only ten feet away and coming fast. Like the last man, his face was contorted in desperation, mouth open and teeth bared. Like pye dogs, thought Joshua as he squeezed the trigger. They were attacking knowing some would die, but still they followed their lust for blood and the kill. The pistol jerked with the recoil and the man's head snapped back.

The rest of bandits were almost on top of him, Joshua no longer even had to aim. He thumbed back the hammer and killed a man only three feet away and spun, shooting another in the face with his last bullet. Dropping to one knee he grabbed Bak's rifle, knowing what was to come, but determined to make them pay until the end came. He could feel the warm morning sun on his face and windblown grass stalks caressing his legs. The smell of the river was distinct, as was the sweet fragrance of the dew-laden grass. It would be a good place to die, he thought. Stephen and the Master Horseman would be with him on their journey to the clouds.

He was lifting the rifle to ward off an attacker when he heard a sound that made the hair on the back of his neck stand on end. It was the metallic singing sound of a sword being drawn.

On his feet, Bak screamed as he staggered forward and swung his blade. "AYEEE!" The blade flashed, biting through flesh and bone. The stunned attackers frantically jabbed with their knives, trying to stop his attack, but the blade sang its death song again as it slashed through the air and struck more flesh.

Joshua fired the rifle point-blank into a young bandit's chest and viciously swung the butt up to strike another in the face. "AYEEE!" he screamed as he stepped forward to hit another man, but the attackers were backing up, wide-eyed. They broke into a run toward the river. Then Joshua heard a sound like thunder. He turned and saw the Chindit and the Horsemen barreling toward him, their swords held high, glistening in the sun. "AYEEE! AYEEE!" they screamed as they rode past, led by Xu Kang, whose blade slashed downward and nearly severed a running bandit's head.

When Joshua saw Bak was still standing, he leaped over the dead and dying to Stephen, who lay still beneath his dead horse.

Unable to move the heavy animal's body, he frantically began digging with his hands. A Horseman reined to a halt beside him, jumped off his mount, and dug with him. More joined and in a minute they were able to pull Stephen's body free.

Joshua brushed the dirt from Stephen's face and saw his friend's eyelids flutter; a second later he groaned.

Xu Kang rode up and dismounted. Seeing his son was moving, he raised his chin and commanded to the Horsemen behind him, "Collect the women and bring them here." He turned and strode toward Bak, who was being attended by Horseman Lante. The Horseman gently laid the old man down on his side and looked into the Chindit's eyes, shaking his head.

Xu Kang knelt and placed the sword hilt back into the old man's hand. "You have honored our ancestors this day, old friend."

Bak smiled through his pain, raised his hand to his Sawbaw. "Bring Joshua to me," he said in a raspy whisper.

Xu Kang turned but Joshua was already kneeling down. Seeing his Teacher's injuries were worse than he had thought, he tore at Bak's shirt to find the wounds, but Xu Kang reached out and touched his hand. "They are calling for him," he said softly.

Bak lifted a trembling hand and took hold of Joshua's shirt. "This . . . this day and forever . . . you . . . you and Stephen are Horsemen." His eyes floated to Xu Kang. "Old friend . . . bestow on this student my band. . . ." Gasping, he looked back at Joshua as if in desperation. "I . . . I have lov—" His eyes stayed locked on Joshua, but the light of life began to fade.

Joshua grabbed the old man's hand, which remained wrapped around his sword hilt, and whispered, "I have loved you, too. The ancestors are rejoicing. . . ." He hugged the Horseman to his breast. "No, please God, no!"

Xu Kang removed the silver bracelet from the old warrior's wrist and stood. Backing up a step, he lifted his eyes to the sky. "The gods are smiling for they have in their presence the Master Horseman. Every campfire will speak his name—he will live forever!"

The mounted Horsemen raised their sword points skyward.

Xu Kang wiped tears from his eyes and bent over to lift Joshua to his feet. "I and my Horseman saw you fighting. You gave your heart to the Ri this day. Joshua Hawkins you will wear the Master Horseman's band. No man deserves this honor more. You and this band have truly been forged in honor."

Xu Kang lifted Joshua's arm and placed the silver bracelet on his wrist.

"Joshua!" Sarah cried out. Jumping down from a Horseman's pony she ran toward him but Joshua motioned to Stephen laying behind the dead pony. "I'm okay, Mom, but check Stephen. He still hasn't come to."

Xu Kang and Joshua watched Sarah as she checked Stephen's vital signs. She lowered his eyelids after inspecting his pupils and relaxed her tense shoulders. "He's unconscious but he'll recover. Thank God he . . ." She stopped in midsentence seeing the Horsemen lift Bak's body. "No!"

Joshua put his arm around his mother's shoulders and gave her a gentle squeeze. "He is with his ancestors, Mother . . . he will live forever."

Xu Kang knelt by his son and took the silver bracelet from his own wrist and placed it on Stephen's. After patting his son's shoulder he stood up and clapped Joshua's shoulder. "Horseman Hawkins, please tell my son he has made me very proud." Xu Kang looked once more at his son before rolling his shoulders back and taking the reins of his horse. Swinging up into the saddle he sat erect looking down at Joshua. "The gods have smiled on us all. We found U Wat last night as we rode toward the village to warn Pastor Henry the army was coming." The Chindit leaned forward in the saddle, his eyes misting. "I must return now to the north and prepare my soldiers. We do not have much time. My spies tell me the army is coming within days. I . . . I fear I will not see you again. My spies also have told me all missionaries will be ordered out of the country. The time has come for us to say farewell. I have failed as a father with my son, Joshua, but I feel I have not failed with you. It was good to see you grow and appreciate the old ways. They are gone, Horseman Hawkins . . . the old ways are gone forever . . . but by wearing the Master Horseman's band you will remember them and I pray to the gods when you smell the smoke of a campfire you will think of me. Good-bye . . . Good-bye my son."

Before Joshua could speak the Sawbaw spurred his horse into a gallop toward his beloved mountains.

PART II

CHAPTER 7

PRESENT DAY

9 A.M. 3 June, Rangoon, Burma

"Couldn't they give you more warning? Can you at least tell me where you're going this time?" Stephen Kang's wife did not hide her anger.

He avoided her frigid stare by sidestepping her but spoke over his shoulder as he made his way to the bedroom to pack. "Like I told you on the phone, they only let me know thirty minutes ago. They said the United States, but they didn't say where." Now the deputy minister of finance for the Union of Burma, his responsibilities were great.

She followed him into their bedroom. "I can't take this anymore, Stephen. The sudden trips, the secrecy, coming home from work at midnight every night. Jacob hasn't had a father and I haven't had a husband for a year. It has to end."

Stephen pulled the suitcase from beneath the bed and tossed it up to the mattress. "Mya, please, don't start. I've told you before you'll just have to believe in me. Our country is facing ruin. I've been trying to save us all. Please don't make my leaving any harder than it already is." He saw she needed more than words and reached for her. "They've promised this will be the last trip, and—"

Mya stepped away from his embrace, not ready to give up. "Your father is worried. He still says you should not trust them."

He froze and his eyes narrowed. "He contacted you again?"

"Yes, I was slipped a letter from one of his people while shopping at the market. Stephen, he's right. You can't trust them. Just look what they've done to our people."

Stephen was about to retort when a seven-year-old boy ran into the room and grabbed his leg. "Don't go, Papa, please don't go."

Stephen forced a smile although his heart was breaking as he patted his son's shoulder. "I don't want to go, but I must. Jacob, you're now the man of the House of Kang. Take care of your mother while I'm gone."

Jacob looked up at his father. "Papa, can I visit Grandfather while you're gone? He said in his letter he would teach me to ride his pony and I can go hunting with him. Please?"

Stephen's eyes turned cold again, and he looked at his wife accusingly. She ignored his look and patted Jacob's back. "Give your father a last hug, then go to your room and play. Your father and I have to talk."

She waited until Jacob had embraced her husband and left the room. "Your father said if you were to leave again that we should leave the city and go to him in the mountains. He doesn't trust them as you do."

"Damn him!" blurted Stephen. "He endangers us with his secret notes. You know how they watch us!"

Mya's eyes watered. "He's worried about us, Stephen. He says—"

"He doesn't know what he's talking about! Don't you see what he's doing? He'll make any excuse to have Jacob with him to corrupt with his foolishness! I won't have it! His army and people have abandoned him for good reason. He makes promises that can never be fulfilled. Even now he's causing problems in the north trying to be the 'Great Chindit' again. He was, and is now, nothing but a thief! And now he tries to steal my son."

Mya stared at him accusingly. "Your father sacrificed everything for you. He knew what he was and made sure you would be different. But for what end, Stephen? Who are the thieves and who are making the promises now?"

Her words and fiery eyes impaled his heart. He lowered his head, knowing she could never understand why he was working for the government. He walked to the closet, picked out several sets of clothes, and put them in his suitcase.

Mya's eyes filled with tears. She walked over and leaned her head against his back. "I'm sorry . . . I'm so sorry. I love you so much. It's just that it breaks my heart to hear you speak badly of your father. I can't bear lying to him and making excuses for you. He loves you more than anything in this world. He's so worried. Please read his last letter to you."

Stephen turned and cupped her chin to raise her head. "I'll take the letter with me," he said softly. "Things will be different when I return—I promise."

She backed away and resigned herself to his going. "I'll get your shaving kit. Stephen, please call Joshua when you are there. He writes you every month and you haven't written back in a year. Please, he misses you."

Hearing Joshua's name caused Stephen to glance at the picture on his dresser. He picked it up with a reflective smile. "Those were the best times of our lives."

Mya stepped up beside him to look at the picture. "We were all so naive and foolish when we were young. I miss being able to laugh, Stephen, and not having a care in the world. They've taken that away from us. Everywhere I go I know I'm being watched. I can't go on like this."

Stephen handed her the picture and opened the dresser for his socks and underwear. "It's going to be like it once was. You'll see."

Minutes later on the front porch he kissed her gently on the lips and backed away, trying to smile. "I love you. I'll call every day." He gave her a last, lingering look and then headed for the waiting staff car.

11 A.M.

Five miles from the smoldering U.S. Embassy, on the second floor of the Directorate of Defense Services Intelligence's ultramodern building, Major General Ren Swei stood at his office window listening to the distant sounds of wailing sirens. Minutes before he had heard and felt the rumble from the bomb explosion. In his early fifties, Director Swei of the secret police looked every bit the aristocrat he was. Dark pink scars from a battle fought with Shan mountain rebels when he was a young major etched his chin and left cheek. He wore no medals or decorations but rather let his shrapnel scars show his sacrifice and devotion to his country. Tall for a Burmese, he wore a perfectly tailored uniform that accented his fit, trim body. Distinguished splashes of gray streaked his short black hair. He shifted his intense, dark brown eyes to his deputy, who stood nearby with the telephone handset to his ear.

Brigadier General Tan nodded and spoke quickly. "Well done. I will pass the information on to the director." He hung up and smiled. "The bombing was executed flawlessly."

Director Swei lifted an eyebrow. "It's unfortunate they were so inquisitive. It was their *kan*, I suppose. You did excellent work with such little notice. I am indebted as always."

Brigadier Tan, a short but powerfully built officer, accepted the compliment with a slight head bow. "It was very close, my general. Our special operations unit was assigned the mission. They used a Shan heroin addict to drive the truck. He was so desperate for his white powder he believed he would have time to ignite the detonator and get away."

Swei sat down in his large executive chair and nodded reflectively. "It bought us time. It will take the American intelligence replacements weeks to pick up where the others left off; by then it will be too late. Has our Sao taken off for Seattle?"

Tan's chest tightened and his nostrils flared. "Yes, Kang is finally gone. He departed an hour ago. If only we could rid ourselves of his father so easily."

Swei allowed himself a rare smile and waved Tan to a chair. "Colonel Sak Po will be with Kang, and he knows what must be done once the funds are transferred. Forget Stephen Kang. Now, bring me up to date on our operation. I'll have to call the prime minister in several minutes and tell him about the 'terrorist attack.' He will not be pleased. He's having problems enough now with the minority leaders, and he's been pressing me for a date to announce the loan guarantees."

Tan took a small notebook from his pocket and flipped to his notes from the morning briefing. "The first freighter left Singapore a week ago; the second left this morning. The third's cargo is being moved to a Malaysian-registered ship like the others. The cargo has been 'purchased and sold' three times and is now Malaysian. It has all the necessary supporting documentation and cannot be traced back to us. You will meet with the Triad representative in a week, the day the first shipment arrives in Seattle. As of today the operation has had no setbacks. White Storm is on schedule."

Swei felt a rush of pride course through his body upon hearing how smoothly his meticulously planned operation was running, but it was more than the update on the freighters. It was hearing the code name he had given to the operation years before. The name was spawned in his mind when, like a storm, a sudden, unexpected chain of events occurred and made the operation possible. The Soviet Union crumbled and China needed allies. She came offering what she had never offered before, support and recognition of Burma's military government. The junta accepted and became a legitimate government in the eyes of the world. Within a year, with China's help, the army was finally able to crush the rebel insurgencies that had plagued the country for forty-five years.

But Swei and his colleagues had to face facts. The junta had consolidated power throughout Burma, but it was a hollow victory. There was nothing left to rebuild the country, now one of the world's poorest. Then came another reality: The rebels had provided the Hong Kong Triad with its opium. With the insurgents scattered, the Triad had come to Swei, the director of the DDSI, and made a proposal that would give his country renewed hope. These events led him to design and propose a master plan to his leaders—White Storm, a symbol of change.

Swei smiled inwardly, knowing his leaders didn't appreciate the powers his storm was capable of unleashing. But soon they would learn.

Seeing his general's distant stare, Tan coughed to regain his attention and picked up the phone receiver. "You need to make the call, my general."

Swei took the phone handset. He pushed two numbers to access his direct line and waited only a moment. "Prime Minister, I'm afraid I have bad news. It appears the U.S. Embassy was the site of the explosion. At this time we don't know what caused it, but it appears the damage was very severe."

Northern Burma

The ground rumbled from the hoofbeats of galloping ponies, and the yells of the riders echoed down the valley. "AYEEE! AYEEE!"

Colonel Banta got out of a new Toyota four-wheel pickup to watch the hunting party and smiled at the war cries. He had joined the Chindit twenty years before, and yet he still marveled at the old leader and his gray-haired Horsemen's dedication to the old ways. Weapons and tactics had changed over the years, but not the Horsemen. They still wore their useless swords and rode horses as the ancient ones had done hundreds of years before. Of the original one hundred, only eight remained; battles had claimed many, but now time was their enemy. Not one was under sixty.

Xu Kang broke off from the others and reined his stallion up just short of the pickup painted in camouflage. "Greetings and blessings, Colonel. Are you the only one left?"

"Greetings and blessings, Chindit," Banta said, bowing his head. Looking up, he motioned behind him down the rutted road. "Only half from the camp are coming. The others deserted and went back to their homes. They think the government will honor its agreements this time."

"By the gods, they are fools! How many do we have left?"

"Maybe four hundred men. We were able to load everyone and all of our equipment in the trucks. They will be here shortly."

Xu Kang's old black Mexican saddle creaked as he shifted his weight to his left stirrup and climbed down from his black horse. He untied a dead *gyi* from the back of the saddle and tossed the small deer onto the hood of the truck. "There will be meat in the pot tonight, my friend. It was a good hunt. The long truce has softened me. I can still ride, but I must admit my old bones prefer the Land Rover." He laughed and gestured toward the lush valley. "It's good to be back in my old camp. The army has done me a favor by forcing us deeper into the mountains. What times we had and what battles we fought from here! It is the gods' will for me to return to where it all began."

Colonel Banta smiled. "The people have heard the great Sawbaw Xu Kang has returned to the Ri. You will soon have another army to lead."

The old warrior smiled a wolfish grin. "Four hundred men left, eh? We had ten thousand strong only two years ago. They'll all come back soon enough! The lying pye dogs are up to no good with their promises. I can smell it."

Xu Kang took off his turban to reveal silver-white hair that he pushed back with a liver-spotted hand. He didn't feel sixty-nine at that moment but he knew later, once he rested, his old body would feel the effects of the long hunt. He turned once again and gazed down the valley where he had marched in 1945 as a twenty-year-old lieutenant in the Chinese Army. So long ago, he thought. Motioning for the colonel to join him, he strode to the shade of a towering teak beside his small bamboo and thatch headquarters and sat in his old campaign chair. An aide brought a chair forward for Banta, and a young Shan corporal poured two cups of cool green tea.

Xu Kang leaned forward in his chair. "Our small army is not what's important. Our secret army in Rangoon is our real source of power. We must use it and find out what the junta is doing. Also, I must have forty here who speak Burman. Send them to Rangoon to establish multiple radio bases. They should provide guidance, money, and whatever is necessary to help the others watch the DDSI and the army."

Colonel Banta unfolded a map. "And what of these *lai* labs?"

Xu Kang's brow furrowed. "The fools! I warned those Sawbaws that dealing with the DDSI was like sleeping with a cobra. We should patrol the *lai* houses and ensure there are no cobras lurking about."

Banta sipped his tea until he decided the time was right. Then he asked, "Chindit, why are you so sure DDSI will not keep the agreements? Your own son is—"

Xu Kang's eyes dimmed. "Stephen is like the others. He wants desperately to believe in them. . . ." He slowly shook his head. "Stephen doesn't understand them as I do. They're lying pye dogs! We control the mountains! The silver, tin, jade, tungsten, teak forests, and ruby mines are owned by us, the minorities. Do you really believe after all these years that they will give us independence and lose those resources? Never! Their agreements and honey words of rebuilding the country are worthless! They will strike as soon as our guard is down!"

Banta smiled and said, "The hunt has filled your heart with bloodlust."

The old soldier raised a silver eyebrow. "The Shan women say I'm too old for pleasuring them and would rather fight. There is some truth to it. I have fought too many years and know these cobras want us to believe they are tame. They only want us to become docile and expose our throats."

Banta heard the rumble of engines in the distance and stood. "I'll see to the arrivals and have the equipment stored; then I'll begin planning the Rangoon intelligence campaign."

Xu Kang rose and patted the colonel's thick shoulder. "Keep faith with this old man a little longer. I smell treachery. The cobra will strike very soon."

1400 Hours, 3 June,
Ministry of Defense, Rangoon, Burma

Director Swei was escorted into the prime minister's office and came to attention in front of the desk. The general of the army and prime minister of Burma, Aung Mawg, motioned his old friend to a chair. "The Americans are demanding more information on the terrorist attack. Do you have anything yet?"

Swei tried to look disturbed that he was letting his leader down. "I'm sorry, my general, but we have come up with very little. The cassette tape sent to the government television station is our only lead at this time. This 'People's Communist Battalion' that claimed responsibility for the bomb is new to us. We are working with the police and the army on the matter. I can assure you I have my best men on this."

Mawg sighed with resignation. "We didn't need this, did we? Our operation is still on schedule, I hope?"

Swei raised his chin. "White Storm is on schedule—soon you will be able to lead us to greatness."

Relieved, Mawg began to smile but remembered his other problem. He frowned instead. "I need to give the minority leaders a date for the announcement of the loan guarantees. Without those agreements, they will break the truce. Xu Kang has already fled to the mountains and is calling for others to join him. I fear that old man the most. Many listen to his claims of treachery on our part."

Swei nodded in sympathy. "Yes, I heard the old Chindit had returned to the mountains. It's just as well, for he will be made the bigger fool. Tell the others the date for the announcement will be Martyrs' Day, the nineteenth of July. The people will be home for the public holiday and you can make the announcement on television with the minority leaders in attendance."

Mawg's eyes brightened. "Excellent. So the plan is going well?"

"Only a few setbacks, but nothing for you to worry about. I can guarantee the nineteenth. You will be able to announce the new loans from the People's Bank in Hong Kong and can begin implementing the economic rebuilding programs immediately."

The prime minister nodded reflectively. "It is our last hope. We've strived for this day. I've given you complete authority in the execution of your master plan and have never doubted that you will see it through. We have made too many mistakes in the past my friend . . . too many."

Sensing that the meeting was over, Swei stood and gave a respectful head bow. He was about to walk out when the general said quietly, "Find the terrorists, General. They killed more than Americans. My wife's sister was shopping across from the embassy."

Swei showed grief yet resolve in his eyes. "They will be found," he said confidently and walked out. The prime minister's executive aide stood in the anteroom, and Swei motioned for the man to follow him into the hallway. Once there Swei lowered his voice to a whisper. "I told him the nineteenth—that should hold off the minority jackals until we can deal with them."

The aide whispered back, "We are ready for the word."

Swei patted the man's shoulder. "It will come sooner than you think. Keep me informed of whom he talks to."

Minutes later Swei was in the underground tunnel that ran from the Ministry of Defense to his own Directorate complex. He strode past the guards into his underground command center, where General Tan was waiting.

Tan raised an eyebrow. "Was he satisfied with the date?"

Swei allowed himself a small smile. "Of course. He trusts us."

CHAPTER 8

5 June, Washington, D.C.

"How'd you do today, Josh?" asked the old boathouse custodian.

Joshua Hawkins placed the scull on the rack and looked back at the river. "I think I'll be ready, Fred. I think maybe this is my year."

The old man motioned to Josh's eighteen-foot, flat-bottomed bass boat tied to the pier. "I gassed her up for ya. Looks like ya made a good haul on your hunt this morning. By any chance ya see him?"

Josh strode toward his boat as he put on a dirty khaki shirt. "Naw, but I've designed a new trap. I'll get him."

"Sure you will," said the old man with a smile.

Josh checked the tie-downs over the rectangular wire traps in the front of the boat before climbing in the back. He pulled down the bill of his faded blue ball cap and smirked seeing the old man's disbelieving grin. "Just you wait and see, Fred. You're a disbeliever just like the others. I'm tellin ya he's out there."

"Sure he is, Mr. Hawkins. Have a good trip home."

Josh cast off the line and started the outboard. He pushed his Conway Twitty tape into his old eight-track player that was rigged to the console and gave a last wave as he headed the small boat down the Potomac.

Fifteen minutes later Joshua tied off at the back pier of the Emporium fish market and rang the service bell. Seconds later a small, Oriental man opened the back door and stepped out. As usual he was wearing his beat-up baseball cap, ragged sweater, low-riding dress slacks and dirty, calf-high rubber boots. Mr. Ky, the owner of the Emporium, scanned the interior of the boat before barking, "How many you got?"

"Well, hello to you too, ya old goat," Josh said dryly. "Be nice to me. I had to work hard at it today, but I got ya a dozen that'll go at least three pounds apiece." Josh bent over and pulled back the wet tarp at his feet to reveal a writhing jumble of green shells, elongated necks, and clawing feet. He picked up one of the water turtles and held it up. "This one will go four at least."

Ky's eyes remained impassive as he stepped back inside the door and yelled out. Seconds later two young Vietnamese boys came out and began unloading the catch. Josh followed Ky inside, past mounds of crushed ice, stacks of iced-down fish and crabs, cleaning tables, and plastic buckets brimming with unwanted fish and crustacean parts. Ky entered his small, cluttered office. He motioned to a rusted metal chair stacked with papers. "Sit, sit, sit."

Josh settled himself on the lip of Ky's desk, knowing the pirate wanted to deal.

Ky smiled a toothy grin and held up two fingers. "You bring two dozen next time, okay? Chinese cus-ta-mers like. They want more."

Josh wrinkled his face. "Naw, a doz a day is all I can handle. They're gettin' smart. I'm having to hunt downriver as far as Fort Belvoir to get ya the dozen."

Ky kept smiling. "O-kay, o-kay, I give you fifty cent more a pound, you bring more, o-kay?"

Josh looked casually at his fingernails but spoke with an unmistakable warning tone. "I know you raised your price to your customers, so I expect the fifty-cent increase on *this* load." He looked into Ky's narrowing eyes. "Or as your *only* supplier, I might be forced to go to your competition next door. Antonio says he'll beat your price."

"Antonio no have Chinese cus-ta-mer! No deal, no deal!" blurted Ky.

Josh nodded absently and pushed off the desk. "Better have your boys load 'em back in the boat. I'll go over to Antonio's and see what he says."

Ky exploded into loud, singsong Vietnamese, slapped the desk, kicked the trash can, and stomped in place in his rubber boots.

Unimpressed, Josh stood by the office door, waiting. Seeing that he wasn't fazing the supplier, Ky threw up his hands. "O-kay, o-kay, fifty cent more. You big-time thief, Josh. You take advantage of poor, old refugee, trying to make living."

"Save it for the customers, ya old goat. Pay me," Josh said with a wry smile.

Ky's worn face cracked into a small smile. "You deal like Vietnamese." He opened a desk drawer and pulled out a wad of bills. He counted out $120 and handed it over. "Tomorrow I leave buckets of bait for you on back pier as usual."

Josh stuffed the money into his dirty khaki shorts pocket as he strode through the prep area. Ky followed him back to his boat and patted his back as he got in. "You see him to-day?"

Josh started the outboard and spoke over the grumbling engine. "Naw, but the bastard ruined another trap. I'll get him. I've built a special trap. I'm taking it out tomorrow."

Ky grinned. "You say same last week. You catch him, I pay hundred dollar."

"Deal," Josh said, casting the line. He raised his hand in farewell and turned the boat up the channel for the nearby Capital Yacht Club docks and home.

Stefne Hawkins saw her father leave the distant fish market and could hear Conway Twitty's twangy voice over his rumbling outboard. She strode down the side deck of *Lil' Darlin'* toward the bow. A small, willowy young woman, only two inches over five feet, she tossed her short auburn bangs from her eyes as she stepped over chicken wire and assorted piles of metal rods before finally reaching the prow. Her cobalt-blue eyes narrowed as she waited for her father with her hands on her slim hips.

Josh reduced power and turned into the marina's first row of slips. He saw his daughter and waved but silently braced himself for what was to come. Aiming for the second slip, he pushed the Stop button on his eight-track player, then cut the engine and glided in.

Stefne threw down a line to him, scowled, and said, "It's six; you're late as usual. You'd know that if you wore your watch. You've got to brief the summer hires at six-thirty. Simson called in sick, but I got Postroski to take his place. Harry called and says he'd like extra coverage tonight for a group of high rollers. Don't be lookin' at me to help. I've got finals to study for. You're out of milk again; Clifford drove me crazy. You owe Meg half a quart of milk." She took a step to lean over and help him up, but her boat shoe caught in chicken wire. "Damn, Dad, when are you gonna clean up this mess?"

Josh climbed up to the deck and looked around at the clutter with pride. "It takes time to design the right trap. He's big and mean and—"

Stefne rolled her eyes and stomped toward the catwalk, barking over her shoulder, "Twenty-eight minutes until your briefing. At least change and take a shower. You smell like rotten fish."

Josh watched her, but he did not see an attractive, twenty-two-year-old woman. Rather, she was the little girl who had stolen his heart years before.

Stefne turned around once she reached the cockpit and saw the look in his eyes. She gave him an understanding smile. "Tough day, huh? I put a Cutter's in the fridge for you."

She was looking and sounding more like her mother every day, he thought. He forced the ache out of his heart and put on a smile. "Thanks, hon, I'll be just a sec. I have to stow the traps."

Stefne nodded with a sigh and stepped down into the hatchway. "Twenty-six minutes until the briefing, Dad!" she said loudly, then disappeared inside the cabin.

The chairman of the Waterfront Restaurant Association glanced at his watch and anxiously looked down the sidewalk. He broke into a nervous sweat and mumbled to himself, "Damn Hawkins, damn him, damn him. Why is he always late?" The chairman hurried back up the steps to the covered patio where a young woman was just wrapping up her presentation to new employees on the Waterfront's courtesy policy. The chairman signaled the woman to keep talking and kill time. She understood, having had to do it before.

"Now I think it would be helpful to know more about where you are working. The famous Waterfront of Washington is where tourists and locals come to enjoy the scenic Potomac River, take a pleasure cruise, see a play, eat in a fine restaurant, buy fish at the Maine Avenue fish market, or just sit back and watch the boats glide by in the Washington Channel. Only blocks away from the bureaucratic bastions of Washington, the Waterfront is a place for locals to get away for a while and for tourists to come and be guaranteed a good meal and friendly service. The Waterfront, bordered by the scenic Washington Channel, offers a relaxing atmosphere without the noise and normal city distractions. Once turning off Maine Avenue onto Water Street, the customer is on what we affectionately call the Front. We have the open fish market, the Channel Inn motel, river cruise, small office complex and the wonderful restaurants where all of you are now employed. Where else can customers come and have a panoramic view of the harbor, the Washington Monument, and the beautiful Jefferson Memorial? Yes, you new employees are indeed fortunate we . . ."

The chairman had returned to the sidewalk, and he sighed in relief when he saw his tardy next briefer step out of the marina's security gate. "About damn time," he muttered and hurried back up the steps. He gave a sign to the woman to wrap it up before taking his place in front of the small audience.

"Thank you, Miss Evans, for that illuminating presentation. Folks, your next and last orientation speaker is the president and founder of Hawk Security Services, Joshua Hawkins. Mr. Hawkins's company has been employed by the Waterfront Restaurant Association for four years and has been so successful his company has become the model of other associations throughout the United States. Mr. Hawkins, like his company, is unique. He formed his company after retiring from the army as a Special Forces colonel. He served our country for over twenty years. Here, he has eliminated the problems we had with criminal elements and has made our area one of the safest in Washington, D.C. Mr. Hawkins will brief you on his company's responsibilities and what part you play in helping him protect our customers. It is an honor to present Joshua Hawkins, president of Hawk Security Services."

The young men in the audience were disappointed at the man who walked up the steps and came onto the patio. They had envisioned a tough-looking ex–Green Beret type. The short, blond man didn't fit their image at all. Needing a haircut and dressed in faded khaki work pants and shirt, he looked more like a down-on-his-luck construction foreman. The women employees were not disappointed at all. The broad-shouldered, short but good-looking man who appeared to be in his early forties was a stockier and younger version of Paul Newman. His tanned face, grayish-blond windblown hair, flat stomach, and intriguing light blue eyes made him look like a model for an outdoor-clothing catalogue.

Josh was met by polite applause and leaned over to whisper in the chairman's ear. "What the hell did ya tell 'em, Charlie?"

Charlie whispered back, "I lied. I said you were hot shit. Go get 'em."

Josh mumbled a sarcastic "thanks a lot," then smiled at his audience of thirty or forty people. As always, they were of all races, colors, and ages, typical summer hires, dressed in the different uniforms of the restaurants. The classy tuxes from the Channel Inn's Pier 7 restaurant and bar, Mexican garb and peasant dresses from the El Torito, sailor-suited Hogate's employees ... Just looking at them made him feel hungry. He ignored the podium and stepped closer before casually sitting on the edge of a table.

"Congratulations for landing jobs on the Front. You're gonna enjoy it and make good money. Don't worry, I'm not gonna take long. I know you wanna get to work and start making the big tips you've all heard about."

He got smiles from the comment and motioned to himself. "I'm Josh; that's what everybody calls me and what I prefer. 'Mr. Hawkins' makes me feel old, and at my age I don't need the reminder. I run a security service for your employers. Since you now work for them, my service extends to you as well. My service is responsible for keeping the Front free of working girls, scam artists, car thieves, derelicts, drunks, drugs, and gang problems. In short, I ensure that your customers have a safe, enjoyable meal without threat of their cars being broken into or stolen and that they can walk the strip without fear of mugging or being offered a snort of coke. I achieve this by employing off-duty, experienced MPD, Metropolitan Police Department officers to patrol the Front in civilian clothes. My crew is made up of men and women who can be recognized by a small gold hawk lapel pin on their sport jacket or blouse. Posted on the walls in your work areas is the company telephone number. If you ever have problems when you're working, you call that number. All of my staff carry hand-held Motorola radios, and we can have someone there within minutes."

Josh scanned the faces of the workers and lowered his voice an octave. "I said I work for you as well. What that means is you could be victims just like our customers. You can be victimized by your fellow employees. The restaurants you work in are successful and profitable because they have a good rep. A few slick employees can ruin that. We've had a few employees who decided to keep the dropped wallet, the forgotten credit card, or the expensive coat in the cloakroom. Not smart. Some have provided a rear take-out service of food and equipment to waiting buddies, or they've hidden stuff in their cars. That kind of activity hurts business and hurts you. My people have seen it all and know all the tricks. There is no discussion of a second chance when we catch a slicky. It's jail. I'm saying this because we need your help. If you see this kind of activity or know it's happening, call us. Those kinds of people are not 'cool.' They are stealing money and business from you as well as your employers. Okay, that's it. I said I'd keep it short. You'll be seeing me and the officers making the rounds every night, so we'll see each other again. Enjoy your job and help us make the Front a nice, safe place. Good luck."

Minutes later Josh was walking back to his boat to change into his work uniform. Ahead of him he saw a cluster of pigeons and timid sparrows gathered around a seated woman on a park bench. He couldn't help but smile. Megan was at it again. She was in her late fifties but age had been kind to her. She'd been a dancer on Broadway and made the big time for a while, but a bad divorce and a bad knee ended her career. She now ran an uptown dance studio off New Hampshire that kept her bills paid. Her hair, dyed flaming red, was tied back with a blue bandanna that matched her sleeveless denim shirt and shorts. She could have passed for normal if it hadn't been for the black leotard she wore beneath the shorts. Meg always looked as if she had just left a long Broadway rehearsal. She never wore make-up, or normal clothes. She was considered weird by many on the Front, but to Josh she was a gem. Meg had come to the Front three years before and within a few months had adopted him and Stefne as family. She was like a mother hen and had become one of his closest friends. Josh could hear her as he closed the distance.

"Not you, fatty! Let the little one have some. Damn you! Stop it! Here, cutie, here's some for you. Get back, leave the sparrow alone. You want some? Forget it. Here, you get some instead, sweetie."

"Hiya, Meg."

The woman glanced up. "Hey, I've been lookin' for you, neighbor." She stood, tossed her huge Indian-blanket bag over her shoulder, and kicked at the pigeons, scattering them in a flurry of beating wings. "They're nothing but flying rats—filthy." She took his arm, changing expression. "We gotta talk. First thing I gotta know is, has the marina board already been complaining to you about me?"

Josh sighed. "Don't worry about it. A couple temps mentioned a few things, but it's nothing serious."

Meg snickered as she walked alongside him. "The uppity bastards haven't seen nothin' yet. I'm gonna sunbathe naked soon as it gets a little warmer. That'll make the temps squirm."

Josh tossed his arm over her shoulder and gave her a gentle squeeze. "Look, you gotta quit declaring war on the temps. We live-ins are outnumbered and can't win. Just accept it. They're only around four months out of the year."

Meg threw her hand in the direction of the moored yachts and cruisers nestled in the Capital Yacht Club's marina. "It's criminal, Josh. The temps write the damn things off on their taxes as second homes. They come prancing down here all dressed in their Land's End yachting clothes once a month just to show off and throw parties to impress their rich, snobby friends. Dammit, we live here! They've got no right complaining that I dry my clothes on the boom and shrouds. And what's it to them that *Windsong* needs paint? I like her rustic! I don't want to paint her. I love it that she's flaking. She's like me!"

Josh walked up to the marina's security gate and punched in his code. "Meg, their complaints don't mean anything. We'll do what we did last year. Every time they have a party or watch television on deck we'll make written complaints about the noise. Tit for tat, remember? They'll back off just like they always do—but hey, if you do decide to get naked, call me, huh? I wanna see ya without those leotards."

Her lips slowly turned up into a smile. "Thanks, Josh. I needed a boost. Come on, I have to talk to you about Stef." She hurried down the steps to the pier, leaving him two steps behind. He saw why she had dashed ahead, for her lingerie was drying on the boom. He slowed his pace to give her more time to clean up and looked down two slips to *Lil' Darlin'*. He knew the temps would soon be complaining about his boat too. She needed paint and a good cleaning. Both *Windsong* and *Lil' Darlin'* were older sailers modified for full-time living. Mostly wood, they were classics—but no modern yachtsman would touch them. They were outdated antiques compared to the slick fiberglass sailers that were made for speed and show. Josh didn't care about speed or show—his forty-two-foot "antique" was bigger and roomier inside than the modern boats. *'Lil Darlin'* was home.

"Hey, Josh, come on board," Meg called.

Josh stepped down to the aft deck into the cockpit, where Meg motioned to the pilot's seat. She handed him a nonalcoholic beer— knowing he would accept nothing else before work—and wrinkled her brow. "Tell me about this new assistant of yours. Bob, right?"

"I thought you said you wanted to talk about Stef?"

She gave him a "humor me" look. He shrugged. "Yeah, it's Bob. Bob Stevenson. He started to work part-time a few months ago up in my front office. He graduated from college a couple of years ago with a criminology degree and got a snuffy job with the Drug Enforcement Administration. He found out soon enough he needed a master's degree to get ahead in their organization. He got a release and is going to Georgetown. He works for me around his classes."

Meg raised an eyebrow. "Did you know Bob and Stef have a thing for each other?"

Josh rolled his yes. "He's too busy to be interested in Stefne. Hell, he's at least five years older than—"

"Three."

"What?"

"He's three years older than Stef. I asked."

"Why are you askin' stuff like that? When did you talk to Stef, anyway?"

"Look, Josh, she came over and borrowed some milk, alright? We talked—girl talk, y'know? The subject came up about this Bob guy. She says she likes him a lot and isn't sure how you'll take it and—"

"She said that? Stefne doesn't say stuff like that."

"Not to you; you're her father. Give her a break, will ya? She's a grown woman, and a darn good-lookin' one at that . . . or haven't you noticed?"

"She said that? I'm gonna have to talk to her and—"

"Don't you dare! What women say during girl talk is privileged.

I'm just warning you to take some time and look at your daughter. Heaven forbid, she's like you. She does what she wants and is hard-headed, but don't be surprised when one day she tells you she's in love."

Josh waved the last comment away. "Thanks, but Stef isn't even close to fallin' for Bob. She's going to law school once she graduates this summer, remember? She has her life all planned, and fallin' for Bob or anybody else isn't on the list—at least not until after law school."

Meg frowned and pushed her red bangs from her eyes. "Josh, you're as stupid as they come, and I've known a lot of stupid men. Listen to me. I'm trying to be subtle here but you're not listening to what I'm saying. Stefne *really* likes the guy. When you're off playing the great white hunter, those two talk a lot."

Josh looked over the wheel toward *Lil' Darlin'* with a distant stare. "I—I had no idea."

"Because you're stupid," said Meg with a smile. She slapped his back. "Cheer up, it's not the end of the world. Your daughter is very happy. Be happy for her."

Josh's jaw tightened as he lowered his eyes to the beer bottle. He didn't want to lose her, too. He faked a smile, put down the beer, and got up. "I'd better go get dressed." He took two steps before looking over his shoulder at the redhead. "Thanks, Meg. I'll drop by the milk I owe ya later tonight."

Meg began to respond but he had already jumped to the pier. She shook her head, wishing there had been another way.

Josh entered the cabin hoping Stefne would be there. She wasn't, but a Post-it note was on the computer screen. He took a step toward the desk and leaned over to read the note.

Dad—
   I'm at the library picking up some books. Your pork chops are in the oven and corn is on the stove. Baked potato is in the microwave (remember to stab it with a fork). Be back later.

Love ya, Stef

Josh sat down in the leather office chair and looked around the cabin. It always seemed empty when she wasn't there. Slowly his eyes panned from the cabin door across the bookshelves to the small galley that had her touch everywhere. The little wooden rainbow hanging on the light over the sink, pictures stuck to the refrigerator with tiny bear magnets, the smell of her perfume that lingered in the cabin. His eyes shifted back to the desk where her school notebook lay open. He leaned over, studying her handwriting, the perfectly made loops and twirls of the letters and the exact spacing between words, not an erasure mark anywhere. She was just as meticulous and organized as her mother had been, he thought. He glanced at the work calendar and saw names in each block of every day for two weeks, along with the times for the shift changes. She did it all—wrote the checks, made the calls, and organized the shifts, all while a full-time *A* student at Georgetown.

Josh lowered his eyes to his callused hands in thought. His baby girl was falling in love? How come he hadn't seen it? He should have seen it, he saw her every day! Closing his eyes, he knew he hadn't really been seeing her, he'd been seeing his little girl.

He felt something brush his leg and opened his eyes. "What ya been doin', Clifford?" He bent over, picked up the fat yellow cat, and scratched its head. "I hear you been drivin' Stef crazy."

"Jesus, boss, aren't you dressed yet?"

Josh turned and looked at his new assistant, Bob Stevenson, who stood in the hatchway. Yes, he thought, he was fairly good-looking—tall, broad-shouldered, athletic. Josh could still whip his ass in racquetball two out of three games, but—

"Boss, you alright? Come on, the shift will be here in ten minutes," Bob said, uncomfortable with his boss's stare.

Josh got up and motioned toward the cabin door. "Go check the radios. I'll be right there." Without waiting for a reply, Josh walked down the narrow passage past the galley and entered the master sleeping berth. Minutes later he was dressed in his work uniform of gray slacks, starched white button-down shirt, regimental tie, and blue blazer. He picked up his thirty-five-dollar Casio digital diver's watch and strapped it to his wrist. Turning to the mirror, he brushed back his hair with his fingers, then glanced over his shoulder at the picture of Jill hanging over the dresser. He smiled and whispered, "She's growing up, hon. You'd be real proud."

The small office in the Waterfront Restaurant Association building was packed as Josh walked in and nodded to the seven waiting people. He strode straight to the compartmentalized battery recharger and pulled out a Motorola radio. Facing his part-time employees, he quickly inspected their civilian dress as he spoke. "It's business as usual tonight. Harry, from Hogate's, wants a little extra coverage 'cause he's got a group of high rollers, but I'll take care of it. Who's base tonight?"

A hard-faced blonde lifted her hand. "I am, Josh. I drew it again."

He patted her shoulder. "Betty, give us all commo checks every thirty minutes—the radios have been actin' up." He smiled at the others. "Okay, let's do it."

Bob waited with Josh until the others had departed for their assigned beats, then followed his boss out the door. Josh glanced at the younger man once outside. "You don't have class tonight?"

"Nope. I've got finals next week."

Josh nodded absently and began walking up the sidewalk toward Hogate's. Bob fell in beside him. Josh stopped and asked, "Where you think you're goin'?"

"With you. You said you wanted me to tag along tonight and see how you ran things, remember?"

"When did I say that?"

"This morning, boss. Are you alright? You've been out of it this evening."

Josh suddenly remembered. It had been when Bob checked in at the boat that morning before opening the office. Damn, the kid was right. He *was* out of it. The headlines in the morning paper had got to him. Reading about what had happened in Burma had blurred his brain.

The two men walked along in silence and entered Hogate's, the famous seafood restaurant. They strolled past the line of tourists waiting for tables and turned right, into the crowded bar.

Harry, the manager, saw Josh and rushed up to him. "Damn, I was just about to call and see what was holding you up. I already have problems."

Josh glanced over the crowd and noted most were wearing expensive suits and stylish ties. "They look like money to me."

Harry lowered his voice. "They're all lawyers attending a convention. At the window table, number six, there's a couple of lookers wanting to cash in."

Josh nodded and motioned for Bob to follow him. "We'll take care of it, Harry."

The blonde saw him coming and lifted a perfectly painted eyebrow. "Hiya, Josh. Don't worry, we're just having a couple of drinks."

Josh sat down and gave the stunning woman a knowing smile as his eyes took in her low-cut, sequined dress. "You're looking really good, Wanda, but you know the rules. Once they're off the Front they're open game, but here you so much as bat an eye at one of these ambulance chasers, it's the street. Finish your drink and be a nice girl and do business elsewhere."

"Who is this bozo?" the raven-haired looker across from the blonde said with a sneer.

Wanda batted her eyes at Josh. "Meet the White Knight, Dakota. He's the Mr. Clean of the Front. Isn't that right, Josh?"

Josh extended his hand across the table. "Pleasure to meet you, Miss Dakota. You must be new in town and don't know the rules. Wanda knows them, so listen to her. It'll keep you out of trouble."

Wanda sighed and pushed back her chair. "Okay, White Knight, we're out of here." She reached for her purse but Josh touched her hand and winked. "It's on the house, good lookin'."

Wanda gave him a lingering look before smiling wanly. "I had to try, Josh. It's business, ya know."

Josh got up and pulled back her chair for her. "I know. Take care of yourself. You know my number if you get in over your head."

Josh watched the women walk toward the door and then acknowledged the grateful nod from Harry, who was standing at the bar. Bob grinned as he stepped up beside his boss. "I'm glad you wanted me to tag along tonight. I knew the company did this kind of thing, but seeing it is . . . is . . ."

"Our job," Josh said with a sigh. "They were easy, but it'll get rougher. You'll see what I mean when the Front heats up. Watch and listen to me tonight. Knowledge will give you strength."

Bob squinted. "Huh?"

Josh sighed again. He was *really* out of it. The phrase he had spoken countless times in his past had slipped out. He glanced at his right wrist at the thin, worn silver bracelet that he had worn for thirty years. Like his memories of the Master Horseman, the silver band had become a part of him.

CHAPTER 9

JUNE 5

10:40 P.M., SEATAC (Seattle-Tacoma) International Airport

The passengers of Flight 803 from Japan wearily gathered their luggage from the carousel and made their way to the Customs counters. Booth nine's Customs officer finished processing a Japanese businessman and motioned for the next passenger. A tall, Oriental man the officer judged to be in his late thirties stepped forward and held out his passport and visa. Seeing the passport was from Burma, the Customs officer eyed the passenger more closely. Since the bombing of the American Embassy in Burma, everyone coming in from that country was to be checked and logged. He scanned the passenger's face and compared it to the passport picture. The high, chiseled cheekbones, prominent nose and chin, and aristocratic face all fit. The officer handed the passport back and motioned behind him. "Mr. Kang, please proceed along the blue line to the tables behind me."

The officer watched the passenger's eyes for a response. There were no signs of nervousness or distress. He was very good or he was clean, the officer thought, as he motioned for the next passenger.

The black female Customs officer waiting at the table took Stephen's visa and handed it to her assistant, who strode toward a distant office. She opened his passport to do a routine check and flipped through the pages, looking at the stamps. "You visit Hong Kong quite a lot, Mr. Kang. Are you a businessman?"

"Deputy minister of finance," he said without inflection.

"This is your first trip to the United States, I see. Is it business or pleasure?"

"Pleasure. I'm going fishing in your glorious mountains."

She smiled as if being friendly. "Your English is better than mine. Where did you learn to speak our language without an accent?"

Stephen gave her a soft smile, knowing her questions were not just idle curiosity. "English is the second language of my country. We were a British colony for many years."

The officer nodded and glanced at his declaration form. "You have nothing to declare?"

"No, nothing."

She carefully went through his luggage and confirmed what she already knew—he was clean. As she closed the large suitcase, her assistant returned with the visa and handed it back to her. Smiling again, the officer handed Stephen his passport and papers. "Welcome to the United States, Mr. Kang. Have a nice stay."

Stephen nodded without reply, picked up his bags, and walked toward the exit.

In the reception area, standing behind the throng waiting for the passengers, three Burmese men waited for Kang, the last member of their team. Their leader, Colonel Sak Po, was Brigadier General Tan's deputy special operations director. Like all the senior leaders in the DDSI, his aristocratic family had sent him to a United States college. A 1975 graduate of Washington State University, he had returned to Burma and been appointed a lieutenant in the army. Four years later he was recruited into the DDSI for his keen intellect and his expertise in financial matters. In 1987 he trained in East Germany with the Stasi. Upon returning to Burma, Po became the principal architect of the special operations department of the DDSI. A small, slender man with almost feminine features, he was continually underestimated by those who knew nothing of his background.

Po genuinely liked Stephen Kang, for he was extremely intelligent and could be depended on for independent and original thought, rare attributes within the DDSI. A year before as the deputy finance minister, Kang had briefed the prime minister on several proposals he had written for restructuring the country's massive debt. His proposals had been brilliant, showing his analytical and meticulous mind. His proposals had been approved and he'd been asked to join the government's Recovery Planning Group to represent the minorities of Burma. In just a matter of weeks, he had become the principal architect of the recovery plans and leader of the Group. Since he was half Shan and his father was the government's enemy, the opposition and minority party leaders believed he would represent them fairly. For the past year he had worked long hours, unaware that he was in reality in charge of a small portion of a much larger operation—White Storm. Po had kept the Recovery Planning Group compartmentalized so the other members knew nothing about the overall operation, its purpose or even its name.

Stephen saw Colonel Po and made his way through the crowd toward him. He liked the small man because the colonel respected his abilities and treated him as an equal. As Stephen approached, the colonel's grin enlarged and he held out his hand, Western-style.

"Stephen, so good to see you! I trust your flight was a good one?"

Stephen took the offered hand and returned a weary smile. "Greetings and blessings. Yes, but it was very long."

Stephen then noticed the other two men, whom he knew all too well. They stepped up to flank their superior and dipped their chins, but neither spoke. They were both captains from the special weapons and security detachment, selected from the army for their size, intelligence, experience, and all-important family background.

Po clapped Stephen on the shoulder. "Come, we must get you to the hotel, where you can rest. Sing, his bag please."

Captain Su Sing stepped forward and took Stephen's suitcase with hidden disdain. To assist a minority, especially a Shan, was beneath him.

Stephen's brow furrowed as he began walking alongside Po. "During my night layover in Japan I heard reports on CNN of the American embassy bombing . . . who would do such a thing?"

Po's face contorted in feigned anger. "The filthy communists were responsible."

"Communists? They have never been a threat to us," said Stephen, surprised by Po's accusation.

The colonel slowed his steps. "Stephen, you of all people know our country is on the verge of economic collapse. . . . the communists are trying to hasten our fall."

Po stepped closer to Stephen and lowered his voice. "Now that you are here we can save our country. . . . Stephen, you are here because we are going to be negotiating with some very influential American businessmen. The prime minister approved your plan for opening our country to Western business."

Stephen stopped in openmouthed shock. "He approved my plan?"

Po took his arm and kept him moving. "Yes, almost four months ago. We had to keep it a secret for security reasons. Until we hold free elections it is against American policy for these businessmen to deal with us. To keep the American authorities from knowing we are conducting negotiations, I and the others have identification making us Thai-American citizens. We must secure the loans and guarantees now."

Stephen nodded reluctantly, knowing all too well how much they needed the loans.

Outside a minivan was waiting. Stephen recognized the driver, a DDSI sergeant. Once the other four men were inside the vehicle, the sergeant pulled away from the curb. Po motioned toward the driver. "Sergeant Shin will be with you from now on, for security reasons."

Po opened a briefcase and handed Stephen a thick packet. "Inside is your cover background paper. Read it and memorize all the information. You are now an American citizen. Inside you'll also find a driver's license, credit cards, and five hundred dollars. You also have a rental car that Shin will drive for you. Your new identity will be used from now until you return here to the airport. I've been here the past month finalizing the arrangements and have had no problems, so don't be concerned. Captains Sing and Bwin will be monitoring our overall security."

"You have found American businessmen willing to take such a risk?" asked Stephen.

Po smiled. "They want to be ahead of their competitors. Profit always outweighs the risk. The oil and mining representatives are very eager to acquire exclusive rights. We will get the loans from them with no problem." Po patted Stephen's leg. "Sit back and rest, my friend. The nine-hour time difference plays havoc with your system. Shin has already checked you into a room that adjoins his, and I put some pills on your nightstand that will help you get a full eight hours of sleep. Take them, Stephen. I need you ready. The negotiations begin in three days. Your plans for the future of our country will soon become a reality. You can be very proud."

Sergeant Shin took Stephen's bag and led him through the side entrance of the Holiday Inn's Holidome. Once inside, Stephen stopped in awe. He had never seen anything like it. The huge glass ceiling forty feet above completely enclosed a large swimming pool partially surrounded by rock formations and junglelike gardens. Large tropical trees, ferns, and flowering plants gave the surreal effect of being in a tropical paradise.

The sergeant smiled at Stephen's expression. "It is very nice, yes? Our rooms are just ahead. We can walk out our front door and enjoy this beautiful place." He led Stephen to a door just thirty feet from the pool and motioned to his right. "I'm next door and the others are in the next three rooms. Let me show you how lucky we are."

He opened the door and tossed Stephen's suitcase onto the king-size bed. "Have you ever seen such a bed? And if hungry or thirsty all you have to do is pick up the phone and dial room service. They will bring you almost anything you desire."

At the mention of "phone" Stephen shot his eyes to the husky sergeant. "I must call my wife. How do I get through?"

Shin frowned. "Yes, I understand, but you cannot call. To phone our country would violate security. Records are kept of such calls and would tell the authorities we are here. Tomorrow morning I will drive you across the city and you may phone her and explain that you will not be able to call again. You will tell her the reason is security. Sleep now. Tomorrow you can relax and enjoy the pool and other wonders this place offers. Our rooms adjoin and the door will always be open. If you need anything just call for me, night or day. I'll always be with you."

Weary from the long trip, Stephen nodded in silence, knowing that nothing had changed. Despite being in the United States he was being watched and told what he could and could not do—he still wasn't trusted. But a few minutes later he lay down and smiled with pride. They had accepted his plan! Soon his country would be open and have a freely elected government. Mya would be so proud of him . . . and perhaps, so would his father.

9 P.M., *Washington, D.C.*

In an executive conference room of the State Department, Gordon Thorton, the White House deputy national security adviser, sat down at the table facing three men who made up a very select special committee. Thorton glanced first at the crusty, silver-haired man directly across from him whom he knew well and secretly admired, Director William Jennings of the CIA. Jennings was a no-nonsense leader who was known for not pulling punches. The second man was Lieutenant General Nathan Summer, head of the Defense Intelligence Agency. A tall, broad-shouldered West Point ex–football star, he was, at forty-nine years old, the youngest man in the room. The third man was James Cutter, the State Department's former chief of Southeast Asian affairs and now State's newly appointed bureau chief of International Narcotics Matters. Cutter, a Harvard man, was a bookish type; he even wore small, wire-rimmed glasses and a bow tie to add to the stereotype. Despite not being a backslapper or a people person, Cutter was considered one of the most steady men in the State Department.

Thorton cleared his throat and spoke somberly. "Gentlemen, I appreciate your attendance at this late hour but I'm sure you understand why the president gave me permission to call this committee together. The president has had time to digest your updates and now wants you to give him options."

Director Jennings casually lifted his hand from the table. "Gordy, the updates we've been giving you and the president have been just that, updates. We also just got in some new information that you and the president haven't seen. Before you start pressing us for options I want to make sure you understand what we're up against." Without waiting for a reply, Jennings nodded to his assistant. "This is Harv Irving, one of our desk men for Burma. Harv, go ahead and give Mr. Thorton the latest poop."

The Burma desk officer looked at Thorton. "I will quickly recap the events as we presently know them, then discuss the newest information. On 3 June, an agent from the CIA's Counter Narcotics Center assigned to work with the DEA country team was reported by the Rangoon police as having been seen by several witnesses in his car prior to veering off a road, breaking through a guardrail, and plunging into a Rangoon river canal. His body was not recovered. None of our embassy staff were allowed to interview the supposed witnesses of the accident. An hour after the accident the embassy was attacked by a bomb-laden truck. You have seen it on CNN, so there is no need to go over what the press has reported thus far about the events. The loss of life has been placed at nineteen embassy staff personnel killed and another thirty-six wounded, nine of them critically. Twenty-two Burmese were also killed, twelve working in the embassy and the rest outside the front gate in cars, on the sidewalk or shopping in the stores across from the American compound. What the press does *not* know is the following: Television security cameras at the main gate recorded the entire event up to the explosion. The security control room in the basement of the chancery was not destroyed, and the tape of the events prior to the explosion was saved."

Irving stepped over to a television and VCR set up on a metal stand and pushed the Play button of the VCR. "Our technical support people have copied the tape in slow motion for analysis. What you are seeing now is Chief of Station Alex Manning's staff car pulling up to the gate. Our technical staff enlarged the frames and we have identified the occupants of the vehicle as the Defense attaché, Colonel Abbot, right front seat; agency case officer Robert Jobaski, driving; Alex Manning, the COS, right rear passenger seat; DEA chief Gilbert Halley, left rear passenger seat. Note the Marine guard, now."

Thorton cringed as the back of the young Marine's head exploded toward the camera. He was about to avert his eyes from the screen when the truck came into view. "Oh, God," he murmured aloud, as in slow motion, the small staff car collapsed around the truck's extended bumper and the DEA chief was flung from the vehicle. The camera view changed to one obviously of a camera attached to the roof of the building for the truck was seen from an above angle. The television screen turned to static just as the front portion of truck disappeared behind the front entrance awning.

Irving took a cassette from his pocket and inserted it into a cassette player on the table. "This tape was also recovered from the control room. Prior to leaving the embassy the COS had his staff make two copies of this conversation. One he placed in a envelope to be sent to us, the copy I have now; another copy he took with him. The tape you are about to hear is a call from the agent who later would be involved in the canal accident and is believed dead." He pushed the Play button.

The four men exchanged glances after listening to the words of agent Peter Drisco. Then Irving returned to the head of the table. "Mr. Thorton, as you know, we sent aircraft for the remains of the deceased. The first aircraft returned early this morning with the bodies and all the case files of the COS and Colonel Abbot. Those records are at Langley and are still being studied."

Irving dipped his chin and returned to his seat behind Director Jennings, who raised one bushy silver eyebrow. "Gordy, based on the security camera tape, this was not a random terrorist attack. There are too many coincidences. First, the call from the agent at the airport that you heard. Second, his subsequent wreck and disappearance. Third, the shooting to ensure that the chief of station's vehicle was stopped at the gate. Fourth, the truck striking that particular car at that particular moment. We believe this was a hit to specifically kill the members of the embassy's intelligence community. It is our opinion that this drastic action was ordered by elements in the military government of Burma who are directly involved in the production of heroin and are trying to cover it up."

Jennings let his words sink in before speaking again. "As you and the president have read in our recent updates, we believe the junta is producing heroin. Manning's mission had been to find us hard proof. His cables of the past week indicated he had a lead. The agent's recorded tape confirms he had found something." Jennings nodded toward the uniformed officer across from him. "Nathan has been providing us with the satellite photos, so I'll let him give his opinion on this."

General Summer leaned forward in his chair. "Mr. Thorton, the National Reconnaissance Office is taking more shots as we speak, but with the photos we've taken over the past two years our imagery analysts and those of the Agency agree that there appear to be five major production facilities operating in northern Burma. The DIA agrees with the CIA assessment. We believe the junta killed our people to cover up their illegal heroin production activities."

Thorton nodded slowly and leaned forward, placing his elbows on the table. "Alright then, what I need from you now are options for the president to consider on how to handle the situation. He's going on national television tomorrow to respond to the press about what happened in Burma. Do we have enough for him to accuse their government of a cover-up?"

Jennings's face showed his surprise, "Wait a damn minute. You're jumping ahead of us on this. What we just explained is our opinion based on the information we have. But it's too damn early for the president to accuse them of anything."

Thorton stared at the director. "Do we have enough to make the accusation, or don't we?"

Jennings shook his head. "The junta has got us by the balls. There isn't hard proof they were directly involved in the bombing or the disappearance of our agent, and we sure as hell don't have the assets to find anything without their cooperation. The bastards have us in a box and know it."

Thorton's eyes widened in surprise. "Hold it! You're telling me your agency doesn't have spies, or whatever you call them, in Burma! What the hell have you been doing, for God's sake?"

The director bristled. "I'm telling you they've shut us and our allies' intelligence efforts down. Their fucking secret police has had years to tighten the controls and build an informant network so tight a flea can't get into that country without them knowing about it. We're not talking about a half-assed, two-bit organization that can be bribed or co-opted. These bastards are more high-tech and five times more brutal than what the East German Stasi used to be. They don't imprison informers, they kill them."

Thorton's eyes darted to the other two men. "Is this committee telling me the president is going to have to accept the junta's explanation when we all know it's bullshit? The lying bastards have killed nineteen of our people! Jesus Christ, one of you has got to have people in Burma that can get us proof. State, Mr. Cutter, what about your embassy staff contacts?"

Cutter shook his head in silence.

"General Summer, surely the Defense Intelligence Agency has informers in their military?"

Summer's lip twitched before he spoke. "Sir, I'm afraid with the draw-down of strength and fund cuts we've experienced in the past four years, our Defense attaché staffs have been cut to bare minimum. Burma was not a high priority."

Thorton's shoulders began to sag. "Somebody better have something, dammit."

Jennings ran his hands through his silver mane before leaning back and speaking tiredly. "Gordy, none of us have assets in place, at least informants who are willing to talk. This situation is like the Lockerbie Pan Am bombing. We knew the Libyans were responsible but couldn't get the proof until much later. Forget about quick answers on this, there aren't any. To find undeniable proof is going to take time, just like it took to get the Libyans. All of us know what must be done and eventually we'll get them, but—"

"Goddamn it, the president is going to be grilled tomorrow by the press corps!" Thorton blurted. "Did you read the *Washington Post* this morning? The bombing was front-page news, for God's sake! The people want answers and the president must respond!"

Jennings glared hard at the national security adviser. "Then tell them the truth! Tell the press that the administration wouldn't approve our requests for more people and funds. Tell them how the White House and Congress told this committee to cease covert operations in Burma because their friends the Chinese had aligned with the junta. The same fucking Chinese that were, and still are, pouring in arms and advisers. Tell the truth, Gordon, and don't come here looking for answers and insult us when you damn well know you cut the intelligence community's balls off years ago."

Thorton glared back. "Don't sit there and blame our policies, Mr. Director. All of us in this room know China is this nation's last real threat. Burma is nothing but a pimple on the ass of an ant. The decision to keep relations friendly with China is in the best interests of this nation. You and everybody else in this room agreed with the president's foreign policy. Don't avoid the problem by giving me excuses. I need to give the president this committee's recommendation tonight."

Cutter pushed back his glasses on his nose and spoke softly. "Mr. Thorton, I understand the need for the president to respond. I suggest you explain the facts to the president and have him take a cautious approach that gives him latitude to come back later and take action. You must give this committee time to find the answers."

Thorton lowered his head in thought. Several seconds passed before he looked up with a distant stare. "I'll advise the president to play it down the middle. He'll accept the junta's explanation but will say he expects from them an agreement to form a cooperative American-Burmese task force to find and bring the terrorists to justice. That approach will give you at least a week to find some proof before the press demands a status of Burmese cooperation."

Jennings shook his head as if dealing with a child. "That's ridiculous. We'll need months to build a case. You're suggesting a cowboy operation that breaks the first rule of the community—-plausible denial. Gordy, in our business we must establish a cover story so that our government and the Agency aren't fingered if an operation turns sour. We can't mount an operation without—"

Thorton shook his head. "You don't get it, do you? The president doesn't give a shit about plausible denial. He knows his so-called drug war is a toothless tiger; he knows it and wants to take some real action. These assholes killing our people gives us an excuse to do something that will eliminate at least the heroin problem once and for all. Plausible denial is not a factor in this. It's in this country's national interests to eliminate the junta and shut down its drug production, and no third-world country's whining to the U.N. is going to mean a flying fuck to us. I'll give you three weeks. That's as long as I can keep the press from knowing we're stalling. Gentlemen, I have to brief the president on this. Find him something that proves or disproves the Burmese government's involvement in the bombing. I will ensure that the president gives you the authority to do so, tonight. Now if you will please excuse me." Pushing back his chair, he stood, dipped his chin toward the three men, and walked out the conference room door.

The CIA director looked at the other men at the table and slowly shook his head. "The president might want to get tough, but the congressional oversight committee will have to have its say."

"They'll approve it," said Cutter flatly. "The mood has changed in Congress since Senator Walker's wife was killed by the junkie last month at Tyson's Corner mall. And don't forget that *Post* article revealing those four congressmen's kids being addicts. My guess is they'll let the mission go and jump on the president's bandwagon. Burma doesn't have any friends in the international community except for China, and when it comes to drugs they wouldn't dare protest U.S. action. The president smells blood and sees an easy, quick solution. He can get rid of their government and at the same time get rid of one of the world's principal heroin producers."

General Summer furrowed his brow. "This is not how we've done business in the past. It's a major shift in policy that, frankly, I think has been needed for a long time."

Jennings looked at the two men with a rigid stare. "The immediate problem is that Thorton has just told us to throw together a cowboy operation. That's asking for a damn miracle in the time he's given us."

Cutter stood with a weary frown. "I suggest we take a break, order some sandwiches up here, and then see what miracles we can come up with."

General Summer pushed back his chair and stood up, signaling a unanimous decision.

Hours later, Director Jennings puffed on a cigar and paced back and forth in front of the other two committee members. "Alright, we've discussed this thing to death. Let me try and summarize what we've decided tonight. First, we all agree that the military government was involved in the murders of our people. Second, based on the evidence we have, we're going with the theory that the bastards ordered the hit to cover up their involvement in heroin production. Third, we agree that our efforts in finding proof should be directed at linking the government with heroin production or trafficking. Fourth, we agree to send in teams to find the proof as soon as we can assemble assets. Fifth, we agree to bring in Justice and Treasury so the FBI, Immigration, and Customs boys can work on the tape. We all feel the tape of the agent's phone message is the key to this whole mess. FBI and Customs will have to confirm or rule out that we have Burmese nationals in the United States with bogus visas. If they are here, the FBI will find out why." Jennings stopped pacing and faced the other committee members.

"Anything else?"

Cutter looked over the rims of his glasses. "We'll need to bring in the DEA. We'll need their resources and backing on the heroin theory."

Jennings's brow furrowed as if he were in pain. "Yeah, you're right, but we're going to have to put up with them screaming foul when they find out they weren't brought in from the beginning. John T. will stick it to us and go crying to the president. You know him as well as I do."

Summer raised an eyebrow. "I'll try and settle his ruffled feathers."

Jennings blew out another cloud of smoke. "Good luck trying to talk to that asshole. Alright, I think we should go home, clear our minds, and get some sleep. But first let's contact our staffs and have them put together folders on assets for the infiltration. I'll take care of the calls to Justice and Treasury. Nathan, you call John T. and see if you can smooth the waters. We'll have a full working group meeting at ten to get them all on board, then afterward the three of us will meet again to compare assets and begin initial planning for the operation."

"Have you thought of a name for this operation?" asked General Summers.

Jennings took the cigar from his mouth. "Yeah. We'll name it what it is. We'll call it Operation Miracle."

.   .   .

Josh glanced at the crowd in the bar at Pier 7. The shift was almost over. He nodded toward two men sitting at a table. "The one on the right is the one they called us about. He might be trouble."

Bob gave the man a casual glance and turned back to the bar. "He's big and he looks drunk."

"He is," Josh said. He leaned against the bar but kept his eyes on the heavy customer. "Okay, we've made the rounds twice and I've explained the business. You think you've got it down?"

Bob's brow furrowed. "I think so. You've got two officers watching the two access roads off of Maine Avenue onto Water Street. Their job is to report anything out of the ordinary like cars making multiple passes or gang cars. They also keep a watch on the cars parked on the street for break-ins. Three officers are rovers and make the rounds of the parking lots and the restaurants, checking the bars, kitchen, receiving area, and back. Base's job is to screen the incoming calls and notify us if there are real problems. Base is also responsible for calling the First Precinct if we need backup, right?"

Josh still kept his eyes on the customer. "Yeah, it's a simple but effective operation. You've been working the day shift where all you do is answer calls and pass them on. I thought it was time you saw what we really do. The reason is this: I want you to start taking over for Stefne. She's been able to manage school and the admin stuff, but she starts law school in the fall. I'll up your salary to five hundred a week for the extra work. You think you can handle it?"

Bob began to respond when Josh pushed off the bar and nodded toward the customer. "Now we're gonna see if our boy starts trouble."

A waitress had gone to the table to pick up the empty glasses. The big customer ordered more drinks. The young, miniskirted waitress smiled and followed procedure. "Sir, I'm sorry, but we're not allowed to serve more than six drinks per customer."

The big man gave her a lopsided smile. "Get the drinks, honey, and you'll find a big tip waiting."

"I'm sorry, sir."

His smiled turned into an angry scowl. "Get us the damn drinks or—"

Josh stepped up to the table with a pleasant smile. He sat down uninvited and spoke evenly. "Sir, this young lady is just doing her job. She is trying to protect both herself and you, since the law says it's illegal for her to serve you more drinks. Please understand and have coffee instead."

The customer snorted through his nose. "Who the hell are you? I'm not drunk, and you have no right to insinuate I am."

Josh kept his smile. "Sir, I am the chief of security for the Waterfront. I didn't say you were intoxicated." He raised his hand from beneath the table to expose the slender Motorola. "But according to the law, you have consumed enough alcohol to be in trouble if you were to drive. Please have some coffee on the house."

The other customer leaned over to his heavy friend. "Come on, let's get a cab back to the hotel."

The big man leered at Josh. "What would you do if I said 'Fuck you, shorty'?"

Josh's smile turned into an exaggerated frown. "Then you would be causing a scene, sir. I would be forced to demand that you leave and you'd probably say no, and I'd have to call the police and then, sir, you would be embarrassed, because you would be escorted out by Washington's finest and—"

"Shut up. I'm going. I can't stand your voice." The big man got up and glared down at Josh. "I could shove that little radio up your ass if I wanted."

Josh lowered his head to avoid eye contact. "Yes sir, you probably could, but that would be assault and get you five to ten from the judges in this town. Don't forget to pay your tab on the way out."

Only after the men left did Josh get up. He walked straight to the bar and told the cute cocktail waitress, "You did a good job. I'll pass it on to your manager."

The waitress looked at him worriedly. "What would you have done if he got violent?"

Josh smiled. "He didn't—that's my job."

A woman's voice came over the Motorola. "Hawk One, this is base. We have an India Charlie situation at El Torito's, over."

Josh held up the radio to his lips. "Roger, base. I'm inbound. Out."

Bob looked puzzled. "India Charlie?"

"Intoxicated customer."

"Looks like it's your night, boss."

Josh motioned toward the door with one hand and held out the radio to Bob with the other. "Not anymore, the rest are yours. I wanna see if you've learned anything."

Josh walked along the lighted pier down to *Lil' Darlin'* and stepped down to the deck. It had been a relatively quiet night and he'd found out Bob had what it took, at least in understanding the business. He was an alright guy, thought Josh. He stepped up onto the top deck and sat down, leaning against the mast. It was a beautiful night. He'd seen hundreds of such nights sitting in the exact same spot, but those times had been very special because Jill had shared them with him.

He shut his eyes and could see them on the boat, working, laughing, not a care in the world.

"Darn you, Dad, you scared me. I heard the footsteps and . . . What are you doing up here?"

Josh looked at his daughter, who was standing on the catwalk. "Just sittin' here," he said in a whisper as if he were in church. "It's beautiful out. How come you didn't go back to your apartment?"

"I got caught up studying. I'll just sleep on the couch tonight and go back in the morning."

Josh patted the spot beside him. "Come on, sit down. Did I ever tell ya about the old Shan teacher I had?"

Stefne sat down and cuddled against him. "About a hundred times. 'Knowledge will give you strength,' right? You told me and Mom those stories so many times we used to pretend we were asleep so we wouldn't have to hear them."

"She wouldn't have done that. You would—you don't appreciate anything—but not my Jill. She loved my stories."

"Da-aad?"

"Okay, maybe a few times she pretended."

Stefne laughed softly and looked up at the stars. "I miss her, Dad. I really miss her."

Josh felt a familiar ache. "Me too."

They remained silent for a long time, each absorbed in memories. Finally Josh broke the spell. He reached out and patted his daughter's hand. "I know I'm not doing a very good job of being a 'Father Knows Best' kind of dad, but I wanted to tell ya . . . well, I'm real proud of how you turned out."

Stefne smiled in the darkness and took his hand. "You're doin' okay." Leaning over, she kissed his cheek and laid her head on his shoulder. "Dad, it's been a long time since Mom passed away. I want you to know that if you find someone who makes you happy . . . it's okay with me."

Josh gave her a gentle hug. "I'm happy, hon, but thanks."

"Are you, Dad? I mean, are you happy living on a boat all alone with just the Front for a family?"

"I've got you."

"But I'm not going to be here all the time. What will you do when I'm gone?"

Josh hugged her tighter. "I'll think about it when that day comes. Let's not talk about it."

She sat back and looked at him. "Dad, I'm worried about you. You're getting as weird as Meg. You won't wear a watch except at work, you putter up and down the river all morning playing that god-awful music. You scull or play racquetball in the afternoons and then work all night. You own only two ties and drive a rusted-out Jeep. And *nobody* owns an eight-track anymore. Dad, you need to get a life."

Josh shrugged. "I enjoy what I do. I'm as normal as the next guy. And I want you to know my eight-track works great. I get the tapes for almost nothin.' "

"You call catching turtles normal? Dad, people are talking about you."

Josh stretched his arms and looked back up at the stars. "Don't worry about me, hon. Your old man ain't over the hill. Not yet, not by a long shot." He pointed at a star. "That one is yours, remember?"

Stefne nodded. She was wasting her time trying to change him . . . but she'd known that for years. She saw that he was still looking at the stars and knew he was with her mother again. She got up and walked quietly to the cabin, telling him in a whisper that she loved him.

CHAPTER 10

6 June

The waitress saw her regular walk in and sit down at his usual table at the window. She poured a cup of coffee, picked up the morning paper, and walked over to set them both in front of the early riser. "The usual?" she asked, smacking her gum.

Josh glanced at the headlines, then at the waitress. "Yeah, Jean, and don't forget the—"

"Yeah, yeah, hot sauce. I know. You don't have any taste buds left, Josh. You've burned them off with that stuff."

Josh's eyes gleamed. "Just feed me; I need it for strength. Today is the day."

Jean eyed him as she chewed furiously on her gum. "You said that last week and the week before that. You remind me of my husband when it comes to taking me out. He says yeah, sure, but he don't deliver."

Josh took a sip of coffee and waved his hand as if brushing her away. "Go away, nonbeliever."

She rolled her eyes, swung a hip into his shoulder, and strode for the kitchen. Josh read the first three paragraphs of the lead story and felt his chest tighten. Burma again. If the press only knew the truth, he thought.

A disheveled, middle-aged man with a receding hairline walked into the cafe and pulled up a chair beside Josh. He took a gulp of Josh's coffee and held out his hand. "Gimme the sports."

Josh tossed the sports section down without looking at his new tablemate and continued reading the front page. Jean headed for the table but the balding man waved her back and barked, "The usual, Jean, but how's about not burning the toast this time, huh?"

Jean smirked and smacked her gum. "Yeah, yeah." Sticking the pencil behind her ear, she turned around and headed back toward the kitchen.

Josh finished reading the front page and turned to the second. "Who won?"

Detective Terrance Kelly, of the Narcotics and Special Investigations Division for the District of Washington's Metropolitan Police Department, shook his head as he read down the box scores. "Nobody that counts." He lowered the page and tapped the paper in Josh's hands. "Who's winning in the world?"

Josh sighed and dropped the paper to the table. "Nobody. Hey, tell me the truth. Am I gettin' weird?"

Kelly gave his friend of four years a "what the fuck?" look but saw that he was serious. He shook his head and picked up Josh's coffee cup again. "Well, you're a little strange, but compared to the weirdos I deal with every day on the streets you're a regular A number-one citizen. What's up? Stef worried about her ole man?"

"How'd y'know?"

" 'Cause, you wouldn't listen ta nobody else. I know you, remember? I carry your ass on the racquetball court and make the excuses when you fuck up."

Josh took the cup away from his friend and took a sip before looking out the plateglass window. "It's tough gettin' old . . . how's it feel when you're over the hill?"

Kelly bristled, "Hey, I'm not even close, look in the mirror, Hawk, and answer that one."

Josh began to retort, but Jean set a plate in front of him. "One Hawk special, cheese and onion omelet, hash browns and sausage gravy over it all. Eck, what a mess. How can y'stand ta even look at it, let a'lone eat it?"

Kelly frowned as he looked up at the woman. "Last week it was a 'Kelly's special,' you playin' favorites, Jean?"

She cocked up a painted eyebrow. "Josh 'tips' and he says 'today is *his* day.' "

Kelly snorted a half-laugh and picked up his fork. "Yeah, he said the same thing last week." Reaching over he cut an end off of Josh's omelet and stuck in his mouth. Chewing, he looked up at Jean and waved his fork at her to emphasize his words. "He ain't never gonna catch him except in his dreams."

Josh gave them both a sneer. "Today *is* the day. Just you both wait and see."

Jean and Kelly exchanged looks and shook their heads, knowing he was hopeless.

Ten minutes later both men had finished their meals and second cups of coffee. Josh glanced over at his friend. "Any new skinny on the streets."

Kelly picked his teeth with a toothpick. "Same old shit. Crack went up another quarter a bag, hero is gettin' a little scarce. Better keep the boys checkin' the parking lots. The freaks can get a kick by tradin' in a car CD player. Oh, yeah, the Intel boys say we got a bunch of new Chinks in the city. The Intel weenies are puttin' the scare tactics on us, sayin' it looks like a takeover. They told us all to read up on that report about the Chink takeover in that Canadian city. When you fucked off that six months with us, you told me all about it. You know."

"The Vancouver model?"

"Yeah, that's it. The Vancouver model. Remember it, Hawk? You knew it inside and out and even briefed my guys on it."

Josh shrugged. "Sure, it's the report on how the Chinese syndicate took over Vancouver."

Kelly gave his friend a sidelong glance. "Look, be a buddy, huh, and tell me about it again. I didn't get a chance to read it last night 'cause—"

Josh rolled his eyes. "Mary on your case again?"

"Hey, just get to the bottom line, will ya? I don't need the third degree here. Mary wanted me ta have some quality time with the twins. I took the whole crew to Chuck E Cheese's, spent a fortune playin' their gee-whiz arcade videos and even ate their lousy pizza. I need a little refreshing, that's all."

Josh shook his head as he leaned back in his chair. "Poor Mary. I don't know why she even bothers with you. Okay, for Mary's sake. The Vancouver model is a study on how the Chinese syndicate moves in and takes over the action. They work in at least six layers. The first layer is the pushers and recruiters. They get their dope and exchange the cash from sales with the second layer, the block lieutenants. We're not talkin' Chinese unless it's in Chinatown. The syndicate uses the existing locals, paying them a little more money for their loyalty. These local lieutenants work for the third layer, the district captains. These captains are tough, no-shit action boys who pack serious hardware and do the enforcing. They make big bucks and keep a stable of enforcers, muscle, and informants. They do the bribing and whacking if necessary. According to the Vancouver model, the district captains are usually the best of the Jamaican, Latino or black players who know and totally understand the game. The captains take all the risks; they distribute the product and keep a close eye on their lieutenants. These captains report to the fourth layer, the majors, who stay clean and do the wholesale business. Now we're into the smart guys. These majors work through a series of front men, all previous captains who earned the right to move up. These front men are super loyal to their majors, and are your principal wholesalers of product. They keep it stored and accounted for. The majors are where you find your first Chinese syndicate boys, and from here on up we're talkin' strictly family members. They make themselves untouchable by the law and let the front boys take the fall if anything goes down. Unlike the Mafia, these guys didn't work their way up the ladder picking up dirt along the way. They don't swing, party, booze it, throw money away, or do anything that makes them blackmailable or usable by the law or competitors. The majors report to the colonels, who run respectable businesses and supply their assigned majors with dope, set priorities, and make the payrolls. Here we also find specialty colonels who do nothing but handle the books, money laundering, shipping, packaging, et cetera. The colonels report to the San, the lord, the big boss. He is the number one and has on call a complete stable of high-priced lawyers who cover his family with paper if the feds or police get lucky. This San is a boss for the Triad in Hong Kong, which means unlimited funds. This guy pulls all the strings and makes all the big decisions, but he never gets personally involved in anything dirty."

Kelly had kept nodding his head as Josh was speaking. He shrugged his shoulders. "Yeah, I know that stuff. I thought it was more scientific, y'know? Thanks, Hawk. I owe ya."

Josh's interest was now aroused. "Wait a minute, you don't get off the hook that easy. Do your Intel boys really think they could have a Vancouver model moving into D.C.?"

Kelly tossed down his old toothpick and picked up a new one. " 'Fraid so. The Chinese gangs down in Chinatown have straightened up their act big-time. Somebody who has discipline has set them straight. The word is that the independent wholesalers have been told to play ball with the new boys in town or get out. We've put a couple of teams in to keep an eye out, but right now it's all talk and no action. The West Coast sent us some books of photos of the guys who are supposed to have moved in here. My boys have spotted a few, but so far they're playin' it cool. Hawk, you wouldn't believe the names. They're all Wang and Dong and Ye and Fe. Shit, I'm gonna have to get a Chink cop from the West Coast just to keep the names straight for us if they start some action. I'm not real worried yet, but something is definitely going on. The independents are runnin' scared, and they don't scare easy."

Josh looked out the window with a vacant stare. "That's not good news, my man. The Triad boys don't play around. They go for the jugular early to make a statement. When I was on the task force I went to Hong Kong for two weeks for some briefings from the British, who laid it all out for us. The Brits had been trying for years to penetrate the Triad but couldn't get past first base. Whenever the police started getting close, the Triad would go after the cops' families or blow up a few bombs in buses full of civilians. That way the authorities knew the price of waging war against them was going to be very high. The Triad doesn't play by any rules, and in every case the cops had to back off. The Brits said the only way to get to the Triad was to expose its leadership. Cut the snakes' head off, as it were."

Kelly smirked. "Fat chance of that in the good old U S of A. The Hong Kong cops ain't got the American Civil Liberties Union lookin' over their shoulders. Enough of this Chink shit. What about you? You pick up anything I could use?"

Josh lifted his coffee cup with a wry smile. "Yeah, maybe. The Chizo brothers had a pair of high-priced working girls with them while they were throwin' big bucks around in La Rivage last night."

Kelly's eyes narrowed and he became all business. "How big? What denominations?"

"Three hundred a pop for premium vino. They had four bottles plus the best meals in the house. They paid in hundred-dollar bills."

Kelly's upper lip crawled back in an evil smile. "Those boys are dumber than a box of rocks. I'll pass it on to Whitey. He needs a stroke. Thanks. Hey, our game is at two so—ah shit, why am I tellin' ya the time?" He glanced at Josh's bare left wrist. "Be there, asshole, on time for a change. Take a sundial out with you on the hunt, but be there. It's the D-ones down in Vice who beat us last week."

"We didn't lose, we were just settin' them up," Josh said with a crooked grin.

Kelly rolled his eyes, got up, and headed for the door, talking over his shoulder. "Get the check, will ya? Mary forgot to give me my allowance. I'll get it tomorrow. See ya at two."

Josh shook his head slowly, knowing his cheap friend would have the same lame excuse tomorrow. He tossed a ten onto the table and nodded approvingly at Jean, who approached carrying a string that was threaded through the handles of seven plastic gallon milk containers. She handed the bundle over and screwed up her brow. "I can't believe I'm helping you."

Josh winked. "He's mine; I'm gonna get him today. You just wait and see."

Jean stuffed the ten-dollar bill in her apron and picked up the plates. "Yeah, yeah."

Holding the string of bottles in one hand and a bag of ice in another, Josh strode to *Lil' Darlin'*. He was almost there when he heard a familiar voice behind him. "Boss, I need the keys to open the office."

It hit Josh like a bolt of lightning. He turned around and tossed the string of bottles to the startled young man. "And I need a witness. Come on, you're coming with me."

Confused, Bob Stevenson looked at the bottles, then at his boss. "Where?"

"The hunt."

"But the office?"

"We have an answering machine. Stef will be here in a couple of hours; she can handle it. Come on, you're gonna see it happen."

"What happen?"

"Him, I'm catching his big ass today. Just shut up and follow me."

Bob's new Docker slacks and his shoes were ruined as he sat disgruntled in the bouncing bass boat as it made its way around Haynes Point into the Potomac River. Minutes before, two buckets of Ky's rotten fish had splashed all over him. The whole thing would have been a little better if his boss had at least helped him rather than just snickered and rolled his eyes.

Josh turned upriver toward the busy Rochambeau and George Manson Memorial bridges, which contained the usual Interstate 395 bumper-to-bumper traffic. He steered the boat between the pylons and glanced over his shoulder to make sure he wasn't being followed. Looking back, he shouted over the rumbling outboard and Conway Twitty singing "Julia," "I've never taken anyone with me before. You'll have to swear secrecy."

Bob looked at his pants and wrinkled his nose. "I swear I'll never tell a soul you stole the fish heads."

"I didn't steal them! Ky puts the buckets out for me. Hey, I'm serious. You can't tell anyone about how or where I hunt."

"Fine," Bob said, wondering what the hell he was talking about.

Reading his look, Josh patted his assistant's shoulder. "You still upset about the spill?"

"No. I'm upset that you talked me into going."

Josh smiled in understanding. "It's good ta get away for a while. You're gonna love it. How do ya like the music? Conway sure can wail, can't he?"

Bob nodded with a tight, forced smile.

They passed beneath the bridges and Josh motioned to their right. "Over there's the tidal basin. We can't hunt in there." He nodded to an opening just ahead. "We're going in there—Lady Bird Johnson Park

and Marina. Just on the other side of the marina is the riverfront entrance to the Pentagon; you'll see it on the left as we go by."

Josh steered into the small harbor and cut back the power, bringing
the boat to a crawl. "There's a waterway ahead, a kind of canal we're
gonna take. It's the hunting ground. Remember, this is all secret. If Ky
knew I got the turtles less than a mile from his Emporium he would
shit a brick. I tell him I hunt up and down the river. Great con, huh?"

"Yeah, great," Bob said without feeling.

"Here we go. There's the first float marking one of the traps."

Josh cut the engine and glided up to the floating milk container. He
reached into the water beneath the bottle, grabbed a thin nylon rope
tied to the handle, and gave a little tug. "Yeah, we got some," he said
excitedly.

Bob found himself caught up in his boss's excitement. He grabbed
the rope and helped haul the trap up, surprised at the heavy resistance. The chicken-wire and steel-framed trap looked similar to a lob-
ster trap; to his horror it was half full of flopping fish, a snake caught
within a chicken-wire loop, and what must have been five or six very
angry, muddy turtles.

"Hot damn!" yelled Josh, who held the trap level with the water.
"Pull the snake out and help me get the trap into the boat."

"Are you crazy?" Bob exclaimed in a high-pitched voice.

"It's just a water snake. Pull him out!"

"No way!" Bob backed away from the slithering reptile.

His arm muscles trembling with the strain, Josh worked his hands
down the rope hand over hand until he could grab the top of the trap.
He took a breath and suddenly lunged backward, bringing the trap with
him. The snake's body slapped Bob's face and shoulder as the trap tumbled into the boat. Josh grabbed the snake and flung it over the side in a
single movement. "Is this fun or what?" Josh asked, looking into the
trap with glee.

At that moment Bob knew his boss was totally insane. Josh saw
what he was thinking and laughed. "Come on, help me get 'em out.
You'll learn to appreciate this, I promise. We keep only hard-backed
turtles that weigh three pounds or more. Toss everything else back."

Bob knew there was no way out. He'd have to humor the lunatic
until he was safely back at the pier. He looked into the trap of flopping fish and clawing turtles. "Do they bite?"

Josh was already unwiring the top. "Yeah, so watch how I do it.
Forget the fish until we get the turtles out, pick one out aaaand . . .
grab him like that! See, get the back foot or tail and lift him quickly
before he has time to fight." Josh dropped the turtle into the weld between the seats. "No sweat. Okay, your turn."

Bob took a breath, squared his shoulders, squinted, and reached in. His scream echoed up and down the canal until Josh calmly reached over and squeezed the turtle's elongated neck and it let go of Bob's little finger.

The young man waved his hand as if it were on fire, but he'd at least quit the bloodcurdling scream. Finally he looked as his finger, and a sudden stillness settled over him. His eyes slowly shifted to his mentor. "It didn't even break the skin."

Josh tried to keep a straight face but couldn't, and he broke up laughing. Bob tried to act hurt but couldn't and joined him.

By the fourth trap Bob was as excited as his boss. But the wire contraption he pulled up was just a battered ball of twisted metal. "What the heck happened to this one?" he asked, lifting it up into the boat.

Josh's jaw tightened but a gleam sparked in his eyes. "Him . . . he's here." He quickly stepped forward to the front of the boat and untied the special trap. "Today's the day. I've designed a secret weapon to get him," Josh said as he spun around and reached for the bucket of rotten fish.

Minutes later Bob watched his boss lower into the water a heavy-duty steel trap that looked to him like a small shark cage. Josh attached three milk bottles to the rope and dropped them overboard. He steered the boat to shore, got out, and motioned Bob to follow him. "Come on, we'll wait on shore and see if we get him."

Bob carefully stepped over the turtles between the seats and joined his boss. He asked, "What or who is 'him'?"

Josh gazed out at the floating bottles. "About a month ago I tried to pull up a trap but it wouldn't budge. I tried harder and nearly broke my back hauling it in. When it surfaced I saw him. He looked directly at me with his huge black eyes. He'd bit through the wire to get the bait, but caught his front foot in the chicken wire."

Josh turned and looked at his mesmerized assistant. "He's big, a monster—the king of the turtles. He must be 100 years old and weigh at least 150 pounds." Josh's eyes slowly shifted back to the water. "The King looked at me, kinda daring me to reach down for him. I made the move but his eyes rolled back and he suddenly kicked free and was gone. The old King tears up two or three of my traps a week. He does it to show me who rules the river."

Bob closed his gaping mouth. "You're exaggerating, right? I mean about his size?"

Josh shook his head in silence, sighed, and leaned back against a tree.

Bob looked at the still water with a greater respect for what lay beneath its tranquil beauty. He leaned back and spoke quietly. "So we just wait?"

Josh looked up at the tree limbs above him. "I'm going to let you in on another secret. I don't hunt all morning like everybody thinks. I sleep here a couple of hours, just lay back and rack out. Ky thinks I work hard at catching them, and I add to the con by telling him I can catch only a dozen a day."

"We've got that now," Bob said, sitting up.

"Right, and that's the big secret. We could bring in twenty if we wanted, but then Ky would know they're easy to catch. To protect my business, I keep the secret from getting out."

"Boss, why do you do it? I mean, you've got a good business. It's not like you need the money."

Josh shrugged. "It's a challenge. An old teacher of mine once told me a man has to have one now and then just to know who and what he is. It probably seems stupid to you, but . . . but I like it out here. I like knowing I'm doing something nobody else does."

Bob looked at Josh's profile and made up his mind. "Boss, I guess it's as good a time as any to ask you something. It's about Stefne. I . . . well, I would like to ask Stefne out. I'm asking you because I don't want you to think I'm trying to get ahead by asking out the boss's daughter. She . . . she's a . . . a . . . ."

"A challenge," said Josh, helping him find the word.

"Yes, kind of . . . She's different from other women I know. She's beautiful and yet doesn't know it or doesn't seem to care. She doesn't play the usual games, just looks you in the eye and tells you what she thinks."

Josh smiled. "Some would call that opinionated. You don't have to ask me for my permission. Hell, you're old enough and so is she. But I gotta warn you about Stefne. Beneath that know-it-all exterior is a very sensitive woman. Her mother was like that, hard as a rock on the outside. People thought they could say anything to her and it wouldn't bother her, but it did. I know—I hurt her a few times. I could see the loss of a small spark in her eyes. It tore me up and I never forgave myself." Josh picked up a small stone and cast it into the water. "They seem to be tough, yet they're fragile, so goddamn fragile. I wish I'd known before she . . . ." He broke off and glanced at Bob with embarrassment. "Sorry, I was just tryin' to warn you that Stefne has a heart that breaks easier than most, that's all."

Josh lay back against the tree and lowered his old cap's bill to his nose. "I'm gonna rest a little while. Wake me up at twelve, huh?"

"Sure," Bob replied. He lay back and looked up at the tree limbs, knowing he'd seen a side of his boss that few ever were allowed to see.

State Department

General Summer stood in front of a projector screen briefing the Coordinating Subgroup for Narcotics about recent satellite photos taken over Burma.

"... and here you can see a huge number of poppy fields in the northern mountain area, making it the largest poppy-growing area in the world. Based on the size and number of fields, analysts believe that this region is capable of producing upwards of seven hundred tons of raw opium a year, which can become almost seventy tons of heroin. How much is that? American addicts consume only six tons a year. Next slide, please. This photo was taken yesterday. You can see in this close-up a valley; if you look closely you will see camouflage nets. These nets are extensive and cover what we believe to be a large heroin production facility. Next photo, please. Here you see the same area, but it was shot with an infrared camera to pick out hot spots. You can clearly see a very large building that shows up as a red rectangular box—it's the metal roof of the building, which retains the sun's heat. Note these smaller red areas. These are vehicles. When we compare the previous photo and this one, we can see that they are trying to hide a very large complex, complete with motor pool. Gentlemen, in the interest of time I've showed you just one probable production facility. We have photos of four other such facilities, all located in the northern mountains. Lights, please. Gentlemen, do you have any questions?"

The director of the DEA, John Tuckerman, pounded the table with his fist. "Goddamn it! What in the hell are you intelligence people trying to pull? I get a call last night and *this* is what you people wanted me to come here for? This? A wild goose chase? You people are overreacting! Your cockamamie heroin theory doesn't stand up to the facts. The Burmese government is *not* trafficking heroin. In fact, the reverse is true! In the last two years the flow of heroin from Burma to the States, or any other country for that matter, has been next to zero. We know this because we monitor the drug flow and seizures throughout the world. The junta has been cooperating with our people in eradicating the poppies, and—"

"Goddamn it, John, we're not here to listen to how successful your eradication programs are!" Director Jennings said coldly. "The Intel photos, and the killings of our people—including your country team chief—support our theory."

Red-faced, Tuckerman snapped back. "Your theory stinks, and not bringing my people in on this earlier stinks!"

"What do those photos tell you? Are you blind? Those are drug factories!" Jennings yelled.

The DEA administrator waved his hand at the screen. "Those pictures don't prove a thing! They could be producing fertilizer, for all we know."

Cutter from State leaned forward and calmly spoke. "Gentlemen, isn't that the point? That we don't know? I suggest that we stay on track here. This subgroup was brought together to look at the evidence thus far produced and discuss how to confirm or deny Burmese government involvement. If we send teams into those areas, we will find out whether the buildings under the nets are producing heroin or fertilizer."

Director Jennings softened his glare at Tuckerman. "John, we should have brought you in—we screwed up and we apologize. You're in now, and we're wasting time arguing. We have to send some teams in and find out exactly what is going on."

"The president will never approve such an operation," Tuckerman said smugly.

Jennings looked the DEA director in the eyes and spoke in a steely monotone. "He already has."

Tuckerman was a political animal and knew when to change course. His face changed expression and he found a spot on the wall to stare at. "In that case, the DEA will support you in any way we can."

Jennings smiled inwardly at the small victory as he shifted his gaze to the deputy director of the FBI. "Carl, you heard our agent's taped call. We need your help in running down any Burmese nationals who may be in the country on bogus passports and visas."

The deputy director shifted uncomfortably in his seat. "Of course we'll do it, but you know as well as I do that if they are any good at all they'll have changed identities once they cleared Customs. We'll see what we can do, but unless they're real stupid I wouldn't be counting on much in the three-week time window you've given us."

Jennings nodded. "It's a tough one, Carl, but try." He leaned back and took a cigar out of his pocket. "Gentlemen, that's it. You now know all that we do. Please keep me informed if anything pops up in your areas. If you'll please excuse us, the Intel committee members have other matters to discuss. Thank you all for your cooperation."

Tuckerman eyed the director. He had just been politely told to leave along with the Justice and Treasury representatives, but he wanted the director to say it to his face. "Do I stay for this or not?" he asked, as if unsure.

"Sorry, John, this is need-to-know only," Jennings said matter-of-factly without looking up from the notes he was reading.

Tuckerman bristled and shoved back his chair. "Fine. But I better be kept in the loop on all matters concerning the DEA."

Jennings nodded to let the DEA director know his comment was noted, and Tuckerman, satisfied he'd shown the proper amount of indignation, left quietly with the others.

As soon as the conference room door shut, General Summer stood, moved back to the screen, and faced Jennings and Cutter. "We have a problem. My staff consolidated the folders of possible candidates that your deputies provided, and I'm afraid we have only ten submissions. It's not easy to find qualified personnel who have ever lived or worked in northern Burma. The country has been closed to foreigners since 1960, so the problem is age. Most of our people who worked there in the 1950s and 1960s were in their late twenties and early thirties at the time. Those people are now in their fifties and sixties." Summer nodded to his assistant, who put up a slide that showed the file summary and a small photo of the first candidate. "Here's the most promising candidate. He retired from the army just four years ago, and he is uniquely qualified—he speaks the language and grew up in the northern part of the country."

"Boss? Boss, it's noon."

Josh raised his head and looked toward the creek. "If he's around, he's in the cage eatin' Ky's fish heads. It's time."

Within minutes they were back in the boat in the middle of the canal. Both men grabbed hold of the nylon rope beneath the bottles and Josh whispered, "On three. One . . . two . . . now!"

They pulled upward with all their might. For an instant nothing happened; the trap seemed to be full of concrete and wouldn't budge. But then they felt it slowly begin inching up with each hand-over-hand pull. Josh grabbed another handful and yelled crazily, "I got you! I got you!"

He excitedly reached down for another grip and pulled but felt a powerful jerk, then hardly any resistance. Josh's heart dropped to the pit of his stomach as he kept pulling, hoping that somehow the King was still inside. When the trap surfaced, Josh took one look and yelled at the water, "Laugh now, ya bastard, but we *will* be back!"

Bob leaned over to inspect the cage and saw that the bottom grille was gone—the spot welds had not been able to take the weight of whatever had been inside. He looked at his seething boss and knew he was already designing a new trap in his mind. Bob shut his eyes and could still hear his mentor's challenging words echoing down the tree-lined banks. The word "we" seemed to echo most clearly, and it reverberated in his head until he realized what it meant. Oh shit, he thought, this must be how the crew felt when Captain Ahab spotted Moby Dick.

Cutter worriedly looked at the others. "We don't have a choice."

"Let's go over the other files again. Maybe we were too quick in rejecting some of them," General Summer said, trying to stay optimistic.

Jennings took the cigar out of his mouth and shook his head. "Look, let's cut the shit and face reality. We have only two qualified candidates. The rest of them are good men but they're over fifty. We're talking about an infiltration into rugged mountain terrain. The team will have to hump to the site after being inserted and hump back to a pickup point. They're going to have to move fast while carrying at least fifty pounds of equipment, food, and water. Hell, the two candidates we do have are in their forties. Even they may not be able to do it. We've got only three weeks to find the damn answer and we don't have time to get them in shape if they've gained weight or gotten lazy since their photos were taken. Christ, they might both be dead for all we know."

Cutter looked at the director in disbelief. "Are you saying we're wasting our time?"

Jennings snapped his head around. "Hell no! You were right when you said we don't have a choice. We'll have to find these two men and see what we've got. Either way, we need their experience at least to brief my men about the area. We'll use our Special Reconnaissance Unit to do the mission. They don't know anything about Burma but they're damn good."

Cutter looked over his glasses. "The two candidates might not have to go in?"

"Depends. If they know the area around one of the facilities then we'll use them because it ups our chances of success. Both candidates are trained pros; we couldn't ask for anything better. If they're willing and able, they go in." Cutter nodded and shifted his eyes to General Summer. "Both men are retired army and are receiving retirement pay. Am I correct in assuming your people should have no problem finding them?"

Summer smiled confidently. "If they are living in the United States, we'll have both men here within twenty-four hours. That's a guarantee."

Jennings stuck his cigar in the side of his mouth and mumbled, "Poor bastards."

·   ·   ·

Ky heard the bell ring and tossed down the basket of crabs he'd been carrying. He strode to the back door and flung it open. "Who you?" he barked.

"Sir, I'm Bob Stevenson, Mr. Hawkins's assistant. He told me to drop off this load of turtles for you."

"Where Josh?"

"Sir, Mr. Hawkins had an appointment. I'm sorry, but he told me to tell you, 'You old goat, if you don't pay the agreed full amount I'll use your hide as bait tomorrow.'"

Ky looked at the squirming turtles in the boat. "They not very big. How many?"

"Thirteen, sir. I believe they will all weigh more than three pounds."

Ky shook his head. "No, no, I weigh fish all time. It my business for many year. I know weight of fish, crab, turtle. They weigh no more than two maybe two-half pound. Wait here, I get money for you."

Bob turned around, started the outboard, and reached down to untie the line.

Ky yelled to be heard over the engine. "What you doing?"

"Going to Antonio's," Bob yelled.

Ky threw up his hands. "O-kay o-kay, three pound!"

Bob killed the engine with a smile.

The court door opened and two sweat-soaked men walked out. One turned, looked over his shoulder, and said smugly, "If you two old-timers wanna quit, me and Ski will understand."

Josh and Detective Kelly walked out the door, and Kelly said, "You two kids go and have your water break. You've won two, but it's best out of five, remember?"

"Think about it, old-timers. We'll be back in just a minute," said the younger of the two vice detectives with a laugh.

As soon as the young men were gone, Kelly faced his sopping-wet partner. "Remember what ya asked me this morning about being weird? I take back what I said. You're not only weird, you're fuckin' *crazy*! What the *hell* ya doin'? Look at you. You're covered with welts. That kid playing the forehand is hittin' you with his shot on half his forehand returns and you're not even tryin' to get out of the way!"

Josh shrugged. "I've been settin' him up. He's the strongest player, and we can't beat 'em unless I shut down his forehand shot to the corner. I get in the way of his shot enough he's gotta start hittin' it up over me and we'll kill it when it comes off the wall."

Kelly grimaced. "Josh, gettin' hit with that kid's forehand shot is like gettin' stung by a fifty-pound bee. Your back must look and feel like it's been hit with grapeshot. Knock it off, man, it ain't worth it. So we lose. We'll get 'em when the hard hitter is havin' a bad day."

Josh looked into Kelly's eyes and winked. "They're goin' down, Kelly. They never shoulda called me an old-timer."

The two younger men returned. "Well, you old-timers had enough?" the younger cop said.

Kelly and Josh exchanged glances and opened the court door.

Surprised at hearing the familiar grumbling outboard so early in the afternoon, Stefne got up from the desk and walked out on deck.

"Hi. Throw me a rope, will you?" Bob yelled as he approached in the bass boat.

Stefne closed her gaping mouth. "Wha . . . What are you doing? Oh no! He took you, didn't he? *Where* is he?"

Bob killed the motor and grabbed hold of *Lil' Darlin*'s rail. "I dropped him off a while ago for his racquetball game. Throw me a rope so I can tie this thing off, please."

Stefne ignored his plea. "I thought you were sick or had an accident, but no, you were out playing with my dad on the river while I had to take twenty phone messages. I've been on the phone all morning instead of studying."

Bob leaned over the rail, grabbed a line, and tied off the boat. He crawled over the rail and shrugged his massive shoulders. "Today was the day, he said. He wanted me to go and witness him catching the King, and we almost did. He was definitely in the cage, and we almost had it to the surface when—"

"My God, not you too?"

Bob excitedly pointed to the bottomless trap on the flatboat. "There's the proof. We had him. I swear he's real and—"

Stefne backed away, shaking her head. "You sound like him *and* stink like him."

Bob straightened up and rolled back his shoulders. He gave her a cold look and snapped, "I didn't volunteer to go on the hunt. The boss said 'go,' and so I went. And believe me, the King is out there." He spun around and headed for the pier. He took two steps and looked over his shoulder at her. "And we're gonna get him!"

Stefne sighed with indifference until he turned his back and continued up to the pier. Then she smiled.

•   •   •

Josh dropped his racquet on the bench and leaned against the locker to rest and build up his courage before trying to sit down. One of the vice cops walked over and said, "Good match, Hawk. I still can't believe you guys beat us the last three games. You surprised us."

Josh forced himself to fake it a little longer and straightened his back. "Next time ya might get lucky."

The detective nodded with a smile and walked out of the room.

Kelly, seated at the other end of the bench, glanced over at his partner. "Ya look like shit. How ya feelin'?"

Josh winced as he carefully sat down. He let the wave of nausea pass before he lowered his head and spoke in a half whisper. "You're gonna have to help me. I can't move my arms to untie my shoes."

Kelly shook his head and got up knowing he was serious. "Face it, we're gettin' too old for this shit. No more body sacrifices, ya hear me?"

Josh's head slowly came up and his lips drew back in a smile. "We showed 'em, huh?"

Kelly kneeled and began untying his friend's sweat-soaked high-tops. "Yeah, we showed 'em."

Holidome, Seattle, Washington

Colonel Sak Po smiled as he approached the two men sitting at a poolside patio table. Nodding to Sergeant Shin, he walked up behind Stephen and patted his shoulder. "So, Sao, how are you feeling?"

Stephen turned with a smile. "Much better, thank you. I had no idea jet lag could be so devastating. Where have you been? I haven't seen you the past two days."

Po glanced at the people lounging around the pool before motioning Stephen to follow him. "Come, it is time to talk. Shin, remain out here."

As soon as Stephen walked into the hotel room, Po nodded to the two waiting captains, who shut the door and drew the curtains. He motioned for Stephen to sit down at the table and took a seat facing him. "You asked what I've been doing. I have been making the final arrangements. Stephen, I'm afraid the story I told you about the American businessmen and the negotiations was just that, a story."

Stephen felt his stomach begin twisting into knots.

Po sighed. "I didn't want to discuss our true purpose here until you were fully recovered from your flight. Stephen, listen carefully and don't speak until I'm finished. We have been planning an operation for three years. Its code name is White Storm. The operation is now in its last phase—phase six. Within two and a half weeks it will be over, and if it is successful, you will be taking part in the rebirth of our country. The plan came into being three years ago when the Triad approached General Swei with a proposal for our prime minister. Our success in ending the rebel insurgencies had stopped the opium flow. The Triad offered our government a percentage of the profits if we would allow the mountain people to continue growing and harvesting the poppies and allow the trafficking to continue. General Swei told the prime minister of the Triad's proposal but strongly advised him to refuse. Swei explained that there would be no way to control the trafficking and that the word would sooner or later leak out that the government was involved. Such a revelation would force the prime minister and the junta out of power. Swei then offered the prime minister a plan of his own to give the Triad as a counterproposal: White Storm.

"Swei's plan would minimize the risk to the junta while increasing the percentage of profits fortyfold. You see, the Chinese had offered a below-market price for our raw opium. Swei told the prime minister that if *we* produced the heroin and took the risk of shipping it, then we could take a much greater share of the profit. That was just part of Swei's plan. More important, our enormous profits would not be traceable or questioned, for they would come to us in the form of loans. Do you see the beauty of it? Our profits would be placed in banks the Triad controlled and they would offer us dummy loans that would never have to be repaid. Swei is truly a genius. White Storm would give our government the funds necessary to pay off our other loans and begin rebuilding the economy. The prime minister agreed, and Swei proposed the plan to the Triad. As businessmen they saw they had everything to gain—they would even make an additional profit since the tools and machinery we would buy for rebuilding would come from their legitimate Hong Kong companies."

Po smiled. "Swei promised the Triad ten American tons of heroin a year for six years, beginning this year. What the Triad does not know, my friend, is that the shipments coming in the next three weeks total our entire six-year commitment and much more. We are bringing in over 120 American tons of heroin in three freighters over the next two and a half weeks."

Colonel Po looked into Stephen's shocked eyes and continued, "Once the delivery is made, our country will be credited with more than two and a half billion American dollars. Upon the safe arrival of the first shipment, the funds will be transferred to our accounts and our heroin production facilities will be torn down. The poppy fields will be destroyed and the mountain people will be compensated with

a salary equal to what they would have received for poppy production for four years. Also, the rebuilding programs you proposed will be put into effect. Wells will be dug and the necessary irrigation systems and machinery will be provided to grow rice and other crops making the mountain people self-sufficient. And you, Stephen, will be the one who implements the plan for the prime minister."

Stephen's face held a look of disbelief. For the past year he had worked on the economic rebuilding plans. He had had no idea he was actually supporting drugs and the Triad.

Po fixed his stare on Stephen. "As I'm sure you know, you have no choice but to support us. You are critical to this phase of the operation, and for that reason your family is being very closely monitored."

Stephen's face paled. "You are holding them hostage?"

"Stephen, please, of course not. They are fine and know nothing of all this. I just wanted to remind you of your responsibilities to us. When you return you will be considered a hero by the prime minister, and he will place you in charge of the rebuilding programs for the minorities. Stephen, none of us have a choice. As deputy finance minister you know that within six months our country will be bankrupt. Without money to pay the salaries of the government workers and our armed forces, our government will collapse. Such a disaster would trigger riots that could only end in starvation and despair for hundreds of thousands. Then China would step in as a helping big sister and impose her will on us. Stephen, don't you see this is our last hope? The opium is our country's only asset. General Swei is not a heartless man. He knows how destructive the white powder is, but this is the only way to save our country. Once we receive the funds from the Triad, it is over—nobody will ever know."

Po nodded to Captain Sing, who drew back the curtains. "Look at those people out there, Stephen. The most decadent people in the world. They are rich beyond belief, and most of them don't know it. They throw away food after a meal that would feed a Burmese family. To them the *lai* is nothing but forbidden candy that gives them pleasure."

"It will kill them," Stephen said, skewering Po with an accusing stare.

Po avoided the heat of his eyes by looking at the pool. "Perhaps some. It is not your concern. Think about the future of our people and what White Storm will provide for them."

Stephen felt as if he were caught in a whirlpool, but he knew there was nothing he could do. If he refused, his family would be killed.

Po turned from the window looking at Stephen with a searching stare. "Are you still concerned about the Americans?"

"No," Stephen replied, setting his shoulders and straightening his back. "Like you said, this is our country's last hope."

Po smiled. "Good. I knew we could count on you. I'm going to need your help tomorrow. We are responsible for processing the shipments when they arrive and will hand off the *lai* to the Triad representatives. Thirty men from the Directorate have flown in over the past three weeks and are billeted at our rented processing plant. Our workers will break down the cargo once it arrives. As for you, tomorrow we have a meeting with the Triad representatives. If they begin speaking among themselves in Cantonese, I want to know everything that is said. I've dealt with them before, and they like to talk among themselves. At this meeting I will surprise them with the news of the three large shipments. They should be quite pleased to hear that the first shipment will arrive in just two days."

Po looked again into Stephen's eyes. "Do you have any questions or doubts about the operation or the part you play? If so, speak now, Stephen."

Stephen glanced at the silver bracelet on his wrist, praying the Teacher would understand. He leaned back in his chair. "I have only one concern. What is to become of my father?"

Po's eyebrows lifted. "I thought you hated him."

"Yes, but he is my father," Stephen replied, realizing too late his heart had spoken rather than his mind.

Po's eyes hardened. "He was one of the few Sawbaws who did not accept our agreements. The others agreed to our truce and have helped us by running the *lai* facilities. Your father has caused us too many problems to be forgotten when this is over."

Stephen kept his eyes on the small man until Po sighed and said, "Your work for us is far more important than petty revenge. As a gesture I will make the necessary calls to ensure that he is not harmed or imprisoned. But Stephen, he will not be allowed to lay claim to Sawbaw status anymore. He will have to live out his days in the mountains where he will be no threat to us."

Stephen got up and bowed. "I am indebted to you. Thank you, my friend. I am your servant and will do whatever is necessary."

Po stood and clapped Stephen's shoulder, using the Shan way of expressing that he had made a vow and could be trusted.

Stephen ached to grab Po's throat, but instead he just smiled. He would become like them and lie and act as if they were his friends. He would bide his time.

The Waterfront, Washington, D.C.

Meg saw him coming and turned her bag of popcorn upside down on the sidewalk for the sparrows. She hurried up the walkway and grabbed his arm. "Are you in trouble?" she snapped in an accusing, high-pitched whisper.

Josh kept a straight face, knowing Meg must be having one of her really weird days. "I'm not pregnant, if that's what ya mean," he retorted.

She dug her nails into his arm. "I'm serious, dammit! Two suits were here an hour ago looking for you. I told them you weren't here and that Stef had gone shopping. They came over to my boat and started asking questions about you. I think they're IRS . . . or maybe hoods . . . or maybe FBI. What did you do?"

Josh tapped her hand to remind Meg that her nails were still embedded in his skin. "Relax. Some of the boys from Vice probably wanted to follow up on some information that I gave Kelly."

"No, Josh, these weren't cops. They weren't wearin' polyester and they didn't know you from Adam. They showed me a picture of you. You were in uniform, short hair, cute. They asked if you looked the same."

Josh gave her shoulder a light squeeze. "And you told 'em I was better lookin' now, right? Hey, don't worry, it's nothin'. I haven't done anything wrong, and if I have I'm tellin' them *you* made me do it."

Meg shook her head and walked with him to the security gate. "I don't know why I bother trying to take care of you. You're hopeless, Hawkins. I mean it. You—"

She stopped in midsentence. The two men she'd seen before were walking down the steps from El Torito's outside cafe and heading directly toward them.

Josh saw her worried stare and turned around. The tallest of the two men reached into his inside suit-coat pocket and flipped out his identification badge. "Colonel Hawkins, I'm Captain Sooter, DIA. Sir, you have been ordered to report to—"

Josh held up his hand. "Whoa! First of all, Captain, I'm *Mr.* Hawkins, and second, *nobody* orders me to do anything, especially the DIA. Get lost."

"Sir, we have orders to—"

"Son, don't make a scene. I don't care what your orders are or who they came from. I'm a civilian and don't want to talk to you. Go back and tell that to whoever sent you."

Josh took Meg's arm, walked her up to the marina's heavy metal security gate, and punched in the code. He swung the gate open for her and glanced over his shoulder at the two men, who were walking away.

Meg didn't speak or look back until they were even with her boat. Then she whirled to face Josh and whispered, "I told you, I told you they weren't cops—or were they? What is DIA?"

"Defense Intelligence Agency," Josh said, grimacing as if the words tasted bad.

"Intelligence? They sure came looking for the wrong guy on that score. What did they want from you?"

Josh's jaw muscles rippled. "I don't know and don't care. I want nothing to do with those people."

As he turned and began walking to his boat, Meg asked worriedly, "Will they be back?"

"Probably," Josh said as he continued walking.

Stefne stepped down into the cabin and saw him sitting at the desk with his back to her. "Well, I hope you're happy! I was on the telephone all day instead of studying because *you* decided to take *your* assistant to the happy hunting grounds. That's not what you promised me, Dad. You said Bob was supposed to help *me* out."

Fully expecting her wrath, Josh swiveled the chair around with an apologetic frown. "Sorry, hon . . . but did he tell you we almost had him? If the damn trap hadn't broken, we'd—"

Stonefaced, she raised her chin and marched past him into the galley. Slamming a bag of groceries on the counter, she took out a box of crackers, opened a cabinet, and threw the box inside. Next, a can of green beans got equal abuse.

Josh sighed and got up before she got to the eggs. "I'm sorry. I got a little carried away this morning. Anyway, I wanted to check him out and see if he had what it took." Whistling, he walked back to the desk. Sitting down, he turned on the computer and tried to look busy.

Stefne couldn't take it and turned around. "Well, did he pass?"

"What? Oh . . . You talk about a sissy. I'll start lookin' for somebody else tomorrow. I can't have a wimp like Bob working for—" He paused to take in the stricken expression on her face, then winked. "Gotcha! He did real good. He was even man enough to ask my permission to ask you out."

Stefne blushed. "He didn't."

Josh stood. "Yeah, he really did. But don't you let on I told ya. He was sayin' things like you were 'beautiful' and 'different' to suck up to me. The guy must be desperate."

Stefne lowered her head. "What did you say?"

"What any dad would say. 'Boy, what are your intentions?' Naw, I told him you were old enough that this old man's opinion didn't matter."

Stefne walked over and wrapped her arms around his neck. "Your opinion will always matter to me."

He gave her a gentle hug and whispered, "He passes, 'cause he believes me now. Unlike some I know."

"Daaad."

Josh finished a complete tour through all the restaurants on the Front without receiving a single call. It was going to be a slow night. He pushed open the door of the Channel Inn, waved to the night clerk, and strolled back to the Pier 7 bar. The place was almost empty. Still feeling the effects of the racquetball game, he sat down on a tan leather barstool to take it easy for a while.

Lester, behind the bar, nodded. "You skatin' tonight, Hawk?"

Josh gave the gray-haired black bartender a wink. "And gettin' paid for it, Les. Ain't that some shit?"

Lester poured him a tonic water. "You got him yet?" he asked with a twinkle in his eye.

Josh's brow furrowed as he picked up the glass. "I was close today, real close." Out of the corner of his eye he saw a middle-aged woman across the bar slide off her barstool and give him a once-over. He ignored the look and shifted his full attention to Lester. "Les, you know any welders? I gotta modify my special trap and can't do it myself. I wanna get a professional this time and—"

Lester backed away and gave Josh a nod. "I'll talk to you later, Hawk. Looks like you got some company." Josh turned, and there was the woman he'd seen checking him out.

She smiled disarmingly and said, "I'm sorry, but I couldn't help overhearing the bartender call you 'Hawk.' I was wondering, are you the Hawk of Hawkins Security I've heard so much about?"

Josh made a quick scan. The lady in front of him was in her early or mid-forties, with nice auburn hair cut in an easy-to-manage pageboy, not a lot of makeup and not too much perfume. Five-five, maybe six, in black pumps that matched her suit. An expensive, white silk blouse showed no cleavage, telling him she wasn't on the make. The left hand was the one problem. She was unmarried, so she was making a move on him or wanted something else. He guessed she wanted something else, for her brown eyes weren't flirting.

"Yep, I'm the guy," he said and waited for her next move. He figured she'd get around to what she really wanted in three.

The lady stuck out her hand as if she did it a lot. "It's a real plea-sure. I'm Glenn Grant. I live across the street in the apartments. A friend who works at Phillips Flagship has told me a lot of stories about you."

He shook her hand. "I'm Josh. I hope the stories were good ones. I bet you thought I was younger and bigger, right?"

She winked. "You're just what I pictured. I was wondering . . ."

Josh smiled inwardly—three on the nose.

". . . if you would do me a favor."

"Depends."

"Would you mind if I asked you to show me which boat you live on in the marina? I know it's strange, but my friend said you lived on a boat. We strolled down the channel walk the other day and were try-ing to guess which one was yours. Dumb, isn't it?"

Josh shrugged. "We can see my boat from the window. Come on." He slid off the stool and put his radio in his jacket pocket. Taking her arm, he guided her to the large windows overlooking the channel. All lady, he said to himself, feeling more than seeing how she walked with him. Not too close but close enough, yet something was wrong with the picture. Her clothes were nice but she didn't look quite com-fortable in them, and she had an athletic look, strange for a woman her age. But he liked the distraction and her company, so he decided to play along a while longer. He looked into her twinkling brown eyes and asked, "Before I point her out, which one did you think it was?"

She looked him over before tilting her head to the side. "Let's see, you don't wear pinkie rings or gold chains so that means you wouldn't have anything that's real big or flashy. Your clothes aren't tailored so you wouldn't care about fine lines or detail. You're defi-nitely not a cruiser type, so it would have to be a sailboat. Older, I think—you'd like the security and reassurance of something that was made when things weren't mass-produced." She looked out the win-dow, her eyes searching down the slips, assessing each craft. "I would say it has to be one of the two older motor sailers moored at the last pier," she said, pointing at his boat and its neighbor.

Josh could tell when he was being set up—there were at least three or four other motor sailers older than his moored in the marina. He smiled and pointed at a sleek fifty-foot cruiser moored in the slip right in front of them. "Sorry. You'd better not quit your day job. That's her—*Sweet Thang.*"

She shrugged and sighed, acknowledging that he had seen through her. She lifted her purse, took out a folded piece of paper, and handed it to him. "I'm sorry too, Colonel. Since you wouldn't talk to the team, my boss sent me to ensure you got this. You have been recalled to active duty by order of the president of the United States. The order in your hand is effective immediately. Tomorrow a staff car will pick you up in front of the Channel Inn at zero eight hundred."

Josh crunched the orders into a ball and turned to look out the window at the channel. The woman stepped closer and joined him in watching a cruiser glide by with all its lights ablaze. "I'm Lieutenant Colonel Grant, and it wasn't a complete lie. I do have a friend who works at Phillips Flagship, and she did talk about you. Yes, I fudged on the boat—I read your file and talked to the team that was sent out to make contact. If it's any consolation, I didn't volunteer for this job. Since I live nearby they asked me to deliver your orders."

Josh continued to stare out over the water and spoke as if he felt sorry for her. "You were used, Grant. They use everybody." He squared his shoulders and walked away without looking back.

CHAPTER 11

0840 Hours, 7 June

It hasn't changed, Josh thought as he walked down the A wing corridor off the Pentagon. It was still drab despite the new paint and woodwork. The Pentagon was like a forty-year-old whore trying to change her ways; the makeup and clothes couldn't conceal what she was. The escort officer directed him into an office and then into a small conference room. He recognized Colonel Grant from the night before, even though she was now in uniform, but he didn't know the others seated at the table.

A too-young and too-good-looking brigadier general motioned to a chair and said, "Please, Colonel Hawkins, sit down and let's get acquainted."

As he sat, Josh heard the door shut behind him and knew it was going to be a while.

The one-star picked up a folder and began reading aloud. "Let's see, you lived in Burma and went to missionary school until the age of eighteen. Your parents moved to Malaysia, where they established another mission, and you were sent back to the States and attended the University of Virginia. You joined ROTC shortly after your family was tragically killed in a plane crash. Upon graduation you were commissioned and went straight into Infantry Officer Basic course at Fort Benning, Georgia, followed by Airborne and Ranger training. In 1971 you were sent to Vietnam, where you earned two Silver Stars and two Bronze Stars as a platoon leader. You were wounded in your eighth month and sent to Japan to convalesce. Once released, you volunteered for duty at the embassy in Burma. You married another American there and after two years returned to the States and went into the Special Forces, had various stateside assignments, and attended a variety of military schools. In '83 you were assigned back to Burma because of your unique qualifications. You stayed two years, until you had a little trouble and their government asked that you be removed from the country. Then more stateside assignments plus the business in Grenada and later in Panama, and you were involved in operations in Colombia for a few months. You were assigned to the Pentagon from '89 to '91, when you asked to be retired. Does that pretty much sum up your past history, Colonel?"

Josh ignored the question and asked the colonel seated next to him, "Any chance I can get a cup of coffee?"

The general's brow furrowed, and he snapped, "Colonel Hawkins, this is just a get-acquainted session. Don't get offensive—we may all be working together."

Josh leaned back in his chair, shifting his eyes to the other four officers seated around the table. "Is anybody going to explain why I'm here?"

The officers' eyes all went to the scowling general, who said, "Hawkins, you'll address your questions to me. This is just a preliminary session to get an update on what you've been doing since you retired. Later you'll be meeting with those who will discuss why you were asked back to active duty."

Josh turned, and his stare burned holes through the general's forehead. "I wasn't 'asked' to come here. I didn't 'ask' to be retired in 1991 either. You people ordered me here just like you ordered me to retire. If you want to be my buddy, General, start by telling me why I'm here."

The general met Josh's glare for only an instant before lowering his eyes. "I'm sorry, we've gotten off on the wrong foot. I'm Gus Faraday, and the officers in this room work for me in the Southeast Asia branch over at Bolling. We brought you here to the Pentagon because we thought you might feel more comfortable. Plus, it's closer to the State Department, where you're going to be meeting with some very important people in our government in an hour. We just wanted to talk to you first and update your file."

Josh again looked at the colonel beside him. "I still need that coffee."

Faraday approved with a nod, and the colonel got up and left the room. Josh leaned back in his chair and seemed to deflate. "What do you want to know?"

"Begin with why you were retired and what you've done since," Faraday said in a measured tone.

Josh sighed first and looked up. "In 1989 I was assigned to the Department of Defense's Drug Task Force here at the Pentagon. As a part of my training, they sent me downtown to work with the D.C. Metropolitan Police Department to learn the basics. I worked for six months with the Narcotics and Special Investigations Division and learned a lot. Too much. After working on the streets I could see that our so-called war on drugs was a joke, and I told my military bosses that. Let's see, that was in 1990. I wrote papers and even talked to congressmen. I made waves to try and change things so that we could really be effective. Nobody listened except my bosses, who thought I was disloyal and insubordinate. In January of '91, I was told I wasn't a team player and that I should retire for the good of the service. I sold my house and moved to my boat in the marina. I'd made some contacts with the local police while on the Drug Task Force, and one of them, a good friend, suggested I start a security service for the Waterfront. He knew they needed help, made the intros, and helped me get the company started. I've been doing the job ever since. End of story."

"Any foreign travel?" Faraday asked, knowing the colonel had left out some important details concerning his wife.

Josh shook his head.

Faraday picked up a piece of paper. "This is a copy of your financial report. Could you explain the rather substantial amount of funds you've acquired since your retirement?"

Josh's jaw muscles rippled up his cheekbones. Faraday saw the reaction and raised his hand. "I'm sorry, I know I'm asking a lot, but it will save time. We can get the information from the IRS, but it would take us a week."

Josh took a breath and let it out slowly before speaking. "My wife was a CPA and made a good salary. She knew taxes inside and out and used a universal life insurance policy as a tax shelter. When she . . . when Jill passed away . . ."

Seeing Josh struggle, Faraday nodded and said, "Thank you, that explains the large account you have in trust for your daughter. I see you have two other accounts. One is for your business and the other is a personal account, correct?"

Josh nodded in silence.

Faraday set the financial report aside and motioned to the female officer at the end of the table. "Colonel Hawkins, Lieutenant Colonel Grant has some questions for you. She's assigned to the Burma desk in our branch and is working on the Drug Task Force panel for the DIA. I've assigned her to be your escort officer. Because of your experience in Burma and your time on the Drug Task Force, we thought it might benefit you both."

Grant opened a folder in front on her. "Colonel Hawkins, do you presently have any Burmese friends living in Burma?"

Josh glanced at the silver bracelet on his wrist before answering. "Yes, I have a very good friend who I grew up with. He's half Chinese and half Shan, but you could classify him as a Burmese. He loves his country."

"What's his name and profession, sir?"

"Stephen, Stephen Kang. The last time I saw him was in 1985, the day I was ordered by the Burmese government to leave the country. I haven't seen him since, although we still write each other now and then. He is the deputy minister of finance for the country."

Grant made some notes and looked up. "Your file doesn't indicate the reason you were asked to leave Burma in '85. It just states you and another member of the Defense attaché staff were asked to leave by Burma's government. What was the reason?"

Josh's jaw tightened again. "I can't discuss it. You're going to have to ask the Strategic Reconnaissance Office for the file. If they release it to you, then I'll talk about it."

Grant exchanged glances with General Faraday, who nodded and spoke kindly. "I have the file, Colonel. I know you and another member of the attaché staff conducted an unsanctioned reconnaissance of northern Burma, and that you made contact with several rebel leaders. Your reports were quite detailed. The only thing that is not mentioned is how their government found out you conducted the recon."

Josh placed his hands in his lap and ran his fingers over the bracelet. "My friend Stephen Kang . . . he told them."

General Faraday leaned forward in his chair. "But why would a friend turn—"

"Because he loved his country more," Josh said in a low voice. He lowered his head, remembering that day.

Grant closed her folder and spoke softly. "One last question, Colonel. When was the last time you saw Sergeant Major Dan Crow?"

Josh raised his chin and couldn't help but smile. "Hondo a sergeant major? No way; you got him mixed up with somebody else."

Grant smiled for the first time during the meeting. "According to the file, he accompanied you on the recon of northern Burma and was also forced to leave the country. He made sergeant major in 1990 and retired in '93. When did you see him last?"

Josh shook his head and smiled reflectively. "I'll be damned, that ole bastard beat the system. . . . I saw Hondo last during the action in Grenada. My Special Forces team linked up with a Delta Force detachment to secure the students. He was a master sergeant then, working as the detachment leader. Where the hell is he now?"

Grant motioned to the door. "He should be waiting outside. He's our other candidate."

Josh's eyes widened, and he began to push back his chair. Just then, the door opened and the colonel who had been sent to get the coffee entered with a frown and empty hands. He motioned over his shoulder. "Sorry, but—"

"I want some goddamned answers! Who the hell is in charge?" a voice bellowed. A second later, a balding man wearing a sport jacket two sizes too big and a clip-on tie walked into the room. "Is this the place I get the damn answers?" he demanded.

Josh stood up and said, "You always did know how to make an entrance, Hondo."

The small, wiry man halted in his tracks. His eyes widened in recognition and his mouth dropped open in surprise. A moment passed before he yelled, "Hawk! You son of a bitch, ain't nobody called me Hondo in years."

The two men embraced. Then Josh pushed his friend away but held his shoulders. "Ya look like shit. You must not be getting any zu."

"Aw, hell, Hawk, the old lady made me swear off the booze a week after I retired. Ain't that a pisser? I'd been plannin' my retirement for years—sittin' back on the lake drinkin' zu and dyin' happy—but she ruined it for me. How 'bout you, is Jill still keepin' ya straight?"

Josh's smile dissolved. He put his arm around his friend's shoulder. "She died, Hondo. It was four years ago next week. She went in for a normal checkup and they found a tumor. She was gone a month later."

"Shit, Hawk, I'm sorry. I loved that gal."

The general cleared his throat to get their attention. "Gentlemen, we'll take a break for ten minutes so you two can get caught up." The officers all left except for Grant, who stayed in her seat.

She met Josh's stare and raised an eyebrow. "Sorry, I have to stay. I'm your escort. Just pretend I'm not here."

Crow grabbed Josh's arm, walked him to a corner of the room, and whispered, "What the hell is going on? I was fishin' yesterday afternoon when two MP officers show up outta nowhere and tell me I gotta go with them. Jesus, you shoulda heard my ole lady when I showed her the orders. They gave me all of ten minutes to pack, then drove me to San Antonio and put me on a plane with a major for an escort."

Josh leaned closer. "I think it's got something to do with Zuland. These people are all from the DIA's Southeast Asia branch. After that bombing, I'd bet we're being brought in to advise and consult with the big boys."

Crow's drawn face brightened. "Shiiit, that ain't bad. Hell, with the money I make from this consulting stuff, I'll be able to build on that addition I wanted on my cabin. Hey, tell me about Stefne. How is she? I bet she's all grown up, huh?"

Josh reached for his wallet. "Wait till you see her picture. She's . . ."

Grant led the two men through the main entrance of the State Department. Two Ivy League types met them and motioned them toward an elevator. Crow looked at all the national flags of the world hanging in the huge glass lobby and poked Josh in the ribs. "I've had a beer and a piece of ass in almost every country they got a flag for. I think I'll pick me up a miniature set for the cabin to help me remember when I'm too old ta think about poontang."

Josh stepped into the elevator and whispered to his friend, "You caught every strain of clap, too."

Grant looked away to hide her smile—despite their whispering, she'd heard the conversation.

Two minutes later Josh and Crow exchanged confident looks and walked through the just-opened doors of a VIP conference room.

Josh sipped coffee from real china as the men seated at the table were introduced. He was impressed; he had heard all the names before and had even seen the CIA director on the television news a few times. He glanced at Crow, seated beside him. The old soldier was sketching on a notepad. The drawing looked like the beginnings of an addition to a cabin.

Director Jennings sat down and leaned back in his chair. "Our country is in a dilemma. We need information, and you two men have knowledge of Burma that we desperately need. This committee is asking for your help. I'm going to have my assistant explain what has happened and bring you up to date on the current situation. When he's finished, I'll explain what services we need from you."

Two minutes into the briefing, Josh's face had turned to stone. At the conclusion ten minutes later, he felt as if he were going to explode.

Jennings shifted his eyes to the two men. "As you've just heard, we have serious problems and need answers. This committee needs your help."

Josh couldn't take it anymore and snarled, "He didn't brief the truth."

Taken aback by the unexpected response, Jennings uncharacteristically stammered. "Wha . . . what are you talking about?"

Josh pointed at the briefer. "He conveniently left out the fact that *your* agency provided the rebels with guns and advisers to fight the government. He didn't mention that the United States condoned the growing of poppies so the rebels could make money from the opium to hire mountain tribesmen to fight the Burmese government. You, Mr. Director, you and the DIA and the State Department are partly the reason our country is having this problem."

Jennings glared back. "We helped the rebels in the sixties, Colonel Hawkins. We did what was necessary then to stop communism. The situation we face now is different."

"Bullshit," Josh retorted. "I saw weapons your agency provided for the rebels in '73. You established base camps and hired mercenaries for cross-border ops into China. I saw the whole thing."

General Summer had become red-faced. He stabbed his finger across the table. "You're out of line, Hawkins! Don't bring that up again."

Josh looked at the other members of the committee and shook his head in disgust. "In '72 soldiers in Vietnam were buying dope being brought into Saigon from Burma. You people knew it, but you looked the other way. You helped the rebels, who you knew were trafficking, and now you people are upset because their government is involved?"

Jennings slapped the table. "They killed our people! They can't do that and get away with it. Our policies of the past were based on the threat to this nation. I wish to God we had done things differently, but we didn't."

Sergeant Major Crow gave Josh an understanding pat on the arm before shifting his eyes to Jennings. "We understand the problem. We just wanted to make sure all the cards were on the table. You gotta understand Hawk; he likes the truth. Now, what exactly do you want from us?"

Jennings motioned for the lights. As soon as the room darkened, a satellite overhead of a mountainous area flashed up on the screen. The next picture was a close-up of an area Josh recognized immediately. The church mission where he went to school was situated in the lower right-hand corner, but there was something new, a road beside it that made its way north before ending at the small river where he and Stephen used to fish and swim.

Jennings stood and walked to the screen. "I understand that both of you know this particular area very well. Here you can see camouflage netting. This committee needs to know what is under those nets. That is the reason you both are here. We want you to go in and find out."

Crow sat back in his chair and cast an accusing glare at Josh. " 'Consultants' my ass," he muttered.

Josh closed his open mouth and looked at Jennings in disbelief. "Are you serious?"

General Summer spoke for the director. "We're very serious. The

Agency has its operations planning group working up the details as we speak. We're asking you to help with the planning and to take a team in yourselves. Your mission won't be the only one—we're sending in four other teams from the Agency with the support of some elements from the Special Operations Command. The operation's execution phase begins in only twelve days. That will give us time to brief and rehearse the teams and make the necessary arrangements for infiltration assets to be flown into India. As you can see, time is critical."

Jennings locked a stare on Josh. "Are you in or out?"

Everything within Josh's being screamed *"Out"* except for a small inner voice that was whispering to him, "You are sworn to protect the people and the Ri." Josh lowered his eyes to the bracelet on his wrist and heard himself say, "In."

Crow shrugged. "I've been wantin' some good zu, anyway. I'm in."

Jennings stood and put out his hand. "This nation is indebted to you both."

Both men stood. Crow shook hands with Jennings, but Josh turned his back and walked for the door.

Seattle, Washington

Captain Sing stood outside the restaurant with one of the Chinese Triad security men. A red Corvette Stingray swung to the curb and the driver hurriedly got out. Sing took a step forward to stop the impeccably dressed man from going in, but the Chinese guard stepped in front of him and bowed. "They are waiting, San."

"I should hope so," the driver said as he strode past the two guards and entered the restaurant.

Stephen and Colonel Po sat at a table with two embarrassed Triad representatives who were still making apologies for the missing host. Stephen had expected older, more traditional men—not the young, polished barons before him. With their near-perfect American English, they obviously had been schooled and had lived in the United States. They spoke as if relaxed, but their eyes were like those of hungry wolves. He felt sorry for the United States, for he knew now the Triad had planned well ahead before moving into its new territory. They had sent young wolf pups to live among the naive American sheep.

Quan Jie, the senior of the two, turned to Stephen. "I hope you are enjoying your sta—" Jie's eyes abruptly locked on the doorway and turned cold.

"A thousand pardons for my tardiness," said a voice behind the Burmese.

Stephen turned and his eyes widened in surprise. The man in the doorway moved forward after making his apology. He saw Stephen and froze for a moment, then stepped toward him and extended his hand. "I say, haven't we met?" he asked as his eyes instructed Stephen to play along. Then he continued, "Yes, I have it—you attended the University of Hong Kong. I never forget a face. How are you, old boy?"

Stephen smiled politely and replied, "Very well, thank you."

"I am Ke Ping. I was senior to you, I believe."

Stephen bowed his head. "Yes, I vaguely remember you, U Ke. I believe you were in the Horse Club. I am Stephen Kang, deputy finance minister. It is an honor to see you again."

Ke nodded, turned, and broke into a friendly smile. He offered his hand and said, "So we meet again, Colonel Po. I'm quite sorry to be late, but I had difficulties breaking away from another meeting, you understand. Did you bring along this old school chum of mine to impress me?"

Po smiled as he shook hands. "It is a surprise to me that you know my assistant. But yes, U Ke, I did plan to impress you."

Ke took his seat and grinned mischievously. "Ah, yes, I believe you are referring to the very large shipments you are bringing in." Chuckling as Po's face paled, Ke raised an eyebrow. "Come, come, Colonel, did you actually think we wouldn't know? We've been monitoring your shipments with great interest for some time now. It has been rather exciting, I must say."

Po regained his composure and sighed with resignation. "I suppose it was childish to hope we could keep it a secret from the Triad."

"Yes . . . but your reasons were pure, so no harm is done. We've been quite impressed with your leader's mettle in attempting such a feat. Quite sporting, actually. I suppose you have a plan if the first shipment should fail inspection?"

"Yes, of course," Po said, almost as if offended.

"Right, well then, let's get down to it. When your shipment arrives we will conduct the handoff as per our agreement. The wholesale market price as of today is twenty-five point five per kilo. Would you like to lock that price in today or see what the market does in the next few days? I give you the option as a fair businessman."

Po appeared to be contemplating the decision, but inwardly he was rejoicing. The price per kilo was a full $1,500 more than he had expected. He let another moment pass before giving a short nod. "I believe it would be better if we locked in the price today."

"Done, then," said Ke. "Quan Jie will take care of the administrative details."

Colonel Po kept his stoic business expression. "We expect the first shipment in two days. I have the address of the—"

Ke's eyes sparkled. "We know the address of your processing plant, my friend. As we know where you are staying."

Again Po's face paled. "I took every precaution. How could you—"

"Elementary, my friend. You rented the building from one of our subsidiaries. You couldn't have known, so don't look so distraught. We are businessmen, not American gangsters who would rob our friends. There is enough profit for us all. Right, now I believe this meeting is over." Ke looked toward the other end of the table. "It's Stephen, right?"

"Yes, U Ke, Stephen Kang."

"Right, well, Stephen, would you care to join me for a dash to my residence? I would like to introduce you to my wife and prove to the good lady I really did attend an institution of higher learning. We can rummage through the old times and all that."

Stephen bowed his head. "It would be an honor, U Ke."

Ke stood and shook Po's hand vigorously. "Always invigorating, don't you think, making money? Sorry about borrowing your assistant, but it's seldom one sees a fellow Hong Kong University graduate here, you understand. Colonel, others will attend to the handoff, so this is our last meeting. It has been exciting."

Po held on to Ke's hand. "U Ke, please, Stephen requires security and—"

Ke rolled his eyes. "Of course, my people will deliver him back to the door of your hotel. Does that satisfy you?"

Po nodded quickly, afraid to offend him. "Yes, thank you."

Quan Jie lowered his head after the two men left the cubicle and were safely out of earshot. "I'm very sorry, Colonel Po. I apologize for Ke's behavior—he is very abrupt."

Po waved off the apology. Impolite or not, that whirlwind of a man had made his country almost a million dollars richer by giving him the top price.

Stephen waited until they were in the shiny, tight-fitting Corvette before exclaiming, " 'Ke'? Did you change your name, Chen, the same time you got some brains?"

The driver burst into laughter and peeled away from the curb. He wasn't able to speak until he was in third gear, and even then he was still cackling. "Ah, Stephen, what times we had, eh? Women, horse races, and now and then even school. What happened to those good days?"

Stephen smiled and ran his hand over the car's leather upholstery. "It appears you haven't changed a bit, except for the 'Ke Ping' and the exaggerated British accent. You sounded like old Professor Walthrop Arragno-Thorton, who taught us the classics."

"Ah, still my conscience are you? You haven't changed a bit either, Stephen. I was overly theatrical perhaps, but believe me when I tell you, I saved your life. I am one of them now, my friend. I know I swore I wouldn't, but here I am, in deep enough I can't get out. My father saw to it."

Chen suddenly swerved into the right lane and turned into a paved lot beside a park. He turned off the ignition and said, "Let's take a walk." He got out before Stephen could respond.

Stephen joined him on the sidewalk. "What did you mean, you saved my life? Were you serious?"

Chen smiled as he began walking alongside his old friend. "I am now Ke Ping. If you knew this 'Sheng Chen' fellow and were very close to him, then you would obviously know his father, and that would be a very bad security problem. You see, no one in the Circle uses his real family name when conducting business. I am now in business, thus 'Ke Ping.' But I am just a colonel in the Circle. My father is another matter, and he would be the reason you would have to die if you knew me well."

"You *are* serious," Stephen said incredulously.

"Ah, Stephen, you are still the naive Sao of the mountains. Secrecy is everything to the syndicates. Failure and ruin are accepted in business, for they can be explained as bad joss . . . but a violation of secrecy? No, it's the ultimate sin and totally unacceptable. Secrecy is the essence of the syndicates' being. If my assistants back in the restaurant thought for a moment you knew who my father was, let alone had met him, you would have to be eliminated. But it would be a quick death. Friends and all that."

Stephen swallowed hard. "But I knew your father in Hong Kong. Why wasn't I—"

"A different time, Stephen. You were a harmless young man with no connections to anyone, and you were my friend. My father was running a legitimate export business for the Circle. Just one of many of its enterprises. Things are now different." Chen looked at Stephen with a searching, almost sad stare. "Why are you here, Stephen? You are involved in something you shouldn't be. You were the smart one and got me through my studies. You were going to change the world, and now you are working with the Circle. Why?"

Stephen took Chen's arm and led him to a park bench. They sat in front of a small lake ringed by pines. Stephen looked up at the blue sky, then said, "I was a fool and believed them. I thought I was going to help my people and our country. Now I know the truth, but they hold my family hostage."

Chen nodded slowly and leaned back. "Do not be ashamed, Stephen—they are smart, exceptionally so. They have impressed the Triad with this plan of theirs. At least they will save your country, so take heart in that." He lowered his head. "I too am being used. How were we to know things would turn out this way? Perhaps it would have been better to have refused to go to school and been cast out of my father's house."

"No, my friend, then we would not have known each other," Stephen replied, patting Chen's shoulder to console him.

Chen slowly smiled and his eyes began twinkling again. "Yes, and there wouldn't have been those educated women who loved my simple mind. Ah, Stephen, the times we had! It is our joss to be sitting here. We are both in it up to our fool necks. So be it, then! We have this day to remember the old times. I have to leave tomorrow to attend a meeting and visit my esteemed father in Washington, D.C., so let's enjoy our time together."

Stephen couldn't suppress a reflective smile. "How is your father? The last time I saw him he was so angry with you, remember? You were in his bed with those two premed students."

Chen laughed and shook his head. "Ah, our graduation party. Yes, I can still remember the little one with magic fingers. She smelled of ginger and tasted of honey. She loved me for my pectoral something muscles, she told me. My father, now that subject is truly dangerous. But what is dangerous to us who knew glorious passion with women in his bed? He is now the San Chu, the lord of the mountain, in charge of the Circle's interests on the East Coast. A true legend in the making. He too has a new name. Dorba. Just a single name, easier to remember—and fear. I have been assigned here to the West Coast as a liaison between my father and the West Coast San Chu. I am to ensure that my father's interests are kept in mind and that he receives his share of your white powder. The Circle has been waiting patiently and is ready to expand its market."

Stephen remembered a gentle man who loved and raised *koi* fish for his garden pond. The elder Chen had always had a kind word for him for helping his son in school. Stephen lowered his head. "Are you and your father here in the U.S. because of our arrangement? Are we responsible for the Circle coming here?"

Chen smiled patiently. "No, my friend, the Triad is having to look beyond Hong Kong. When the Chinese take over in '97, we know they will make changes that will impede business, despite what they promise. There are many business opportunities here. In fact, we have established many legitimate businesses that are quite profitable. The white powder you bring us is important only because it gives my father much respect. His is the largest syndicate and therefore receives a larger portion of the powder. The quick and very high return on investment will ensure a seat for him on the council of elders. He moved from Hong Kong to Washington, D.C., only five months ago. He said, where better a San Chu than in this country's seat of power. He told me a few weeks ago that his cook even found fresh turtles for his favorite soup. He is very happy, and profits from your white powder will give him more of what he wants—power. To be a member of the council of elders is to be remembered for generations."

Chen dug in his pocket, took out a penny, and tossed it into the lake. "The Americans say it is for good joss. I will need it. Next year when I have amassed enough wealth to keep me in sweet-smelling women, I'm telling him I want out. I don't like the business, Stephen. I never did." He turned toward his friend and said softly, "You always hated your father for sending you away. I hate mine for forcing me to stay. For a time, at least, you were your own man. Now I fear your country owns your soul."

Stephen lowered his head and patted Chen's leg. "I hope the coin brings you good joss, my friend."

Chen stood and took Stephen's arm, pulling him to his feet. "Enough deep thoughts. It is time for you to meet my wife. Don't make a face when you see her plumpness. It was an arranged marriage; everyone is happy. Her father's family and ancestors are proud and my father assured himself of the East Coast position. My fat wife is happy because she can shop at the finest stores, and I am happy because she has given me two wonderful children that I adore. And she is a wonderful cook and asks no questions of my evening activities. I have more women here than is possible for a man to please. These American women love my British accent—they say it is cute. You must try one, Stephen. These women are not the submissive night hens we knew in Hong Kong. They are so aggressive you wonder who carries the seed."

"I already have more than I can handle," Stephen said with a reflective smile. "I married a beautiful Shan girl who is modern and does not believe in the Shan custom of the husband having three wives."

"A modern woman! Stephen, did I not teach you anything in the four years we roomed together? Modern women are to make love to but not to marry! What about the American brother you spoke of all the time?"

"Joshua?"

"Yes. That name, how could I forget it? You talked of no one else, him and that damnable Shan teacher of yours. I would go to bed nights and dream of opening your head and plucking those two out. They put a curse on you for the first year. No women, no wine, no ponies. It took time and all my devilish tricks to convert you."

Stephen smiled. "And you still owe me for when you lost on the ponies that last time."

"What happened to him, this Joshua?" Chen asked as they approached the car.

Stephen kept his smile. "He was still his own man when I saw him years ago. Unlike you and I, he had no father, and his stepfather had died."

"Then I envy this Joshua. Come, we must be going. You drive; I want you to know true decadence. This red machine is like American women: It is very fast and gives untold pleasure." Chen tossed Stephen the car keys and got in.

Stephen climbed behind the wheel and started the engine. "By the gods, this *is* a powerful beast," he exclaimed after depressing the accelerator just a fraction.

"And she is a willing beast," Chen chortled. He waited until Stephen was back on the road before dissolving his smile. He stared straight ahead and spoke as if in a deep tunnel. "Stephen, when we arrive at the house I become Ke Ping again, and you will be a polite but boring guest. I will drink too much and go to bed drunk, and you will ask my wife to have my security men take you back to the hotel. Make advances—she will like that, for a true friend would not do so. She may even respond and pleasure you, but whatever you do, speak nothing of me. You do not remember me, but since we attended the same school you felt obliged to come. The servants will report everything to my father's people. Remember—I carry the memory of those good days with me always. You helped me far more than in my studies."

Chen's face slowly brightened and he managed to grin again. "Seduce this red demon and let her show you her wonders!"

Washington, D.C.

Josh, Crow, and Grant got out of the military sedan in front of the Channel Inn. Grant faced the two men as soon as Crow's suitcase was unloaded. "I know you don't like having me around, but it's the way it has to be so there is no question of compromise. I'm here to help with the cover stories and assist you in clearing up any matters you have to take care of before you leave for Camp Pickett. I suggest we all have dinner in an hour and talk over how I can help."

Josh lifted Crow's suitcase and spoke coldly. "Just pick us up tomorrow. We don't need your 'help.' "

Grant met his glare. "Look, Colonel, I've got a job to do. You know as well as I do I'm supposed to play nursemaid and watch you two until you get to the training camp. Give me a break and cooperate. I won't be in the way, and I won't even speak if you don't want me to."

Crow nudged Josh with his elbow. "Knock it off, Hawk, she's right. We know they gonna have us covered tonight anyway. Let her do her job. Shiiit, they coulda assigned us an ugly infantry major."

Josh kept his hard stare on the woman. "Okay. We're going to the boat to drink a few beers, change, and get Hondo settled in. Any security problems with that?"

Grant ignored the last question. "That's fine. I'm going to my apartment and change clothes. I'll come back and meet you at the boat. There's a team inside the lobby watching you right now. When we link up I'll have them back off. And please don't make any phone calls. I'll see you in an hour."

Crow watched the lady officer walk away and leaned over to Josh. "If we had officers built like that in our day, we woulda followed 'em anywhere."

Several minutes later Josh approached the *Lil' Darlin'* cautiously; Crow had hung back just far enough to listen and wait for a sign that it was safe.

Wearing knee-length khaki shorts, a Hawaiian flowered shirt, and a scowl, Stefne tapped her foot until Josh stepped within range. "All I get from you this morning is a note? A note saying you're going to be gone all day and for me to wait until you get back. What's going on, Dad? I called Detective Kelly, the boathouse, and even Mr. Ky. They hadn't seen you. How come you didn't call me? And why are you wearing your watch? You never wear your watch."

Josh put down Crow's bag and shrugged. "I've been recalled to active duty for a few weeks. They need help and picked me because of my experience on the Drug Task Force. Bob will be here in a little while and we'll talk about how you two will run the business while I'm gone."

"*Gone?* Gone where? They can't ship you off like that! You're retired," she exclaimed loudly.

Josh picked up the bag again and glanced over his shoulder. "I've got a friend here you haven't seen in a long time. He's gonna stay with me tonight. I'll explain all this later, when I get him settled in. Relax, will ya? It's only for a few weeks, and then it'll be a business as usual. I promise."

After introducing Crow, whom Stefne didn't remember from their time in Burma, Josh led his friend into the cabin. Crow looked over his shoulder and grinned. "Damn if she don't look and sound jus' like—"

"I know," Josh said with a smile of pride. "Isn't she something? Well, this is it. Home. I'll take the couch. The head is in the passage on your right, and my berth, where you'll crash, is straight down the passage. You change first. We'll eat fancy tonight 'cause it may be our last good meal for a while."

Crow ran his fingers along the lapels of his too-big sport jacket. "This is the best I got. I picked it up at K-Mart for a funeral the old lady made me go to a couple months back."

Josh smiled. "It's fine. Damn, you haven't changed a bit. I've missed you, Hondo. I'm glad you're here."

Crow slapped Josh's back. "We're a team, Hawk, jus' like the old days. We can do it. They was smart enough to at least get the best."

Josh kept smiling, although he didn't mean it anymore.

Stefne eyed the attractive, auburn-haired woman sitting across from her at the restaurant and raised an eyebrow. "So you're in charge of my dad while he helps out the army?"

Grant smiled. "I think we both know that nobody could be in charge of your dad. No, I'm just assisting in the task force and providing input from the Defense Intelligence Agency. Your dad will be an adviser because of his experience. Don't worry, I'll keep an eye on him for you."

Stefne liked the answer as well as the woman her dad had introduced as Lieutenant Colonel Glenn Grant. She felt better knowing the woman would be keeping an eye out for her dad. Stefne shifted her eyes to the seedy-looking man her dad seemed to like very much. He was crusty in a cute way and reminded her of her father. She just couldn't put her finger on exactly what it was that made them alike.

Josh picked up his wineglass and nodded at Bob, who was seated at the other end of the table. "Bob, this is to you. I wish you luck in running the shifts while I'm gone and especially luck in having to put up with my daughter. And remember, only a dozen a day to Ky, and leave the King alone till I get back."

Bob raised his glass. "Boss, come back quick. I think I can handle the company business and Ky, but Stefne is—"

"Shut up, Bob," Stefne snarled.

Bob winked at Josh. "I think that makes my point."

Josh laughed. He had seen a big difference in Bob since going on the hunt. He seemed more confident and was meeting Stefne's barbs and verbal swordplay with equal skill.

Grant furrowed her brow. "Who is Mr. Ky?"

Stefne frowned. "Don't ask. It will get Dad started."

Crow said, "Yeah, I wanna know too. Nothing worse than being left out of a conversation."

Josh sighed and leaned back in his chair. "Ya see, I've got this little business on the side, and . . ."

After dinner Grant and Stefne followed Josh and Crow toward the boat. Grant chuckled and brushed against Stefne's shoulder. "Was your dad kidding about catching turtles?"

Stefne rolled her eyes. "Don't I wish. He's been doing it for about two months. We were at the fish market and Ky asked Dad if he ever saw turtles when he was out on the river. One thing led to another and now it's his new diversion. Before that he hired out as a fishing guide and would take fishermen to good spots on the river; before that he taught small-boat classes for the park service. I could go on, but you'd get bored. He just has to be busy . . . but not like when he used to work at the Pentagon. That job almost killed him."

Grant noticed the change in her tone. "He worked long hours, huh?"

Stefne stopped and looked across the channel in the direction of the ugly, five-sided building. "He'd go in at six in the morning and wouldn't come home until eight or nine. He lived for the weekends, when we could all go out on the boat and relax. It was the only time my mother and I ever got to talk to him. He'd come home from work with a briefcase full of paperwork and stay up till midnight. I remember waking him up at his desk and—" She stopped herself and took Grant's hand. She looked into the other woman's eyes and said, "Don't let them do that to him again. Please don't let them."

Grant squeezed her hand and felt sick to her stomach for what she was about to do. Lie. "I won't, Stefne. I'll make sure of it."

Back on the boat, Josh handed Crow a beer. "Sit and keep Grant busy for a few minutes. I gotta go say good-bye to a friend."

"Lady friend, by any chance?"

Josh rolled his eyes. "It's not like that."

Grant saw him coming toward her, but he veered off and climbed down to another motor sailer. "Where's he going?" she asked.

Stefne smiled. "Meg's. He's gotta tell her what's going on or she'll worry herself to death."

"I didn't think your dad had a girlfriend."

"Meg? Oh no, it's not like that. Meg is like family, kinda like a nosy aunt. You'd have to meet her to understand. She looks after us, and Dad does things for her. He *has* to tell Meg, believe me."

Once Josh returned, Stefne said good night and walked toward the wharf. A little later, Crow yawned and handed Josh an empty beer bottle. "Hate to leave you two up here alone, but I gotta get some sleep. See ya in the morning, Colonel."

"Good night, Sergeant Major," Grant said.

Josh settled back on a cushioned seat and took a sip of his beer, feeling uncomfortable with the woman. He wanted her to go so he could be left alone to enjoy the evening. "Grant, you gonna stay here all night and guard us?" he said, hoping she would get the hint.

She smiled, seemingly impervious to his cold tone. "No, I was just enjoying the stars. It's funny, they seem brighter here on the water than from across the street in the apartment."

Josh decided to try something different and got up. "I'm gonna have a couple more beers."

"Could I have one too, please?"

Shit, he mumbled to himself. He returned seconds later with two beers, handed her one, and gestured toward the cabin. "You oughta hear Hondo, he's already snoring. Poor guy oughta be home on his lake."

Grant took a sip as Josh resumed his position across from her. "Tell me about the unsanctioned mission you two went on," she asked. "It *was* authorized, wasn't it?"

Josh gave her a cautious look and thought what the hell. He took a long pull from his bottle and looked up at the stars. "Yeah. The Company needed some information. It actually worked out fine. My friend Stephen Kang was taking a lot of heat about that time from the DDSI for being a minority and especially being the son of a warlord. I volunteered for the mission as long as Stephen could turn us in afterward to prove his loyalty to the government."

"Was he an Agency informant?" asked Grant.

"Stephen? Hell no. He wouldn't do anything against his government. For better or worse he loved his country more than anybody I know. The only thing he did for me was tell me where to find his father, Sawbaw Xu Kang."

"Sawbaw?"

"Yeah, it's Shan for 'warlord' or 'leader.' In Xu Kang's case it definitely means warlord. Hondo and I slipped our secret-police tails and took off for the north in a pre-positioned Company Land Rover. We were posing as photographers for *National Geographic*. Jesus, you should have seen us. Hondo didn't even know how to load the film in the cameras they gave us, let alone use them. It took us eight days, avoiding the army checkpoints, and we hadn't made it even to the foothills when Xu Kang's people spotted us first."

Grant got up and sat down beside him so he wouldn't have to talk as loudly. "What information did the Agency need?"

Josh took another sip of beer before answering. "The junta was claiming the communists were taking over the north. The Company had some of their indigenous Intel people telling them it was bullshit. They needed to confirm or refute the information. I was a logical choice 'cause I spoke the language and had lived up in the area. Their all-important plausible denial story was that if we got caught the embassy was going to say I had taken off with a buddy to check out my old home. Anyway, Hondo and I were escorted by Xu Kang's people to his camp in the mountains. I'd been there before, in '73, when I was first assigned to the embassy. The camp had changed a lot. The Company had put tons of money into new radio equipment and weapons for the Chindit's army. 'Chindit' is what everyone calls Xu Kang. To get an idea of what he looks like, think of Anthony Quinn but six feet tall, broader-shouldered, and Chinese. He has a lordly, charismatic presence and a quick laugh. He rides a black horse, and when I saw him last he had a Mexican saddle all tricked out in silver and—"

"Where did he get a Mexican saddle?" Grant interrupted.

Josh smiled reflectively. "The CIA gave it to him back in the sixties to impress him. God, do the Shan love their horses. Ponies, they call 'em. Nobody can ride like a Shan Horseman."

Josh yawned and continued, "We found out the government was lying as usual. They had hired Sawbaw Kang's little army to fight the communists for them. There were a few pockets of hard-core Marxists but nothing the mountain tribes couldn't handle. The junta was making the threat up to get support from the U.S."

Grant shook her head. "Wait a minute. You say the Burmese Army hired this Sawbaw to fight the communists? I thought the army was trying to destroy the mountain rebels."

Josh wiggled his brow. "That's what we all thought. You see, the army knew better than to go after the mountain rebels. They had been trying for years, and for years they'd been getting their asses handed to them. They made a deal instead. The deal was Kang would fight the communists and the army would stay out of the mountains and not interfere in his black marketing. Xu Kang was a sly old dog—he had changed sides with the army three or four times before. He didn't deal in opium, but he moved jade, rubies, and silver from the government-owned mines. Most of his work for the army was turning in competitors who had tried to move in and take a piece of his action. He was the best con man I ever saw, but make no mistake about it, he was taking care of the people who lived under his protection. That old man took his title of 'the Protector' very, very seriously."

Grant smiled at the look on his face. "You really liked him, didn't you?"

Josh nodded without hesitation. "I loved him and still do. He always treated me like a son. When my folks died in the plane crash, I was here in the States going to school. It tore me up pretty bad. A few weeks later I got a letter from him. He reminded me that my mother and stepfather had died fighting and that I should rejoice. The Shan gods and their Christian God were blessed with their presence, he said, since they had died fighting to save souls."

Joshua sighed and looked at his empty beer bottle. "You don't understand what that means . . . but to me, at that time, it was what I needed to get through the pain." Josh forced a smile. "Sorry, you asked a simple question and I took off on a tangent. The answer is yes. I love the old warrior. He's like a father in many ways to me."

"And Stephen really did turn you in when you got back from the mission?" asked Grant.

Josh nodded. "Yeah, after we got back to Rangoon I told Stephen what we did and made him call it in to the DDSI. Their government protested our trip, and you know the rest. The embassy kicked us out to show the Burmese they didn't condone that sort of thing. The Company made sure the written reprimands were pulled from our records as soon as we were back in the States."

Grant folded her legs under her. "Tell me about how you came to live in Burma as a boy. And Stephen, when did you meet him?"

Josh gave her a questioning stare. "Are you working now, Grant?"

She raised her hands palms up and smiled innocently. "No, just interested. I was given the Burma desk because I studied the country in college and wrote a paper on its history, but I've never been there. Hearing this helps me understand the people."

Josh could tell she was being honest. He leaned back again in the seat and looked out toward the dark waters of the channel. "In the summer of 1960, when I was eleven, we left Leavenworth, Kansas, and began the 'great adventure'—at least that's what my mother called it. Jesus, what a pistol she was." Josh couldn't help but smile as he remembered those first days on the river. "My mother and I . . . ."

Grant listened to his entire story without saying a word or moving a muscle so as not to break the spell. She could see the Master Horseman and his bushy white moustache and could see Henry preaching before his Shan congregation. The image of the village was clear in her mind, as was the mission and the rugged mountains that Joshua so lovingly spoke of. She felt his sadness when he and his family bade farewell to the Ri.

Josh's eyes focused back on the dark water of the Washington Channel, then he shifted his gaze to the woman beside him. "I'm sorry if I've been rattling on too long. It's just been a long time since I thought about those days. Have I bored you?"

"No, the opposite. It's a fascinating story. Please don't stop. What happened to Stephen? I mean, you told me this morning you still wrote to each other."

Josh shifted his eyes back to the channel and a passing boat. "After we left Burma, Henry was assigned to a mission in Malaysia. Stephen flew over that summer and stayed until school started again. That fall we both left. I went to the States and he went back to the University of Hong Kong. You know some of the rest. I went into ROTC and—"

"Whoa," said Grant, raising her hand. "That's the part I don't understand. Why would a missionary's son join ROTC?"

Josh took a sip of beer and shrugged. "The money. When my folks died they didn't have much to leave me. ROTC paid a hundred dollars a month and offered scholarships to those who worked hard. I wanted to finish school so I worked hard. It worked out for the best, 'cause I knew it was a way to keep moving and see new things. It's funny—I thought Vietnam cured me of that . . . Vietnam and Jill. I met her in Japan while I was convalescing. She worked for the army in the post finance center. We were both gypsies—I guess things turn out that way. They found out I spoke Shan and a little Burmese and sent me back to Burma. That's where I caught up with Stephen again. He had gotten a job in the Ministry of Finance as the Shan affairs officer in Rangoon. It was like we'd never left each other. Jill came over and joined me in late '72 and I had to make her an honest woman to keep her there. Stephen had met Mya, a beautiful Shan girl who worked in the ministry. We all lived together in a house near Royal Lake. He married her a week after Jill and I were married. In '73 Jill was pregnant with Stef, so we went back to the States. I joined the Special Forces, and we all went back to Burma in '83. It was like old home week except this time Stef was ten. We had a wonderful time together, but Stephen was having trouble advancing because of his background. Like I told you, Hondo and I kinda made him a hero."

Grant lowered her eyes. "It's a wonderful story, but I feel sorry for Xu Kang. He gave up what he loved most."

Joshua smiled. "You're good, Grant. Xu Kang *was* the loser, and it's always bothered me, too. I know from experience it's hard to give up what you love most in the world." Josh looked back at the channel with a reflective gaze. "Some of us still try to hold on . . . even though it's time to let go."

Grant put her hand on his. "I'm sorry about all this, Colonel. Now that I know you and have met Stefne, I know what we're asking of you. I'm truly sorry."

Josh finished the last of his beer and stood up. "Do me a favor and look in on her when I'm gone. She likes you."

Grant forced a smile. "I was going to anyway. I like her too."

Josh looked up at the stars and stretched out his arms before giving Grant a light pat on the shoulder. "Thanks. I guess I'd better try and get some sleep. See ya in the morning." He looked back at the channel one more time as if saying good-bye before turning and disappearing into the darkened cabin.

Grant climbed up onto the pier and slowly walked over the creaking planks toward the wharf, praying she wouldn't be needed to comfort Stefne if something went wrong with the mission. She stopped and looked over her shoulder at the boat. Come back to her, Joshua Hawkins, she said silently before turning toward her home.

CHAPTER 12

8 A.M., 8 June, Seattle, Washington

The U.S. Customs officers walked up the rusting steps to the bridge, where the captain of the freighter waited with a young man who would interpret. The officer in charge glanced at the papers on the clipboard in his hands. "Your papers say you've got a little over forty-eight hundred tons of teak plywood. That right?"

The young Malaysian quickly translated for his captain, who bowed his head and spoke only a few words the officer took as a yes.

The officer held out the clipboard and a pen to the translator. "Have him sign the bottom of the inspection form saying he understands that any nondeclared cargo found on this vessel will be confiscated. And if we find drugs aboard, his vessel will be confiscated and he will be incarcerated pending trial."

The young man translated without expression and handed the captain the clipboard. The middle-aged captain signed the form as he spoke in an accommodating tone. The young man interpreted.

"My captain say, he understand and will assist you in any way possible. He say he has crew standing by to open cargo holds, and will open any pallet you wish."

The officer nodded his thanks and turned to his three assistants. "This should be pretty easy. The plywood is three-quarter-inch stuff stacked twenty-four sheets per pallet. Each of you take a hold, pick three to four pallets at random, and have 'em cut the bands. Get the crew to unstack enough to check if they've hollowed the stack out for contraband. We've got only two hours before we have to inspect that

148

load of Taiwanese bike parts on pier three. Questions? Okay, let's do it."

In a car facing the wharf, Colonel Po's two captains watched the freighter for almost two hours. The Customs crew walked down the gangplank and the lead officer gave a thumbs-up to the waiting stevedore crew chief. The two men knew the sign meant the ship was clean and the crew could begin off-loading. Captain Sing picked up a portable phone and punched in a number. Colonel Po picked up on the first ring.

"The first is in, no complications," Sing said. Then he hung up and drove away.

Camp Pickett, Virginia

Josh and Crow sat in the dark in the first row of a converted army movie theater turned briefing hall. Seated all around them were men from various departments of the Central Intelligence Agency and a group of soldiers wearing civilian clothes from the Special Operations Command (SOCOM) in Fort Bragg, North Carolina.

The operations officer walked up a short flight of steps to the lighted stage, and all talking ceased. He faced the audience and rocked back on his heels.

"Gentlemen, you have all been issued your equipment and been briefed by our security officer. It's now time to tell you what Operation Miracle is all about. This is an intragovernmental operation using assets from the Agency and SOCOM, with the Agency having the lead. Our mission is to conduct a point reconnaissance and surveillance of selected targets within the country of Burma."

A murmur rolled through the audience like a breaking wave. The ops officer raised his hand for silence. "The SOCOM helicopter crews are already inbound to a temporary base and will join us at the operational staging base when it is established. Departure from this location will be in seven days. Execution of mission, depending on the weather, will be in ten days."

Another murmur, louder than the first, stopped the officer for several moments. He waited patiently and placed his hands on his hips. "I know it isn't much time, but the mission demands we execute as soon as possible. This will be a sterile, quick, looksee-and-get-out op. Five teams will be inserted; judging from satellite photos, there are plenty of landing zones so you won't need high altitude or low-opening parachute refresher training. You'll be airlanded by the Pave Low III's. I'll go into details later, but first I'll give you a general overview of how it's going to go down. We'll base out of a staging camp inside a neutral country. Once air assets are on hand we will begin a night air infiltration of the five teams into the target country. An emergency base will be established in-country in a remote area for use in case of compromise. Communications will be . . ."

After the briefing Josh and Crow walked into an old barracks that had been converted into the operation headquarters. They entered the first room off the hallway, the ops commander's office. Waiting for them was Buck McCoy, an Agency strategic operations officer. He eyed the two men as they approached and leaned back in his chair with a scowl.

"What now? You old vets going to complain that we don't have hot water or that the afternoon chow was cold?"

The two men ignored the comment and sat down in the cheap metal chairs without being asked. Josh handed over the notes he'd made at the operations briefing. "I didn't want to make your planner look bad, but you'll need to make some changes."

McCoy glanced down the single page before looking up. "Why do we 'have to' change the time of the insertion to later?"

Josh lowered his head and inspected his fingernails as he spoke. "It's the planting season for most of the mountain people. They'll plant and clear land till dusk and will be all over the lower valleys. If you want us, and the other teams, to go in low level, you'll have to do it later at night so we're not detected. If the locals hear a chopper they'll think it's the Burmese government's, but if they can see our birds they'll know they have company."

McCoy nodded noncommittally and pointed to the second item. "And you think the other teams are too big."

Crow furrowed his brow and leaned forward. "This ain't a combat mission, Buck. Your boys are going in too heavy. They need to be like our team, no more than three people. Less chance of detection, and it makes the cover story better if they're caught. Six-man teams are asking for trouble. Since your boys don't know the lay of the land and are going in cold, they're gonna have to move only at night and very early in the morning. The rest of the time they're gonna have to hole up. Like we told your planners, there's more than their army to worry about. The hill bandits are all over the mountains, and they don't fuck around asking questions of strangers. Hawk and I saw them in action once and had to shoot our way out. They ain't what ya'd call nice people."

McCoy tossed the paper on his desk. "I'll talk to the team leaders. I think you're right that the teams are too big. How's your radioman working out?"

Josh exchanged glances with Crow before looking back at their commander. "He's not. He's too big and talks too much. He's not listening.
No offense, but we want one of the Special Forces radiomen rather than
your man. We want the Vietnamese sergeant, Nguyen Vee."

McCoy sighed as he ran a hand through his short hair. "I don't
mind tellin' you old-timers I don't like the pressure they're putting on
us for this op." He leaned forward and pinned both men with his eyes.
"There's not enough time to get the other teams ready. I'll give you
Vee, but you've got to help the others out more. Talk to them and
give them the benefit of your experience."

"Tell your trainers that," Crow snapped. "Every time we open our
mouths with suggestions, your boys hammer us."

"I'll talk to them tonight," McCoy replied with a frown. "It's the
same old story of professional jealousy, and we don't have time for
that shit. We just received word the government of India approved
State's request for a temporary base on India's border with Burma.
State's cover was that we need a temporary base to recover an inbound errant telecommunications satellite. It cost our government a
diplomatic bundle, but at least we know for sure we have a staging
area. To tell you the truth, it's still not close enough for me. We're going to be at least three hundred kilometers from the farthest insertion
point. Yours."

Josh got up and took Crow's hand, pulling him to his feet. "Ya hear
that, Hondo? Buck is worried about the insertion."

Crow winked at McCoy. "That's the only part I *ain't* worried
about. I just hope I can hump enough batteries to keep all that high-
tech shit you're givin' us runnin'. What I really need is a new set of
legs, and about three more inches of—"

"Come on," Josh said. "Let's go find something else to complain
about."

Once the men had left the office, McCoy again picked up the list of
suggestions, knowing they were all needed changes. Reaching for the
telephone, he wished he had thirty more of the old-timers—then, he
thought, this operation might have a chance.

Chinatown, Washington, D.C.

Sheng Chen stood by the huge darkened plate-glass windows overlooking H Street seven stories below. He heard footsteps behind him
and knew it was time. Glancing slightly to his right, he could see the
reflection of the tall, sixty-five-year-old tycoon coming toward him
dressed in a perfectly tailored black suit. His father's dark gray hair

was swept back and he was wearing new gold-framed, blue-tinted glasses that masked his cold, impenetrable eyes.

"Come, we're about to start the meeting," Dorba said, taking his son's arm. "I want you to sit behind me at the great table."

Hating the weakness he felt in the old man's presence, Chen forced a smile. "Thank you for the honor."

The recessed lights radiated a golden glow that reflected off the huge, lacquered rosewood table where ten men stood waiting for their San Chu. Dorba entered the windowless room, took his position at the head of the table, and bowed. The others bowed deeply and took their seats as Chen and the rest of the compradors, or advisers, filed in and sat behind their respective leaders.

Still standing, Dorba looked down the table at the expectant faces of his appointed deputies who were responsible for the major East Coast cities of the United States. Behind the tinted glasses his eyes were smiling. "The first shipment is in," he said flatly. "We can expect to begin our new business within a week, so make the final offers. All of you have reported there are those who are bad-mannered and do not wish to do business with us. Give them one more opportunity. If they persist, make examples of some and report the others to the authorities through your lieutenants. Our new business will be like a fragile flower needing much care in the beginning until the roots have gone deep into the soil. The beauty of our flowers is they will bloom in all seasons and spread and grow stronger with each passing year. Our garden will provide seeds for expanding rapidly in our other interests and ultimately give us the strength to end our need for the flowers completely."

The leader of the New York syndicate, ten years younger than Dorba, dipped his chin in respect. "San Chu, I understand making examples of some of our competitors, but I am concerned about the authorities' response."

Dorba nodded. "Yes, we can all expect weeds to try to choke our garden in the beginning. We will pull them early. These American officials are no different from those in Hong Kong. They will learn that the cost of pursuing our organization is too high. Find the authorities' leaders, target their families, and take immediate action to make an example for the others. Yes, you can expect to lose some of your lieutenants, but that is the price of business. They can be replaced easily. We all must do whatever is necessary to ensure that our flowers grow."

Sitting behind his father, Chen felt a chill run up his spine and across his shoulders. Shuddering, he closed his eyes.

·   ·   ·

The black Chrysler Town Car turned into the estate driveway and slowed just long enough for the ornate metal gate to slide back before proceeding past the two guards in the stone keyhouse. Sitting beyond the manicured lawn and geometrically shaped English gardens stood a two-story gray stone mansion. The car stopped in the circular driveway at the front entrance, and a waiting security man opened the right passenger door.

Dorba stepped out and looked back toward the front gate a hundred yards away. He smiled and pointed at the squirrels beneath a huge maple close to a rock wall. "They are full of such energy."

Chen had gotten out of the other side of the car wanting only to change clothes and begin drinking the many gin and tonics that would get him through the night.

Seeing his son wasn't listening, Dorba walked over to take his arm and guided him toward a red-graveled path that led to the back of the estate. "I see you're troubled. Let's take a walk in the garden and talk."

Chen nodded submissively, caught off guard by his father's gentle tone. He walked alongside him in silence, trying to find the strength to tell him he wanted out. His previous plan to wait a year had changed once he heard his father would be using the old methods of control.

"You didn't approve of my words today. Why?" Dorba asked, again in a fatherly tone.

Chen took a breath, steeling himself. "Father, I think you're making a mistake by using the old methods. These Americans are not like our people; they have never known true suffering or defeat. They are proud people who won't scare as easily as you seem to think."

Dorba squeezed his son's arm in a rare show of affection. "I have found that all men have a weakness, and it's just a matter of finding it. Most cherish their families; others, their work."

They had entered the estate's rear Oriental gardens which Dorba had had planted upon his arrival five months before. Stands of bamboo hid the surrounding security walls, and climbing honeysuckle filled the evening with its delicate sweet scent. Dorba slowed his steps and stopped on the arched wooden footbridge. Bending over, he peered into the crystal-clear water and smiled at his prize *koi* that had gathered in his shadow.

"These are like children to me," he said in almost a whisper as his fingers rippled the water above the large, brightly colored fish. "I love caring for them and ensuring they have only the best of conditions. There, you see the pair of reds nibbling my fingers? They're my favorite—they are a weakness within me, for I have a deep desire to watch them grow, produce young, and give me years of pleasure. You see, even I have a weakness. I think most fathers have a weakness in watching their children grow."

"Why is this necessary?" Chen asked desperately. "We could become completely legitimate and not have to do business in the white powder. Why must we teach lessons and take unnecessary risks?"

Dorba rose, still watching his *koi* with a loving smile. "It is time for these Americans to pay." He turned to look into his son's eyes. "They and the British brought the opium to our mother country almost two hundred years ago. They made huge sums of money by enslaving our ancestors with addiction in dens that they established. Their pockets were lined with gold while our ancestors and our country slowly died. Only the strongest of our families survived and became their servants—but also their students. We could not defeat them then, but now it is our turn to teach the lessons."

The old man's eyes had become full of fire, but he smiled. "Our business is nothing more than what these people did to us. Yes, some will die, but only a fraction compared to the countless numbers of our people who suffered. You are asking yourself, don't I, your father, have feelings? I say yes, I grieve for my ancestors who were turned into opium eaters years ago. These Americans will pay, my son. They will learn what our ancestors learned—it is only business."

Chen felt a wave of nausea, but he lowered his chin as if in agreement. He strolled in silence with his father along the path lined with fiddlehead ferns, umbrella palms, and wildflowers until they came to the polished round stone porch where a servant waited.

Dorba motioned Chen to a patio chair and sat down beside him as the white-jacketed young Cantonese servant poured green tea into black-lacquered wooden cups.

Dorba reached out and patted his son's hand. "As you know, I selected no San for this city, for I wanted to run the business here myself. I have revisited my decision and think it unwise. I have decided you should be the San here. It is time for you to take your place in the Circle."

Chen kept his stoic expression, not letting his inner emotions show. Picking up a cup of tea in both hands, he offered it to his father and bowed his head, hating himself for what he would soon become. "It will be an honor," he said.

Seattle, Washington

A dark blue Lincoln turned off the highway onto a blacktop road and traveled three hundred yards before coming to a smooth stop behind a semitrailer truck loaded with plywood. The big diesel truck had stopped beside a security guard shack in front of a chain link gate. A large, white-and-red-bordered sign attached to the adjoining fence read:

RED DRAGON
SPECIALIZED WOOD WALL PANELING CO.
a subsidiary of Dragon Inc. USA-Korea

A lone uniformed guard opened the gate, waved the truck through, and motioned for the Lincoln to come forward. The Burmese guard looked at Sergeant Shin, then at Stephen in the backseat. Recognizing them both, he motioned for Shin to proceed. The car rolled forward along a two-lane road to a large brick building attached to a huge metal one that extended back for almost a hundred yards. The truck had taken a side road toward the long building's loading docks, where a forklift and crew were waiting.

Shin parked in the lot between two Mercedes, got out of the car, and opened the door for Stephen. "U Kang, I will be helping to unload the shipment. When you are ready to leave let me know."

Stephen nodded in silence and strode toward the office building, where another guard opened the glass door for him. Inside he passed by the offices that had been turned into dormitory rooms for the DDSI men who had flown in over the past three weeks to do the processing. Po had made sure they stayed in the old cabinetmaking plant for security reasons and had provided for their every need. Televisions, VCRs, and small refrigerators were in every room, and the largest room had been made into a kitchen complete with tables and chairs for all thirty workmen and guards. Stephen strode through the kitchen toward double doors leading to the work bay, stopping only to grab one of the rain jackets hanging from pegs on the wall. Putting on the jacket and tossing up the hood, he pushed through the doors into a torrential man-made rain shower. Far above him a fire sprinkler system was raining down sheets of water onto pallets of plywood that had already been unloaded. He walked down a narrow corridor formed by the pallets of wood until he came to the center of the bay, where a large foreman's office bisected the huge work area. Through the glass windows he saw that the four representatives sent by the Triad were taking off their rain gear. He stepped in and quickly took off his jacket.

Po motioned Stephen forward and introduced him to a tall, well-dressed black man who called himself Mr. Lassen. Stephen waited to be introduced to the other three men, but Lassen only smiled and made light conversation. Then Po pointed toward the work area and said, "One sheet of plywood is being brought into the processing area to show you how the processing will work. As I'm sure you saw, the trucks are still arriving and we are placing the remaining pallets on the dock. We plan to work until we've finished this shipment, which we estimate will take two days. Ah, here comes the first sheet."

DDSI workmen brought one of the soaked plywood sheets from a stack in the "raining" bay and placed it on one of the large tables in the dry work area. Other workmen used chisels to loosen the top veneer of teak, then pulled off the thin, flexible sheet to expose eighteen rectangular white bags between the wood support strips.

Lassen nodded in admiration. "They said you were good, but this is a real piece of work. Let me guess, the veneer was bonded with water-based glue and the soaking causes the bond to disintegrate, right?"

"Correct," Po said with obvious pride. "We went to considerable expense in perfecting the method of shipping."

"Yeah, well, now I see why you were so confident the shipment would arrive undetected. How much in each bag?"

Po replied, "Each bag is a half-inch thick and ten inches square. It holds one point zero one American pounds, or half a kilo. Nine kilos per sheet of plywood, and there are twenty-four sheets per pallet. We calculated 216 kilos per pallet. This shipment contains just over fifty tons of the product."

Lassen puckered his lips and let out a low whistle. "Hot damn. Now that's what I call a load of smack. Your boss is a genius . . . or has one helluva set of balls to bring this much stuff in. No one has ever tried anything like this before. Damn, we're all going to be busy getting the product weighed and logged. I'm supposed to run periodic checks for purity and reweigh every bag. Business, you understand?"

Po smiled. "But of course. Stephen will be our ledger keeper and will work with your assistants in the handoff."

Lassen shifted his eyes to Stephen. "My people are ready to get started as soon as you are. Like you, we wanna get this done as soon as possible."

"What about transport?" asked Stephen.

Lassen held out his hand. One of his men put a cellular phone in his palm. He dialed a number and spoke into the receiver. "It's show time. Send one over now." He tossed the phone back and nodded toward a stocky, dark-skinned man with a gold tooth. "Stephen, this is Chigger, our scales man and bookkeeper. He doesn't know where your country is but he knows numbers."

Chigger stepped forward and put out his hand with a smile. "Nice to meetcha, Steve. Let's do the thing."

Directorate of the Defense Services Intelligence,
Rangoon

Brigadier General Tan entered the office of his director and came to attention.

General Swei glanced up from his paperwork. "Yes?"

"Colonel Po called and gave the code word," Tan said with a contained smile. "The first shipment arrived with no problems."

Swei leaned back in his chair and smiled. "Then it has begun." His eyes slowly turned to Tan. "Is phase seven ready for execution?"

"Yes, my general. I have placed our Strike units on standby, and the engineers will begin moving north tomorrow to their pre-positions. We have located all those on the list except for Sawbaw Xu Kang. We are only waiting for the order to move."

"We'll have time for Xu Kang later," Swei said with a quick wave of his hand. "Once the second shipment safely arrives we will execute the first part of phase seven. And you, my friend, will be the one who will unleash White Storm's power."

Tan bowed his massive head, no longer bothering to contain his smile. "It will be an honor."

CHAPTER 13

15 June, Camp Pickett, Virginia

"I'm doin' just fine. Yeah, I know, Stef, I said I'd call last night but we were in meetings till late. Look, I'm callin' to tell ya we're flying down to Panama for a conference with some Central American government officials and . . . I didn't know I was going to have to go either. Just listen a minute. I won't be in touch for a week or so, but I'll call as soon as I get back. . . ."

Josh held the phone away from his ear and whispered to Crow, "She's not takin' this too good."

He put his ear back to the phone and nodded and nodded some more. "You finished bitching?" he said finally. "Hey, I love you, Stef. Keep things straight and make sure Bob ain't screwed over by Ky. I'll call when I get back. I gotta go . . . Yeah, I'll be careful. Love ya— good-bye, hon."

Josh hung up and took a deep breath, then let it out in a single rush of air. "That was a tough one."

Crow smiled. "She's a pistol. Ya done good with her, Hawk."

Josh shifted his eyes to the small Special Forces sergeant standing beside the sergeant major. "How old is your daughter, Sergeant Vee?"

"She's four."

Josh nodded and put his arm over the young soldier's shoulder. "Start workin' on a son as soon as we get back. Daughters grow up and try to change your life."

Nguyen Vee grinned. "My wife does that enough already."

Crow picked up the bag of equipment at his feet and tossed his head toward the distant helicopter landing pad. "It's time. They're loadin'."

Josh and Vee hefted their bags to their shoulders. Vee looked at Josh with a searching stare. "Do you really think we're ready for the mission?"

Josh exchanged glances with Crow before forcing a smile. "You bet."

Three CH-47 Chinook helicopters from Fort Pickett landed at Andrews Air Force Base's ready ramp and were immediately surrounded by armed Air Force security police. The passengers from the helicopters walked down the rear ramp holding bags of equipment and followed Air Force escort officers who led them to a waiting C-141B Starlifter. The large, four-jet-engine monster was sitting on the runway with its turbines whirling. The passengers leaned into the blast of hot air and walked up the rear ramp into the fuselage. Minutes later the engines screamed as the white bird broke its bonds with earth and soared skyward.

Josh unfastened his seat belt and reached down into his flight bag for the folder of satellite photos. Opening the folder, he thumbed through the glossy eight-by-tens until he came to the one he was looking for—his team's assigned recon area. He studied the picture for several minutes, looking for the best way to approach the hidden building, but it was not easy. He had constantly to fight off images of his past. Finally he tossed the photograph down. It was no use trying. He knew the ground all too well. The suspected drug production plant was on the plateau where he and Stephen had taken the Horseman test. It was the ground where his mother had watched him pass the test and cried. It was his home.

Northern Burma

Xu Kang reined his pony closer to Colonel Banta, who was getting out of his pickup. "Greetings and blessings, Colonel. Who is this bleeding all over the back of your truck?"

"Greetings and blessings, Chindit." Banta casually waved toward the wounded soldier wearing camouflage fatigues. "A pye dog who we caught doing a reconnaissance of the Shaduzup *lai* house. There were three others, but they are with their ancestors. They made sketches and had cameras. This one is gutshot and will die soon, but he was able to tell an interesting story I thought you should hear."

Kang climbed down from the horse and opened the tailgate to look more closely at the feverish young soldier. He patted the boy's shoulder. "I am Sawbaw Xu Kang. You've heard of me, eh? If you don't speak the truth your entrails will be fed to the pigs while you still live to watch them feast."

The young man's eyes widened. "I will speak the truth, Sawbaw. I beg you in the name of Buddha, don't—"

"By the gods! I'm not Wa! I don't kill wounded men who speak the truth. Have pride and accept the gods' will." Kang spun around, motioning to two of his nearby Horsemen. "Take him to the shade in front of my headquarters." He looked again at the colonel. "Is the cobra about to strike?"

Banta nodded with a frown. "His story proves you right, Sawbaw. Our spies in Rangoon have also reported the DDSI's Strike Battalion is on standby alert. One of our young women is sleeping with a sergeant in the unit and reported he has been gone for two days."

Xu Kang hastened his steps. "I must hear your prisoner's story."

Minutes later the old soldier's wrinkled face became a stone mask as he spoke to the young man who was laid on the ground before him. "Now tell me and my Horsemen what you told my colonel. Keep in mind my pigs are hungry. If you are truthful I will see to it that a doctor attends to your wound."

Kang listened for ten minutes as the soldier's voice got progressively weaker. Finally he could barely move his lips. The old man bent over the soldier and brushed his wet hair from his forehead. "I will see that you rest now." He nodded to the two Horsemen, who gently picked up the limp man and walked him carefully toward the dispensary.

Kang shook his head as he sat back in his campaign chair. "He will die within the hour . . . but now we know an attack is planned. By the gods, I warned the Sawbaws about this! They were all fools to believe the government. Now it's too late for them."

Banta's eyes widened. "But they must be warned! You must try, or they will all die."

Xu Kang slowly shook his head and said sadly, "They won't listen to me. To them I am nothing but an old man crying wolf. Greed has blinded them and made them deaf." His eyes suddenly focused and locked on the colonel. "We must save the others. Get my son and his family and all the Shan leaders out of Rangoon. Give them no choice. It will be happening soon."

"Chindit, it will take several days to contact our people in Rangoon," said Banta worriedly. "The army is using jammers to make radio transmission very difficult."

Kang closed his eyes and prayed to the gods that he had not received the information too late. Nodding in resignation, he stood. "Send some of your men as backup immediately—we don't have much time."

"It will be a bloodbath when it begins. So many fools . . . so many," Banta whispered.

Xu Kang raised his head and looked back at the valley, knowing that after all the years and all the battles he had fought, nothing had changed.

CHAPTER 14

1 A.M., 18 June, Rangoon

The night operations officer gently shook Brigadier Tan's shoulder. "General, the call you've been expecting from Seattle is on the secure line."

Tan, fully dressed, stood up from his office couch and hurried down the steps to the basement operations center. He paused only long enough to glance at the wall clock with Seattle's time and noted that Colonel Po was calling at 11 A.M. in the States. Praying to Buddha that the call would be good news, he picked up the phone and placed the receiver to his ear.

"This is Tan. . . . Excellent! . . . Yes, we will move forward with phase seven immediately. When the last shipment is in and the hand-off is complete, finish the business of the loose ends. . . . Yes, I will be expecting your call in four days. Thank you for making this morning one to remember. I will pass the good news on to the director." Tan hung up the receiver and turned to his operations officer. "The second ship arrived in Seattle and cleared Customs. Contact our Strike units and have them execute their orders immediately."

The officer motioned to the wall where a chalkboard and map were hung. "Those on the list will be no problem, since our teams have each target pinpointed except for Sawbaw Xu Kang. We can begin strikes on facilities one through four, but our reconnaissance units report clouds over facility five."

Tan waved his hand impatiently and spoke quickly. "Notify the commander of five to have his recon units cut the phone lines and block all road entrances to the factory so that they won't know about the other attacks. Tell him to go in as soon as the clouds clear. Forget about Xu Kang for now—we'll find him later."

The major acknowledged his instructions with a quick dip of his chin and strode toward the waiting radio operators. Tan looked at the map and rocked back on his heels, knowing that all the evidence of the government's involvement in producing the white powder would be gone within a few short hours. He smiled inwardly and shifted his gaze to the list of names on the chalkboard. The names were those of the Shan Sawbaws and administrators whom he'd paid handsomely to keep the heroin factories full of workers and to ensure the harvested raw opium was transported to the production facilities. They would all be eliminated, for they knew the junta had sanctioned the labs.

Tan walked to the board; beside the name of Xu Kang, he wrote "FIND HIM!" Tossing the piece of chalk back onto the rail, he strode confidently toward the phone to report to General Swei that the wrath of the White Storm had begun.

0235 Hours, Northern Burma

"Oh shit," Josh moaned as the huge helicopter dropped and bucked back up, forcing his stomach into his throat. The two remaining passengers beside their team leader made the mistake of smiling. Their faces were eerie enough in the red glow from the interior lights, but smiling made them look like red-faced ghouls with black eyes and mouths. He cussed them both, along with the Air Force Special Operations Command's Pave Low III crew and everybody else who had told him the ride would be "a piece of cake."

Seeing his team leader squirming, Crow leaned closer to be heard over the roaring twin turboshaft engines. "Hawk, don't embarrass me. The crew bet me you'd toss your cookies in this bad weather. They say we'll be busting out of this little thunderstorm in just a few minutes. Hell, enjoy the ride—some people pay to be bounced around like this."

Josh looked at Crow's red, glowing face and wanted to smash the old soldier's teeth in. His own friend was making fun of his weakness! The bastard! They were all bastards! He clenched his jaw tighter and clamped his eyes shut.

He wanted to remember every detail for the scathing report he would write once the mission was over. Paragraph one, the fucking Agency had rehearsed the infils at Fort Pickett in CH-47s. He knew Chinooks. Hell, he loved Chinooks. They were slow, reliable, and weren't filled with computers—the pilots actually had to fly them.

But when he arrived at the staging base in India what did he find? Fucking monster helicopters he'd never seen before except in pictures! Pave Lows? What the fuck are Pave Lows? he'd asked. They'd said they were the newest and best thing going for special ops. Hadn't he been in one before? they'd asked. What else could he do but lie? Sure, he'd said. Then he found out the goddamned things were flown by fucking computers! Here he was in a fucking multimillion-dollar machine flying two hundred knots per hour at treetop level, at night, in a small thunderstorm while passing through the mountains of Burma! *And the fucking pilots were probably reading fucking comic books!*

Crow patted Josh's trembling hand. "Hawk, snap out of it, the crew chief says we're four minutes out from the LZ."

Josh filed his future report away and opened his eyes. His partners were unbuckling their seat belts, so Josh forced himself to believe in the computers and tried to lift his hand to pick up the pack at his feet. He found he was frozen to the seat.

The crew chief materialized from somewhere and held up two gloved fingers in front of Josh's face. "Two minutes out, team leader!" he yelled over the engines.

Josh nodded and unbuckled his seat belt. He hadn't realized he was moving until he saw he was holding his pack. He smiled inwardly, knowing his past experience and training were finally overcoming his fear. Feeling better and more confident, he allowed his eyes to move toward his team members. He gathered even more strength and yelled, "Last equipment check!"

He patted his pockets and all the equipment attached to his body, feeling for the items that were essential for survival and necessary for successful completion of the mission.

"One okay!" Crow yelled.

Sergeant Vee checked his shirt pocket once more to make sure his compass hadn't slipped out and was still tied to his lapel. It was. He nodded. "Two okay!"

Josh stood and barked, "Team leader okay! Stand by!" He threaded his arms through the pack's straps and hefted the weight to his shoulders. He tapped Crow's shoulder. "How much they bet ya?"

Crow held up five fingers. Josh turned and looked at the embarrassed crew chief, who shrugged.

Josh felt the bird beginning its flare to slow its forward air speed. The crew chief stepped forward and yelled into Josh's ear. "Pilot says he scanned the area with infrared coming in and didn't pick up any human activity for miles around. It's clean, so you're good to go. Good luck!" He turned and opened the side door. Josh moved closer to the door and saw a moonlit view of a wind-whipped grassy field he knew all too well.

The bird was still four feet from the ground when Josh jumped, followed by his team. He hit the ground and screamed in silent joy as he ran a few paces; then he dropped to his knees and turned to check if Crow and Vee were with him. They were, and he ducked his head and closed his eyes as the huge bird lifted off like a mini-hurricane and shot forward over the treetops.

The team remained perfectly still, giving their ears and bodies time to adjust from the constant sound and vibration, while Josh scanned the moonlit valley. He was in his element now with the Pave Lows just a bad memory.

He waited another full minute and then whispered, "Get me a GPS check to confirm."

Crow pulled out a small device from a pouch on his web belt and pushed the Position button. The Global Positioning System's digital display began showing numbers behind a small backlit screen. The high-tech device was like everything else they carried—nonmilitary and non-American. It was a sterile operation, meaning that if they were captured, nothing they were wearing or carrying could be used as proof they were a U.S. government–sponsored unit.

The high-powered binoculars and night-vision goggles in their packs were German; the freeze-dried food and their boots were French; the camera equipment, watches, and radios were Japanese; their knives were Swiss; packs, canteens, and dark brown, lightweight hiking clothes were Spanish. They carried no identification and nothing personal in their pockets. For personal protection they were issued small, Italian-made .22 semiautomatic pistols with silencers, concealed in covered holsters that looked like canvas map cases.

The GPS finished its data exchange with circling satellites above them and gave a ten-digit grid coordinate. Crow compared the display with the numbers written in washable ink on the back of his left hand.

He shook his head as if disgusted and whispered harshly, "Leave it to the Air Force to fuck up a good op. They put us down twenty feet from where we were supposed to come in."

Josh couldn't help but smile. His thoughts of the Pave Low went from hate to love. The chopper had flown three hundred kilometers, at night, low level, and placed them within a few steps of where he had put a small X on a planning map a week before. That was really somethin', he thought. He turned and whispered to Vee, "Give 'em Charlie Mike."

Vee had already taken the small radio out and unfolded the miniature satellite dish. He punched in the code words on the keyboard for Continuing Mission and pushed the Send key. A satellite received the secure data-burst transmission and sent it back to the staging base in India within seconds. Josh smirked, thinking this high-tech shit wasn't half bad. He stood and whispered, "With the moon's light I don't think we'll need the NVGs for a while. Your call. Check equipment and give me an up, then we'll move out. I'll take the point."

Vee took out his night-vision goggles, not as confident as his team leader about seeing in the semidarkness. He put them on his bare head and quickly patted and touched his equipment again. Both he and Crow whispered at the same time, "Up."

Josh took out his compass, looked at the luminous arrow, and turned to the south. It was all the direction he needed. He had memorized the route and recognized the dark mountains to his left and right. He was in the valley where he and Stephen had gone on their first boar hunt without the Teacher. They were only five kilometers from Shaduzup. Setting his shoulders, he took a breath, let it out, and took the first step.

3 P.M., Seattle, Washington

Stephen stood on the dock watching as the first trucks loaded with the second shipment of plywood arrived at the plant dock. He felt a strange chill and for some reason glanced at his bracelet. He pushed thoughts of those days from his mind and turned to Colonel Po beside him. "You did say they have shut down the production facilities, didn't you?"

Po wrinkled his brow, surprised at the question. He had to think for a moment to remember what he'd told him. "Yes, of course, as soon as the first shipment came, the facilities were closed. Why do you ask?"

Stephen shrugged. "I just wanted to make sure I understood you correctly. Last night I thought of my wife and son and how different things will be when I return. My people won't be growing the poppies anymore. I admit to you I'm torn between joy and sorrow. We are doing a great thing for our country but are bringing a horrible plague to America."

Po nodded as if in agreement, knowing full well phase seven was under way. He felt the same feelings of joy and remorse. It was going to sadden him to have to order Stephen's death, but Tan considered the deputy finance minister a loose end. Po put his hand on Stephen's shoulder. "I was in contact with headquarters this morning and asked about your family. They are doing fine."

Stephen lowered his head. "I miss them terribly."

Po smiled and patted Stephen's back. "And you will see them very soon, my friend. In three days the last shipment arrives—I received word last night. You'll be home within a week and all of this will be behind you. The economic programs you developed will soon be a reality."

Stephen gave his chief a muted smile. "I guess I'd better buy some presents after I've finished with this shipment. My son wants something called a skateboard."

6:30 P.M., Washington, D.C.

Seated behind his desk, Anton Simmons, known as "Cage" to his forty-two street dealers, looked up at B-Ball Thomas with a sneer. "What da fuck they want now?"

B-Ball tossed his thumb over his shoulder. "They wanna talk again. Them Jamokes is a pain, man. They ain't listen ta English, y'know. They sayin' somethin' 'bout it being good business to talk over the dispute, and dis is our last chance."

"Dispute? What da fuck they talkin' about, dispute? The nigger muthafuckers ain't got no dispute. I ain't givin' up shit! Who da fuck they think they are to threaten us?"

B-Ball glanced at the two men seated in easy chairs beside the desk. "Tell him. Don't be sittin' there starin' at *me*."

Wease Elkins fondled the heavy gold medallion hanging from his neck as he spoke with his customary whine. "They got a bad rep and got connections with the Chink heavies out west, Cage. They real bad, man. We might oughta talk to 'em. Check 'em out, y'know. See what they gonna offer, man."

Jimmy the Spoon nodded in agreement. "I been checkin', Cage. They been puttin' pressure on all the players and got most to work for 'em. They organized, man. Real connected. The Chinks been movin' in to New York, Philly, Boston, Baltimore, Miami, and here, man. They hired them Jamokes and some no-fuckin'-around Latinos who carry some heavy shit. You bes' talk to them Jamokes, 'cause they got big-time friends."

Cage shook his head in disbelief. "No Gook, or Chink, or Latino, or jive nigger muthafucker takes *my* territory. Wease, hire some help for your territory. Spoon, you do the same. Give 'em our good shit. The mac-tens and all the ammo they can carry. We'll see who da fuck is bad."

B-Ball looked down at his size 14 Air Jordans. "Whatcha' want me ta say ta them Jamokes waitin' downstairs?"

Cage leaned back in his chair. "Tell 'em ta get fucked. We ain't dealin'."

0355 Hours, Northern Burma

Josh stopped and looked up a nearby slope feeling sick to his stomach. Once blanketed by towering pine trees, the hill where he and Stephen had hunted *gyi* and hares was now covered with jagged black stumps. Horseman Lante had been right—greed had prevailed. The Shan had slashed and burned their land to plant poppies.

Crow nudged Josh's shoulder. "It's gonna be light in a couple of hours. Are we gonna take a break or go all the way in?"

Josh knew they were only a little more than a kilometer from the river, but they could use an hour of rest before moving into position. The last kilometer would be the most dangerous part of the move, and they needed to be 100 percent alert. He spoke in a low whisper. "We'd better take a break. There's a trail just ahead on the right leading up to a ridge. We'll climb up there and find a spot to hole up for a while. From there we'll follow the ridge all the way down to the recon position by the river."

Vee stepped closer. "Do you smell something?" he whispered.

Josh nodded in the darkness. "I've been smelling it for thirty minutes. It's the chemicals they use for processing. I'll explain it when we get to the hide position."

Thirty minutes later the three-man team had cleared themselves a space in the middle of a stand of four-foot-high ferns. Josh leaned over to Vee and whispered, "As a kid I ran across a couple of small mom-and-pop opium huts, but I didn't know what they were then. When Hondo and I were assigned to the embassy back in the eighties, we took a little trip up here to check out the action. We linked up with a couple of rebel leaders, and one of them showed us how they made their money. They had an opium production refinery. What we're smelling is what Hondo and I smelled back then when we visited their crude refinery."

Hondo leaned over and whispered, "Man, I forgot about this stink once I left Zuland. Hey, based on what we're smellin', looks like we're gonna get what the spooks wanted, huh?"

Josh nodded in silence as he listened to the morning sounds of the awakening forest. The smell of the chemicals meant they'd found the evidence, but it also meant the people he loved had given in to greed. The wind was bringing the smell from where the facility was located alongside the river, and just past the plant, three hundred yards up the ridge, was the village of Shaduzup.

4:10 A.M., India Staging Base

The moon's glow reflected off large American helicopters, newly painted white, and two C-130E Combat Talon refuelers, all of which had *NASA* stenciled in blue on their sides. The white birds were parked beside a dirt runway surrounded by two miles of chain link fence. Combined Indian and American guards patrolled outside the fence of the old air base, while inside, marine guards dressed in civilian clothes made their assigned rounds in Jeeps to check the fence and stationary guard posts. There were only four permanent buildings. One was an old tin hangar, two were small mud huts for flight and maintenance crews, and the last, and largest, was the flight operations building. The old terminal was made of mud and straw but had a substantial tin roof and observation tower that now held antennas and satellite dishes. The once sleepy, almost deserted Indian outpost had been transformed—tents had been erected beside the hangar, and floodlights turned the once dark buildings and runway into what one flight mechanic called "Las Vegas East."

Buck McCoy sat in the flight operations building with his operations officer and four radiomen who were monitoring a bank of radios. Behind the table was a work area with a large map of Burma posted on the wall. A tall, stately man entered the room, having been wakened minutes before by a radioman sent by McCoy. The new arrival was the Agency's chief of station for India, the senior representative in the Area of Responsibility, or AOR. By virtue of his rank, the COS had overall responsibility for the mission from the time the task force had arrived, days before. McCoy was in charge of the actual mission, but he was subordinate to the chief of station, who would make the nonoperational decisions and report to and confer with Washington.

McCoy set down his coffee cup and walked to the wall map. "Sorry to have to wake you, sir, but something is going on." He motioned to the map, where five red markers were placed representing the five teams' locations. "Sir, a few minutes ago teams one and three reported that they had moved within a few klicks of their recon targets. They both reported hearing gunfire and explosions coming from the direction of their target locations. While John was getting you, team four called in and reported the same thing."

The chief's eyes widened. "Are they sure it's gunfire?"

"They're posit—"

"Sir, team two reports gunfire!" a radioman said loudly.

McCoy shook his head in frustration, motioning toward the red stickers. "The teams are separated by over forty klicks, so they're not hearing the same action. It's got to be a simultaneous attack of some kind on the production facilities."

"But who is doing the attacking?" the COS asked, stepping closer.

"Hell if I know, maybe rebels?" McCoy offered.

"They're not organized or sophisticated enough to hit four locations at once," the COS said with a frown. "Damn! I'll call it in and see what Langley makes of it. Jesus, this changes everything. Can any of the teams move in and see what the hell is going on?"

McCoy wrinkled his brow. "That's why I called you here, sir. That decision is above my pay grade. I wanted your approval to proceed. It could be very dangerous. I suggest we tell the teams to move in closer but take no risk of being compromised. They sure as hell aren't armed with enough to disengage from a firefight."

The COS looked back at the map. "I see team five is still moving into position. We'd better warn them of the other teams' reports. I'm going to fill in Langley and see what they say."

He got up from the radio minutes later and gave a nod to McCoy. "They said to proceed with the mission. They have no idea what is happening either but are going to scramble a recon bird and see if they can get some pictures."

McCoy sighed and sat back down in his chair tiredly. "Just when it was going so smooth. Shit!"

4:55 A.M., Northern Burma

Josh cautiously settled to the ground behind a large boulder and motioned the others up. The team had been moving down the ridge for thirty minutes, taking it very slow and easy, scanning their front and flanks with the night-vision goggles. The radio warning they received before leaving their rest position made them doubly cautious.

Josh whispered, "A few meters beyond this boulder, the ridge ends and falls almost straight down to the river about a hundred meters below. On the other side of the river is what we came to see. We know our rear is secure for a while, so we'll all move into position under the boulder, where there is a shallow cave. . . . I know 'cause I used to play here. Once in position we're going to scan the valley below us for patrols or guards, then quickly set up the cameras and radio. Vee, once your gear is set up, come back here and pull rear security. We won't be here long. Once it gets light we'll take the pictures and get the hell out. Okay, let's do it nice and slow."

Josh crept forward and got halfway around the huge boulder. He looked across the river but his vision within the goggles suddenly became blurred by bright green balls of fuzzy light. He froze, lowered himself to the ground, and slowly took off the goggles. What he could plainly see with his eyes caused his heart to skip a beat. He took a deep breath to try and stop his shaking and was about to move again when Crow grabbed his arm. "We got company!" he whispered. "I see some people just down the ridge to the right . . . a hundred meters back from the riverbank."

Josh couldn't see anything in the darkness in that direction and put his goggles back on. It took him several seconds to find them, but there was no mistake about it. There were four armed men lying prone behind small boulders close to the riverbank. He whispered to Crow, "They're facing away from us. Once we're in position, keep an eye on them. Come on, you're not going to believe this."

Crow took off his pack and hurriedly took out the camera and telephoto lens case. He set up the equipment and then joined Josh at the lip of the small cave. Despite a light fog he could clearly make out a long tin building beneath a huge camouflage net held up by long bamboo poles. The lights inside the building shone brightly through the large open windows and a set of open garage-type doors. Crow scanned the building one more time with his binoculars and counted at least thirty people working inside. He let out a rush of air. "Christ, Hawk, is what I'm seeing for real?"

Josh lowered his binoculars. "It's too real—our worst nightmare."

Vee had been listening as he unpacked the video camera and now whispered, "What's wrong?"

Josh handed him his binoculars. "The refinery down there is a fully operational production facility, *including* a lab. It makes the finished product. Look at the markings on the fifty-gallon drums just inside the open double doors. It's alcohol. That's used only in the last stage of making number four heroin."

"Number four?" Vee repeated, not understanding.

Josh stared at the distant building and replied, "It's the highest grade, 85 to 99 percent pure."

Crow spoke in a whisper as he moved his binoculars back to the men he'd spotted earlier. "What in the hell are those four guys doing down there? They aren't guards; they look more like a reconnaissance team watching the place like we are. I've spotted four guards and a patrol of six men so far, but they're all on the other side of the river." He swiveled his glasses back toward the building and shook his head. "It's a helluva big operation to be workin' around the clock. Jesus, they look like ants at a picnic the way everybody is moving around inside."

Josh turned to Vee. "Get on the radio and tell 'em what we see. Tell 'em we'll get pictures as soon as it's light, then we'll pull back to a hide position. I'll pull security while you're sending it."

Washington, D.C.

Cage told his two security guards to walk out first and check the street. They approached their boss's white Cadillac, checked the surrounding parked cars for occupants, and looked up and down the street for signs of danger. Seeing nothing unusual, they nodded toward the dilapidated brownstone.

B-Ball Thomas sauntered out first, followed by Cage, who kept his eyes in constant motion and his hand close to a nickel-plated .357 stuck in his belt.

Across the street, watching from a window, a seventeen-year-old boy brought a portable phone to his mouth and spoke into the receiver in Spanish. "The niggers are moving to the car."

The person on the end of the line hung up.

Cage and B-Ball got in the backseat of the Cadillac and the two security men got in the front. The car pulled away from the curb and turned off K Street onto New Jersey Avenue. They traveled only two blocks before entering the 395 underpass toward Garfield Park. They were halfway through the underpass when the driver suddenly slammed on the brakes to avoid colliding with a truck that had veered into their lane from the other direction. Two more cars behind the truck pulled out and skidded to a halt, blocking the road.

Cage reached for the .357 just as bullets raked the right side of the car. As the last act of his life, the driver twisted the wheel left and stomped on the accelerator. A split second later the front windshield shattered and he and the other guard jerked spasmodically as nine-millimeter bullets ripped through their upper bodies.

Spattered with blood and covered in crystallized glass, Cage lay on the floor, screaming from pain and fear. B-Ball bounced on the blood-covered backseat and held his neck to try to stop the stream of dark blood shooting from his ruptured carotid artery. The Cadillac careened off the concrete underpass wall, struck one of the blocking cars in the rear, and finally stopped when it hit a light pole. Cage felt the vehicle come to a sudden jolting halt and was about to move when he heard someone running toward the vehicle. He lay perfectly still, hoping they would think he was dead. Something hard hit his shoulder and rolled to the floor in front of him. He looked at the grenade and tried to scream but nothing came out of his mouth. Frozen, he shut his eyes just as the small bomb exploded, ending his fear forever.

Fifteen blocks away, Wease Elkins lay in bed with a fifteen-year-old junkie who had needed a hit. She had performed to his satisfaction and he was reaching for his trousers when the door to the bedroom burst open. He saw their faces and managed only to say "Muthafuc—" before his body and that of the girl were riddled with bullets.

Jimmy the Spoon was on the street doing what he did best, talkin' shit with his dealers, boosting morale and profits. Jimmy was a people person until he saw the fast car approaching. He grabbed one of the boys he'd been talking to and tried to use him as a shield. It didn't work. The boy took six rounds, but one hit Jimmy just above his right eye and killed him before he took a single step.

5:45 A.M., India Staging Base

Buck McCoy froze in place as he listened to team two's report.

"Base, this is scout two. We are five hundred meters from the target, except there is no longer a target. What used to be a large building looks as if it was hit by a bomb and is still burning. There appears to be a village nearby. We hear gunshots and people screaming but cannot get any closer because of the open terrain between us and the burning building. Over."

McCoy picked up the mike. "Scout two, this is base. Roger, I have a good copy. Take pictures of what you can, then pull back to hide position. Out."

Putting down the mike, he turned to the chief of station. "That's the third team to report the buildings were destroyed. It has to be the army that made the strikes. It's the only logical answer."

The tight-lipped COS looked at the map with a distant stare. "I knew Alex Manning, the chief in Burma. I saw his file and satellite photos. He knew they were involved, dammit! The bastards must have found out about the operation somehow and decided to destroy the evidence."

McCoy shook his head. "Sir, there was no leak on our end. There's got to be another answer." He rapped his fingers on the table for a moment, then made up his mind. "Sir, the teams have the information we came for. I'm calling to tell them to pull back to hide positions. Tonight they can move to their pickup zones for exfiltration. There's no sense in taking any more risks."

The chief of station nodded in silence.

Crow saw the light flickering and knew a message was coming in. He quit taking pictures and pushed the Receive button. Then he read the message that rolled across the small backlit screen in a whisper loud enough for Josh to hear.

"Mission is terminated. Repeat, mission is terminated. Move to hide position until nightfall, then move to PZ for exfiltration. Acknowledge."

Crow exchanged glances with Josh and smiled. "Let's get the hell outta here."

Crow began to rise, but Josh put his hand up. "Listen. Do you hear what I hear?"

Crow had heard that particular sound too many times in his life not to recognize the distant sound of incoming helicopters. He crawled over to Josh. "You see them yet?"

Both men scanned the horizon and valley until Crow put down his binoculars and pointed. "There, at ten o'clock, coming in low, five Chinese-made Mi-4 Hounds."

Josh lowered his glasses after spotting the choppers, which were designed to carry infantry. He glanced down toward the river. "Look, one is about to shoot a star cluster." Just as he spoke, one of the soldiers in camouflage fatigues hiding by the river stood and hit the bottom of a hand-held tubular device. A small rocket shot skyward and exploded in a bright shower of miniature reddish-orange fireballs.

Josh began to shake with anger and frustration as he realized what was going to happen. "Oh God, no!"

Two of the helicopters swooped in just above the tin building's camouflage net and the other three hovered over the village, all shooting their door-mounted machine guns. Above the racket of beating blades and the staccato gunfire, another sound joined the din. Josh turned to stone, unable to move as he heard the pathetic sound that tore through his heart like searing shrapnel. It was the sound of Henry's church bell, but it wasn't a call to services. The bell from the old mission was being rung repeatedly as a warning of danger. Josh could see terrified people running out of the tin building trying to find cover and could hear bloodcurdling screams from the direction of the village. The four sharpshooters on the bank had more targets than they could shoot at. The panic-stricken Shan workers, seeing their friends shot down as they headed for the river, ran in the other direction toward the village. Josh thought they might escape, but a sudden burst of machine-gun fire from the ridge to their front cut the running people down like stalks of wheat.

Crow lowered his head after seeing some of the survivors with their hands in the air being riddled. "Jesus, Hawk, it's not an attack, it's a massacre."

Josh fought back the bile in his throat and growled. "Get it on the video camera."

The killing lasted five minutes more. The helicopters had landed and troops swarmed out, some of them hauling boxes full of small white plastic bags. Other troops led or carried screaming, fighting men and women to the riverbank and executed them. Five prisoners dressed in Western clothing were taken at gunpoint from the building and placed on board a helicopter, but when the chopper rose to several hundred feet in altitude all five were pushed out of the olive-drab bird and fell into the forest behind the now burning building. Smoke billowed up not only from the lab but also from the village.

Tears streaming down his face, Josh swung the camera, looking through its high-powered lens to search the faces before taking pictures of the dead. He'd recognized a few and kept moving the camera to look for others.

Crow put his hand on his friend's shoulder. "Hawk? . . . Hawk, there's nothing you could have done. Come on, Hawk, you've been out of film for the last two minutes. We've got to get out of here."

Josh could hear screaming from the distant village and twitched when a single gunshot echoed down the valley. One less Shan. Then there was another shot, and another. Each shot reverberated in his head and tore through him. Finally there was silence, but he could hear the faintest of echoes of his and Stephen's laughter when they would play on the ridge. Now other echoes joined those in the serene valley—the screams of his adopted people. Now they too were just echoes.

Crow took the camera from Josh's hands and gently put his arm around his shoulder. "Hawk, we gotta go."

Josh looked with pleading eyes at the sergeant major. "Why, Hondo? Why did they murder them?"

Crow picked up Josh's pack and handed it to him. "I don't know. Come on, let's get out of here before we're spotted."

Minutes later, a stone-faced Josh led the other two men back up the ridge. His cold eyes were constantly moving as he concentrated on the sounds and smells of the forest. After an hour at a steady pace he slowed and waved the others toward a stand of dense bamboo to rest and hole up until it got dark. Crow moved up close to him and whispered, "How you feelin'?"

"I'm okay. It got to me, that's all."

"Glad you're back; you had me worried. I'm gonna take a dump in that other grove just ahead." Crow motioned to another large stand of bamboo twenty feet up the trail.

"Me too," said Vee.

Josh nodded. "I'll pull security here. You two cover each other."

Taking off his pack, Josh watched his two men until they disappeared in the yellow bamboo. He thought he heard a hawk screeching somewhere above in the trees and was about to look up when gunfire erupted from the direction in which his men had gone. Spinning around, he pulled his silenced semiautomatic pistol from its holster and crept forward, following the sound of laughter.

Crow lay still on the ground as a dark-skinned, flat-nosed Wa cackled and nudged the prone figure with an M-16. "This one is bleeding like a pig. I lay claim to him, for I saw and shot him first."

The leader laughed, turned to the three men behind him, and motioned to Vee, who stood with his hands in the air. "Look at this wide-eyed one—he puts his hands in the air like a woman. Pu, kill him and let's see what is in his pack."

Pu raised his rifle but his knees suddenly buckled and he dropped to the ground like a rag doll. The leader heard a metallic clink and turned just in time to take a small hollow-point bullet below his right eye. The Wa holding his rifle on Crow lifted his weapon and fired toward the bamboo clump, but Josh fired once more and he fell beside the other bodies. The third Wa landed face first and lay twitching with a bullet lodged between his eyes.

The remaining two men stood back to back and were firing from the hip at any clump of ferns or bush that seemed a likely place for the invisible killer. Crow bit through his lip in pain as he grabbed a dropped M-16 and fired one-handed at the startled men, who had thought he was dead. The bullets stitched both men's legs, toppling them over. Screaming, Vee pulled his pistol and emptied the magazine into their jerking bodies. He was still squeezing the trigger of the empty weapon when Josh commanded, "Get me the first-aid kit!"

Drooling blood down his chin, Crow was shaking like a leaf. "I . . . I'm sorry Hawk, Je . . . Jesus, I . . . I didn't see . . . 'em until it was . . ."

"Forget it, they'd made camp and were resting in the bamboo. There was no way you could have known," said Josh as he finished tying a knot over Crow's exit wound. One bullet had ricocheted off Crow's rib cage and grazed his underarm. The second had drilled a neat hole in the old soldier's right side below the rib cage and had blown out his back just above his hip bone. It looked as if he'd been attacked with a mini post-hole digger that had taken a two-inch bite out of his flesh. Josh didn't think any major organs were hit, but his old friend had lost a lot of blood and was already in shock. He patted the sergeant major's chest with a sticky, blood-covered hand and forced a smile. "Relax, I gave you half a shot of morphine. You won't hurt as bad in just a few seconds. We'll have you out of here in no time."

Crow's eyes became glazed and he tried to talk, but his jaw went slack and he just drooled more blood from his swollen lip.

Josh snapped his fingers and whispered to Vee, who was pulling security. "Did you get them on the radio?"

The young sergeant nodded and stuck his thumb up. Josh stood and gently rolled Crow over onto the litter he'd made out of a poncho and bamboo poles. He tied his friend onto the litter, picked up the poles at one end, and began dragging the litter forward. He came alongside Vee and whispered, "You move out a good twenty meters in front but stay where I can see you. If you see or hear anything, signal. It's all downhill. Once we get to the valley floor there's plenty of places for the chopper to land."

Vee glanced down at Crow. "They said they'd be here in about an hour, Hawk. Will it be too late?"

Josh shook his head and motioned to the bandit's M-16 in the sergeant's hands. "Remember what I told you. The Wa hunt in groups of two. There are probably more around who heard the shooting. Keep your eyes and ears open. Go."

Crow opened his eyes and saw blue sky. He shut them again, feeling very weak, and knew he must be delirious. He'd dreamed he'd been shot and . . . His eyes snapped open and he tried to move, but a wave of pain hit him and nearly made him faint. Vee appeared over him.

"Sergeant Major? Can you hear me?"

Crow shut his eyes and let another agonizing tremor pass. "Y . . . Yeah, what happened?"

"Don't move, Sergeant Major, or you'll start bleeding again. Lie still. The chopper will be here in a little while."

Crow's eyes shifted right, then left, searching, but he didn't see his leader. "Where is he?" he asked in desperation.

Vee glanced around, holding the rifle ready, and whispered, "Just lie still. He's making sure we'll be able to get you outta here. He'll be back."

Josh silently switched off the safety of his small pistol with his left hand and held his breath. The four approaching Wa he had spotted from the ridge had taken the valley path in an attempt to cut them off. He'd left Crow with Vee and run ahead to do what they least expected—attack. They were jogging in single file by the tree he was hiding behind, holding their rifles to their front. As soon as the last one passed, Josh stepped out from behind the tree, aimed at his target only three feet away, and fired. He kept moving forward, shot the second in the back of the neck and watched the next man as he turned, wide-eyed. Josh shot him in the face. The fourth ducked down and spun but could not bring his rifle barrel around in time. For an instant he looked into Josh's eyes as if pleading. Josh fired.

Buck McCoy glanced at the chief of station after Sergeant Vee finished his report. Both men turned to the team leader, who sat sipping coffee. The chief looked into Josh's eyes and said, "Tell me again about the bandits that attacked your two men."

Josh lowered his coffee cup and spoke tiredly. "They were Wa, not bandits. They're like vultures; they feed on anything dying or dead. The tribe used to be headhunters, but they got civilized in the 1940s. Then they began reverting to their old ways in the sixties when some of them moved back to the mountains to reclaim their homelands from the Shan. Hondo and I ran into a group of them in '83."

The chief nodded silently and nodded to McCoy to continue the questioning.

The commander looked at the notes he'd made during the debrief. "And you're sure the men you saw attack the facility were DDSI Strike soldiers?"

"Yes sir. They wore their uniquely patterned brown and green fatigues. It was a company-size force from their Strike Commando Battalion that I know works for the DDSI on special operations. I saw them training a couple of times when I was assigned to the embassy. They're selected from the army for their loyalty and wear a brown beret with a silver coiled-cobra badge on the side like we wear a flash and rank on our SF berets. The bastards shot the workers as if they were dogs and wiped out the village."

McCoy turned to the chief. "Sir, do you have any more questions for these two? We need to get them cleaned up and let 'em get some rest."

The chief stood. "Just one more, for you, Colonel. The Company could use your experience. You're the most knowledgeable American on northern Burma that I've ever met. This isn't the end of our problems by a long shot. Would you be interested in—"

Josh lifted his hand to interrupt. "No sir, I've already got a job. Now I have a few questions. First, where'd they take Hondo?"

The chief glanced at McCoy before giving Josh an apologetic look. "I'm sorry, I thought you knew. They flew him to New Delhi in one of our helicopters. We sent a doctor with him and he said before he left that the sergeant major would be fine."

Josh sighed inwardly in relief and stood, eyeing both men. "Is our government going to get involved and get the fuckers or not?"

The chief turned and looked out the window toward the dirt runway. "I don't know. We hope so."

Josh began to walk toward the door but stopped and spoke over his shoulder. "If I were you, sir, I'd try to find out if Sawbaw Xu Kang is still alive and still has his army. Once the Shan hear about the massacres, they'll flock to him for protection. He'll need your help."

The chief looked surprised. "How do you know about Kang?"

Josh patted Vee's back and pulled him to his feet. "Go get cleaned up and I'll join you in a few minutes." He shrugged and told the chief, "I know him from a long time ago. If he's alive, and that's a big if, he's your last chance to keep a pocket of resistance alive in Burma until our government makes up its mind."

The chief nodded once. "We're working on it, Colonel, believe me. Think about what I said. We need you."

"So does my daughter," Josh said as he walked out the door.

As soon as the two men left the room, the chief's searching gaze settled on McCoy. "What's the story on Hawkins? He sat here and told us he killed seven men without so much as blinking an eye."

McCoy looked out the window toward the two men as they walked to their tent. "He was in 'Nam, where he picked up two Silver Stars. The citations in his file read like something out of a war comic book. I didn't believe them and had him checked. They were true. In one instance the NVA overran a firebase he was on. He had been wounded lightly and was in a hospital ward. When the Dinks hit the base in the middle of the night, he got out of bed, picked up a .45 from a dead MP, and hid by the entrance of the hospital ward. In the space of five minutes, he greased four sappers who were trying to throw charges through the doorway." McCoy turned and looked at the older man. "I've seen his type a couple of times before. He's a shooter. He looks like a normal guy, but once in action he becomes ice. No feelings. His type are rare, and lethal. It's something that can't be taught; you just have it or you don't. The weapon becomes an extension of his mind. Men like him are deadly in a firefight because everybody else is scared and trying to stay alive. Hawkins's type don't think about dying. Their minds are locked onto one single conscious thought: Kill them first."

The chief shook his head as if disappointed. "He's a psycho, then."

McCoy looked back out the window reflectively. "No, he's just different from the rest of us. Shooters have a gift, and a curse. They know they have it, and their problem is living with it. In reading Hawkins's file, I'd say he's been trying real hard to forget he has it."

6 P.M., Northern Burma

Colonel Banta saw the old man sitting in his campaign chair by the campfire with his Horsemen and approached cautiously. He could see from his leader's haggard face that he was not taking the news well.

All afternoon scouts had been reporting the casualties from the Strike Battalion's attacks on the facilities and the villages that had supported them. The old Sawbaw had accepted the deaths of those who worked in the *lai* houses, but hearing of the murders of the villagers had wounded him as if he'd been shot with a rifle.

Banta slowed his steps, for the news he had just received would devastate his Sawbaw.

Xu Kang looked up from the coals of the fire; seeing his operations officer, he quickly rose to his feet. "Did they get them out in time?" he asked almost pleadingly.

Banta stepped closer and looked into the old man's eyes. "Our people got your grandson, but . . ."

Kang lowered his head. He sat down and gazed at the burning embers with a sad, faraway stare. "What happened?"

"We were able to get your grandson while he was playing in a park, but the DDSI beat us to your son's house. The house mother had been beaten badly but said they took Mya. Stephen is in the United States. The house mother said he was picked up by a DDSI staff car over a week ago."

Xu Kang's drawn face twitched. Gathering strength, he raised his eyes and asked, "How many of the others did we get out?"

"Twenty plus your grandson. The junta is declaring a great victory in the evening papers. They are claiming they have eradicated the last of the drug lords and put an end to poppy production. The information minister even went so far as to say the Sawbaws supported the communists who bombed the American embassy. They are blaming the Shan for everything to cover their own wrongdoing."

Xu Kang closed his eyes. "My son is dead or will be killed. So will Mya. We'll be next. We are their last threat."

Banta began to speak, but Horseman Lante stepped up and put his hand on the colonel's shoulder and whispered for him to be quiet. Lante and the seven other Horsemen gathered around their leader to offer him their strength. Lante motioned to the mountains and said, "Chindit, the people will flee their villages and head for the mountains to save themselves. They will come to us as they have before. We are their last hope."

Xu Kang shook his head wearily. "We can't stay in this camp any longer. The army will be coming to finish us. Tell the others to load the equipment and weapons in every available truck. We must leave tomorrow at first light and seek refuge in Thailand."

"But the people?" Lante asked in an anguished whisper.

Xu Kang rose as if he had a heavy weight on his shoulders. "The people made their decision years ago and must live and die with it, like my son. We'll go to the old Thai border camp to rebuild. We Shan are just the beginning—the DDSI will also go after the other minorities. They will try to destroy us all, as always."

Xu Kang took a step toward his hut but stopped. He rolled his shoulders back and turned to face Colonel Banta, his smoldering eyes filled with hatred. "Have our people and informers in Rangoon begin preparing for an attack on the Defense Ministry. Use them all and find out everything possible about the army bases, their communications, and the routes they would use. We will not die without fighting. We no longer wait for the enemy to come to us in the mountains. We will take the fight to their lair and show them what fear is."

Banta inwardly smiled at his old leader's rekindled spirit and replied, "We will have help from the students and other minorities who have been protesting against the government. I will ensure they know where to find us if they want to join the fight."

Xu Kang's chiseled face seemed to glow in the firelight. "Many Burmans will come to us, for they now must see nobody is safe with the bastards in power. Have our people bring my grandson to me at the border camp. He will need me, and I need him. Take care of telling the others about the move." The old soldier didn't wait for a response before he strode into the darkness. Only when he reached his hut did he let tears of sorrow flow for Stephen, Mya, and his people. He lay down in the hammock and cried for them all. There was not enough time or enough of the enemy to kill to fill the void in his old heart.

India Staging Base

Josh sat up as McCoy pulled a chair up to his cot. "I thought you'd be sleeping," McCoy said.

"I was listening to the choppers come in."

"Yeah, the other teams are all back safely. We just got a secure radio message from our Burma embassy. The Burmese TV news reported the DDSI Strike Battalion wiped out five drug labs and is saying the Shan were involved in supporting the terrorists that hit the embassy. They even showed a Shan leader admitting he provided the explosives."

Josh slapped the side of the cot. "We're not buying that shit, are we?"

The commander lowered his eyes. "That's why I'm telling you, Hawk, to warn you. It's going to be hard to dispute a witness who says to the world that he and his people did it. On Langley's orders, we're flying out tomorrow at first light for Guam to rest a few days and repaint the birds. The director is going to talk to us once we get back to Washington, and he wants to talk to you personally. The station chief told him you knew Xu Kang. He's going to want you in."

"He's wasting his time," Josh said angrily. "I want no part of it. We've made promises to Xu Kang before and never followed through."

The commander stood. "Sleep on it, Hawk. You've got three days before you see Director Jennings." He turned and walked out of the tent.

Vee sat up on his cot, having heard the conversation. "Hawk, it sounds like they really need you."

Josh lay back down and closed his eyes. "Naw, they want to use me to get to the Chindit. They'll make promises and then leave him out to dry if it turns sour. Believe me, the old man has a better chance if we stay out of it."

"But Hawk, you told the chief that, if Xu Kang was alive, they should help him."

"Yeah, with weapons and equipment, nothing else. If the Company just gives him the stuff he needs, that's fine. But if they want me it means there's more. I don't want any part of them and their harebrained plans. I've seen what they can do. How are you doin', anyway?"

Vee rubbed his temples as if in pain. "I can't sleep. Every time I shut my eyes I see those poor people and hear their screams."

"Think about your wife and family and take a couple of these," Josh said, handing over a bottle of sleeping pills. "You're gonna need 'em for the next few days. Once you're home the dreams will go away, at least most of the time."

Vee took the pills and washed them down with canteen water. He lay back down and looked up into darkness. "Thank you, Hawk, for saving me. I—"

"Just think about getting home and talking your wife into having a son. Forget this op. It was all for nothing."

Vee reached out and patted Josh's shoulder. "I met you, Hawk, and that's something to remember."

CHAPTER 15

21 June, Seattle, Washington

The Customs team arrived at 8 A.M. and finished the inspection just after eleven. They walked down the gangway and motioned to the stevedore crew chief to proceed with the off-loading. Once reaching the wharf, the youngest officer threw his thumb over his shoulder. "That plywood sure would make some beautiful cabinets. How much would a sheet of that cost me at a lumberyard?"

The head Customs officer cocked an eyebrow. "I'd say at least fifty bucks. Teak is gettin' hard to find nowadays."

A hundred yards away, Captain Sing lifted the car phone—having already dialed the number—and spoke in a monotone. "The last shipment has just been cleared."

Colonel Po sighed in relief. "Thank Buddha. Report to me at the plant. You will soon have some work to do that I know will please you."

Five miles away, Stephen paid the cashier at a toy store and picked up a large bag holding a yellow skateboard and a Tonka truck. Walking out of the mall, he said to Sergeant Shin, "Thank you for bringing me here. My son will be very happy when he sees these." Just then, the beeper on Shin's belt began buzzing.

The sergeant pulled the beeper free and watched the one-sentence message run across the small screen.

"The shipment has arrived—time to work."

He repeated the message to Stephen and said, "Only three days and you will be home to give your boy those presents."

Central Intelligence Headquarters, Langley, Virginia

Despite the air conditioning working overtime, the room seemed hot and stuffy to Josh. He was seated in a conference room with Mc-Coy and the other team leaders, all of them jet-lagged. They had landed at Andrews only an hour before and had been choppered to the Langley landing pad. The full subcommittee was there and congratulated them on a job well done, then began reviewing the photos the teams had taken. Josh's pictures began flashing up on the screen, and he noticed the committee members were squirming and cringing in their seats as they watched the shots he'd taken of the executions.

Thorton, the deputy national security adviser, had had enough and stood up. "I see no need to show any more gruesome pictures and ruin our dinners. This meeting is now irrelevant. The junta has eliminated the heroin problem and has captured the people responsible for the bombing of our embassy. We owe our thanks to the brave men who went into Burma. Gentlemen, I can assure you your efforts were not wasted. The photos prove the junta did what it said it did—eliminate the heroin labs. Although we don't approve of their brutal methods, it is not for the United States to question the way Burma runs its operations. The photos and videos will not be released to the public nor will any of us communicate any of what we saw or heard here today. Now, I think we can adjourn this meeting and—"

"Hold it. We still have a helluva big problem," DEA Chief Tuckerman barked.

Every head turned to look at the big man. He stared everyone down and pushed back his chair. He strode to the screen and told the assistant to put up a photo of the tin building. As soon as the picture flashed up on the screen, Tuckerman pointed at the structure. "I was the one who doubted the junta's involvement because of the fact Burma's heroin wasn't on the market. This photo proves one very important thing. This refinery is huge by heroin production standards. It could probably produce ten to twenty kilos a day. And that's just *one* refinery. We've seen and heard proof that there were four other almost identical facilities. Gentlemen, where the hell is the heroin these facilities produced? It appears they produced it for some time, but it hasn't showed up on the world market. *Where is it?*"

Thorton gave a frown and a nod to the DEA chief to show he was concerned, but he said, "The problem, Mr. Tuckerman, is yours, not this committee's. I'm sure your colleagues will support you in any way they can."

"Bullshit!" Tuckerman said angrily. "It will be a major national security problem if that heroin shows up in the U.S."

Thorton nodded condescendingly. "Mr. Tuckerman, we are well aware of that, but as you yourself said, it is *not* in the U.S. It's up to you and your administration to make sure it does not reach here. Now if I may, I would like to adjourn this meeting. Is there any more business? No? Good day, gentlemen."

Thorton strode for the door while the other members collected their notes. Josh rose to follow the other team leaders out but felt a hand on his shoulder. He turned and faced the director of the CIA, who extended his hand.

"You did a helluva job getting your team out," Jennings said. "How about coming up to my office to talk about this Xu Kang fellow you seem to know."

Josh held his ground despite the attempts of the director's eyes to draw him in. "I'll talk to you about Sawbaw Kang, sir, but don't ask me to get involved. I won't do it."

Jennings's expression didn't change, but his voice lowered to a whisper. "What you just heard from Thorton was a facade. He's just as worried as you and I are about their government and where the dope went. He had to play it that way because of who was at the meeting. It's not over, Hawkins—we're still going after the bastards any way we can. You think about that, and when you're ready you call me." Jennings took a card from his pocket and handed it to Josh. "I put my direct number on the back, and the operator knows to put you through night or day. Call me, Hawkins." Jennings gave Josh one last, penetrating look, then turned around and walked out.

Josh stuffed the card in his pocket and strode into the hallway, where McCoy was waiting for him. He walked up to Josh and smiled. "How'd it go with the director?"

"He laid it on pretty thick, but he's got a short memory about the last time the Agency tried to help the Burmese people."

The commander's brow furrowed. "Yeah, but maybe times have changed." He held out his hand. "Hawk, this is where we say good-bye. Your escort is waiting downstairs to take you home. Thanks again. You brought your team back, and in this business that means a lot."

Josh shook his hand. "I won't say I enjoyed it because I didn't, but thank you for your support."

McCoy handed Josh a piece of paper. "That's the phone number of the Fort Sam Houston Hospital in San Antonio. Sergeant Major Crow is being flown there to be closer to his wife, and I'm sure he'd want to hear from you."

Josh smiled. "And I thought you were a tough guy, Buck. If you're ever in D.C. and need a place to stay or eat, call me."

"Too dangerous for me," the CIA man said with a wink. He slapped Josh's shoulder and walked down the hall.

Josh looked again at the address and suddenly cringed at the sound of a familiar voice.

"There you are, Colonel. I was getting worried," Glenn Grant called.

"Aw hell, not you again," he said, turning to face the approaching woman.

"It's good to see you again too. I'm still your escort, Colonel. Come on, the car's waiting outside."

Josh held up his hand. "I'm not a colonel, okay? I'm just a mister again, but don't call me that either. I'm Josh. Please call me Josh, will ya?"

"If you'll call me Glenn, and not Grant."

"Deal."

The attractive officer led Josh down the stairs and outside to the waiting staff car. She reached to open the door, but Josh blocked her hand. "Gimme a break, will ya? I'm not the president."

Josh opened his own door and got in. The second he sat down he leaned his head back and shut his eyes.

Grant got in on the other side, sat down, and motioned for the driver to go. She looked her fellow passenger over and sighed. "You look horrible, but we need to go over your cover story again. You just got back from the conference in Panama. Security was tight because of threats, and they made it almost impossible for you to call, and—"

Josh slowly opened one eye. "Grant, shut up. I'm beat, and you're giving me a headache."

"You called me Grant. We had a deal, *Colonel*."

"I take it back, now shut up. I don't work for the army anymore."

"Sorry, but that's not true. You're still on active duty until new orders are cut. In fact, the army is trying to do you a favor. They're keeping you on active duty so that you get a full month's pay to compensate for the loss of—"

Josh opened one eye again. "Grant, you're talking again."

She gave him a frigid glare before looking to the front and folding her arms across her chest in defeat. His eyes closed and he smiled.

"Colonel, we're here."

Josh stirred and slowly opened his eyes. His door was open and Grant was standing on the curb in front of the Channel Inn, holding a package. He got out, ignoring her, and took a deep breath of home. He could smell the river, different foods from the exhaust vents of the restaurants, and even the distant fish market's unique smell of boiled crabs. God, how he'd missed it, he thought, and started walking toward the sidewalk that would lead him to the marina. He took only two steps before he heard pumps on the sidewalk. "What?" he barked, turning around.

She looked hurt as she held out his suitcase and the wrapped present. She dropped the suitcase and tossed him the gift box. "It's a present for Stef from Panama. I had some friends send it up. It'll help your cover." She spun around and strode back toward the staff car.

Josh sighed and yelled, "Hold it, Gran . . . Glenn. Please."

She stopped and looked over her shoulder. He shrugged. "I'm sorry. I've been an ass, and you don't deserve it. Thanks for the present; it was very thoughtful of you. I really appreciate it."

She looked into his eyes without changing expression. A moment passed before she turned, walked straight to the car, and got in without looking back.

Josh had seen that hurt look before. Damn, he mumbled to himself. He picked up his suitcase. He got to the channel walk and couldn't help but smile. Meg was sitting on her usual bench, trying to feed the sparrows. He strolled up and winked. "How ya doin', good lookin'?"

Meg shocked him by jumping up, throwing her arms around him, and planting a big kiss right on his kisser. Backing up but holding his arm, she looked him over. "Ya look terrible. The army didn't take very good care of you. Come on, we've gotta talk."

Josh stopped her, for she was leading him up the steps of El Torito's. "Hey, I haven't seen Stef yet, and I gotta get rid of this bag, and I—"

She pulled him up the steps. "This is important. This is about Stef. She and Bob have been going out since you've been gone and—"

"Surprise!" yelled the assembled crowd.

Josh dropped the suitcase and slapped at Meg's arm, for she had reeled him in like a big fish. Stef, Bob, Charlie, his part-time employees, and all the restaurant managers rushed forward and mobbed him. Above the outside patio hung a banner that read, "WELCOME BACK HAWK!"

After the others shook his hand, pounded his back, and told him he looked shitty, Stefne looked him up and down and shook her head. "Dad, you look—"

"Come here!" He grabbed her and hugged her tightly. Finally releasing her, he handed her the present. "For my girl. You've put on some weight, haven't ya? Or else I'd forgotten you're a grown woman."

"Daaad. Stop it."

He put his arm around her and made the rounds to thank everybody for the party.

Bob came up, put his arm around Stefne, and handed Josh a wad of money. "Ky sends his regards. His exact words were, ' 'Bout time you come back, need two doz-zen bad. Chinese cus-ta-mer willing to pay more mon-ney.' "

Josh laughed although he felt uncomfortable seeing his assistant's arm around his daughter's shoulders. He took Bob by the arm and led him to the patio fence overlooking the channel. "You see him?" he asked in a whisper.

"Nope, but he tore up another six traps. I built more and was able to keep catching a dozen a day. Ky is serious. He says he's got a Chinese customer who doesn't even ask the price per pound. He's raised prices twice. We're gettin' another dollar a pound."

Josh eyed his big-shouldered assistant. "How'd you find out about the price hike?"

"Hell, boss, I checked. I wasn't going to let that old goat cheat us. He bitched and moaned, but he paid."

Josh's face broke into a big smile knowing he'd found the perfect son-in-law.

Stefne came over and joined them, scowling playfully. "That's it, you two, no more business talk. Dad, Glenn made it. She's over there talking to Meg. She checked on me every day while you were in Panama and told me when you'd be back. The party was really her idea." She moved closer and wiggled her eyebrows. "Dad, I really like her. . . . Don't you?"

Josh rolled his eyes. "Don't push your ole man, dear. These things take time *and* the right person."

Stefne turned to look at the officer, who had changed into thigh-length shorts and a Hawaiian shirt. "I don't know how you old men judge women, but I'd say she's at least a nine, maybe a nine and a half. What do you think, Bob?"

Bob gave Josh a lewd smile. "She looks like a big ten to me, boss."

Josh waved his hand at the young couple. "You two go find something to do." He headed toward Glenn, but when he saw Kelly walking up the patio steps, he changed direction and faced the unkempt man. "Don't say it, I know I look like shit. How ya doin', Kelly? Who's been carrying your ass on the courts?"

Kelly smirked, walked past him, and attacked the food. Once he had his mouth and plate full, he looked at Josh with a scowl. "They didn't have papers in Panama? Christ, didn't you watch CNN? Josh, there's a war on the streets. Racquetball? Shit, I've been lucky to see my family six hours in the past week."

Josh moved closer. "What war?"

Kelly looked at him with genuine surprise. "You really haven't heard? Hell, we've got nineteen stiffs in the city morgue, all unsolved homicides. The Chinese have taken over the dope market. Christ, it's worse than we ever imagined. It's not just D.C., either. In New York, they had twenty-two wholesalers whacked in four days. The whole East Coast is blood alley."

Kelly set his plate down but took a burrito and walked with Josh to the patio steps. "I gotta get back to work. I just wanted ta come over and get some free chow. How's about breakfast tomorrow as usual?"

"You bet. I want you to fill me in on what's gone down."

Kelly began to take the first step down but looked over his shoulder. "Ya do look like shit. Didn't the army feed ya?" He smiled. "Good to have you back, Hawk. I missed ya." He waved his hand, stuffed the burrito in his mouth, and hurried to a waiting squad car.

Josh watched the car disappear onto Maine Avenue. As he turned around, he nearly bumped into Grant as she walked toward the steps.

She stopped and said tightly, "Don't worry. I promised Stef I'd stop by, but I'm leaving."

Josh began to step out of her way to let her pass but reached out and took her arm instead. "Look, Glenn, I'm really sorry. Coming over and checking on Stef was way beyond the call of duty, and I can't tell you what that means to me. I apologize for being an asshole. Forgive me. If you want I'll get down on my knees in front of everybody and beg."

Grant patted his arm with a cautious smile. "I forgive you. I wouldn't want the famous Hawk to make a scene. Get some sleep, Josh. You look like you're about to drop. I'll be over tomorrow to see you—sorry, but it's my job." She winked and walked down the steps.

"Hey, wait a minute! What time? Dammit, Grant!" He saw her fling her hair back as she walked and couldn't help but smile. She had spunk; he had to give her that.

Meg came up beside him and followed his gaze. She bumped his shoulder. "She's your type, Josh, and you sure ain't getting any younger. Come on, you've got to get to bed. You've had it, I can tell."

The pair had taken only two steps when Stefne stepped in front of them wearing a halter top with colorful bright fish sewed on almost sheer white material. She grabbed Josh, kissed his cheek, and backed up, spinning around. "I love it, Dad! I never thought you'd get me something like this."

Josh closed his open mouth—the halter top exposed more of his daughter than he'd seen since she was six. "Uhhh . . . I thought it had more material, but . . . uhh . . . it looks good on you."

Meg held up her hand. "Sorry, he's had it. I'm going to walk him to the boat, but I'll be back in a little while. Save me some margaritas."

Josh hesitated. "But what about work tonight?"

Bob smiled. "No sweat, boss. I got it. Get some sleep."

Charlie, the Hogate's bar manager, stepped up and put his arm around Bob's shoulder. "You ought to see him in action, Hawk. He's got the look down cold."

Meg pulled him forward and they walked down the back steps. Reaching the wharf seconds later, Josh took a deep breath. "You smell that, Meg? There's nothing like the smell of home, is there?" She put her arm around his waist and gave him a gentle hug. "We've missed you, Josh. Nothing is the same when you're gone. Stef looks wonderful, doesn't she?"

Josh smiled and said, "Yeah, she really does. She's in love, huh?"

" 'Fraid so."

"Guess it's not so bad. I like Bob. And he likes her for the right reasons."

They reached the *Lil' Darlin'*, and Josh sat down on the cushioned pilot seat to look at his biggest love besides Stefne. He took the old girl in with loving eyes, noting that she had been cleaned recently and even had a fresh coat of spar varnish on the upper deck. He leaned his head back and looked up at the darkening sky. "I love it here."

Meg smiled. "I know. I'm gonna get back to the party. I don't want you sitting here very long. Get some sleep. And Josh? Welcome home."

Seattle

Stephen placed another bag on the scale and took a step to the right. Chigger took Stephen's place, glanced at the scale weight, and nodded. "Yep, it's good. Next. Man, I'm hungry. How 'bout you?"

Stephen made a mark in his ledger book, as Chigger did in his. The handoff process was complete as soon as Chigger's assistant took the half-kilo bag from the scale and placed it in a large soap box. Once the box was full he would load it on a truck backed up to the loading dock.

Stephen smiled. He was used to Chigger's voracious appetite. Over the past two shipments the two men had worked night and day weighing and keeping count of the shipment's half-kilo bags with occasional breaks for purity testing. Not liking the meals served in the kitchen for the workmen, Chigger had taken it upon himself to teach Stephen about the culinary delights available at American fast-food restaurants. Just three miles from the plant was a strip full of such places, and they had been to them all several times for breakfast, lunch, dinner, late dinner, and early-morning meals.

Stephen placed another bag on the scales. "Where are we eating this time?"

Chigger cocked his head to the side in deep thought. "How's about pizza?"

"Didn't we have that for lunch?"

"Oh, yeah, okay, then Kentucky Fried Chicken, without the skins—I gotta watch my weight, y'know." He looked at the scale and nodded, and made an entry in his ledger.

His assistant picked up the bag but rolled his eyes. "Man, let's check out the steak place. I'm tired of fast food."

Chigger gave the man an evil glare to remind him who was calling the food shots. "Shut your face. We ain't got time for steaks or we'll fall behind. Right, Steve?"

Stephen put another bag on the scale and shrugged. "You are my culinary teacher, U Chigger."

"See?" Chigger said, emphasizing the point by patting Stephen's back. "My man agrees—it's KFC or the fish heads they got in the kitchen."

The assistant shook his head in defeat. "Shit, man, them fish heads ain't food."

Chigger checked the weight, nodded, and made an entry. "One more and then we're outta here for chow."

The assistant sighed as he took the bag from the scale and dropped it into the box at his feet. "This one's full, and this box fills this load. Where's this shipment goin' again? I gotta tell the driver."

Chigger glanced at Stephen and saw he was busy with the scale. He had been told not to let the Burmese know where the shipments were going. He leaned over the table and whispered, "Don't be askin' them questions in front of these dudes. It goes to Carlisle, P-A, dummy. Damn, we're only shippin' to three warehouses. Can't you keep it straight? The last load went to Sacramento and the one before that to Kansas, remember?"

The assistant rolled his eyes. "Fuck, man, I can't keep all this shit straight. We been keepin' such weird hours I don't even know what day it is anymore."

Despite the whispers, Stephen had heard the conversation, but he paid little attention. All he thought about when Chigger wasn't talking to him was going home.

Chigger looked at the scale, nodded, made an entry, and picked up his jacket from the table. "Come on, Steve, I'll drive this time. You picked up your kid's skateboard yet?"

"Yes, I went to the mall like you advised and purchased it on sale."

"Good. Ole Chigger don't give no bad poop. I'm gonna make you into a regular K-Mart shopper by the time you get outta here."

Captain Sing strode out of the glassed-in office and stepped in front of Stephen. "Where are you going, U Kang?"

Chigger turned around and tapped the broad-shouldered security man's back. "What's it to you, man? You've always got an attitude. Steve is going with me to get some real food. Now how's about gettin' out of the way?"

Sing turned and looked at the stocky black man as if measuring him for a casket. "Don't speak to me in that tone of voice. I am doing my job."

Chigger stepped closer with his own bad-news stare. "Well, do your fucking 'job' outta my face, and don't be talkin' shit 'bout my tone of fucking voice."

Sing's eyes narrowed and his lips tightened. He opened and closed the fingers of his right hand as if he were waiting for Chigger to draw. He took a step to the side instead and motioned with his hand for Stephen to go on but kept his cold glare on the black man. "You have very bad manners."

Chigger snorted a half laugh. "And you got fish-head breath, asshole." He stepped back and took Stephen's arm. "What you gonna have? I suggest their chicken nuggets and corn on the cob. They got beans or cole slaw, and for dessert you got a choice of . . ."

Captain Bwin stepped out of the office and watched the men walk out the loading dock door. He turned to look at Sing. "Be patient. The handoff will be complete tomorrow night, and the colonel wants it done once the Shan returns to the hotel. I think the parking lot would be best."

Sing calmed himself by taking several deep breaths. "I would like to kill the Wa American as well. What does it mean when he says I have an 'attitude'?"

CHAPTER 16

26 June, Washington, D.C.

Josh walked into the cafe and took his usual seat by the window. He heard Jean coming by the smacking of her gum. He looked up and smiled. "Hi, pretty lady, did ya miss me?"

She set a cup of coffee in front of him and tossed down the paper. "Yeah, sure, you up and take a vacation without so much as warning me. Kelly Special or what?"

Josh faked a pout. "I missed you. I thought about you every morning."

She smirked. "Yeah, sure ya did. You and Kelly been gone and nobody else ate that crap you two eat so I had to throw it out. How's about tellin' me next time you decide to take off to see the world, huh? Must not have been too good a vacation. You look like our gravy, kinda puny." She swung her hip into his shoulder and bent over to give him a hug. "I'm just kiddin'. You bet I missed ya. I got a whole storeroom full of milk bottles saved up for ya."

Josh put his arm around her hip. "Give me the Hawk Special with double gravy and—"

"Get your hands off my woman!"

Josh and Jean faced Kelly as he approached the table with his hand resting on the grip of his old police .38 special.

Jean waved him off and bent over to hug Josh's neck again. "He knows how to talk to a woman, Kelly, plus you're spoken for."

Kelly sat down and picked up Josh's coffee. "Stop hugging him before I run your skinny butt in for lewd and indecent acts."

She smiled as she smoothed down her dress over her ample but-tocks. "Now that's the first compliment I ever got from you. 'Skinny butt'? You do know how to talk to a woman, don't you?"

"Hey, I lost my head, okay? Just get me a Kelly Special, don't burn the toast, and how's about a pitcher of coffee."

Jean rolled her eyes and walked toward the kitchen. Josh took his coffee cup away from Kelly and tossed him the sports section. "So you been busy, huh?"

When Josh put down his cup, Kelly picked it up again and took a long drink. "Busy? Is a one-legged man in a butt-kicking contest busy? I was on more crime scenes last week than I could count. The bad guys are playin' for keeps out there. All hell busted loose, but it's finally calmed down. Everybody musta learned the lesson 'cause the last three days it's been business as usual. Just us cops still working overtime."

"The Vancouver model?" asked Josh.

"Yeah, they took over the turf of all the hero players but so far just been makin' promises. The stuff ain't on the market yet, but word is it's coming and the price is gonna be right. We're worried, Hawk. This new bunch in town don't mind whackin' people to make the others pay attention."

Josh glanced at a headline, STILL NO LEADS ON GANGLAND KILLINGS, and looked back at Kelly. "The paper right?"

Kelly rolled his eyes. "Fuckin' press is houndin' us big-time. You'd think it was a church choir that got whacked instead of hardheaded players who'd sell dope to their mothers. Screw 'em, we ain't givin' the press shit." He leaned closer. "We got a lucky break a few days ago. One of our stoolies lives next door to a couple of Jamokes who've been braggin' about making a hit on some players. We tapped and wired their room and hit the jackpot last night. We got some good stuff, so tonight we're going to pay those boys a visit."

Josh eyed his friend with concern. "You take care, huh? You're not a spring chicken. Let the kids knock the door down. You just be there and talk to the press when it's over."

Jean set two plates and a pitcher of coffee in front of them. She winked at Josh and walked back toward the kitchen.

Josh poured coffee into a cup for Kelly. "I'm serious—no hero shit. Let the D-ones earn the right to be D-twos."

Kelly grinned. "This is gonna be a piece of cake. Them boys ain't gonna know what hit 'em. Relax, I've got good people for the job."

After their meal Kelly glanced at his watch. "Aw shit, I'm late. Let's plan on playin' tomorrow. I'll get us a game with some easy marks so we won't have to work so hard."

Kelly reached for his billfold but stopped and shook his head. "Damn, Mary forgot to give me my—"

"Your allowance," Josh finished. "Get outta here. Tomorrow I wanna hear all about the bust."

Kelly picked up Josh's paper and made his way toward the door, purposely brushing by Jean, who had her hands full with a tray. "See ya, skinny butt."

Josh was loaded down with plastic milk bottles as he approached *Lil' Darlin'* and didn't see Glenn Grant waiting on the deck until he almost ran into her.

"What are those for?" she asked.

Josh put down the bottles and stared at her in disbelief. "You were serious?"

"Yep, I'm supposed to debrief you. Plus there's a big drug conference at the end of the week here in the city and I thought I could pick your brain. I thought I'd go on the hunt with you this morning and—"

"No way, Grant. It's man's business. You can talk to me while I'm making the rounds tonight."

"Sorry, Colonel, I'm not staying up all night to walk around and watch you sweet-talk drunks and prostitutes. I go with you on the hunt, or tomorrow you get called into the Pentagon, all day, and talk to my boss. You decide."

Josh's jaw muscles rippled in frustration. "Damn you!"

"Is that a yes?" she asked softly.

"God, it stinks."

Josh set the bucket of rotten fish in front of her, pushed in his eight-track tape, and started the outboard. "Start asking your questions; you're wasting time."

Grant turned around on the seat to avoid looking at the rotten fish. She raised her notebook. "Could you turn down the music? I like Conway, but not when it's that loud. Besides, we have business to discuss, remember?"

"You like Conway Twitty?" Josh asked as he turned down the music.

"Sure, I like all country-and-western music. Now, tell me what you thought about your orientation on Burma. Was it adequate for the mission?"

Josh gave her another point on his woman scale because she liked Conway. Shrugging, he answered, "N.A."

"What's N.A.?"

"Not applicable. I knew more about Burma than they did. I ended up giving the orientation briefing to the other teams. What state are you from?"

"I thought I was asking the questions."

"I wanna know who I'm huntin' with. Plus, it's only fair. You've read my file and know all about me. Answer my questions and I'll answer yours."

"Louisiana, I'm from Plaquemine, Louisiana. Was the training you received on new equipment adequate?"

"Hell no! You ever see a Pave Low III?"

"Well . . . I've seen them, but not up close," Grant replied.

"Neither had I until I got in the one that took us into Burma. You have any kids?"

Grant gave him an evil glare. "No, Colonel, I *don't* have any children. You could have at least been a gentleman and first asked if I had been married."

"Well, have ya?" Josh pressed, enjoying her discomfort.

"Yes, I was married, for six years. My husband was a captain and I was a captain. He wanted children, and I couldn't give him any children. Also, I loved the military life, so we went our separate ways."

Josh nodded. "Let me guess. You were a fast burner and doing better than he was. Am I right?"

"Colonel, I answered your question, but I'm *not* going into details."

Smiling, Josh bobbed his head. "I thought so. He couldn't handle your success."

Fuming, Grant angrily flipped to a new page in her notebook. "Was the equipment you were provided adequate for the mission, and . . ."

"Don't just sit there, help me!" Josh yelled as he tried to pull the trap into the boat.

Grant set down her notebook, grabbed hold of the rope, and pulled along with Josh. Her sour expression disappeared as soon as the trap broke the surface and they pulled it into the boat. Her eyes darted back and forth at the flopping fish and squirming turtles. "It really works! Look at that one—it's huge!"

Josh was put out. He really hadn't needed any help getting the trap in, but he'd been looking forward to seeing her scream and back away from the full catch. He smiled inwardly as he unwired the top of the trap, sure this would do the trick. "Get the turtles out, will ya? I need to change the float."

She shocked him when without hesitation she leaned over and deftly grabbed the biggest one by the rear foot, lifted him, and dropped him in the weld. Without coaxing, she reached in again and grabbed another.

Josh closed his open mouth. "Have you done this before?" he asked suspiciously.

"Not exactly, but we used to trap crayfish when we were kids. My brother and I made our spare money that way." She smiled and tossed the last turtle into the weld. "This kind of reminds me of those days."

Josh watched as she expertly grabbed the fish in the trap and tossed them over the side. "Where's your brother now?" he asked.

Her happy eyes dimmed. "He didn't make it back from Vietnam. You want me to rebait the trap?"

Josh nodded in silence and reached down for a new plastic milk jug. He didn't like admitting it to himself, but once again he'd totally misjudged the lady officer. She was okay.

As he lifted the third trap out of the water, Josh yelled, "Oh shit." He'd made the powerful upward pull to bring the trap in and was committed before he saw the snakes inside. He dropped the trap on the boat's floor and backed up as far as possible to avoid their striking heads. It was then that he heard the splash.

Grant's head popped up seconds later, and she was in Olympic form as she stroked for the nearby shore. Josh used his seat cushion to slap at the snakes that were slithering out of the wire loops into the boat. He kept slapping and kicking until they were all over the side; then he looked toward shore. She was standing on the muddy bank, and her dripping T-shirt was very revealing. She stared at him with eyes that could have killed, but he smiled and said, "You know, you don't look half-bad wet."

Grant angrily folded her arms across her chest. "You're an idiot, you know that? They could have killed you!"

Josh started the outboard and guided the boat toward her. "Naw, they were all water snakes. It happens sometimes; I forgot to warn ya. Sorry."

He beached the boat and hopped out, then took off his shirt and handed it to her. "Put this on. Come on, we'll walk up the bank to that grassy area in the sun so you can dry out. One more trap oughta do it anyway."

She put the shirt on and followed him up the bank. She saw the scars on his back and knew from his file they were caused by shrapnel in 'Nam. When she caught up, he was already sitting, facing the canal.

She sat down beside him. "Sorry I jumped, but back home when we saw snakes it was usually water moccasins."

He surprised her by reaching over and patting her back. "You did fine. I'm really impressed. Since you lost your notebook you won't be asking any more questions, right?"

Her eyes widened and she spun her head toward the boat.

He kept patting her back. "Yep, you dived in with it. I saw it floating by as I came to shore."

Grant turned and slugged the arm doing the patting. She eyed Josh coldly. "Pentagon, tomorrow, be there!"

"No way! I cooperated. It's not my fault you're scared of snakes."

Grant began to speak but laughed instead. Josh liked it. It was a deep, honest laugh.

She shook her head, still chuckling. "Can't you just see the general when I tell him I don't have the debrief done because of a turtle hunt?"

Josh's bemused expression changed to a scowl. "What's so funny about that?"

She cracked up again.

Ky stepped out and looked at the two muddy people in the boat. "How many?"

"Yeah, I had nice time in Panama and it's good to see you too. Ky, don't you ever say 'Hi' or 'How are you doing?' or 'Who's the lady?' How come it's just business with you?"

Ky kept his eyes on the squirming catch. "Hi, how doing, who lady? Now, how many?"

Josh threw up his hands. Grant kicked at one of the turtles. "We have one dozen, Mr. Ky."

Ky gave her the once-over. "Who you?"

Grant rolled her shoulders back. "Actually, I'm with the Department of Fish and Game. The Department was concerned about the recent depletion of water turtles along the Potomac. Mr. Hawkins agreed to an inspection, and based on what I've seen it's clear that there is a problem."

Ky shifted his eyes to Josh. "She talk bull-sheet like you."

Josh shrugged and got out of the boat to give Ky a warm hug. "I missed you, ya old goat. I understand business is good."

Ky pushed Josh away, looking embarrassed. "It okay, your assistant big-time cheater. I glad you back. Who is talking lady?"

"Ky, meet Glenn Grant. She's a crayfisher up from Louisiana getting tips from the best turtle man on the Potomac."

Ky rolled his eyes and extended his hand to Grant to help her out of the boat. He motioned with his head to Josh. "He nothing but pirate who take advantage of old refugee." He gave Josh a poke with his elbow. "This assistant bet-tar than Bob—she have better legs. Come, we talk business. I need two dozen next time. I have . . ."

Josh expected the worst when he saw Stefne in her usual hands-on-hips position on the bow of *Lil' Darlin'*, but she smiled, threw down the line, and asked innocently, "Well, how was the hunt, you two?"

Josh saw the mischievous glint in his daughter's eyes, and warning bells sounded. She helped Grant up and waved a hand in front of her own face. "You smell terrible. Did you have fun?"

Josh pulled himself up to the deck and spoke before Grant could respond. "Huntin' isn't 'fun,' it's work."

Stefne ignored him and said to Grant, "I cooked too much dinner for just Dad and me. Why don't you go home and clean up and come back over and join us? I'd like to hear what Dad does from a woman's perspective."

Grant said she'd love to and would be back in forty-five minutes. As she strode for the pier, Josh's warning bells were clanging so loudly he had to shake his head.

Josh faced his daughter. "What's this about cooking too much? You've never cooked too much in your life."

Stefne avoided his eyes and ducked into the passageway, calling over her shoulder, "I picked up a few things for you. They're on the bed."

Josh felt uncomfortable in the new shirt and slacks as he listened to the two women laugh and talk. He wondered if his daughter thought he really was dumb enough not to know she had set him up.

"Well?" Stefne said, looking at him.

Josh had not heard the question. "Well, what?"

"Is it true Glenn jumped in the water?"

Josh nodded. "Yep, she left me all alone to fight off the water moccasins."

"Whoa, Josh. You said they were water snakes."

" 'Water moccasins' sounds better," Josh replied with a wink.

Stefne glanced at her watch and pushed back her chair. "Sorry, but I have to get to the library. You two talk and relax a while. Dad, Bob said he would take the shift tonight to give you more time to rest up. See ya."

Josh had to laugh. Stef had set the whole thing up like the Hawkins she was—perfectly. He admired her attempt and liked Grant's company, so he figured he'd just go with it. It would keep his mind off Shaduzup for a little while.

Grant saw his distant gaze. "You're still tired, aren't you?" she asked, misreading him.

He smiled tiredly. "Kinda. How about we go up on deck and enjoy the evening for a while?"

Grant picked up her wine and pushed back her chair. "Lead on, 'best turtle catcher on the Potomac.' "

Josh winced. "It kinda just slipped out today. Don't tell another living soul I said that, okay?"

She patted his back as he led. "My lips are sealed."

In the cockpit they sat on deck chairs facing the channel. They sat in silence for a long time, just taking in the beauty and gentle rocking of the boat. Then Grant chuckled lightly. "I think your daughter is trying to set us up."

Totally relaxed, Josh nodded, keeping his eyes on the channel's tranquil waters. "It was a little obvious. She means well. I guess she's worried about me."

"You're lucky you have someone who cares that much. She's sweet."

"Sweet," repeated Josh, rolling his eyes toward her. " 'Sweet' is *not* Stef. 'Determined' is a much better description."

Grant lifted an eyebrow. " 'Sweet' was pushing it. You're right."

"Thanks for being a good sport tonight, and today on the hunt. You were 'sweet,' " Josh said sincerely.

Grant took the compliment with a slight nod. "I enjoyed your company." She tilted her head to look at him. "I understand now why you didn't want to help. You've managed to escape by creating your own little world here on the river. I like it, it's warm and homey."

"Are you making fun of me, Grant?" Josh asked, looking into her eyes.

"No. In fact, I envy you. Can you always keep it this way?"

Josh slowly shifted his eyes back to the channel. "I'm trying."

She reached out and touched his hand. "Is there room for a Louisiana crayfisher to visit your world now and then? I'd like to be a part of it. It reminds me of home."

Josh lifted his beer as if in a toast to her and winked. "Welcome to the world of Joshua Hawkins—and his dream."

Grant raised an eyebrow. "What's the dream?"

"That it never changes," Josh said quietly.

Grant finished her third wine cooler and stood. "I guess I'd better go. It's getting late. I have some reading to do to get ready for the drug conference, and I know you're still beat from the trip."

Josh got up, yawned, and took her arm. "I'll walk you. I was gonna check in with Bob anyway."

"That's nice, thank you. It's been a long time since a man walked me home."

Josh smiled tiredly, feeling the effects of the beer and jet lag. "If you didn't live across the street I'd let you take your chances. Come on, before I change my mind."

Josh found himself enjoying the walk, for she stayed close to him. He'd almost forgotten what it was like to feel a woman beside him, especially one who honored his silence. Their steps became slower, and several times they stopped just to look at the gifts above them. Upon reaching the entrance to her high-rise building, they paused but knew it wasn't over. Grant pushed in the code on the security lock and took his hand. "You're going to love the view from my balcony."

The elevator ride and walk down the hallway were just blurs to Josh, for he was floating in her fragrance and closeness. Her apartment was somehow what he had expected. It was warm and filled with things that were important to her—an old oak rolltop desk her father had given her, a painting from a close friend, the Oriental carpet picked up from a dealer in Turkey who had charged her too much, but whom she had liked because he lied so well. It *was* Glenn Grant, things with meaning, each with a story, a face, each a memory to treasure but no one to share them with. They sat on the balcony, and she talked of her home, her brother, her dreams.

At last, Grant got up from her patio chair and stood watching the sleeping man. She gently took the wineglass from his hand and smiled as she bent over and kissed his cheek. "Good night, Josh. Thank you for letting me in for a while." Leaving the balcony, she walked into the living room and got an afghan her mother had knitted, then returned to spread it over him. With a last, lingering look at her sleeping guest, she walked back into the apartment.

8:05 P.M., Seattle

Bone-tired, Stephen placed the last bag of heroin on the scale and made the final entry in his ledger book. Chigger glanced at the weight, picked up the bag, and tossed it to his assistant. "That's a wrap. Be ready to roll as soon as we finish the business." He quickly marked his book and threw his arm around Stephen's shoulders. "Get your book and let's wrap this deal. You're a righteous dude, my man. I like you. Have a good flight home."

Stephen smiled as he put the ledger under his arm. "You have been a fine teacher of American food, U Chigger. I wish you a good journey as well."

The two men walked into the foreman's office, where Colonel Po and Lassen were waiting. Taking the ledger book from Chigger, Lassen turned to the last page and took a calculator from his pocket. He punched in numbers while Po did the same thing with his own calculator and Stephen's book. Lassen grinned and announced, "We acknowledge the receipt of forty-eight American tons of product in this last shipment."

Po glanced at his calculator screen and said with a smile, "Our numbers agree."

Lassen took a cellular phone from his sport-jacket pocket and punched in a number. He looked at Po and winked. "One ringy dingy . . . two ring . . . Hey, this is Lassen. The transaction is complete and everything is in order. The number is confirmed at forty-eight. . . . Yes, he's sitting across from me."

Lassen handed the phone over to Po, who put the receiver to his ear. "This is U Po. . . . Yes, we are calling now." He handed the phone back to Lassen and picked up the briefcase at his feet. Unlocking the case, he took out an account code book and a cellular phone. He motioned for Stephen to sit down beside him and handed him the phone and code book.

Stephen quickly pushed in the Hong Kong Bank's number. Within three minutes he had reached the special accounts bank officer, given him the coded account numbers, and received back the balances for each account. As he wrote out each balance, he tried to keep his hand from shaking.

"Well?" Lassen asked when Stephen had terminated the call and Po had totaled the numbers.

Po nodded. "The deal is complete."

Lassen spoke into his phone. "It's done." He immediately pushed the Terminate button to end the call and tossed the phone to Chigger. "We're out of here." He stood and shook hands with Po. "Nice doing business with you. I'd stick around and celebrate with you, but we've got to hit the road. Have a safe trip home." Not waiting for a response, he headed for the door but stopped and reached inside his jacket pocket. He turned around and held out a folded note to Stephen. "Sorry, I almost forgot. I was told to give you this note from an old school classmate of yours."

Stephen unfolded the stationery as Lassen walked out of the office.

Po stepped closer to Stephen and saw that the note was written in Chinese characters. "What does Ke Ping say?"

Stephen sighed tiredly as he read the lines aloud. "You must come see me once you complete your business and bid farewell to my wife, who adores you. She has a gift for you and your wife. We are at the Marriott two miles south of your location. Room 200. No excuses, old boy—it is a command performance. Ke Ping."

Po smiled and patted Stephen's back. "You cannot refuse an invitation from such a generous man who helped save our country. Go on, Shin will take you. We'll finish up here. Come to my room once you return and pick up your tickets. You are booked on the early-morning flight for home."

Stephen sighed in relief and said, "I won't be long." He looked at his watch and strode for the office door. "I'll be knocking on your door within two hours."

Po waited until Stephen had left the office before facing the two captains, who were standing against the wall. "Finish it once he returns to our hotel. I don't want to hear his knock."

Both men bowed their heads.

Sergeant Shin pulled into the driveway of the Marriott and was about to let Stephen out at the entrance when Chen stepped out, opened the front car door, and got in. Smiling, he told Shin to park in back. Looking over his shoulder at Stephen, he frowned. "There is a slight change of plans. My wife is with friends and will be finished in a few minutes. How are you, old boy? I hope you didn't work too hard."

Shin pulled into a parking place and turned off the ignition as Stephen finished telling Chen that he was tired but happy to be going home.

Chen nodded as he reached inside his cashmere sport jacket. Turning suddenly, he withdrew a small silenced pistol and fired point-blank into Shin's startled face. Grabbing the dead sergeant's jacket, he pulled the limp upper body over onto the seat and pointed the pistol at Stephen. "Your joss has turned very bad, my old friend. I fear you are a dead man."

Stephen stared at his friend in disbelief. Chen sighed and tossed the weapon into Stephen's lap. "Just listen to me. I last saw my father two days ago. He is making me San of Washington, D.C. I flew back to make arrangements for the move . . . and to warn you. While I was with my father he met with a senior Triad representative who had flown in from Hong Kong to discuss business and bring my father up to date on events. The representative had attended a meeting with your General Swei a day after your first shipment arrived. General Swei is a very good businessman; he understood that he had to inform us of his plans and was seeking our approval. It seems your general laid out a complete plan to take over your government once the last shipment arrived and the funds were all transferred. Swei explained that your current leader was too tainted by his past policies and that change was necessary for the rebuilding programs to succeed. Your prime minister, most of his ministers, and all of the opposition leaders will be removed in a single quick strike operation. Then Swei will take control with the full support of the younger army leadership, who have pledged him their loyalty."

Chen glanced at his watch. "It is now noon in Rangoon, and they plan to strike in the early-morning hours tomorrow. In less than six-teen hours your general's men will arrest the prime minister and army leaders, who will become scapegoats for all of the wrongdoing in the past. Swei will announce the coup and his vision for a new Burma on radio; within days he will announce the new loan guarantees and begin the rebuilding and economic programs. His plan calls for open-ing the borders and letting Western companies in. With the Triad's help he will make your country the new Hong Kong."

"Impossible!" Stephen exclaimed. "There are too many who know of his past involvements. The Sawbaws, minority leaders, and incor-ruptible Burmese won't let that happen."

"Swei saw to all of them in the past week. They are all dead or im-prisoned. All threats have been eliminated . . . except you. Stephen, you know too much. I'm sure you are on their list. Po is going to have you killed before—"

Stephen's eyes suddenly widened. "Mya! My son! What have they done to the families?"

Chen lowered his head. "I don't know, but I'm sure they would be considered a threat as well. Swei can take no risk of anyone speaking out against him. I'm sorry, my friend. You have been used by men who will do anything to attain their goals. The pistol is my gift to you, but it's not much. Po and his men will try to kill you. Then, if you kill Colonel Po, you will become a threat to us as well. We will find you, for there is no place you can go and no place you can hide. I'm offering you a Shan death, Stephen—for our friendship I owe you that. But once I leave you, I become Ke Ping. If it comes to it, I will or-der you hunted down. You are a threat to the Triad and a threat to the Circle, for you know far too much. Good-bye, my friend. I will re-member our days together always."

Chen reached for the door handle but Stephen leaned forward and grabbed his shoulder. "Let us fight this together, Chen! We can defeat them with what you know!"

Chen smiled. "You are still the naive Sao of the mountains. A trai-tor's family is not spared—my son and daughter would die an un-speakable death over many days. Stephen, I have given you all that I can. May your god forgive us all."

Stephen closed his tearing eyes and released his grip. "He can't for-give those who are already in hell."

Stephen dumped Sergeant Shin's body on a back road and parked a block from the large Holiday Inn complex. He walked hurriedly to the parking lot, keeping in the shadows of the trees. Not seeing Po's white Mercedes or the matching black one that the security captains drove, he entered the back entrance of the Holidome and tried to act casual as he passed two boys splashing each other in the shallow end of the pool. Po's room curtains were still pulled and the lights were out, so he quickly retraced his steps back to the parking lot, knowing he had made it back before them. He scanned the partially lighted lot and chose a position in the shrubs next to the entrance they always used. Backing up against the brick wall, he kneeled behind a hedge of evergreens, pulled the pistol from his belt, and took a moment to familiarize himself with the small .22 semiautomatic. He pushed the magazine clip and saw it was only one bullet short, slapped it back into the butt of the weapon, and jacked a round into the chamber. The solid *chuck-link* sound of the working parts boosted his sagging confidence. He prayed they would hurry, for he knew there must still be a way to save his family.

After a minute the black Mercedes pulled into the lot. Stephen thumbed the safety off as the car pulled into a space only twenty feet away from him. He looked toward the lot entrance but didn't see Po's car following. His luck was holding, he thought, until the driver's door opened and the interior light revealed only Captain Bwin.

The stocky officer got out and locked the door. He looked toward the lot entrance and paused before shrugging and turning toward the pool entrance. Reaching into his pocket for his room key, he lowered his head but suddenly looked up hearing movement to his right. Stephen fired.

Bwin's head snapped back, his knees buckled, and he sank to the sidewalk, twitching. Stephen grabbed the officer's collar and pulled the body behind the hedge. As he returned quickly to the sidewalk, he picked up a handful of pine needles to throw on the pool of blood—but there wasn't one. The small bullet had not exited. He tensed as another car entered the lot, but it was a station wagon. Then a second car pulled in—Po's white Mercedes.

Po got out with his briefcase and headed for the entrance. Captain Sing locked the door of the car and hurried to catch up to his boss. Po paused at the door and turned to Sing, who had come up behind him. "Come with me to my room and I'll give you the cellular phone. I want you to call Brigadier Tan from out here while you're waiting for Stephen."

As soon as both men had walked in the door Stephen stepped out, keeping his gun hand hidden in his jacket, and followed them inside. Stopping beside a Pepsi machine, he waited and watched as the two men walked toward Po's room. Once they had unlocked the door and stepped inside, he moved.

Po unlocked the briefcase he had placed on the table and handed Sing the phone. "Get Bwin and—"

A knock at the door interrupted him. "That's him now. You two know what's to be done." The captain opened the door and a bullet struck him two inches below his navel. He doubled over, let out a gasp of air, and fell. Stephen shoved him back and slammed the door while Po stared at the black pistol, stammering, "No, Stephen. No!"

Stephen kicked Sing in the chin, lifted his head, and jammed the silencer into his open mouth. He pulled the trigger before facing Po, who had turned and run toward the hall door. Stephen raised the pistol and shot him in the back of the leg. He went down facefirst, grunting. Stephen stepped forward and grabbed Po's jacket collar. Then he dragged him back to the center of the room and threw him down next to Sing's body.

Po brought his hands up and pleaded, "Anything, anything you want. Don't kill me . . . don't kill—"

"Where are Mya and my son?" Stephen hissed, seething with hate and frustration. "Tell me or I will blow your toes off first and work up your legs."

"I'm bleeding to death," Po cried, writhing in pain.

Stephen placed the silencer barrel on the colonel's right kneecap. "Where?"

"Dinto. They were all taken to Dinto. Tan ordered it to make sure none of them—"

Stephen picked up the cellular phone from the floor and tossed it to the wounded man. "Call Tan and tell him you will die unless they are released. *Do it!*"

Gasping in pain, Po fumbled with the phone. His hands were shaking so badly he misdialed three times before finally getting it right. He got through to the duty officer, who passed the call through to Tan's residence.

"Brigadier, this is Colonel Po. . . . No, listen please, Stephen is here. He has killed Sing and—" His eyes opened wider and he shakily handed the phone to Stephen. "He wants to talk to you."

Stephen snatched the phone away and brought it to his ear. "Tan, he will die unless you—"

Tan snarled, "He means nothing."

Stephen's nostrils flared. He glanced at the briefcase and snapped, "I want my wife and son freed. I have the account numbers, and—"

"Fool, we moved the funds to another bank once the transfer was made. Do you think we would risk Po being stopped and searched by U.S. Customs? You are a fool, Kang, just like your father. I will call our Chinese friends and they will find you. If you go to the authorities, I will personally kill your wife. In fact, it will please me, for there will be one less filthy Shan to worry about. If you have a pistol, put it to your head—it's the only thing that will save her . . . from me."

Stephen screamed in rage and threw the phone at Sing's body. It hit the dead officer's skull and bounced toward the door. Spinning, Stephen kicked the device and cried, "God, no! No!"

Seeing his chance, Po reached for the nine-millimeter pistol holstered under Sing's arm. Sobbing, Stephen turned, dropped to one knee, and fired the entire magazine into Po's twisted face.

1:15 A.M., Washington, D.C.

Kelly put the shoestring necklace that held his badge over his head before facing his men. They carried their badges in identical fashion for easy identification, and each man had a shotgun in his hands. Kelly pulled out his old snub-nosed .38 and nodded. "Show time. We go in like we planned. Keep each other posted on the radio tac sets. Let's do it."

Within minutes the teams were at their posts. Kelly nodded to the team behind him carrying the door buster. They closed up and Kelly exchanged glances with Sergeant David Nolan, his friend and partner of ten years. He whispered, "Slow and easy, Davy."

They turned the corner in the darkened third-floor tenement hallway and slowly walked forward in their rubber-soled shoes until coming to a door marked with a rusted seven. Kelly nodded.

Nolan whispered into the small ball just in front of and below his lips. "We're going in . . . five seconds."

Four other teams located inside and outside the building all received the message on their tactical radio headsets and began the countdown.

Four . . . three . . .

Kelly flattened himself against the right wall. Nolan was on the left. The door team swung the metal ram back in the ready position.

Two . . . one . . .

The ram slammed forward, shattering the door. The busting team dropped the device and grabbed the shotguns they'd leaned against the wall as Kelly raced in yelling, *"Police, nobody move!"* He swung his pistol right toward movement and hollered, *"Freeze!"* An old Jamaican man sitting in an easy chair in front of a blaring television threw his hands up.

Nolan was in a shooter's crouch beside Kelly but was looking into the kitchen, where two men sat at a small table. He yelled, "Get your hands where I can see them, *now!*"

One of the men raised one hand immediately and then brought the other up holding a compact submachine gun that chattered with surprisingly little noise. Nolan fired as he took a bullet in the neck. His one shot went high.

Kelly spun at the sound and was hit in the leg by the burst. He staggered back a step but fired his snub-nose twice before the second Mac10 burst hit him in the chest, knocking him off his feet and back into the television. The door busters came in blasting with their shotguns, turning the kitchen into splinters, broken glass, and bleeding men.

Despite the shooting and screaming, Kelly could hear only the pathetic sound of Nolan gagging on his own blood.

Kelly tried to move and help his friend but he couldn't—a giant invisible hand was pushing down on his chest harder and harder. Unable to fight the pain any longer, he closed his eyes and gave in to the quiet darkness.

Seattle

Stephen washed his hands and looked in the mirror. He hardly recognized the man he saw. Hating the image, he picked up Sing's nine-millimeter and stuck it into the shoulder holster he had taken off the officer's body. He walked into the bedroom and picked up the briefcase holding the dead men's billfolds and other weapons. Ignoring the sickeningly sweet, coppery smell of blood, he strode for the door, placed the Do Not Disturb sign on the outside knob, and shut it. He walked slowly to his room, where he threw his things into his suitcase and left. Getting into his rental car, he placed the key in the ignition, then lowered his hand and stared out the windshield, realizing he had no place to go. The weight under his arm gave him an option—Tan and Chen's option—to kill himself now. He wanted to fight, but whom? His enemies and his family were in Burma, twelve thousand miles away. He could not kill himself, for he knew as long as he lived, they would not kill them, his wife and son were their insurance of his silence. Now it was only a question of how to stay alive and somehow get back to Burma. How? Tan would have called the Triad, who would have contacted their syndicate in Seattle, so they would have people watching for him at the airport. Where could he go? Slowly his eyes lowered to his only hope, the silver bracelet. Joshua.

CHAPTER 17

4 A.M., North Bend, Washington

The ringing alarm woke him up. Stephen picked up the battery-operated clock from the dash and turned it off. It was 7 P.M. in Rangoon. In less than ten hours Swei would become his country's leader. He opened the car door, took a few steps into the trees, and relieved himself. After leaving the Holidome he had turned in his rental car at the airport, gone to a different rental company, and rented another car using the false documentation Po had provided when he first arrived. He had made it only as far as North Bend before he had to pull off at a rest stop to get a few hours of sleep.

Getting back in the car, he turned on the interior lights and looked at his map. The small town of Ephrata was about 250 miles away, just off Interstate 290. It had a commuter airport. If he stuck with flying into other small airports, always heading east, he could wind up close enough to Washington, D.C. to rent a car and drive to the capital city. He closed his eyes for a moment to think. Tan would send his henchmen back to his house or question his wife about if he knew anybody in the States. Even if Mya didn't tell them about Joshua, all they had to do was look at the picture on his dresser. It showed him and Mya with Josh and Jill on Royal Lake in a sailboat. And there were his letters—Mya had kept them all.

Stephen's eyes teared again as he thought about his wife and the questioning she would have to endure. Trembling, and telling himself he had to try, he started the car. The syndicate knew about Joshua by now and would be watching him. He, Stephen, wouldn't be able to call, but if he got to Washington he would make contact somehow. Joshua had written he was living on a boat, so there had to be a way. Forcing his tears back, Stephen slipped the transmission into Drive and pulled out onto the dark road.

Washington, D.C.

Josh awoke hearing a strange phone ringing. Opening his eyes, he saw an even stranger ceiling and realized he'd slept in Grant's apartment. He had gotten up during the night and moved from the patio chair to her more comfortable couch. One glance at the VCR's digital clock told him it was almost 5 A.M. "Ah, shit," he mumbled as he headed for the door to make his escape.

"Josh?"

He turned and saw a vision in a short nightgown standing in the opened bedroom door. The light was behind her, so the sheer material was almost transparent, showing off her slender but well-proportioned body. He stammered and quickly averted his eyes. "Yeah, I'm still here, I'm sorry. I must have—"

"Josh, Stef's on the phone. She sounds upset."

"Ah, shit," he mumbled again. He didn't want to talk to his daughter, who must think she'd caught him with more than his hand in the cookie jar. Grant strode over and handed him the phone. Her being so close in the skimpy nightgown woke him instantly. He took a deep breath for strength and tried to sound innocent. "Hi, hon. I went to sleep on the—"

"Dad, Kelly has been shot. Mary called me ten minutes ago after trying to reach you at the boat. He's at University, but I don't know his condition. Mary was too upset to tell me anything."

"I'm leaving now," Josh said quickly and hung up, feeling as if he'd just been hit in the stomach with a sledgehammer.

Grant saw the anguish in his face. "What's wrong?"

Shaking, Josh looked up at the ceiling. He wanted to put his fist through a wall. "My friend Detective Kelly has been shot. Do you have a car here?"

"In the parking lot."

"I'm not sure my Jeep will start. Can you drop me off at University Hospital?"

Grant was already heading for the bedroom. "I'll be ready in two minutes."

·   ·   ·

Mary Kelly saw him and Grant come in to the waiting area. She ran past the detectives and officers clustered there, fell into his open arms, and buried her head in his chest. "God, I'm glad you're here."

Josh held the small woman close and walked her down the hallway a few steps. "How is he?" he asked, steeling himself for the worst.

She saw his worry and reached up to touch his face. "He's okay, but it was damn close. Nolan is . . . Oh Jesus, Josh, I can't believe it." She lowered her head, crying. He hugged her to him again. Over her shoulder he saw Nolan's wife sitting in the waiting room being consoled by Kelly's fellow detectives.

Mary pulled away and quickly dabbed her eyes as if embarrassed. "Who's this? You said you'd wait till I threw his Irish butt out. Introduce me, will you?"

Josh gave Mary a smile, seeing she was trying hard to get it back together. He motioned to Grant, who was two steps behind him. "Mary, meet Glenn Grant, a . . ."

Grant stepped up. "I'm his army friend. It's nice to meet you, Mary. Sorry we have to meet under these circumstances, but I'm glad your husband is out of danger."

Mary shook Grant's hand and eyed Josh. "Army friend? That's a good one. Do you play racquetball, by any chance? I don't know where else he would meet a lady."

Josh put his arm around Mary again. "You probably want to get out of here, but can I see him?"

"You have to. He's been asking about you. I'll just wait downstairs with Glenn and we'll have coffee. I should stay with Cindy, but—"

Josh shook his head. "She has plenty of people with her. Go on. I'll be down in a little while and we'll take you home."

Josh walked into the room and immediately felt a wave of relief. Kelly was lying back on the hospital bed cradling a phone to his ear, red-faced as always. He nodded, pointed at the phone, and held up one finger, all the while talking in just above a gravelly whisper.

". . . I don't care if they say Freddie ain't gonna talk. Bring him in and scare him. Tell 'im I know about his bad deal that went down on L Street. . . . Yeah, use it. Just get him in and squeeze him. Freddie knows if anybody knows. Do it." He held the receiver out to Josh. "Hang it up for me, will ya? They got me wrapped so tight I can hardly move. What ya doin' here? You tryin' to make a move on Mary while I'm down?"

Josh could see the pain in his friend's eyes despite his playful words. They were two of a kind, he thought, Kelly and Mary, trying hard to cover their real feelings with humor. It might have worked if it hadn't been for their eyes. Josh shrugged. "Naw, Mare said it was a bad time. I'm glad ta see ya, buddy. Shitty night, huh?"

Kelly lowered his eyes. "Yeah. Ya heard about Nolan, right? Christ, I just gave his kid a ball glove for a birthday present. He just turned seven, and . . ."

Josh looked into Kelly's eyes. "Mary said it was close."

Kelly tried to smile but failed, then motioned to his chest. "The vest stopped the bullets. Can you believe it? Mary ain't never gonna let me live it down. She buys me the vest a month ago—insurance, she says—and damn if she ain't right. It worked, Hawk. The impact of the slugs still broke one rib and bruised some others, but the damn thing worked. Ain't that some shit?"

Josh motioned to the bandage on Kelly's leg. "And this?"

"Flesh wound. It's nothing. I'll be able to carry your ass on the courts in no time. Doc says two, maybe three weeks, I'm back at work."

Josh's eyes narrowed. "You went in, didn't you? You led the fuckin' charge."

Kelly waved the accusation away but avoided Josh's stare. Josh shifted his position so his friend would have to look at him. "I gave your twins their presents six months ago for *their* birthday. Am I gettin' through that thick Irish skull? You're a D-two detective—let the others handle the hero shit."

"I don't need this right now."

"Well, you're gonna hear it. If not for Mary and the boys, then for me. I can't win on the courts without you."

Kelly lowered his head. "Okay. Christ, you'd think you were my mother the way ya talk." He slowly lifted his chin. A single tear was trickling down his cheek. "They were loaded with heavy weapons, Hawk. Poor Nolan didn't have a fuckin' chance. They aren't like the others. They fight to the death and that puts us back where we started—with nothin'. The one Jamoke we busted won't talk. He hasn't said a word since they brought him in, and about an hour ago one of the best defense attorneys in town shows up to take his case. We got nothin' on the hits—shit, we don't even know where to start. The guys been roustin' a few walkers in Chinatown, but the fuckin' ACLU is already screamin'. Give me some ideas. You studied the Chink organizations, and none of my guys have ever been to Hong Kong like you."

Josh pulled up a chair beside the bed. "What are you doing to find the snake's head? You have to find the San, the lord, that's runnin' the action here in the city."

Kelly rolled his eyes. "We're workin' it, shit. We contacted Immigration two weeks ago and got a list of all the Chinks from Hong Kong who got green cards in the last year. The fuckin' printout is thirty pages long, so it's gonna take time. We need something else to narrow the field of probables."

Josh took Kelly's notepad and pen from the nightstand. "Bear with me, okay? You've probably already got a profile of what to look for, but here's what I think you're lookin' for. He'd be a high roller, real big-time money. He'd seem legit, with interests in lots of different companies. He'd be working out of a regular office, so that means lots of calls and faxes to and from Hong Kong. His communications systems would all be hooked up to sophisticated scrambling equipment that would encode and decode communications. His security men would be the best there are, but they wouldn't be locals, they'd be Chinks. And the company would be running twenty-four hours a day because of the twelve-hour time difference. He'd want to keep up with news back home, so check out who's sellin' the *South China Morning Post*, Hong Kong's major paper." Josh wrote down what he had just told Kelly, then looked up thoughtfully.

Kelly asked, "What are you thinking?"

Josh shrugged. "It's probably nothing, but Ky says he has Chinese customers who don't even ask the price of the turtles I sell him. Turtle meat is a delicacy to the Cantonese, but only the very rich can afford it in Hong Kong."

"Write it down. I'll try anything right now," Kelly said, motioning to the pad.

Josh added it to the profile, then tore off the page and handed it to his friend.

Kelly smiled for the first time. "Hand me the phone, and tell Alvarez to come in and see me."

Chinatown, Washington, D.C.

Dorba sat behind an intricately carved teak desk and regarded the two men seated before him. Qui, his chief of staff, was wearing a new suit, but the Western clothes couldn't conceal the street fighter he once was. Now in his early fifties, he still made others feel insecure in his presence. Qui had worked as an enforcer for Dorba from the beginning in the Cholon district and had become his most trusted friend and adviser. On the other hand, Michael Woo, seated by Qui, was a suave young man who had been assigned to Dorba's syndicate by the leaders of the Triad to obtain experience and to ensure that their interests were kept in mind. Woo was the son of an elder and had been sent to the United States for his university studies. He went on to graduate from Harvard Law School, became an American citizen, and married an American woman. One month earlier he had left one of Washington's most respected law firms to begin learning the business. One day he would take his place as San in one of the Triad syndicates. He was now Dorba's American affairs and legal adviser.

Dorba shifted his eyes to Qui. "The loss of two of our employees is of concern to me."

Qui nodded somberly, but his eyes twinkled. "It's time for a warning."

Michael Woo dipped his chin. "San Chu, I have great respect for your wisdom, but these two lower workers were expendable. As your legal adviser I strongly recommend that we allow this to—"

Dorba's cold glare stopped him in midsentence. "You must learn that trust and loyalty are the foundations of the Circle. Our other lower employees must know they will be protected. Send the authorities a warning letter. Tell them the takeover of the city's white powder distribution was only business, and if they interfere in our affairs again, they will face the consequences."

Woo bowed his head again. "With all respect, San Chu, the police will laugh at such a warning. I worked for the district attorney's office here and I know the leaders of the police department. They won't heed such a warning."

Dorba leaned forward in his chair and said firmly, "They have never dealt with an organization that could carry out the threat. They will learn. I know the warning won't be heeded—this time. From now on they will know they are not dealing with children. If they continue interfering in our affairs after our warning, we will strike with enough force to bring them to their knees."

Dorba took a piece of paper from the top drawer and handed it across the desk to his young legal adviser. "These are the men that I have already instructed Qui to make arrangements for."

Woo's eyes widened as he read down the list. "With all respect, San Chu, this is . . . is a war you are declaring. An attack on just one of these men will enrage the authorities and the people. The police and federal agencies won't rest until they find and destroy us."

Dorba exchanged a smile with Qui before shifting his eyes back to the young lawyer. "You will learn that we do not exist. Our organization is impossible to penetrate. The anger of the police and that of the people will be turned to a group who will be easy to hate. Qui and I have used the tactic before, as have many of our Triad friends in Hong Kong."

"But why send a warning if another is to be blamed for the attacks?" Woo asked in desperation.

Dorba leaned back in his chair. "Be patient and you will see. Leave me now and come back in an hour. I will help you draft the letter of warning."

Still shaken by what he had read, the young lawyer got up, bowed, and left.

Qui grinned. "These new ones have no stomach for our old ways."

Dorba lowered his head. "My son is like this Triad spy they have burdened me with. He thinks he is an American instead of a businessman. They will learn like we did. Tell me, old friend. Are we ready to begin distribution of the white powder?"

"It begins today, San Chu."

Dorba nodded once and took off his glasses to wipe the lenses with his silk handkerchief. "We might have a problem. One of the Burmese who brought in our white powder killed three other Burmese last night in Seattle, and another is missing. My son called and told me this killer is a man my son went to school with and I had met as well." Dorba picked up a fax message from his desk and handed it to Qui. "This Stephen Kang may come to Washington and seek refuge with an American friend who lives here, according to our Burmese friends. The name of the American and his address are in the message."

"Eliminate the American?" Qui asked, glancing at the paper.

"No, not yet. If he is killed we will not find Kang. Put surveillance on him. If Kang gets to him, then kill the American and find out from Kang who Kang has spoken to. We need this matter cleaned up as quickly as possible. The Burmese are holding Kang's wife, so I don't believe he will go to the authorities. Even if he did, he knows only that my son was involved, but he knows nothing of me and our business."

Qui stood and lowered his head. "I will see to it immediately."

Dorba smiled. "As you always do, old friend."

Grant pulled up to the curb at Josh's office. "You won't have time for hunting, will you?"

Josh shrugged. "I'll have time to check a couple of traps after I get my Jeep running. I'm going upriver later for a workout. It's been a while."

"I guess that means sculling?" she asked, already knowing the answer.

Josh nodded absently and turned to look at her. "I'm sorry about crashing at your place last night. You should have thrown me out."

Grant winked. "It'll give you and Stef something to talk about."

"Don't remind me. Really, I owe ya for your help this morning. Anytime you wanna go huntin', let me know. I enjoy your company."

"My God, I think that's a compliment. Thanks. I'll stop by tonight while you're making rounds. I'd like to see you in action."

Josh got of the car and waved. "Tonight then. And thanks again for this morning."

Josh watched as she pulled away, feeling guilty. While he'd been talking to her he'd kept seeing her in her nightgown. Maybe he wasn't as far gone as he'd thought.

8 P.M., Directorate of Defense Services Intelligence,
Rangoon, Burma

Swei felt a tingling sensation run up his spine as he saw the activity in the underground tunnel complex on his way to the command center.

Brigadier Tan was talking to four of his commanders in the planning room when he saw his superior walk in. He motioned the lieutenant colonels out and smiled. "Everything is going smoothly. The units are all on standby and all targets have been identified."

Swei nodded and took a seat in front of a large map of the city. "My only concern is Kang."

"Which one?" Tan asked.

"Both, actually, but Stephen is our biggest threat for the present. I just got off the phone with our Triad friends. They confirmed Po and the two captains are dead. The FBI is involved and has asked our embassy to identify the bodies and explain why they used false identification to check into the hotel. I've already instructed our embassy team to identify them as members of the army staff. What concerns me is that the FBI is now looking for our Sao as the main suspect."

Tan waved his hand as if not concerned. "How can he be a threat? He thinks we have his wife and son . . . and if he *does* go to the authorities, the *lai* is gone, so are our workers, and the funds are in a different account. He has no proof we were involved in anything."

Swei's eyes stabbed Tan. "Our Triad friends are concerned he will speak of *their* involvement."

Tan's nonchalant demeanor evaporated, and he blurted, "He knows nothing of the Triad!"

Swei shook his head. "You don't understand. If Stephen Kang is caught by the FBI, the Triad wants our assurance he won't speak. I gave that assurance just hours ago, saying we had his wife and son. I didn't tell them she had already died during our questioning and that his son had escaped."

Tan's nostrils flared. "How could we possibly have known the

Shan bitch would hang herself? Kang doesn't know that! He thinks we have both of them, so he won't dare say anything."

Swei rose up from his chair. "See that no one else knows of this. We have come this far and are so close. In less than nine hours we will achieve what we have always wanted, but it won't last a day if the Triad becomes our enemy. They must not know."

Tan had already come to his feet when his superior stood. He bowed his head. "I'll see to it."

Washington, D.C.

Josh looked up at the blazing sun and judged it to be after three. He grabbed the oars again and pulled back. The sound of the seat rolling back was like music to his ears as the scull shot through the water. Sweat dripped down his forehead, gathering on his chin until dropping to his chest. He brought the oars and his legs up and pushed forward again for another bite of the water. With every stroke he was becoming stronger. Just a little more sweat and a little more pain and the faces of the screaming men and women of Shaduzup and the Wa that he had killed would blur, become indistinguishable. The dreams would fade like they'd done after Vietnam and Grenada. The river understood and gave compassion to those who tried to carry on.

"How's it feel to be back, Mister Hawkins?"

Josh smiled at the old boat keeper as he carried the scull up to the boathouse. "It's like I never left. I didn't lose a bit of rhythm, Fred."

The old man raised his hand to shield the sun and looked to the north. "Well, I missed ya, you're about the only one who comes around regular. I thought ya mighta been sick the past weeks. Good thing you made it when you did. Looks to me like we got us a storm coming in."

Josh hung the scull on the pegs and looked toward the north. "Yep, you're right, those thunderheads mean rain and wind. Looks like I'll just make it."

Josh climbed over the seats and the squirming turtles in his flatboat and started the outboard. He raised his hand. "See ya day after tomorrow, I'm back on my schedule."

The old man waved. "You best hurry, you don't wanna be on the water when the lightning starts."

Josh backed up, turned the throttle up and headed for open water.

.　　.　　.

Josh left Ky's Emporium just as the wind picked up, and the first slaps of rain cooled the back of his neck. Pulling his baseball cap down tighter, he steered for *Lil' Darlin'* and his daughter, who stood on the prow waiting.

Stefne tossed him a line and helped him up. For the first time he could remember, she didn't say a word. Josh wasn't sure how to take her silence and said the only thing he could think of. "How ya doin'?" he asked, hoping she would let it drop.

Stefne just nodded and smiled. He threw up his hands. "Okay, I took Glenn home, but nothing happened. I went to sleep on her balcony. That's all there is to it."

Stefne shrugged but kept the knowing smile. "I didn't ask in the first place. Thanks for calling and telling me Kelly was alright. I was worried about you."

"Me?"

Stefne just nodded, thinking of how he had gone to pieces the day they buried her mother. He wouldn't leave the grave. Kelly had stayed with him for almost four hours until finally convincing him to leave. His old crooked smile returned only when he had sold the house, gotten out of the army, and started the business.

Josh realized what she was thinking and put his arm around her shoulder. "He's gonna be fine, just like I told ya. Come on, we gotta batten her down. There's a storm coming in."

Josh was cleaning up in the cabin when he smelled her. He turned and saw Grant in the cabin door, looking at him strangely. "Josh, do you have a TV?"

Stefne came in and asked, "What's wrong, Glenn?"

Grant quickly scanned the cabin seeing that he didn't have a television before looking back at Josh. "General Swei of the DDSI took over the government of Burma an hour ago."

Josh's jaw tightened. "He'll have the power to finish off the minorities, just like he's always wanted. Poor Stephen will lose his job in the ministry."

Grant stepped closer. "Josh, you'd better sit down. There's something else." She shifted her eyes to Stefne. "Stef, this is classified stuff. Would you mind if . . ."

Stefne took Josh's rain jacket from the peg in the passageway and strode toward the cabin door. "Sure. I'll go visit Bob for a while."

Grant waited until she had shut the door behind her. "Josh, Stephen Kang has been in Seattle for the past two and half weeks, and—"

"Naw, wrong guy. Stephen would have called," Josh said adamantly.

Grant sat down. "The FBI sent us a report this afternoon. They've been trying to determine if we have Burmese in our country with bogus visas. Stephen Kang entered the U.S. on the fifth of June, two days after the embassy bombing. His visa was checked and he was logged in the Customs computer. Last night three Burmese Army officers were shot and killed at a Holiday Inn just outside of Seattle, and another is missing. They had checked in early in May and rented their cars using phony names. A fifth man checked in on the fifth of June. The hotel staff describes the new man as having Oriental features, tall, good-looking, early forties. A maid distinctly remembered him because she asked him about the silver bracelet he wore. The FBI checked with the Customs officers on duty that evening. A female officer remembered him because his English was flawless—he told her he was in the States for pleasure and was going fishing."

Josh's face had gone pale. He stared past Grant at a spot on the bulkhead.

"I'm sorry to tell you this, Josh. The FBI has an all-points bulletin out for him for questioning about the killings. The fingerprints in his room match those on a cellular phone found in the room where two bodies were discovered. The third body was found outside, hidden under a hedge. The Burmese embassy identified the bodies as being officers assigned to the staff of the now-imprisoned prime minister."

Josh lowered his head for a moment, then slowly raised it to look into her eyes. "You told them I knew him, didn't you?"

Grant didn't blink. "Yes. I contacted the FBI just before coming over here. They think he may try to contact you. They want your cooperation. I wanted to tell you first before they got here. Josh, I'm sorry, I know how close you two were."

His insides felt like they were being torn apart, but he dipped his chin toward her. "I would have done the same thing if I'd been you. It's your job." He walked into the bedroom and came back with a small framed picture, which he handed to her. "This was taken on Royal Lake in '82. We . . . we . . ." He turned away from her so she wouldn't see his tears. "Please stay until the FBI get here. I don't want to be alone right now."

Scottsbluff, Nebraska

Stephen had checked into a small motel near the airfield after arriving at the county airport. He was sitting in front of the television with tears running down his cheeks.

The television screen was filled with a color photograph of General Swei's smiling face while a newswoman spoke in the background.

"Today marks the end of one more chapter of this Southeast Asian country's long history. Today General Ren Swei became yet another general to become the self-proclaimed prime minister of Burma. Early this morning officers from the elite Burmese Strike Commando Battalion arrested General Maw Mung, the prime minister and general of the armed forces, at his home. At the same time similar arrests were made of his cabinet and of other key government and military officials. At eight this morning General Swei, the former leader of Burma's secret police, spoke on government radio. He shocked his audience not only with news of the bloodless coup, but also by announcing his plan to begin government reforms to help the Burmese people and to rebuild the country. He also announced he will open the borders and cancel all restrictions on foreign travel into and out of Burma within weeks. Most Burmese would not speak to us, but a few did say they fear the general's words are just that, words. The people of Burma are waiting to see if their new leader keeps his promises. They are waiting, and so is the world. This is Connie Hoffman, reporting live from Rangoon."

Stephen got up, turned off the television, and lay down on the bed. He could see his son pleading for him to stay and Mya's teary eyes filled with worry. He bit down on his lip, remembering he'd promised her everything would be alright. Clenching his fists, he cried out, "What have I done? My God, what have I done to them?" Tears began streaming down his face again, for he knew the answer all too well.

Thailand Border

Xu Kang stood as the two men were brought into his office. He motioned for his soldiers to release the two Americans and spoke tiredly. "You're too late. Your trip has been wasted."

The CIA chief of station for Thailand stepped forward and said, "It's not too late if you're willing to try. We have been authorized to assist you with our intelligence capabilities and enough weapons to arm all of your soldiers. We know that—"

Xu Kang sat down and shook his head. "It's too late. I'm too old to lead another attempt at the impossible. My heart is bleeding—my son is surely dead, as is his wife. All I have left is my grandson. Find someone else who believes in dreams. Mine are gone. I seek only revenge."

The agent exchanged looks with the other man beside him before speaking. "Stephen Kang is not dead. He killed three Burmese officers in Seattle, Washington, and is now being hunted by our Federal Bureau of Investigation. We have instructed them not to harm your son when they find him."

Kang had come out of his chair upon hearing his son's name; now he stood staring at the chief of station. "You are lying! How would you know of my son?"

The second man stepped forward. "Sawbaw, I am the chief of station for India. We know of your son because we know Joshua Hawkins. I believe you know him, and—"

"Joshua! You know Joshua? By the gods! If he says Stephen is alive, then by the gods it's true!"

"Sawbaw, Colonel Hawkins was recently involved in an operation to find out if the junta was involved in heroin production. Colonel Hawkins and others were infiltrated into Burma and witnessed the destruction of a drug facility and the village of Shaduzup. After the operation he spoke to me about you. He had previously talked to a member of military intelligence about your son, Stephen. This afternoon we received word that your son entered the U.S. on June 5. We don't know where he is and we don't know why he killed the other men. We have come here today because you are the last hope for your country. Could we at least sit down and talk?"

"Where is Joshua?" Kang asked impatiently.

"Sawbaw, he is in the United States. We believe your son will be trying to reach him."

Kang spun around to face Colonel Banta, who was leaning against the bamboo wall. "The gods have willed it. Stephen and Joshua will be coming to join us."

Banta nodded with sadness. "Yes, Mya and the others will be revenged. Our people in Rangoon are waiting for your orders to begin."

The India chief of station held up his hand. "Wait a minute, you don't understand. I didn't say anything about the colonel or your son com—"

"You're the one who doesn't understand!" blurted Kang. "I am not the last hope for my country—my son is! And Joshua will come as well, for he is a Shan! By the gods, they will return to me!"

"I don't know about the gods, Sawbaw, but I do know your son has a lot of questions to answer and—"

"They will come because you will see to it. I am not a fool. You are here because your country feels threatened by the new government, and I have the only army left to do your dirty work. Help me, then. Bring Stephen here. Tell him his son is with me and that I will help him avenge his wife's death. That is all the assistance I need from you."

The Americans exchanged looks. The Thai station chief glanced at

Banta, then shifted his eyes to Xu Kang. "Your colonel said something about having people in Rangoon. Do you have a network in place? Knowing would help us consider your proposal."

Xu Kang's lips curled back in a humorless smile. "We knew about my son's wife dying in Dinto prison because we have blackmailed the sergeant of the guard for years. We know about all the people they have killed. We have loyal people everywhere within the city, and more join us every day. We also have something that might interest you very much. One of our teams in Rangoon captured a DDSI lieutenant. He and his men shot a marine guard and some men in a car before a truck hit the car and blew up within your embassy. The lieutenant foolishly spoke of his bravery to his girlfriend, who is part Shan. The officer is now without his toes and three of his fingers, but he eventually told our people everything. They are bringing him here to the camp tomorrow. He will be my gift to your government."

The Thai chief of station looked at the other chief, then said, "We will need to contact our headquarters about your proposal, but I must tell you there is no guarantee the FBI will find your son."

Xu Kang walked to the hut window and looked at a small boy playing with two other children. The old warrior said in an emotional whisper, "He will come."

Washington, D.C.

Josh glanced at his watch. "It's slow tonight, Pete."

The off-duty police officer took another peek at the woman beside his boss and said, "Why don't you knock off early, Hawk? This storm has kept most of the customers at home. You look tired anyway. I can handle the rounds, and if something comes up, I'll call you on the Motorola."

Josh patted the officer's shoulder. "Yeah, thanks, I'll be less than five minutes away." He approached Grant and said, "Sorry you didn't see much action tonight."

She smiled. "I saw enough." She changed her voice and repeated what he had said to a drunk customer an hour before. " 'Sir, don't cause a scene, since it will be very embarrassing to you.' Did I get it right?"

Josh rolled his eyes. "Come on, I was good. Don't make light of my performance."

"Let's go to my place and have a beer. I wasn't finished talking to you last night when you interrupted me by snoring."

Josh looked down at his shoes so as not to have to face her. "I'd really like to, Glenn, but . . ." He raised his head and looked into her eyes. "I'm feeling things that I haven't felt in a long time. I don't trust myself alone with you."

She smiled and leaned closer to him. "Don't make a scene—just take my arm and walk me home. We'll discuss this as we watch the storm from the balcony."

Josh didn't know how it happened. He didn't use any lines or make any moves. It just happened. They were standing on the balcony sopping wet, taking in the power of the storm, when she was suddenly in his arms. Lightning flashed and he saw the look in her eyes. They kissed just as the thunder cracked and rumbled across the turbulent black sky. The storm grew more intense, but the couple was no longer there to feel it. Inside the apartment the bedroom door closed, shutting the storm, and the rest of world, out.

CHAPTER 18

University Hospital, Washington, D.C.

Josh set the Styrofoam container on the bed. "Here, Jean says she misses ya, especially your big tips."

Kelly tapped the lid, which had writing on it. "Hawk Special? Tell her I'm gonna wring her neck, then give her a big kiss. Thanks, Hawk. I need some real food."

Josh handed his friend napkins from the bag. "You're lookin' better."

Kelly stuck a big portion of the gravy-covered eggs in his mouth. He closed his eyes, murmuring and nodding as he chewed, then said, "Some storm last night, huh?"

"Have you looked outside, Shamrock? It's not over. The forecast is for another couple days of this. The streets are already flooded."

Kelly took a quick bite of the omelet and stabbed the air with his finger for emphasis.

"You ain't gonna believe this. The commissioner got a letter saying he'd better lay off busting dealers. It was a real piece of work; it says the trouble we had with the players was nothing but business, and we better not get involved. It was a threat letter. No signature, but it had a green circle where the signature should be. He sent copies to all the precincts and departments and told 'em to push harder and find the assholes."

Josh shook his head when he saw his friend had gotten himself worked up. "Why don't you take this time in the hospital to relax? Forget work, read, talk to Mary and the boys, watch television, do puzzles—hell, anything but stay on the phone connected to the job. I saw Mary outside and she said she's worried about you."

Kelly's eyes narrowed. "They made it personal when they killed Nolan."

"They shot you too, Kelly. You're out of action for a while. Take a break; enjoy it while you can."

Kelly eyed his friend as he took another bite. He chewed for a while, then waved his fork at Josh. "You look different this morning. You get that big turtle . . . or you get laid?"

Josh felt his face flushing and quickly averted his eyes. Kelly grinned with his mouth full. "Who, the looker you brought with you yesterday? Mary said she was stacked."

Josh waved the question away and focused on the hospital regulations posted behind Kelly's bed. "Shut up and eat, will ya?"

Kelly broke into an even wider grin. "Well, ain't this some shit? I'm not tellin' anybody, so relax. Hey, I got good news and some bad news. The good is I gave the profile you gave me yesterday to my guys and you were right as fuckin' rain. We've got a list of probables for this head Sancho Chink."

"San," Josh corrected.

"Whatever. The guys have narrowed the list down to six, but I think Mr. Big is number two on our list. The guys came over last night after doin' some checkin'." Kelly picked up a computer printout from the nightstand. "Listen ta this: Mr. Dorba. No last name, just Dorba. An exporter, no less, Far Eastern goods from bikes to rice beer. He's connected, I can smell it."

"How come you're so sure?"

"Just listen to the facts, okay? The guy arrived five months ago from Hong Kong and bought himself, in cash, a mansion over in Bethesda, overlooking the Potomac. It's one of those walled-in estates with security cameras, guards, the works. He's renting an entire seven-story office building in Chinatown, all black glass and stocked with classy Chink lookers. My team tried the fire inspection routine but couldn't get past the Chink security guards on the first floor. We checked with the phone company, and Dorba's company has rented the most sophisticated communications equipment on the market. The business is called the Asian Import and Export Company. And yeah, that Hong Kong paper you wrote down, *South China Morning Post*, is delivered to their front door every morning. Also, the Chink cook from the mansion picked up a basket of turtle meat from Ky's last night. The boys are stakin' out the office to ID all the well-to-do businessmen who go into the office building. This morning, when this Dorba Chink goes to work, the third precinct is gonna sic a roller on him to do a little roust and get a look-see. My bet is the man is dirty. Nobody spends that kinda bucks anymore except connected people. He's syndicate."

"You got him tapped?" Josh asked.

"The judges say no probable cause. Payin' cash for a mansion ain't a crime in this town."

Josh eyed his friend. "I didn't ask if it was legal. I worked with you, remember?"

Kelly shrugged. "Okay, Nolan had friends. Yeah, we got a tap. Nothin'. You know how hard it is to find a badge who speaks Chink? And not just any Chink, 'cause we do have one guy, but he says the house staff is talkin' some kind of different Chink that he doesn't know."

"Cantonese, if he's connected to the Triad," said Josh matter-of-factly.

"Yeah, Cantonese." Kelly took another bite and spoke with his mouth full. "He's just another dirty slicky boy. He'll fuck up and we'll be there."

"Not you, remember?" Josh said pointedly.

Kelly waved it off. "You know what I mean."

Josh's brow furrowed. "Be very careful, Shamrock. The Triad plays hardball. You're not dealing with average scuzzballs here. You should have seen the Hong Kong police officers who spoke to us—they were some really depressed cops. The Triad broke them by putting hits on their families. If you're gonna take them on, make sure Mary and the twins are protected. I mean it. If they sent that letter, it was exactly what it said it was, a warning. The Hong Kong boys got the same thing. The Triad means it."

"This ain't Hong Kong, Hawk, and they can't get away with that shit here. We know how to handle tough guys."

"If that was the good news, I'm sure not sure I wanna hear the bad," Josh said, frowning.

Kelly shrugged. "The heroin hit the streets yesterday, good stuff, 95 percent pure high. The really bad news is, it's cheap. The dealers are almost givin' it away. You'd better warn your people tonight. This town is flyin'."

Josh couldn't take any more bad news. He took a bottle of hot sauce from his jacket pocket, put it on the nightstand, and sat on the edge of the bed. "I gotta go—my super trap is ready for pickup. Kelly, I'm serious. Get Mary and the twins covered. Your name was in the papers, so they know it was you who made the bust the other night. Do it today, and tell your guys the facts. They have to know what they're up against. Okay?"

Kelly rolled his eyes. "Jesus, you act like a mother hen sometimes! Alright, already. Shit, go catch King Kong and leave me alone, will ya?"

Josh got up and walked toward the door. Kelly waited until he had grasped the doorknob before shifting his eyes to him and speaking in a soft whisper. "Hawk, thanks."

Josh winked and walked out.

Bob Stevenson rose up from behind the desk when his dripping boss walked in the office door. He held out a note to him. "You sure know some interesting people, boss."

Josh looked at the yellow piece of paper. "Director Jennings of the CIA called *me*?"

"Well, his secretary did. There's a big druggie conference over at the Roosevelt Hilton tomorrow. The secretary said the director was inviting you as his special guest to watch and listen. He wanted to see what you thought of the programs being proposed."

Josh tossed the note in the trash can. "That's what I think of it. Anything else?"

Bob's eyes widened and he rushed to the trash can. "Damn, boss, the papers have been talking about this conference for weeks. Big decisions are going to be made. Plus, you don't get an invitation from the director of the CIA every day. How does he know you, by the way?"

Josh leaned against the wall and ignored the last question. "Let me tell ya somethin'. I read the articles this morning. If it's in the papers, it means it's a show, ya got it? Sure, the paper says it's a closed conference, but what it means is the big boys are going over stuff the staff did months ago. It's a dog and pony show for the press so the administration can say they're gettin' tough on drugs."

Bob shrugged and said, "It's almost like turning down dinner at the White House. I think you're missing an opportunity, boss."

"Look, if you want to know what happens at the conference, ask Glenn tomorrow evening. She's going."

Bob raised his eyes to his boss with a smile. "Stefne said you were getting along pretty good with the lady colonel. Is this getting serious?"

"I'm too old for serious. Now shut up and quit grinnin' at me," Josh growled as he headed for the door. He looked back over his shoulder. "It's too wet and choppy for huntin' so I think I'll work on my Jeep. I'll be down in the Channel Inn's underground park. Be ready to play raquetball at one. Kelly tells me lots of heroin hit the streets yesterday, so we'd better bring in an extra rover for tonight."

"Got it, boss," Bob said as Josh opened the office door and walked out into the rain.

Meg was nursing a cup of coffee at the table when Josh walked into the cabin to find his tools. She came over all the time and made herself at home. He took off his rain jacket and poured himself a cup of coffee. As soon as he faced her she grinned like a wolf.

"*Windsong* do all right in the blow last night?" he asked, sitting across from her.

She pushed her red bangs out of her eyes and nodded. "I lost my electricity for a while and came over to see if you could help me, but *you* weren't here." Her eyes began twinkling. "It's about time you found a lady. I was getting worried about you. Now tell me everything."

"Meg, for cryin' out loud. I'm not gonna sit here and talk about my love life."

Meg pouted for two seconds before grinning again. "Too bad, I was hoping to get all excited. Hon, you stick with that lady. She's good for you." She locked her eyes on him and leaned closer. "Tell me, what's going on? I saw those men come in here yesterday before you went to work."

Josh sighed. "Nothing gets past you, does it, Meg? I swear, you know everything I do."

"Almost everything," she said, eyeing him. "So who were they?"

"FBI. They wanted to talk to me and bug my phone."

Meg rolled her eyes. "Yeah, sure. Come on, who were they?"

"Meg, they were really, truly, honest-to-god FBI agents. You remember I talked about Stephen, my friend in Burma? Well he's in the States and in some trouble. The FBI thinks he may try and get in touch with me. I'm telling you this because he probably will. There's a couple of agents hanging around so don't get antsy if you see a pair of guys snoopin' around. If you see people you don't know around my boat, just call me. Whatever you do, don't confront them—just call and stay out of the picture."

Meg's face had become pale as he spoke. She grabbed his hand in a vicelike grip. "Are you in danger?"

"Me? Heck no. Stephen is like a brother, but I don't trust the Bureau. They always pull their guns before thinking. Don't look so scared. Probably nothin' is gonna happen, so don't worry about it."

She released her grip slowly and got up with a cold glare. "Great, now I won't sleep nights worrying about you. Damn you, why can't you be like normal people?"

Josh canted his head to the side and looked at her with a grin. "You, of all people, are saying *I'm* not normal?"

She smiled. "Okay, so we aren't like the temps. I'll keep an eye out, but I won't get in the way. Stefne knows about all this, right?"

"Yeah, and bitchin' up a storm. Talk to her, will ya? I can't get her to calm down. It's best for Stephen to come in, and this way nobody gets hurt. I know him, and I'm sure he has a damn good excuse for his troubles."

"I'll talk to her as soon as she gets here. I gotta go, I have classes to teach. And Josh, thanks. I'm glad ya told me."

Josh nodded in silence.

As soon as the cabin door closed the phone rang. All calls were taken at the office, so his phone almost never rang unless it was Stefne calling for him. She, Kelly, and Meg were the only ones who had his direct-line number. He picked up the handset, knowing it wasn't Stef. "Hawkins."

"Why'd you tell her about us?"

" 'Cause she's family and has to know." Josh looked out the porthole toward the Channel Inn's third-floor room on the end. "You guys comfortable?"

"We're a little upset that you said we pulled our pieces before thinking."

"I was trying to make a point. Meg is good people and knows everybody on the Front. She made you two as soon as you showed your faces around the pier."

"Okay, Mr. Hawkins, we understand. Do us a favor, will you? When you use the latrine, shut the door. The mikes we put in your boat are very sensitive, and that song you were singing this morning when you were in the shower just about did us in. No offense, but you're no Conway Twitty."

Josh walked over to the porthole. "Look out your window. Can you see this?" He stuck his middle finger up to the porthole glass.

"Yeah, we see it."

"Good. No offense."

The cruiser waited until the black Chrysler was two miles from the estate before speeding up to close in. The third precinct sergeant behind the wheel glanced at his partner. "Remember, make it look routine, but check 'em out good. You got the paper?"

The partner nodded with a smile. "Yeah, this is a piece of cake."

They followed the car another block before turning on the bubble machine. The big Chrysler pulled into the parking lot of a 7-Eleven.

The two police officers approached the vehicle from opposite sides. The sergeant knocked on the car's roof and spoke loudly. "Lower all of the tinted windows so I can see you and the occupants, but please remain in the vehicle."

He waited until the driver's window had rolled down. "Sir, please step out of the car. I will need to see your license and registration. Please tell the other occupants to remain seated in the vehicle and keep their hands where my partner can see them."

"Why are you stopping us?" snapped Dorba, leaning forward from the backseat.

"Sir, your driver failed to yield for a pedestrian in a walkway one mile back. Please sit back and remain quiet."

The driver, a thick-shouldered Oriental, glared up at the sergeant and spoke Chinese to the front-seat passenger beside him before opening the door.

"Freeze!" the officer said, placing his hand on his holster. He barked to his partner, "This one is carrying. Check yours."

Fifteen minutes later the two smiling officers got back in their car. They'd followed the rules of being polite but had been very thorough in checking all the paperwork, especially the weapons permits.

The sergeant motioned to the Chrysler as it backed up and pulled out onto the road. "Did you hear that? The driver told me he was a driver and gardener. He was wearing an eight-hundred-dollar shark-skin suit and two-hundred-dollar shoes—a gardener?"

His partner grinned. "Mine said he was maintenance man for the estate. I asked him why a maintenance man needed a nine-millimeter, and you know what he says to me? Rats. Yeah, he says rats. Can you believe the balls of that Chink ta say that ta me with a straight face? Mr. Big in the back was not a happy camper. You notice he wrote down our badge numbers."

The sergeant started the engine. "We better call it in and tell 'em what we got. You have your paper?"

The second cop motioned to the top form attached to his clipboard. It was standard practice to make the occupants of a stopped car sign a form that was conveniently dropped so they had to pick it up and put their prints on the special paper. "It got a little wet, but the prints will be fine. I have one Mr. Big signed for me, too. You think the detectives will get these guys?"

"Have you ever worked with the guys in Narcotics and Special Ops? They don't always play by the rules. If these big-money Chinks are dirty, they'll be going down. Bank on it."

•   •   •

Josh shook his head. "You're not trying."

Bob tossed him the raquetball. "You have a problem, boss. You don't feel pain. I'm beat. You've run me ragged and whipped my ass five games straight. This is not fun."

Josh shrugged. "It is for me. Come on, one more game and I'll let up on my serve."

Bob shook his head dejectedly and walked for the door. "I've had it. Find somebody else to humiliate."

"Hold it," Josh said, louder than he had intended. "I'm sorry. I just needed to win today. When you're my age, you'll understand. Come on, I'll buy you a Coke or mineral water or whatever you young guys drink nowadays." He put his arm over Bob's shoulder. "I'm trying to make it right here. Give me a break, huh?"

Bob sighed and walked out with him.

Stefne was seated in the office when Josh and Bob walked in. She gave them both her best evil glare before looking back at her school notes.

"Why aren't you studying on the boat?" Josh asked.

She gave him a sarcastic look. "It's spooky knowing somebody is listening to me breathe. Forget it. I'll stick around here or go back to the apartment later. Dad, I heard at school today that heroin is very plentiful around campus and in Georgetown. The word is it's cheap and really pure. We'd better warn the guys tonight."

Josh looked at Bob and smiled. "God, I love her. She's just like her ole man, always thinkin'." He winked at him. "You heard her, let's put on an extra rover tonight."

Bob played it cool. "I'll get right on it, boss."

Chinatown

Dorba sat beside his desk with his hands folded beneath his chin as he listened to one of his colonels.

"I was stopped by the police after leaving your office. They searched my car as if I were a common criminal. This is an outrage."

Dorba nodded. "It will not happen again. Our lawyers are ensuring that our rights will be not violated anymore."

Dorba shifted his gaze to his young legal adviser. "Michael, do you now see why a lesson is necessary? They have insulted my officers and me. They are obviously watching this building and identifying all those who do business with us. I'm very impressed by the speed with which they have singled us out. They are smarter than I thought. All the more reason for the lesson."

Dorba turned to his chief of staff. "Qui, are you prepared?"

Qui smiled. "The teams have made their reconnaissance where necessary. All is ready."

Michael Woo spoke up with a tremor in his voice. "San Chu, I beg you to reconsider these actions. The police can do nothing, for they have no proof of wrongdoing on our part. Their harassment tactics are a desperate effort on their part. We have nothing to fear, and our lawyers will stop the harassment today. They have had the warning letter for only two days. If you go through with these acts of violence, they will know we are responsible."

Dorba's eyes were cold. "Yes, I know." He looked at Qui. "Tomorrow, when you deem it best."

Qui bowed his head. "The lesson will be delivered, San Chu."

Galesburg, Illinois

A young pilot strolled into the small waiting room and glanced at the seated man before putting two quarters into a soda machine. He pushed the button for a Pepsi, picked up the can, and looked down the narrow hallway in both directions before facing the waiting passenger. "I hear you wanna go east. That right?"

Stephen glanced up from the paper he was reading. "Yes, you know someone heading that way?"

The pilot again looked down the halls. "Yeah, me. I fly for Co-Op Feed Mills. I'm not allowed to take passengers, but if you wanna go to Norfolk, Virginia, I'm leaving in an hour. Two hundred bucks cash sound fair?"

Stephen's alternative was a flight at six that evening going only as far as Mansfield, Ohio. He stood and offered his hand. "Very fair."

The pilot ignored his hand. "Be at the green hangar in thirty minutes, and don't say anything to anybody about this. I could get in a lot of trouble, but I need some cash for my wife's birthday. Half an hour, don't be late." The pilot headed down the hall toward the door.

Waterfront, Washington, D.C.

Glenn Grant found him in Hogate's bar talking to Harry. She leaned against the bar and waited until he was finished talking before winking at him. He walked over and put his arm around her shoulder. "You worked late tonight, I see. You do look good in that uniform, though."

Her eyes searched his face. "Stephen contact you yet?"

"Nope, not a word."

"Well, it's bigger than I thought. The FBI didn't tell us the whole story. I was ordered to Langley this afternoon to see the officer who handles the Burma desk. He gave me a complete rundown on the situation. They've made contact with Xu Kang. They want me to talk to you and get you in."

Josh closed his eyes in relief. "Thank God, the old Lion is still alive."

"Yes, he's alive and in a border camp in Thailand. He has Stephen's son, but there's some very bad news. . . . Stephen's wife died in Dinto prison."

Josh lowered his head, remembering the last time he'd seen her. It was the day he'd been ordered to leave the country. Stephen and Mya had come to the airport. She had hugged him and Jill, crying. Josh felt his eyes moisten, for Mya had become like a sister to him.

Seeing his reaction, Grant spoke softly. "I'm sorry, Josh. Xu Kang wants Stephen back to help lead an insurgency against the government. The Company has agreed."

Josh shook his head. "It's suicide."

"Maybe not. Xu Kang has a big intel network in Rangoon keeping him apprised of the situation. It's not all bad news. Swei is conducting a purge of the minorities who were in the government and all the opposition party leaders. It's caused a quiet revolt. People are leaving the country and joining up with Xu Kang. Lots of people. The Company also has a prisoner given to them by Kang. The prisoner was involved in killing the intelligence community people when the truck hit the embassy. The DDSI did it."

Josh took a deep breath and looked over the crowd. "Let's talk about something else. I've had enough bad news for one day."

"Josh, it's not going to go away. You can't hide in your world and think somebody else will take care of all the problems."

Josh shifted his eyes to her. "I can sure as hell try. I did my part, remember?"

Grant nodded slowly, seeing he was hurt by the news about Mya. She reached up and stroked his face. "Come over when you get off work, and we'll both get away for a while. I promise I'll take your mind off today."

He smiled lightly. "That's the best offer I've had in a long time. I'll be there."

"You know the code to get in and have a key, so let yourself in. Wake me up if I'm asleep—I need you to hold me."

Josh gave her a gentle hug. "I'm not gonna stay here much longer; it's slow."

"Good. I'll see you in a bit then."

He watched her walk away and felt sick inside. It was as if a small piece of him had died when he heard Mya was dead. Again his eyes began to water, and he turned toward the men's room. Before he got there, an FBI agent leaned against the bar and said, out of the side of his mouth, "Go to the kitchen, now."

Josh never looked at the man or acknowledged his presence. He glanced over the crowd routinely and slowly ambled through the kitchen door.

The other agent was waiting for him and handed him a picture. "We're not the only ones watching you."

"Who are they?" Josh asked, studying the picture of two Latino men in a new BMW.

"We're not sure just yet, but they're pros, that's for sure. We spotted them when you left the lady's apartment early this morning and walked back to your boat. These two are just one team—they sit in the apartment parking lot and roll when you drive. Three women and one man in another team are watching you at work. They're good. They change their looks by using glasses and wigs. This is no small-time tail operation. It's strictly pro and is costing somebody big bucks. Could be the mob or—"

"Chinese," Josh said, finishing the sentence.

The agent smirked. "You're way ahead of us. Yeah, it could be the Triad, which means they are looking for Kang too. This is all beginning to stink. Kang must know something, so you're now in big-time danger."

The agent picked up a bag and dumped it on the table. "Take this and wear it. We heard you know how to use it." He handed Josh a shoulder holster with a nine-millimeter Beretta.

Josh took off his jacket to put on the holster. "You takin' them down or gonna watch them and hope for bigger fish?"

The agent held the holster straps as Josh ran one arm through. "The brass says watch them. We have two more teams assigned, including some tech boys. The ones tailing you on the job call in to the guys in the BMW, as best we can tell. Our tech guys will be able to monitor all those calls and any the car boys make to their bosses. We don't think they know about us. We were lucky—our surveillance was loose because we knew your schedule. Which reminds me. Are you going to visit the lady again tonight?"

Josh nodded as he put on his jacket. "Yeah, we're going to talk."

The agent's expression didn't change. "Okay. Just keep an eye out. This is getting big, Hawkins, real big."

                         •   •   •

Glenn was sitting on the couch when he opened her apartment door and walked in. She didn't get up or avert her eyes from the packet she was examining until Josh sat down beside her and said, "Must be good reading."

She made a sour look. "I've been around you too much. I'm getting as cynical as you are on this drug war business. This is a read-ahead packet for the conference tomorrow, and it's all politician double-talk claiming that everything is getting better. Why can't they look at the real issues and do something?"

Josh put his arm around her and gave her a gentle squeeze. "The problem, my dear, is very simple. Nobody is in charge. All the agencies are doing their own thing since nobody is setting priorities or writing out a plan for all of them to follow. They won't dare let another agency take the lead because it could mean a loss of funds for their organization. Don't worry about it. Relax and come into my world. It's the only way you'll be able to keep your sanity."

She yielded to his touch and laid her head back against his shoulder. Suddenly she sat up and pulled back his coat. "So that's what poked me. You're now carrying a pistol on the job?"

Josh reached out and pulled her back to his shoulder. "Naw, it's the last option to make you go to bed with me."

She smiled and settled against him again. "I'm here to be caught, best turtle catcher on the Potomac."

Josh's lips curled back in a grin. "Let's go to bed and discuss really important stuff like traps and bait."

"Whoa, you have to catch me first. What kind of bait are you going to use?"

He pushed aside her robe and ran his hand slowly up her bare leg toward her inner thigh. "I thought I'd coax you into the trap this time."

She shuddered with his touch and closed her eyes, breathing heavily. "It's working . . . Ohh . . . Don't stop . . . Ohhhh yes."

Josh couldn't seem to get close enough as he pressed against her, feeling her warmth and building passion. He felt her every tremor and heard every murmur as they moved faster and harder against each other. He didn't want it to end and strained to hold on to the moment, but he wasn't strong enough.

CHAPTER 19

Kelly looked at the writing on the Styrofoam container and grinned. "She got it right this time—'Kelly Special'. God, I love that wench."

Josh passed him the hot sauce and napkins with an accusing stare. "What'd you do last night?"

Kelly eyed him cautiously. "You're settin' me up. You talked to Mary, didn't ya?"

"Yeah, I saw her outside as she was leavin'. She's going to throw your ass out on the street unless you start payin' attention to her. And I'll snap her and the twins up in a heartbeat."

"The guys came over and we went over some things, that's all."

"Mary said they left at one in the morning."

"Hey, I'm a cop. Get off my case. I got her covered, so I been listening. You wanna hear what we got, or don't ya?"

Josh pulled up a chair. "I'm listening."

"The uniforms rousted the Sancho yesterday, as well as every Chink who went into his office building who wore a suit. We came up with nine businessmen into everything from dry cleaning to restaurants. They must be his colonels or at least his majors. They were all clean, but now we have their prints and they know we're watchin' them. The Sancho got bent with the rousts and called in some heavy hitters. His big-buck lawyers came first, then that Chink businessman association, the Asian-American Group, and finally the fuckin' American Civil Liberties Union boys with their whining song-and-dance routine. I guess it was quite a show in the mayor's office."

"And?" Josh asked with a knowing smile.

"Look, smart-ass. So we took some heat from the brass. They're nothin' but politicians wearin' uniforms. We made the point and that's what's important. The Chinks know we know, so now the line is drawn. We're gonna wait and see who blinks first. It ain't gonna be us."

"You thought about bringing in the Feds yet? If it's Triad, and it sounds like it is, you're in over your head."

Kelly pointed at himself. "I ain't a cowboy. Sure, we been tellin' the Feds what we got so far. But you know them—unless they have hard proof, they stay in a look-see mode." Kelly lowered his eyes. "You're not gonna like this. Some of our undercover boys bought a bag of the new hero and gave it to the DEA for tests." He looked up at Josh as if in pain. "The DEA says it's from Burma. And they ain't happy about it. They told us it could be the beginning of a whole lotta shit comin' in."

Josh's jaw muscles rippled. Too many things were falling into place. Now he knew why the CIA director had wanted him to attend the conference. Their worst nightmare had come true. The missing heroin from the facilities was on the streets.

Kelly saw the reaction and wrinkled his brow. "We're in a war, Hawk, and we're like the British redcoats, all lined up walking down the road while the players are poppin' us from behind legal eagles and the ACLU. We're gonna have to bend the rules and get the snake's head before this gets out of control."

Josh took a breath and told himself to relax, it wasn't his concern. He got up and patted Kelly's shoulder. "You can do it. I'll watch from the sidelines and cheer you on."

"Talk to Mary for me, Hawk. She listens to you. I tried to explain last night how important this is but she wouldn't listen to me. Talk to her. I'm asking as a friend. She needs to hear it from somebody else, and she trusts you."

Josh forced a smile. "I'll run over and see her after sculling this afternoon. I promise."

Kelly looked toward the window with a distant stare. "I wish I was like you and could get away from all this. I don't see an ending to this."

Josh walked toward the door. "You'll figure something out to get them. Take care, Shamrock. I'll talk to Mary and see ya tomorrow."

Josh walked out into the drizzling rain and looked down the street toward the BMW parked alongside the curb a block away. He wanted to walk up, pull his pistol, and make the bastards tell him why they were making him a player in a game he didn't want to play. Instead, he mumbled, "Screw you" and headed for his Jeep.

Norfolk, Virginia

Stephen awoke and rolled over to look at the alarm clock. It was 12:15 P.M. He groaned but knew he had needed the rest. They had arrived at Patrick Henry Airport just after 4 A.M. and parked in front of a small hangar across the airfield from the much larger commercial passenger terminal. A nearby motel sent a van for him and he'd checked in, paying in advance in cash. He sat down at the room desk and looked at his road atlas. It was only three hours to Washington, D.C. by car. He picked up the briefcase, took out the money he'd taken from the bodies, and found he had a little over three hundred dollars left. It wasn't enough to get back to Burma, but it would get him to Joshua. With renewed hope he quickly showered, changed into comfortable clothes, and called for a cab to take him to a car rental agency downtown. Minutes later, he headed for the lobby, saw his cab, and walked out into the circular drive. Handing his suitcase to the cabby, he looked to the north at the dark, rumbling storm clouds and felt a strange shiver run up his spine.

Georgetown Boathouse, Washington, D.C.

As Josh parked his Jeep by the boathouse, Fred stepped out of his small office and said, "You're not thinkin' about goin' out, are you?"

Josh walked over and lifted the scull off the pegs. He balanced the weight on his shoulders. "Fred, I can't let a little rain screw up my schedule."

"Hell, I'm not worried 'bout the rain, but the river's up and runnin' fast. You ain't gonna get a hundred yards upriver against that current. Better come back when she's down."

Josh continued to carry the lightweight craft toward the swollen banks. "I gotta try it, Fred. If it's too much I'll take her downriver to the tidal basin and call you. Can you come get me and the boat in your truck?"

"Sure, but it seems awfully foolish taking the chance of gettin' swamped or worse."

Josh strode back for the oars but stopped long enough to pat the old man's shoulder. "I need this, Fred. I gotta get away for a while, you understand."

The old man begrudgingly nodded. "Yeah, she gets in your blood and it seems you can't live without her. Be careful, Mr. Hawkins, she's bitchy today."

•   •   •

Fred was wrong. Josh fought the current for three hundred yards up-river before he had to turn about. He was drenched, and his baseball cap was pulled down so far his ears stuck out, but he'd done what he wanted—felt the exhilarating pain of trying to beat her. She'd won like always, but he knew she would at least respect him for his attempt. He soon found out that shooting down the river with the churning current was almost as difficult as going upriver, for he had to avoid the debris and rolling swells that could swamp the scull. He barely had a chance to look toward the shore to see where his tails were. He didn't see them, but knowing they were trying to keep him in sight was a pleasure of its own. Below the Theodore Roosevelt Bridge the river calmed down a little, and he dug in his oars and shot forward like a slender rocket. Beneath his light-weight nylon jacket he was drenched with sweat, but he kept up the breakneck pace. Just a little more pain, he thought, just a little more.

Mary Kelly parked the old station wagon in the driveway and looked over her shoulder at the her twin seven-year-old boys in the backseat. "You both wipe your feet before going in the house. And hide the clothes I bought you. Your dad will have a fit if he knows what I paid for those jeans and T-shirts you two had to have."

"Mom, everybody wears Panama Jack shirts in the summer. It's cool," Mike said, unable to believe his mother didn't understand "in" clothes.

"You'll think 'cool' if your dad finds out," she snapped, and glanced at her watch. "Move it, and get the stuff inside. It's four o'clock, time for 'Oprah.' "

She got out and waved to the young officer in the cruiser that had pulled in behind her. He waved and got out in a hurry. "Hold the boys up, Mary. I need to check the house first."

"You heard him, guys. Hold up."

"Mom, it's raining," complained Todd.

"Open the garage and wait there. I'll yell when it's okay." Mary rolled her eyes at the approaching officer and handed the house keys to him. "Skip, whatever you do, don't have twin boys. You have to push on the door when you hear the click."

"Got it," the officer said with a smile. He opened the door with no problem and stepped in with his hand on his revolver. Mary followed a few seconds later and stood in the entryway. He strolled out of the kitchen and shrugged. "Looks fine. I'll check the upstairs and then I'll get out of here."

Mary sighed, looking at the mess in the living room where the boys had set up a Star Wars base for intergalactic warriors. She walked in to rescue her good couch pillows, then heard a crash. She turned and yelled up the stairs. "Skip? . . . Skip, are you alright?"

Josh had pulled in behind the station wagon and saw the boys standing in the garage. He got out and was about to speak when he heard a bloodcurdling scream from inside the house. He spun and grabbed his holstered pistol from the passenger seat of the Jeep and yelled at the boys as he sprinted toward the house, "Run to the neighbors and call 911!"

He dropped the empty holster on the steps, chambered a round into the pistol, and went through the open door in a shooter's crouch. His blood turned cold—Mary was standing five feet away in the hall with a black man holding a nickel-plated .38 to her head.

"Move and she's dead! Drop the piece and get your hands up!" the black man hollered.

Josh didn't move. "You got it wrong, asshole. You want to shoot me, not her. I'm the one in the way of your getting out of here. Now watch me real close, 'cause I'm gonna lower the pistol so you get your chance."

"Fool, I'm gonna kill her!"

"Me, asshole, you gotta kill me!" Josh barked, watching the man's eyes. Slowly, Josh stood up and began lowering the pistol to his side, waiting for a blink or a movement of the other gun. But the man did something unexpected—he smiled as if he knew an inside joke. Josh heard a creak at the top of the stairs and threw himself into a forward roll. Bullets tore into the wood floor where he had been standing. He was now within a foot of the man holding Mary. The assailant pointed his pistol at Josh's face and grinned. "You're dead, muthafuc—"

There was a thunderous *kaboom,* and the man fell back with a bullet through his heart. Josh threw himself on top of Mary knocking her to the floor as he screamed, "Upstairs!"

There was no need for the warning, for the second FBI agent through the door was already firing. The man upstairs got two shots off before a back portion of his skull flew off and shattered Kelly's framed police academy graduation picture hanging on an upstairs wall.

Josh slowly got off Mary, who was still trying to scream although not a sound came out of her open mouth.

"It's over," he said softly, then hugged her.

The Silverado Room of the Hilton Conference Center was filled with conference-goers. On the stage, a panel of national and state agency and bureau chiefs sat behind small microphones. The afternoon session had been made up primarily of briefings about proposed drug enforcement programs, followed by a concluding question-and-answer period. Grant, seated in the next-to-last row, leaned over to another DIA colonel. She pointed at her watch as she whispered, "They've already gone past four. I've heard enough and think I'll slip out."

The colonel nodded and whispered back, "Yeah, you might as well. The directors left their deputies to answer the questions. Nothing's been said that we couldn't have gotten from *Newsweek*. I'll call you if anything important happens."

Grant picked up her purse and raincoat from beneath her chair and stood up. Excusing herself, she scooted down the close row of chairs, finally made it to the aisle, and strode for the guarded rear doors. Stepping into the lobby, she gently closed the door behind her and saw a friend from the DEA leaning against the wall smoking a cigarette. Grant walked over to her as she put on her raincoat. "What'd you think, Shirley?"

The woman shook her head. "We're wasting our time. Nothing is going to work until we get some leadership. Did you hear the way the agencies bickered?"

Grant shrugged. "A friend of mine says we need one person in charge."

"Your friend is right. This is a joke. I'm finishing this cigarette, then going home and try to forget this fiasco. You want to join me?"

"Thanks, but no, I found a little world where I can get away. I'm going there now and—"

An ear-shattering explosion inside the conference room ended their conversation. Both women's eyes closed in nature's response to the horrific noise. Neither one saw the conference room's doors blow off the hinges and become lethal projectiles that slammed into the reporters and attendees unlucky enough to be standing in front of them. The blast cloud roared into the lobby, leveling everything and everybody like a giant tidal wave. Grant and Shirley were not in the direct path of the invisible wave, but were caught in its wake and blown down the hallway like bits of cork.

The 4:15 Blue Line Metro train slowed and came to a stop at the Arlington Cemetery Station. Unlike the previous crammed stops at Roslyn, Foggy Bottom, and McPherson Square, the platform here had only a few waiting passengers. The doors of the train opened and three men stepped out of different cars as the few new riders hunched their shoulders and tried to push their way into the tightly compacted mass of commuters. None of the passengers on board the departing train noticed the briefcases the three men had left behind under the seats.

The three Nigerians walked straight for the exit as the train rolled into the tunnel toward its next stop, the Pentagon.

Hundreds of eager commuters waiting on the Pentagon platform saw the lights flash to warn them a train was inbound, and they began jockeying for position. The Pentagon station was a change-out point. Those who worked in midtown and lived in the outlying communities took the Blue Line to the Pentagon, then they got off and took the escalator to the aboveground Metro bus station. There they could catch a bus to their neighborhoods. Those waiting on the belowground platform and those staying on the train would take the Blue Line to stops in Crystal City and Alexandria.

The train became visible in the black tunnel and the waiting throng began the final press forward. Blue Line Train 23 came to a halt and the doors opened to release the human flood.

Five seconds later, at exactly 4:18, the first car, its passengers, and those waiting to board it disappeared in a flash of light, heat, and debris. Milliseconds later, two identical blasts came from two other cars. Within the huge concrete and steel tunnel, the confined blast rebounded off the ceiling like a rubber ball and roared down the man-made tubes like an invisible locomotive, destroying everything in its fury.

Glenn Grant walked with a painful limp through the wisps of smoke that rose up from the blackened floor littered with chairs and shattered bodies. The pathetic moans seemed oddly louder than the screaming clean people who were shouting as they ran through the debris, searching for survivors. The clean ones were those who had not been inside—they were the living. She approached the shattered remains of the stage and halted. Her burning eyes swept over the carnage and she slowly turned, her eyes capturing it all like an imaginary video camera. The vacant stares, shoeless feet, a notepad, an unbroken glass in the hand of what was left of a man—or a woman; she couldn't tell—it didn't matter. She had to get it all, keep moving, capture it, keep it for . . . for . . .

"Lady, are you alright? Over here! This one's in shock. Get her to the lobby with the others!"

Josh sat beside Mary in the back of a cruiser with his arm around her shoulders and said softly, "It's going to be alright. These officers will take you and the boys to your mother's. They'll stay with you all the time so you can take it easy."

"How . . . how is Skip?" she asked through her sobs.

Josh shook his head. He had found the officer dead in the upstairs hall with his throat cut. "He didn't make it, Mare, but don't think about it, just think how lucky you and the boys are. These officers called in a warning to other precincts, and they're getting the word out to all the families to take precautions. Mary, I have to go now. I have to go downtown and make out a statement. You know the routine. I'll come by your mom's later and check on you." He gave her one more hug and called the boys over. "Okay, you guys get in and take care of your mom."

He closed the door and nodded to the officer behind the wheel, who pulled away from the curb.

A detective motioned him over to the cruiser where he and the two FBI agents were standing. The detective shook his head as Josh approached. "We turned off the radio in the roller Mary is in so as not to disturb her any more. Hawk, the city is so full of code-four emergencies, we can't track them all. There's been a hotel bombing and four or five Metro train bombings in the past couple of minutes, plus it looks like at least two families have been hit."

Josh's face paled and his knees almost buckled. "What stations?" he yelled. "My daughter takes the Metro!"

One of the FBI agents took Josh's arm, seeing he was about to lose it. "She's probably already back at the Front. Go on and we'll follow you. These guys have got to roll to the code fours. They've agreed that we can fill out statements later."

Josh climbed into his Jeep, gunned the engine, backed up, and threw it into first gear. Shifting to second, he saw the white BMW parked next to the curb a block away and floored the accelerator. Screeching to a halt beside the car, he startled the two passengers by jumping out of the Jeep holding his pistol. "Get the fuck out. Now!" he screamed.

Both men opened their doors and stood up with their hands in the air. He lowered the pistol and fired a bullet into the right front tire, took a step, and fired again at the right rear tire. Walking toward the two men, he waved the pistol. "On your faces!"

Neither man moved. Josh slugged one in the stomach and pointed his pistol in the face of the other. "Down!"

As the man began to squat Josh brought the pistol butt down on his head, knocking him to the ground. Leaning over the bleeding man, he jammed the pistol barrel into his forehead. "You tell the fucker who hired you I'm going to kill him. Tell him that!"

Josh backed up, keeping both men covered, then turned and fired into their radiator. The FBI car pulled up behind him and the driver jumped out. "Jesus, Hawkins! What the hell do you think you're doing?"

"I'm fucking tired of this! I'm going, so get back in."

Josh climbed back into his Jeep and pulled away. He drove with tears in his eyes and glanced at the empty space where the radio should be. He'd taken it out a year earlier to fix it, and it was still on the boat where he'd left it. He couldn't even listen to the news. "Shit!" He shifted to second gear and floored the accelerator.

Josh sped into the Channel Inn underground parking lot and jumped out of the Jeep at a dead run for the back exit. The FBI car pulled in and the driver yelled out his window, "We're gonna pick up the other tails!"

Josh ran through the beating rain to the marina gate. As soon as the metal door opened he yelled, "STEFNE! STEFNE!"

He saw a woman on deck and felt a wave of relief but then heard Meg yelling, "She's not here! Oh God, where is she?" Meg ran toward him, her wet hair plastered to her face. "Oh God, Josh! Where is she?"

She ran into his open arms, nearly knocking him over. She was as pale as a sheet and soaking wet. Her body was shaking so hard he could barely hold her. "Jo . . . Josh, I heard it on the ra . . . radio. . . . I've been wait . . . ing on you . . . both."

He hugged her tighter and turned toward *Windsong*. "Did you hear what stations were bombed?" he asked, trying to be calm for both of them.

"N . . . n . . . no. I came . . . up on deck . . . t . . . to wait."

"We're gonna get you out of these wet clothes and warm you up. We'll watch TV and listen to the radio and find out. Think positive— we have to think positive."

Josh shut his watering eyes and hugged Meg, who had collapsed against him when they heard the update over the radio. They were in her cabin, watching the television and listening to the radio for reports. There had been three, not five, Metro stations destroyed by explosions—the Blue Line's Pentagon station, the Orange Line's West Falls Church station in Fairfax County, and the Red Line's Bethesda station. All were outside of midtown, and none were the lines Stefne would have taken from school.

Josh hugged Meg again and opened his eyes to look at the screen. A newswoman from a local station was standing in front of the Hilton. Behind her were fire trucks and ambulances. He pressed the Sound button on the remote control just as the camera panned to the news-woman's right to show a grassy area that was lined with covered bodies.

". . . and due to the shortage of emergency equipment the bodies of those taken from the conference room have been placed here. Many of the injured are reportedly still in the lobby awaiting ambulances, and—"

"They bombed a hotel too?" Meg asked, still trembling.

Joshua was staring at the screen, his face stricken.

Meg was about to ask what was wrong when she heard a familiar voice outside. Josh got to his feet first and ran out of the cabin yelling, "Stefne!"

Stefne watched her father walk out the cabin door. She looked back at Meg and saw tears running down the woman's cheeks. She reached over the table and took Meg's hand. "He'll be fine. He has to find out."

Meg nodded and wiped her eyes. "I know, I know . . . God, I hope she's okay. I told him just yesterday he needed to hold on to the lady colonel."

Seeing a traffic jam ahead, Josh pulled off the road and parked on the grassy center median. Getting out of his Jeep, he began a slow jog, knowing it would be the only way to get there. It took him ten min-utes to reach the sprawling grounds of the hotel complex that now looked like a war zone. He made his way forward through the crowd of anxious people who had come searching for a loved one or a friend. He skirted the crowd that had gathered at the main entrance, which was blocked by a wooden police barrier and a single MPD officer. Josh approached the officer and flashed the old temporary badge Kelly had given him when he worked for the department.

"Crime scene D-one," he said as he walked by. The officer, busy trying to calm the crowd, only nodded.

Josh saw why they had only the one officer at the barrier as soon as he passed the screen of fire trucks. Every available person was tending to the injured or carrying bodies. He saw that even the TV news crews had been pressed into service. Walking along the sidewalk, he saw every imaginable wound within twenty feet, and he knew some would never make it unless they got medical attention quickly. An older man covered in what looked like black soot leaned against the hotel wall, staring blankly up at the grumbling sky. Blood trickled down from an ugly scalp wound and puddled in his lap.

Josh knelt down, took a handkerchief from the man's pocket, and held it against the wound. "You're going to have to keep this in place until you get help," Josh said calmly.

The man's eyes slowly rolled to Josh. "What happened? Do you know what happened?"

Josh lifted the man's hand to the already blood-soaked handkerchief. "There was an explosion. The important thing is that you're alive. Hold that in place and put some pressure on it. You're going to be fine."

Josh got up and walked inside the lobby. The smell hit him first, followed by the silence. It was a living hell—blackened people, lying and sitting against the walls and furniture. Those with their eyes open seemed dazed. Despite horrible gashes and tears in their limbs or bodies, none spoke or made a sound. The marble floor was slick with coagulated blood and mud and covered with shattered glass. The smell of the blood and burnt flesh was overpowering. He gagged, fought back the bile, and continued to search. Paramedics from the ambulances dashed about from one blackened body to the next, moving those with lesser injuries outside. He heard a helicopter landing outside and knew they'd soon be getting them out to be attended to. A minute passed, then five, and he still had not found her. He was about to give up and go out to check the dead when he saw her. She was sitting against a wall in the lobby, and she was rocking back and forth. Beside her a man was writhing on the floor, holding his hands over his face.

Josh kneeled down and lifted Grant's chin. "You ready to go home?" he asked softly. It took a moment for her eyes to focus, then tears began welling. She tried to speak but nothing came out. He gently ran his hands over her body feeling for wounds or broken bones before cautiously lifting her to her feet. She was like a rag doll, unable to stand on her own. He picked her up and walked out the door.

The Waterfront bars and restaurants were packed full of customers, but not the usual tourists. The people who sat silently at the tables or on the floor were stranded commuters. They watched the televisions or huddled around radios brought out by the staff. The Metro trains and buses had stopped running after the first explosions, leaving midtown office workers with no way home. Although they were safe, there was no way to get in contact with their waiting families at

home to tell them they were okay. The phone lines in and out of the city were overloaded with desperate callers seeking word of their loved ones. The restaurant staffs were dead on their feet, since most of the evening shift had not showed up for work. Outside it was a ghost town. People were staying indoors, afraid to leave the safety of homes, apartments, offices, or bars. The city was in shock.

Josh walked into the lobby of Hogate's and spotted Bob talking to a long line of people in front of the phones. "Folks, you're wasting your time standing here. The lines are all overloaded and the news reported their having to dedicate lines for emergency use only. I'm sorry, but everyone is in the same boat. Please clear a passage in the lobby so others can come in. The management will let you know when the phones are working again."

Josh took Bob's arm and steered him toward the door. "We're probably going to be the entire shift tonight, since our people will probably be called out to help in the city."

Bob nodded with resignation and asked, "How is Glenn?"

Josh nodded. "Okay. Stef and Meg are with her at her apartment. They have her soaking in the tub. She's bruised real bad, but she'll be fine. She was lucky."

The voices of the crowd inside the bar suddenly got loud and angry. Josh and Bob strode into the bar to investigate as the television news announcer said, ". . . and I repeat, this is just in from sources at the *Washington Post*. A group calling itself the Islamic Revolution Jihad Committee has claimed responsibility for today's bombings. The cassette tape delivered to the *Post* this evening claims the bombings are retaliation for the Islamic brothers slain by U.S. troops during Desert Storm in 1991. The tape promises more killing until America is brought to its knees. . . ."

Josh abruptly spun around and walked back out into the lobby, knowing it was a lie. Bob joined him seconds later, shaking his head. "It was bound to happen sooner or later, but I don't think any of us really believed it would."

Josh's jaw muscles twitched as he stared out the window into the darkness.

Stephen sat in a Quantico motel bar watching the news along with packed tables of hushed customers who were, like himself, unable to get into Washington. Hours before, he'd pulled off I-95 when he saw the backup of traffic. He had been one of the lucky ones and got a room before the rush began. The news later reported that traffic on I-95 had come to a virtual standstill. There were no police available to clear the accidents and those that were available were trying to keep the left lanes open for emergency vehicles coming in from other towns to help with the large number of casualties. The traffic was reported to be backed up as far as Fredericksburg to the south and Frederick, Maryland, to the north. Stephen sat in a corner booth of the dark room with people he didn't know, nursing a gin and tonic and watching the news updates. The people around him were past mad; they wanted blood. Tears trickled down his cheeks—he knew how they felt. During the past days, realization had set in. Mya and his son would not have been able to take more than a few days in prison. Time had run out. The stories from Dinto were never spoken except in whispers among the people. To be taken there meant unspeakable tortures and certain death. His hands trembled with hatred and guilt.

An older woman sitting beside him leaned over and patted his shaking hand. "I'm scared too. My son works at the Pentagon. I don't know what to do."

Stephen took her hand in his. "We can pray."

CHAPTER 20

Josh awoke when Glenn stirred against him. She patted his cheek and slowly got up, testing her mobility. He reached for her hand to coax her back to the bed but she stepped out of reach. "I've got to go in to work and report what happened. They don't know if I'm alive or dead."

Josh, still fully dressed, nodded. "I'll drive you."

She saw his concern and gave him a smile. "I'd better drive myself. I don't know when I'll be back and I can't call or take the Metro. You take care of Stef and check on your police friend. I'm fine. Really."

He saw in her eyes that she wasn't but also saw she needed him to let her go. He nodded again and got up to kiss her cheek. "Take it easy today," he murmured.

Josh walked into *Lil' Darlin*'s bedroom and abruptly stopped. Bob was curled around Stef on the bed that they had not turned down. It was good to see that she had been protected. He stepped back into the galley and called, "Anybody for coffee?"

Bob came out first, looking embarrassed. He began to speak but Josh motioned to the stove. "Thanks for staying with her. Put some water on, will ya?"

Stefne walked into the tiny kitchen and sat down as if in a trance. "Dad, this is all a nightmare. Bob and I stayed at Meg's most of the night watching TV. It's so horrible."

Josh reached over and took his daughter's hand. "Be thankful we're all okay."

249

Stefne looked at her father. "Where's Glenn? Is she alright?"

"She had to get to work and report in. Look, the city is going to be turned upside down for the next few days. Don't take any public transportation and don't hang around in one place any longer than you have to. Tell the agents where you're going, because they're going to be following you too. Stephen should be showing up any day now if he's coming. Glenn said that you can stay with her for the next couple of days so I won't have to worry about you. You scared me yesterday . . . really scared me."

Stefne pushed her coffee cup away and stood up to give him a hug. "I love you, Dad. I'm going to take your Jeep and run back to the apartment to get a few things. I'll see ya later."

Josh waited till she left before shifting his eyes to Bob. "Keep an eye on her for me, will ya?"

Bob nodded in silence.

Dorba nodded at Qui. "Very well done. I believe we have gotten the desired point across. There will be a few who persist in trying to find us. Locate them and take action. Within a month we should have no problems."

Qui raised an eyebrow. "We still have the problem of this Stephen Kang. He has not showed up as of yet. The American, a man called Hawkins, attacked several members of our surveillance team, and the FBI arrested three other team members."

Dorba's look grew concerned. "Are you saying we have no eyes on him?"

Qui smiled. "No, San Chu. We have others. Now that we know the FBI is protecting him, I placed our best on him last night. It's almost humorous. They reported this morning that the FBI has a team in a room in the inn overlooking the small boat harbor. Our people have already identified the frequency they are using to monitor the conversations on his boat, so we can listen in. Our people no longer have to watch the American but just the FBI team. When they get ready to move in for Kang, we will move first. I am saying this to warn you we will have to take out this FBI team to get to Kang when the time comes. Are you certain you want this?"

Dorba leaned back in his chair and looked at the arrangement of flowers on the table. "They are beautiful, aren't they? Such delicate creations . . . but their beauty only lasts for days. We enjoy them until they wilt, then replace them with others and think nothing of the dead. A shame." He nodded slowly to Qui. "Do whatever is necessary. I leave it in your hands."

Qui bowed. "I will take care of it. You have business now with the San from New York. It seems a lesson is needed there as well."

Dorba looked back at the flowers and sighed. "These Americans are so stubborn. Send him in."

Phone calls started coming through after noon. Stefne and Bob answered them all and checked the names against the shift list. Finally the last cop called in to say he was fine and would be back to work that night.

Stefne sighed in relief. "Thank God none of them were hurt. It would have been terrible to lose someone we know."

Bob lowered his head. "While you were on the phone the radio reported the casualties—there are at least 322 dead, with well over a hundred still in critical condition. And there are over eleven hundred people in hospitals throughout the city and surrounding counties."

Stefne's eyes narrowed. "I'd like to be there when they find the Iraqi bastards that did this. I'd—"

"You and 270 million other Americans," Bob said somberly.

Josh walked into the office and Bob held out a message.

"Boss, Kelly called for you fifteen minutes ago. He says he needs you to call him."

Josh did a double take as he read the number. "This is his office number. Damn his stubborn hide! He should be in the hospital."

Josh tried three times but kept getting a busy tone. He hung up just as the office door opened. He faced the man who entered and said, "I was just tryin' to call ya. What the hell are you doin' out of bed?"

With tears in his eyes, Kelly limped over and stiffly hugged Josh. "I . . . I can't tell you . . . Jesus, Hawk, thanks."

Josh patted his back affectionately. "How are Mary and the boys?"

Kelly backed away, wiping his eyes with his hand. "I just left 'em. They're still shook up but okay." He felt the questioning eyes of the others on him and turned around. "Didn't he tell ya?"

Josh quickly guided him to the door. "I'll tell them later. Come on outside—we gotta talk."

"Tell us what? Kelly, tell us what's going on," Stef demanded.

Josh waved one hand at his daughter and said with finality, "Later." He walked his friend outside. "Everybody was upset enough last night, and I didn't want to add to it by explaining the attempt on Mary and the boys. Anything on the hitters?"

"Nothin'. The fuckers got Cummings's wife and two daughters and Alvarez's wife and son. Hanson's wife was hit but she's gonna make it. They tried on a couple of others but missed. It's bad news in the department. I had to get out of there for a while. The guys ain't gonna take this lyin' down." He took a deep breath and winced. "Jesus, I can't get enough air."

Josh took his arm and led him to the unmarked cruiser. "Go back to the hospital, Shamrock. You're not in any shape to be workin'."

Kelly leaned against the car and looked up at the overcast sky. "There's too much to do. The Feds are handling the bombings, but the precincts are working in the barricade and support role except for the crime scene and bomb boys, who are workin' overtime with the Feds. My guys were told to start lookin' for these Islamic revolutionaries the press is talkin' about."

"You buyin' that Islamic Revolution shit, or are you thinkin' what I'm thinkin'?" asked Josh.

"I ain't thinkin' . . . 'cause they told us not to think. That threat letter that the commissioner sent to us? It's not posted on the bulletin board anymore. The word is ta keep our mouths shut about it. The head shed says there is *no* connection and is going with the terrorist thing. I'm not thinkin', okay? But if I was I'd be asking, Why would terrorists hit the drug conference? Why not one of the military posts or the naval yard? That part of it doesn't make sense. The Metros were pure terror hits, but the conference? Naw, that was a signal. I'd say the big boy has laid out his rules—we fuck with his operation, he drops a bunch of fucking bombs. We play straight, he leaves the civilians alone."

Josh's jaw tightened. "You think that's how the head shed sees it?"

Kelly swung his eyes over to his friend. His look gave Josh the answer.

"Shit," Josh cursed.

Kelly shifted his position and winced again. "I gotta get back to the desk. I had to come by and thank you personally for putting it down for Mary. I owe you everything. Come to the office later and bring your FBI shooters with you. You and them still gotta fill out paperwork. And hey, I wasn't born yesterday. I talked to a friend in the Bureau and he told me why the agents were there. You should have told me you were being shadowed."

Josh shrugged and said, "You had your hands full. If Stephen shows up, the Feds get him and he goes home. Nothin' to it."

Kelly eyed his friend. "Yeah, sure, I ain't askin' any more questions 'cause my Bureau friend told me this thing was at the national level. That puts it out of my league. But it still worries me, so watch your ass, ya hear me? Now help me get in the fuckin' car, will ya? I gotta get back to work."

A hundred and fifty yards away, across Maine Avenue, a wino dressed in filthy clothes and wearing a ragged stocking cap lay on a bench in the small park. Although he looked asleep, he was fully awake and watching an old friend help a man into a car. Despite his inner pain, the memories flooding over him made him smile inwardly. Part of him was ecstatic with joy, but another part felt ashamed. Tears trickled down his cheek as he closed his eyes and prayed he had enough strength to face him.

Josh called it right; the Front was busy. He was in the Gangplank when he felt someone brush against his back. He turned and smiled. "Hi. You look a lot better."

Glenn took his arm and walked him slowly over to a window with a good view of the Washington Monument. "I'm still sore as hell. Thanks for last night."

He winked. "Anytime."

She glanced around the bar with a sympathetic look. "They're trying hard to forget it happened, aren't they?"

He nodded as he looked over the crowd. "It's human nature. They know they have to get past it to go on. But yesterday was a day nobody in this town will ever really forget."

Her eyes sparked. "Can you come over after work and stay? I'll feed you breakfast in the morning."

Josh tilted his head to the side and frowned. "Great offer, but Stefne is staying with you, remember? I gave her the key so she's there now."

Grant winced. "My head must have got bumped harder than I thought. I'm sorry, I forgot. I'd better go and see how she's doing. Be careful, Josh. The FBI is betting Stephen shows up in the next couple of days. I talked to them this afternoon. They haven't spotted a tail to replace the ones they picked up, and they're worried about it." She leaned over and kissed his cheek. "See you tomorrow."

Josh watched her walk away and began to move toward the dining room when an agent brushed past him and whispered, "Follow me."

Ten seconds later Josh stepped into the kitchen and the agent spun around. "The room team spotted a man in a small rubber boat heading toward the marina. They spotted him in their night vision scope just a minute ago. Wait a sec." He took a small radio from his sport coat pocket and inserted an earplug. He spoke into a miniature receiver on his lapel. "This is Alpha one, you still see him? . . . Roger, I have him with me now. . . . Roger, out." He looked back at Josh. "He's heading toward your boat. We think it's Kang because the opposition would send more than one man. It's your call. We can go check, or you can."

"I'll do it," Josh said quickly and began to turn around.

"If it's him, secure any weapons he might have and calm him

down. We'll be listening, and we'll call before we come so you know it's us. You got it?"

Josh pushed the door open and said over his shoulder, "Got it."

Walking quickly, Josh approached *Lil' Darlin'* holding his pistol against his leg. He cautiously stepped down to the deck. Taking one step to his left, he saw by the reflection of the pier lights a black rubber dinghy tied off to his bass boat. He froze when he saw a dark figure rise up beside his traps. His hand tightened around the pistol as he stepped closer and softly asked, "Stephen?"

A wave of relief spread over Stephen as he heard his best friend's voice. He cried out softly, "At last, Joshua."

Josh quickly glanced over his shoulder to make sure no one else was on the pier. He holstered his pistol, and put his hand out. "I've missed you, brother."

With tears in his eyes Stephen grabbed the offered hand and was pulled up to the rail, where the two men hugged each other. Stephen broke from the embrace and hopped over the rail. "We're in danger, Joshua. The Triad is hunting me."

Josh took his arm and hurriedly pulled him toward the cabin. "We'll talk inside. God, I've been worried about you."

They entered the cabin and Stephen spun Josh around and hugged him again. "Joshua, they have Mya and Jacob. You were the only one I could turn to. I'm sorry for endangering you."

Josh held Stephen's shoulders and gently pushed him back to look into his eyes. "I know all about it, brother. The FBI is looking for you too. We've been waiting for you."

Stephen's face paled. "No! If the FBI takes me the DDSI will kill Mya and Jacob."

Josh kept his gaze and grip steady. "Your father has Jacob. He's waiting for you."

Stephen froze for an instant before stammering, "How . . . How do . . ."

"I know, Stephen. I know you were in Seattle and I know you killed three men. My government wants to help you."

Stephen was shaking so badly he could barely speak. "Mya? Is she safe?"

Josh hugged Stephen to him. "She's with her ancestors, brother."

The telephone rang. Josh guided Stephen to the galley, sat him down, and picked up the handset. "Yeah."

"We heard it all. We're on our—*What the—*"

Josh heard loud metallic coughing noises, then suddenly the line went dead. He dropped the phone and looked out the open cabin door just as the pier lights went out. He grabbed Stephen, who was still crying. "Stephen, I think the FBI team has been hit! Come on, we're getting out of here!"

Not waiting for him, Josh pulled his pistol as he rushed to the open door and threw himself on the cockpit floor. Raising only his head, he saw to his horror it was a coordinated attack. Despite the pier and wharf lights being out, he could see four men running toward his boat on the pier. He got up into a shooter's crouch and aimed at the lead figure.

"Hey, who are you people?" Meg barked as she stepped out of the cabin to investigate the loss of the pier lights.

The lead man spun, the weapon in his hand coughing in a deadly muffled staccato.

Josh screamed in anguish, fired, missed, and fired again. The lead man went down, but now warned, the other three began firing as they ran. Josh rolled and came up firing on the stern deck and another went down, but the other two were swinging their barrels toward him. Suddenly another weapon sounded behind Josh and an attacker fell, hit in the chest. The remaining assassin fired a burst at the new shooter and swung the spitting barrel toward Josh, but it was too late. Josh squeezed the trigger and rushed forward. The man staggered but didn't go down. Josh shot him twice more in the heart and put another bullet into one of the men who was trying to get up. He spun around and saw Stephen fall as his knees buckled. Josh rushed to him and raised his chin. His right cheek was laid open as if it had been plowed and his lower ear was gone. Stephen's eyes rolled up to him, and he said, "See to the woman. I'll watch your back."

Josh broke into a dead run toward *Windsong*.

Moaning, Meg lay on the deck in an expanding pool of blood. Josh kneeled by her and lifted her head. "I'm here, Meg. I'm here."

She reached for him in the darkness. "It hurts, Josh. It hurts so bad."

He ran his hands over her body and discovered that a wound in her lower thigh was bleeding profusely. He frantically took off his belt and had just circled it tight around Meg's leg when Stephen fired twice and yelled, "More are coming!"

Josh turned around just as submachine-gun bullets chewed up the planks around Stephen, who was stumbling back toward *Lil' Darlin'*. Two men were climbing over the security gate while two others kneeled and fired their silenced machine guns. Josh aimed and began firing. One of the men climbing the fence was knocked backward by a bullet in the shoulder. The other man jumped from the fence to the wharf just in time to take a round in the groin. The two kneeling men raked *Windsong* with long bursts, then stood and backed up. They got one of the wounded men to his feet, and all three ran down the Channel Walk.

Josh dropped to one knee beside Meg, pulled the Motorola from his pocket, and shouted, "Base, shots fired on pier one! Need ambulance and police *now*! Three armed assailants running north on Channel Walk. Tell police to call FBI and inform them their team on Waterfront is down. I repeat, team is down. Get me an ambulance and help *now*!"

Josh dropped the Motorola and gently picked Meg up in his arms. "I'm gettin' you some help. Hang tough, good lookin'."

She lifted her trembling hand to his face. "I'm sorry, Josh. I didn't listen, did I?"

A man raised his head up from the entertainment deck of a cabin cruiser moored only three slips down. Josh yelled, "Dr. Cole, it's Josh. Help me—Meg has been wounded."

Another head popped up. "We're not moving till the police get here!" a woman screamed hysterically.

Josh headed for the cruiser. "The police are coming, dammit! Help me!"

Ernie Cole, a weekend marina regular, stood up. "Bring her on board. I've got a first-aid kit."

Josh stepped onto the cruiser's deck and laid Meg on the cushions in the weld behind the bridge. He heard voices yelling for him from the security gate and yelled back. "Over here! Watch out for a wounded man in front of the gate."

Cole turned on the bridge light and quickly inspected Meg's wound. "You're lucky, Meg. No arteries were severed."

Josh leaned over to stroke her face. "I gotta go, Meg."

A wave of pain caused her to grimace. She bit her lip until it passed, then focused her liquid eyes on him. "I'm so sorry, Josh."

Brad Rawlins, one of Josh's security men, climbed up on deck with a pistol in his hand. Josh took his rover's arm and walked him back to the pier. "Brad, get the others here to cordon off the pier. Don't let a fuckin' soul past the gate unless they're cops or medics." A thought struck Josh as he was talking and he looked back toward his boat. "A man named Stephen Kang was on the pier. He was hit in the chest and knocked into the water. They'll need to look for his body."

The off-duty cop looked at the dead men sprawled on the planks, then back to Josh. "What the hell happened, Hawk? And where in the hell are you going? You can't leave a crime scene."

Josh's face tightened. "These fuckers just tried to whack me. I'm not going to wait around the pier for a sniper's bullet. Trust me on this. I gotta go."

The cop reluctantly nodded. "I'll handle it. Get outta here."

Josh ran back to *Lil' Darlin'* and found Stephen sitting against the cabin door, holding his wadded-up shirt against his face. Josh grabbed the first-aid kit from beneath the wheel and pulled Stephen to his feet. He guided him toward his bass boat and said, "We gotta move. We're gonna take my boat upriver. It's too dangerous to stay around here, and the cops would ask you too many questions."

Josh throttled back and glided up to the boathouse pier. Quickly tying off, he picked up the first-aid kit and helped Stephen into the huge, barnlike building. Having seen Fred hide the office key plenty of times, he lifted a flowerpot by the door and picked up the old-fashioned key beneath it.

Minutes later in the office, Josh angled Stephen's head back and put the last piece of tape in place to hold the bandage on his face. He patted Stephen's back and sat down beside him. "Brother, it's gonna hurt like hell, but you have to tell me everything you've done, seen, and heard since arriving in the U.S."

Stephen's glazed eyes watered. "I've killed Mya and almost got you killed. I don't want you involved anymore, Joshua. They'll kill you."

"I'm already involved, brother. Think about your son and getting home to him. I can help you if you tell me every detail, just like our Teacher taught us."

Stephen's eyes came into focus as he thought of his son. He lowered his head and closed his eyes. "I flew into Seattle on the fifth of June and was met by . . ."

11:05 P.M., Alexandria, Virginia

Awakened by the ringing phone, Kelly slapped the nightstand twice before finding the handset. "Kelly . . . Christ, yeah, I'll be there in thirty minutes."

He sat up stiffly, replaced the handset, and turned on the lamp.

Mary raised her head from the pillow. "What's wrong, Terry?"

Kelly got up gingerly, holding his bandaged ribs, and turned to look at her. "Josh was involved in a firefight on the pier. He needs me."

She got up immediately. "I'll help you get dressed."

11:18 P.M., Waterfront Apartments

Grant picked up the phone on the first ring, praying it was him. "This is—Thank God! Josh, where are you? The FBI are here and— Yes, one of your men told Stef you were okay. She went to the hospital to be with Meg. . . . Josh? . . . Josh?"

She lowered the handset and looked at the FBI agent standing beside her. "He hung up."

11:20 P.M., Falls Church, Virginia

Sitting in the study in his home, Director Jennings put down the report he was reading and picked up the ringing phone. "Hello? . . . Yes, put him through. . . . Hawkins? Where the hell are you? I heard what happened and—" Jennings's eyes widened and his face reddened. "Don't play games with me, Hawkins! We had a deal! Damn you! Why the hell do you need three days? . . . You can't do that! . . . Dammit, don't hang up. Let's discuss this. I have to hear Kang's story first. . . . I'll come alone, but you're pushing, Hawkins, and I don't like being pushed. . . . Okay, you have my word on it. . . . 1 A.M. I'll be there."

11:35 P.M., Georgetown Boathouse

Kelly walked through the office door and gave Stephen a once-over before pinning Josh with his stare. "I've been listening to the MPD radio. You've been busy, huh?"

Josh motioned to Stephen. "Kelly, meet Stephen Kang. He knows your Mr. Dorba."

Kelly's head snapped to Stephen with an incendiary stare.

Ten minutes later, after hearing Stephen tell his story, Kelly took a deep breath and shifted his eyes back to Josh.

Josh knew what he was thinking and shrugged. "It's all hearsay. No district attorney will touch the part about Dorba."

Kelly raised his eyebrows, but his eyes were smoldering. "But we *know* he's dirty. He's going down, Hawk. Hearsay or not, I'm taking that fucker down. It's his turn for a lesson."

Josh exchanged a look with Stephen. "I thought you'd say that. Stephen and I discussed it before you got here."

Stephen lowered his eyes and spoke from the unbandaged side of his mouth. "I didn't know Dorba was responsible for the bombings and killings of your people until only minutes ago. I am partially to blame and want to help you stop him."

"I'm in too," Josh said.

Kelly looked at the two men for a moment before nodding in silence. He turned and began thinking aloud. "Alvarez and Cummings are burying their families day after tomorrow. They'll want in. So will Hanson and Youngblood 'cause of the attempts on their wives. We're gonna need a plan that—" His eyes suddenly focused, and he turned back to Josh. "I know how we can get in. Remember Michael Woo, the assistant D.A. who . . ."

Director Jennings stormed into the small boathouse office expecting to see two men, not three. He came to an abrupt halt, looked at Josh, then took the cigar from his mouth. He motioned toward Kelly. "Who the hell is this?"

Kelly rolled his eyes as he took out his badge and held it up. "Detective Kelly, MPD, Your Holiness."

Josh motioned Jennings to a seat and put his hand on Stephen's shoulder. "This is Stephen, who you know about. He's told us some things that will sicken you. We need you to help us. If you don't, then—"

"I won't go back," Stephen said with a cold glare. "My country caused this, and I must right the wrong before I can return."

Jennings stuck the cigar back in his mouth. "I can't promise anything. Tell me what you know."

Jennings stood up and shook Stephen's hand, then Kelly's, and then faced Josh. "This conversation didn't take place, understand?"

Josh nodded. "Right. Just make sure the FBI and DEA find those heroin distribution centers that Stephen told you about. And make sure they agree to the cover story."

Jennings took the stub of the cigar out of his mouth. "The cover is no problem. Stephen was killed during the attack. As for the distribution centers, the ones in Carlisle and Sacramento should be no problem for the bureau and DEA to find, but 'Kansas' is not much to go on. There's no guarantee on that one."

Stephen shook his head. "I'm sorry. All I heard them say was 'Kansas.' I wish I could be more specific."

Jennings shrugged. "It's got to be on a major interstate. They'll find it eventually."

Kelly looked at his watch. "Forty-eight hours, Mr. Director. We hit him tomorrow at 1 A.M. regardless."

"I understand," Jennings said. "Just make sure it's done right."

Kelly smirked. "He'll learn."

CHAPTER 21

Chinatown

Qui knocked on the open door and walked into the large office. Dorba leaned back in his chair and motioned toward the morning paper on his desk. "I see they eliminated Kang . . . but it was costly."

The chief of staff furrowed his brow. "The paper is correct. We had four killed. Three escaped, and one wounded man was captured. There must have been more FBI on the boat that our men didn't know about. The American, Hawkins, was wounded and is in the hospital at Fort Belvoir. It will be very difficult to get to him."

Dorba leaned forward in his chair. "Did Kang speak to him about us?"

"No, our people attacked before he could discuss anything."

Dorba leaned back in relief and shrugged. "Forget the American then. We have more important matters to attend to. I see by the reports our profits on white powder sales are higher than expected. The council will be very pleased."

Glad the subject had changed, Qui allowed himself a small smile. "Business is very good. In fact, it is so good we will have to obtain more powder from the distribution outlet in Carlisle very soon."

Dorba's eyes sparkled. "And I will be an elder very soon. The American appetite for white powder will cause our roots to grow very deep . . . very deep indeed."

Fort Belvoir, Virginia

Kelly showed his special badge to the military policeman guarding the entrance to an old World War II barracks and walked in the door. Josh was studying a city map of Washington he had taped to the barren wall. He glanced over his shoulder. "Welcome to our new headquarters. There's coffee and some doughnuts in the back room."

Kelly's eyes swept over the gray furniture and he shook his head. "This is all Jennings could come up with?"

"Whatcha expect on short notice? Hey, he followed through on his part of the deal. Our cover, by the way, is that we're working with the CID on a security problem at the Night Vision Labs just a few blocks over."

Kelly rolled his eyes. "Spooks and their fuckin' cover stories. They can't piss without a cover. Where's Stephen?"

Josh pulled up a chair for his friend and motioned over his shoulder. "He's knocked out in a room upstairs. Jennings sent a doc over to check his face. He had to knock him out with a shot before removing some dead tissue. He's gonna have a helluva scar, but he'll be alright. He'll be ready. Did you see Stef?"

Kelly winced. "Yeah, and I ain't never gonna do that again. Jeez, and I thought Mary could bitch. She laid into me like an ugly stepchild, but I finally convinced her you had to lay chilly for a while. Jennings came through on talking to the FBI—they were over early this morning making sure the MPD had their stories straight for the cover. Kang's body was 'found' in the channel this morning, and you're reported as seriously wounded. The people on the cruiser—the Coles—and Meg are cooperating with the Feds and won't give any interviews to the press. They've been told you were involved in busting a Mafia drug deal and anything they say could endanger you . . . and them. Everything is good to go. Now it's up to us."

Josh leveled his stare on Kelly. "You talk to your people?"

Kelly gave a short nod. "Yeah, Alvarez, Cummings, Hanson, and Youngblood are all in. I told 'em this could end their careers, but they want blood."

"Any second thoughts on your part, Kelly? You've worked a long time for that pension," Josh said, searching his friend's eyes for doubt.

Kelly's face became rigid. "I'm going to two funerals tomorrow. I don't have any second thoughts. Dorba is mine."

Ministry of Defense, Rangoon, Burma

Newly promoted Major General Tan took a seat in front of the prime minister's desk with a smile. General Swei leaned back in his chair. "You must have good news for me."

"Very good news. Stephen Kang is dead."

Swei sighed in relief. "Excellent. Then let's get on with it. All threats to us are eliminated. I will inform our minister of information that Martyrs' Day, the nineteenth of July, will be the date of my announcement to the world that our borders will be opened. I will announce the loan guarantees and detailed plans for our rebuilding programs. Free elections will be scheduled for one year from Martyrs' Day. That will give time for our rebuilding programs to take hold and assure my election as the first freely elected president in forty-five years."

Tan's brow wrinkled. "Sawbaw Xu Kang is still a problem. Many are joining his army."

Swei smiled. "He won't be a threat once I make the announcement to the world press. The western companies will be begging to come in, and every government will send words of praise and support. We have defeated him—we have defeated them all."

Thailand Border

Xu Kang wiped sweat from his brow as he stood in the hot sun observing his newest recruits. He couldn't take it anymore and bellowed to the captain in charge of training, "Enough! Stop yelling at them." He strode forward, motioned the captain back, and waved the formation of young men and women to him. He raised his hands as if surrendering. "I am sorry. I see now we are wasting time by trying to make you into soldiers. You are college students, not soldiers, and we have been asking too much of you. Return to our homeland and go back to school in Rangoon. You will join my secret army and march, but not to cadence. You will need to march in protest when the time is right."

A young woman stepped forward and raised her fist. "We came to fight!"

The other students cheered her in support.

Kang smiled seeing the anger in her eyes. "And fight you will. Do you remember the student protests here in Thailand two summers ago? Young women and men like yourselves brought the prime minister down. He was not removed by an assassin's bullet. Students removed him by marching. You and many more like you are the real force that will cause change. Go back to school, recruit others, and when the time is right, march. March to Swei's headquarters and show the world he is nothing but a dictator and a lying pye dog."

"But who will lead us?" a young man asked.

Kang pointed at the young student who had asked the question. "You will!" He then pointed at the young woman with the angry eyes. "You all will. A leader is someone willing to take the first step. You may be slain or beaten by the soldiers, but another will step forward and take your place. A leader is one who believes and is willing to die for that belief. You are Burma . . . you are her hope."

Kang shifted his eyes and looked into their young faces. "I see in you the leaders our country needs. I ask now that you go back and start becoming those leaders. Your day is coming."

The students didn't move. He thought he had wasted his time when suddenly the girl in front of him snapped to attention and saluted with the wrong hand. "Permission to return home, General."

Kang came to attention and brought his own hand up with tears in his eyes. "Permission granted, young leader."

Another student came to attention, then another and another until all of them were saluting and asking permission to go home. He snapped his heels together and raised his hand again. "Permission granted, leaders."

As he stood in the empty field and watched them walk back to camp to collect their belongings, the Shan captain stepped up beside him. "Sawbaw, they are not Shan. Can we trust them if they *do* become leaders?"

Kang put his arm over the captain's shoulder. "We are not fighting for the Shan this time, my young friend—we are fighting for Burma."

As the old man approached the hut he saw the CIA chief of station for Thailand, John Hobbs, sitting with Colonel Banta on the covered porch. Hobbs rose and bowed his head. "Greetings and blessings, Sawbaw Kang. I bring good news."

Kang felt his eyes misting again. "It is truly a blessing if you bring news of Stephen. You have found him?"

The chief smiled. "Yes. He is with Colonel Hawkins and is safe."

"The gods have blessed me! I will give prayers of thanks to them! When will he be here?"

"Soon, Sawbaw. Perhaps a week, I can't say for sure. The message I received last night said only that he was with Colonel Hawkins and that he was safe. I came to tell you of this good news and ask if you have any more information. My government was very appreciative of your gift of the DDSI lieutenant. But I'm afraid we need more proof than a young officer with no toes."

Kang's beaming face turned sour. He sat down in his campaign chair and shook his head. "You Americans are such fools. You are victims of your own laws. Listen to your heart! Look with your eyes at what is happening! Are you deaf and blind? Proof? My camp is full of proof. The people have voted with their feet. 'Proof' is a word when there are laws, courts, and judges. There is no law in Burma, U Hobbs. There is only despair."

Hobbs pressed. "Sawbaw Kang, my country is trying to help you. With hard proof we will able to show the world what Swei really is and what he has done to the people of Burma. Hard proof will give us—"

Kang raised his hand. "Enough. You know there are deadly cobras in the cave and yet you want my people to go in and fetch one for you. I will not waste a single man to 'prove' what *we* already know. U Hobbs, they have killed thousands over the years and imprisoned thousands more. I am going into their cave very soon. Our deal was for you to bring Stephen to me. Do it. Watch, as your people have done before, and see who comes out of the cave. And pray to the gods, U Hobbs. Pray that you can live with yourself if the cobras prevail."

Xu Kang stood up but his penetrating eyes pinned the CIA chief. "I have other business to attend to. Don't come again until you have my son. I don't need your government's words—I need those willing to enter the cave." Turning around, the old soldier walked down the porch steps and strode for the distant rifle range.

Hobbs shook his head in frustration and turned to Colonel Banta. "Will you talk to him and make him understand? He can't take over the government without our help."

Banta smiled without humor. "You are the one who doesn't understand. We have no intention of taking over the government. We are Shan. The Burmese would never accept a minority 'takeover' of the government."

Hobbs's eyes widened. "Wha . . . what is your intention then?"

Banta stood in the hot sun and walked toward the steps. He paused once and looked over his shoulder with a contemptuous stare. "Our 'intention' is to kill the cobras."

CHAPTER 22

10 P.M., Fort Belvoir, Virginia

Kelly paced in front of the table where six men were seated. "Team one, weapons and equipment status?"

Detective Hector Alvarez, the team leader, spoke up immediately. "We're good, Terry. Chick has the flare and smoke rounds for his blooper. Me and Al have the uniforms, ignitors, and vehicle."

"Tac sets?"

"Yeah, we have the tactical headsets, and each of us has a Motorola for backup. Because of the distance, Chick will stay on the roof so he can keep in contact with you and relay to us while we're inside the building."

Kelly kept pacing with his head down. "Okay, the phone company shuts down their lines at exactly 1 A.M. Bernie could only promise us fifteen minutes so it's critical you begin the operation on time. Chick, are you sure you can get to the roof?"

Detective Chick Cummings's hooded eyes shifted slowly to Kelly. "I went up last night to make a recon. The fire escape in back makes it a piece of cake. It's an easy shot from there to the seventh floor. They won't hear a thing."

Kelly came to a halt and raised his wrist. "It's now ten forty-five. I want radio checks every fifteen minutes until show time. After that, keep me informed of each phase. Questions? Okay, one last thing before we go. Give me your badges. We're not cops tonight."

The detectives tossed their badges to Kelly, who laid them out on the table with his own. Looking up, he nodded. "Alright. Team one . . . roll."

Alvarez, Cummings, and Al Hanson stood and walked toward the door in silence. Kelly waited until they were gone before facing the remaining three men. "Hawk, did you and Stephen get checked out on the stun guns?"

Josh patted the oversize pistol that was holstered on his hip. "Yeah, we fired a dozen darts apiece this afternoon. I just hope they work."

Detective Howie Youngblood smiled cruelly. "They work, alright. Assholes'll go down like they were hit in the head with two-by-fours. You'll be using the full-load darts. Twenty-four hundred volts in each dart guarantee they stay down for at least fifteen minutes. All they'll be able to do is shit their pants and piss all over themselves."

Kelly nodded in agreement. "They'll do the job, Hawk. You and Stephen remember to aim for the stomach or back. Don't hit 'em in the chest or it could be fatal. Alright, any questions before we make our first visit?"

Josh, Stephen, and Youngblood were silent. Kelly nodded. "Let's do it."

Michael Woo was sitting on the couch with his wife watching "Saturday Night Live" when the phone rang. They exchanged glances, each hoping the other would volunteer. His wife yawned for effect, and he reluctantly got up. "Next time, you get it." Her eyes said maybe.

He walked into the kitchen and took the handset from the wall extension. "Woo residence." His eyes widened when he realized the excited man on the line was speaking Cantonese. It took a moment for his brain to engage, but it was clear he wouldn't be watching any more TV that night. "Yes, of course, I'll be there in fifteen minutes," he said. He hung up the phone and hurried upstairs to get his car keys from his other slacks. Hearing his heavy footsteps, his wife yelled, "What's wrong, honey?" Not getting a response, she got up and walked into the hall just as he was coming down the stairs. "What's the matter?"

Woo's face was drawn with concern. "There's a fire at the office," he said as he brushed by her and headed for the door leading to the garage.

Parked one block from the house, Stephen handed the cellular phone back to Kelly. "He bought it. He's coming."

Woo backed his green Jaguar out of the drive, slapped the gearshift into first, and accelerated. He was about to shift into second when he had to slam on the brakes to avoid hitting a dark van that suddenly pulled out in front of him and blocked the road. No sooner had he stopped than his door was jerked open and he was staring into a pistol barrel.

"Hello, Mike," Kelly said amiably. He waved the weapon, motioning for the lawyer to get out of the car.

Woo's initial shock turned into indignation. "What the hell do you think you're doing, Kelly? You can't . . ." His eyes widened when a dark figure approached wearing a black hood with eye and mouth slits. The man pressed his Beretta into Woo's left cheek. "Get the fuck out now or I blow your head off!" Josh commanded.

Trembling, Woo got out and let himself be pushed toward the open side door of the van. Youngblood was waiting and shoved him inside. Stephen moved the van back to the curb and Kelly and Josh got in after parking Woo's car. Kelly sat down beside Woo and shook his head. "I'm disappointed in you, Mike. We had some good times together when you were with the D.A. You shoulda stayed clean."

"Kelly, you'll burn! You can't roust me like this."

Josh took off his black hood. "Hi, Mike. Remember me? When I worked for the MPD, you took me and Kelly to a Capitals game. They lost."

Woo suddenly felt the need to vomit. Josh motioned over his shoulder. "Meet Stephen Kang. He tells us your boss Dorba is very connected. I guess that makes you a slicky boy, huh?" Getting the effect he wanted, Josh nodded to Kelly, who sighed and clapped his hand on Woo's shoulder. "Mike, you're in big-time trouble, my man." He raised his wrist and tapped the crystal of his watch. "The FBI and DEA are making big busts just about now in the three states. You'll appreciate this, having been an assistant D.A. It seems they got a tip about three big heroin distribution warehouses. Funny how that shit happens. Let's take the one in Carlisle, Pennsylvania. The Feds ran a computer check to see what trucking firms and warehouses had been sold in the past year. Guess what? There were only three. And guess what else? The IRS did a check on them and only one wasn't privately owned. You know what, Mike? It seems it was owned by a company that was owned by another company that was a subsidiary of a corporation, and the list goes on. Ahhh . . . I'm boring you, right? You want me to get to the good stuff, right? Well, Mike, my man, the bottom line is you're gonna lose all your hero. Too bad."

"I . . . I don't know what you're talking about," Woo stammered, knowing Kelly was right. He *was* in big-time trouble.

Kelly sighed. "Mike, look at me. Look at me! That's better. You fucked up, my man. I think you are personally responsible for killing four hundred people, and I'm going to kill you, Mike, unless you cooperate. Look at me, don't lower your eyes when I'm talkin' to you. I'm gonna kill you because you went after my wife and family. I honestly hope to God you decide not to cooperate. I want to kill you, but so do some of my guys. You remember Hector Alvarez and Chick Cummings? You should—your boss had their families hit. They want a piece of you too ... real bad. We figure we'll take our time—a kneecap, a wrist, a gut shot—watch you squirm and beg. Tell me Mike. Please tell me that you don't wanna cooperate."

Woo felt it coming and couldn't stop it. He vomited, gagged, and threw up again.

Dressed in black, Chick Cummings walked across the flat roof of the five-floor tenement building, keeping his eyes on the glass office building across H Street. He kneeled by the brick retaining wall and unzipped his bag. When he took out the M-79 grenade launcher, his hands stopped trembling. The short, single-shot weapon was an old friend. He had carried one just like it in Vietnam. Just touching it reminded him of those days when he was young and airborne crazy. He had never told a soul, but he loved those times. His wife and girls had given him better memories, so he'd stored Vietnam in an old footlocker in his mind. But his wife was gone, and so were Carol and Kathy. He wouldn't put their memories away for a long time. He needed them, but he knew that one day they too would be placed in a footlocker, like their clothes and pictures, and stored away.

With tears in his eyes, he looked back at the enemy's building and spoke in a whisper into the small ball in front of his lips. "Charlie one in position."

A voice responded in his earpiece. "Roger, Charlie one. Alpha one and Hotel one are standing by. One minute and thirty seconds, over."

Chick Cummings looked at the luminous hands of his watch and saw it was almost 1 A.M. Opening the breech of the shotgunlike weapon, he slid a .40-millimeter flare round into the chamber. "Roger, good copy. I will give you a five-second countdown. Break, Kilo one, this is Charlie one. Team is in position. One minute till show time, over."

In the van, parked only two blocks from Dorba's gate entrance, Kelly exchanged looks with his three other team members before speaking. "Roger, we monitored and are standing by. Out." Kelly picked up the cellular phone and handed it to the broken man seated on the floor of the van. "Call him. If you fuck it up you'll die very slowly."

Michael Woo took the phone without making eye contact and

pressed the keys. He put the phone to his ear and waited. "This is Michael Woo. I need to speak to Mr. Dorba. . . . I know he's in bed! Wake him. This is important! Mr. Dorba, this is Michael. My father called me minutes ago. He is very concerned and wished for me to talk to you this evening. I am in my car and will be there in five minutes. . . . Yes, it is very important. I can't say more over the phone. Thank you."

Woo handed the phone back to Kelly with dulled eyes. "He'll be waiting."

Chick Cummings lifted his M-79 and aimed at the corner office on the top floor. On the lower floors all the lights were on and he could see office workers, but the top floor was totally black. He whispered as he clicked off the safety. "Five . . . four . . . three . . . two . . . one." He squeezed the trigger. The weapon made a deep-throated *thump*. The black glass didn't shatter but spiderwebbed around the hole made by the round. The shell hit the back office wall and exploded with a muffled *pop* and a burst of white light. Chick had already popped open the breach and pulled out the casing. He slid in another white-smoke round and fired again at the same office. Seeing his shot go through the window, he spoke in a normal tone into the tac set. "The first two are in target. It doesn't look like any more are needed. I'm observing occupants on sixth floor and it appears to be business as usual. They didn't hear it, over."

Detective Alvarez and Al Hanson were parked only a hundred yards away from the building. From their position they had a perfect view of the smoke now coming through the holes in the glass on the top floor. "Roger, Charlie one. It looks good. We're moving now."

Alvarez started the engine of the red car, turned on the siren and bubble machine, and sped down the street. Screeching to a halt for effect, he and Hanson jumped out of the car and ran up to the main entrance.

The Chinese security guards behind their desk leaped up as the firemen rushed in the door. Alvarez yelled, "You've got a fire on the top floor! Clear the building immediately!"

"What fire? We don't have a fire," the chief of security replied, eyeing the men suspiciously. Hanson grabbed the officer's arm, pulled him out the door, and pointed up at the cloud of billowing smoke. "Look there, idiot! See for yourself! Now clear the fucking building! My partner and I are going to get our equipment and go up and see how bad it is!"

The security officer ran back inside and hit the fire alarm. Alvarez had already opened the trunk of the car and tossed Hanson a heavy fireman jacket. The men smiled at each other and put on their fire hats and somber faces, then ran for the entrance.

It took them four minutes using the steps, for the elevators were all coming down full of night-shift workers. On the top floor they quickly checked the offices for people, then used fire ignitors to set two fires in the center offices. They tossed everything they could find that would burn onto the licking flames, then ran down to the next floor, which was filled with computers and telecommunications equipment. After checking again for people, they tossed two chairs through windows to create a draft and started two more fires, then moved down to the next floor and repeated the process.

Cummings watched the smoke pouring out of the three upper floors and spoke into his tac set. "You're doing just fine. Uh-oh, I hear sirens. Looks like you're gonna have company real soon."

Alvarez popped another ignitor and tossed it into an open file drawer "Charlie one, let us know as soon as you see them approaching."

All four team members in the van were monitoring the radio messages of team one on their tac sets. Kelly nodded. "Okay, it's our turn. Stick to the plan." He grabbed Woo's arm and pulled him up as Josh opened the van door.

Kelly walked Woo back to the Jaguar that Josh had driven over. "Alright, Mike, so far you've done real good, but here's where you win the Academy Award. Me and Josh will be down in the backseat. When you pull into the gate do it just like we told ya. Do everything I said and you'll be one step closer to seeing your wife again. You got it?"

Woo nodded as if he were in a trance. Kelly lifted the man's chin. "Look at me and tell me you've got it."

"I've got it," Woo whispered weakly.

"Thatta boy, Mikey. You're doin' fine."

The guard in the key house stood as the Jaguar pulled up to the gate. He pressed the gate's electric button, having recognized the vehicle and driver. Putting on his hat, he stepped to the door and waved as Woo pulled in. Then the car suddenly stopped, blocking the gate, as its motor died. The Chinese guard sighed and walked toward the car. "What's the problem, Mr. Woo?" He saw the rear door of the car fly open and reached for his pistol. He felt as if he'd been poked in the side by a burning knife; a millisecond later came a jolt of excruciating pain. He knew he was falling face first toward the gravel but could do nothing but scream in silence.

Josh rolled the shaking man over and cuffed his wrists behind his back with a special plastic tie that could only be cut off. He did the same to the guard's ankles, then ran toward the distant house following the Jaguar, which was already moving. He looked over his shoulder—like clockwork the van was already through the open gate with its headlights off.

As soon as the Jaguar entered the lighted circular drive in front of the mansion, one of Dorba's security men stepped onto the porch to escort the lawyer in. Kelly peeped over the seat, then ducked down but kept his stun pistol pointed toward the open window. "Delay, Mike," he whispered. "Act like you're having trouble with the seat belt."

The guard waited for several moments before deciding to see what was holding up the boss's late-night visitor. He was within three feet of the car when Kelly sat up and fired through the open window. The big guard went down like a bag full of rocks. Kelly opened the car door and got out, then spun and shot Woo in the shoulder with a dart. Turning again, he reached the entrance just as Josh threw himself against the right side of the open front door. Kelly took the left side and nodded. Josh rushed inside with Kelly on his heels. The second bodyguard was standing in the entry when Josh went in. The thick-chested Chinaman's mouth partially opened as he fell backward in a deathlike paralysis. Kelly saw no other targets, so he took the lead and continued down the hall.

Wearing a silk robe, Dorba sat in his dining room drinking tea. He heard footsteps and turned in his chair, expecting Woo. Instead he saw a man dressed from head to foot in black pointing a huge pistol at his forehead. Dorba's face went slack and his bowels turned to water.

Kelly didn't hesitate at all. He used his forward momentum to backhand the old man across the face, knocking him to the floor. Forgetting the pain in his ribs, he bent over and viciously grabbed Dorba's thin shoulders. Kelly picked him up and slammed him back into the chair. He stuffed the belt of the old man's robe into his bleeding mouth, pulled his arms through the rails of the chair, and bound his wrists with a plastic tie.

Josh came into the room with Stephen and Youngblood. Kelly motioned to the other detective and whispered, "Howie and I will clear the upstairs—you two take the rest of the downstairs."

Five minutes later the team reassembled in the dining room. Kelly and Youngblood had awakened two sleeping bodyguards with twenty-four hundred volts apiece. Josh and Stephen had found and tied up two sleeping servants.

Kelly nodded to Stephen, who left the room. Pulling up a chair,

Kelly sat down facing Dorba and pulled the belt out of his mouth. "Look at me, asshole. We're gonna talk."

"Who are you?" Dorba hissed, as blood dribbled from his split lip.

Kelly motioned to himself, then Josh. "I'm John Wayne and this fella is the Lone Ranger. The other guys are Clint Eastwood and the Cisco Kid. We represent the cowboys of America."

"Are you thieves? What do you want?" Dorba asked, knowing that if they were going to kill him they already would have. He wanted to know all he could so his people could find them.

Kelly's eyes narrowed. "We want four hundred lives back, asshole! We're cowboys seeking vengeance for what you did. You fucked up, Dorba. That's right, we know your name. You fucked up 'cause you pissed us off. Now we're going to teach you a little lesson—Don't ever fuck with us again! Next time, you will die. Now let's get on with the lesson."

Kelly nodded at Josh, who pulled a fish knife from a scabbard on his belt. He stepped forward and stuck the point of the blade inside Dorba's left nostril. "First lesson, asshole," he said. "We're smarter than you. Your name is not Dorba. You are Chin Fe Dang. You've been proclaimed San Chu by the Circle. You have a son in Seattle who is moving here to become your San for the city. Chen is your son's real name. He has a fat wife named Su, who has given you two grandchildren. You recently received seventy tons of white powder that was stored in a warehouse in Carlisle, Pennsylvania. Yes, *was*! It's all gone now. We cowboys told the FBI and DEA about it. We also told them about your other heroin distribution centers—you know, the ones in Sacramento and Kansas? You run your operation from an office in Chinatown. Your office is gone too—we cowboys burned it tonight. You pay for bringing in the white powder with this."

Josh flicked his wrist and the razor-sharp knife sliced through the skin between the left and right nostrils. Dorba's head snapped back as blood gushed from the wound.

Detective Youngblood stepped forward wearing a black hood like the others. He hissed in the bleeding man's face. "Lesson two, turtle breath. We know what you are, who you are, and what you've done. You ordered the bombings of the conference and the Metro stations and you ordered hits on the families of police officers. You could never repay us with enough pain for that." He slipped on a pair of brass knuckles. "But this is a start." He brought his fist back and slugged Dorba in the mouth, shattering his upper teeth.

Youngblood and Josh picked up Dorba with the chair, carried him into the kitchen, and dropped him by the sink. Kelly doused the San Chu's face to keep him conscious and wash away the teeth fragments, blood, and drool. Kelly kept spraying him as he leaned over and raised Dorba's chin. "Look at me! I hope these lessons are getting through to you. We're letting you live so you'll tell your Triad scum they'd best not mess with us again. See, you thought you could come to our country and hide behind our laws. Sorry, asshole, but cowboys don't play by the rules. They see a wolf or a snake and they don't think twice about killing it. We don't care about laws when it comes to people like you. Time for another lesson."

Stephen walked into the kitchen with a large plastic bucket. He turned on the garbage disposal and lifted one of Dorba's prized *koi* out of the plastic container. He dropped the fish into the drain headfirst. The disposal's whining became a loud, grinding roar. Stephen looked into the swollen eyes of the old man and felt no sympathy. "You have taken those we loved. If you do not cease operations, you will lose much more than your fish." He picked up another flopping fish, deep red in color, and began to lower it into the sink. Dorba cried out through his broken teeth and tried to get up, but Kelly held him back. Stephen dropped the fish into the grinding hole and picked another red one from the bucket. "These are your favorites, I see. Good." He set the flopping fish on the old man's lap. "You will watch this one die."

Kelly leaned over again. "The last lesson is coming up. In just a minute you won't feel any more pain—for a while. Look at me. No matter what you do, we'll find you if you stay in the United States. If you order one more hit, sell one more nickel bag of heroin, or so much as spit on our sidewalks, we cowboys will know it 'cause we'll be watching every fucking move you make. Tell the Triad to get out. If they don't, they're gonna go down, and hard. You live—this time. We killed none of your people—this time. Next time you die, asshole. This cowboy is gonna personally drill you between the eyes after I shoot your kneecaps, your wrists, and your balls. You don't know who I am and you never will. And you know the funny thing? There are 270 million of us cowboys in the U S of A—remember that."

Youngblood stepped forward and handed Kelly a syringe. He pushed out the air bubbles in front of Dorba's wide eyes and nodded. "Yep, this is the good stuff. It's going to make you fly just like the junkies do. We're gonna hide a kilo bag in the kitchen and leave a note on the door saying 'Stay out of our territory.' It's for the cops, ya see? We cowboys figured you oughta get a chance to use your big-buck lawyers to try and spring you. See, after we leave we're gonna call the cops and tell 'em we heard there was a territory fight over the heroin action, and you lost. When the cops get here, they'll think you were hit by a rival dealer who was teaching you a lesson. Of course, they're gonna find you high, and your security men high, and the stuff. You're gonna go to jail, my man. Ain't that some shit?"

Kelly held the needle against Dorba's arm. "Don't forget our lessons. As the cowboys always say, this town ain't big enough for the both of us." He plunged the needle in and nodded. "Shitty dreams, asshole!"

CHAPTER 23

". . . ashes to ashes and dust to dust, we commend these souls to . . ."
The pastor's words echoed softly across the gently rolling garden of
stones. Josh and Stephen stood hidden within a stand of oaks fifty
yards away from the crowded graveside service, watching the family
of Detective Chick Cummings being put to rest. The three bronze
caskets gleamed in the sun as the MPD honor squad raised their rifles.

"Ready . . . aim . . . fire!"
The volley's echo was joined by the sorrowful sound of "Taps" as
played by a lone bugler on the hill. The city of Washington, D.C. had
given full honors to the detective's family. The mayor had proclaimed
that all of the families had been on the front line when struck down
in the line of duty, supporting their husbands or fathers. It was a kind
gesture, for the entire city was mourning its dead. In every cemetery
in every district and every town within twenty miles, thousands gathered in black to pay their respects to those killed in the bombings.

Standing by the grave, Kelly put his arm around Cummings's
shoulder as the detective tossed a handful of soil first on his wife's
casket, then on his two daughters'.

As the crowd of mourners walked back to their cars, the department captain stepped away from his wife and walked up alongside
Kelly. "Where were you last night, Terry? We had a hell of a night. I
tried to get you at your wife's mother's to see if you could help us
out."

Kelly winced as he took a breath. "Sorry, Cap. I checked myself
back into the hospital last night. I think I pushed too hard too early. I
heard a big-timer went down. Territory fight?"

"Yeah, a bigwig Chink lost. Is Cummings going to be okay?"

Kelly's eyes misted. "I don't know. I keep asking myself how he can go home after this. I don't have the answer."

The captain nodded. "Once Alvarez's family is buried tomorrow, we'll have to work hard to get past this. It'd help if we could find the bastards that did it." He patted Kelly's back in consolation, seeing he was taking it hard. "Take it easy, Terry. You can't let it get to you. See ya in a couple of days."

Minutes later, when the last of the mourners had left the cemetery, Josh and Stephen walked down the knoll and joined Kelly, Youngblood, Hanson, and Alvarez. Still standing by the grave of his wife, Cummings slowly turned and faced the six men who were waiting for him. His tear-filled eyes settled on Kelly. "I heard Dorba is out on bail. Why do we even try?"

Kelly shook his head. "You heard only half of it. His lawyers and two of his doctors convinced the judge they should release him from County General to go to Mercy Hospital, but he never made it. They took him to the airport instead. He skipped bail and flew out with eight of his men on a private jet. We won, Chick. He's history."

"And the others?" Cummings asked, looking into Kelly's eyes.

"Woo has given the DEA the names of Dorba's key players here in town and all the leaders in the other East Coast cities. Like I said, we won this one, but you know as well as I do somebody else will come along to take his place. We ain't out of a job." Kelly took the detective's badge from his jacket pocket and tossed it to him. "Here, Chick. You ain't a cowboy anymore—you're a cop."

Cummings caught the badge and ran his trembling fingers over its shiny surface. "I'm not sure I make a difference anymore, Kelly. We win a few battles, but never the war."

Kelly nodded toward the three mounds covered with flowers. "*They* thought you made a difference. It ain't gonna be easy, but we gotta keep trying. There are a lot more people out there who need us."

Cummings rolled back his shoulders, took a deep breath, and faced his family. Raising his head, he whispered, "Good-bye, kittens. Daddy is going to miss you. Good-bye, Linda. You made it worth living. Take care of them. I love you all."

Kelly watched as his detectives walked to their cars. He turned and put his hand out toward Stephen. "Good-bye, Stephen. I pray things work out for you in your country. You've made a difference here. Thank you."

Stephen's eyes became distant. "Like you told your friend, I have to try. Good-bye, Terrance."

Kelly's gaze shifted to Josh. "Come by my mother-in-law's after you hand Stephen off to the Agency. Mary wants to thank you again with a dinner."

Josh smiled grimly. "I'm going with Stephen. Keep an eye on Stefne for me until I get back."

"Wait a damn minute! What do ya mean, you're goin'?"

Josh shrugged. "It's just somethin' I gotta do."

He turned to walk up the hill but Kelly grabbed his shoulder and spun him around. "What the fuck are you talkin' about, 'gotta do'? You don't *have* to do shit!"

"Drop it, Kelly. This is personal. Like Dorba was personal for you. Okay?"

Seeing Josh's look, Kelly realized there was nothing he could say to make him stay. "Take care, huh? I . . ." He threw his arms around Josh and hugged him. "Take good care of yourself. Mary would be real pissed off if somethin' happened to ya."

CIA Headquarters, Langley, Virginia

Jennings entered the office having come from funerals for two of his department chiefs who had been killed at the conference. He lit a cigar, then shifted his gaze to the two men seated before him. "You finish up your business?" he asked, obviously already knowing the answer.

Neither of the men spoke. Jennings blew out a blue cloud of smoke and focused his eyes on Stephen. "I have a debriefing team ready to hear and record what you told me at the boat house. Afterward I've scheduled some briefings for you to bring you up to date on the last month's events in your country. One particular upcoming event is also very important. General Swei has sent invitations to the world media inviting them to a press conference in Rangoon on July 19, Martyrs' Day. He will then announce the opening of the country and probably the loan guarantees you told me about. I'm telling you this because once he makes those announcements, our best guess is that most countries will formally recognize his new government."

"After what he's done to the people?" Stephen snapped, not believing what he was hearing.

"Stephen, the simple fact is that nobody knows what happened. No outside press has been in Burma to report what went on over the years, and Swei has killed or imprisoned anyone who could speak out against him. The people who watch CNN on July 19 will think they see a man trying to help change his country for the better. He will be a hero to many of them."

"When do I leave?" Stephen asked impatiently.

"In two days," Jennings replied. "We've got to get you a passport and paperwork made and—"

"Count me in too," Josh said matter-of-factly.

Jennings's eyes widened. "I didn't think you wanted to go back."

"I'm in."

Stephen put his hand over Josh's. "You've done enough for me, Joshua. You should stay. Go back to Stefne and your boat. You've found happiness, brother."

Josh shook his head. "I'm going."

Jennings said, "Hawkins, under the circumstances I have to agree with Mr. Kang. His father intends to strike Swei too soon. We believe such an undertaking is doomed to fail. We hope that when Stephen returns he can reason with Xu Kang and convince him to take the time to recruit and train a proper force."

Josh's jaw muscles twitched as he stood up and walked to the window. "No, Xu Kang is right—he has to attack soon." He turned toward Jennings with an icy, accusing stare. "The U.S. will be one of the countries to recognize Swei's government, won't it, Mr. Director? You know they killed our people at the embassy, and you know what they've done to the Burmese people, but we will recognize his government, won't we?"

Jennings lowered his eyes. "Probably. An open Burma means new markets. There are those in our government who believe we have to live with Swei to help American companies get into the country before the Japanese or the Germans. I've argued against it for the reasons you've stated, but they won't listen without solid proof. Industrial competition for markets is another kind of war, and America's businessmen don't like to lose."

Josh knew Jennings was not the enemy, so he simply shrugged. "I'm going, Mr. Director."

Jennings nodded slowly in resignation. "We'll help you in any way we can, until the nineteenth. I'm sorry, Hawkins. I'm truly sorry."

". . . so do just like last time. Keep an eye on Stef and keep the business running."

Bob's eyes were fixed on his boss. "And you can't tell me why or where you're going?"

"Like I told ya on the phone, it's all legit. I asked Glenn to bring

you over here so I could take care of things before I go. Take this. It's a letter of instructions if—"

"Christ, Hawk, don't do this to me. You're workin' for the CIA, aren't you?"

Josh handed him the letter. "You're a smart guy, Bob. You know better than to ask me that. But no, I'm not working for the Agency. It's just something I have to do. Trust me. Don't tell a soul about my leaving except for Stef. She's not going to like it, but she'll understand. Tell everyone else I'm still recovering from my wounds and the location is being kept secret for security reasons."

Bob lowered his head. "I still don't like it, Hawk. I don't like bodies on the pier and those four agents getting killed in the motel. I don't like it that Meg is in the hospital and that Stefne is worried sick about you. This is out of control and it has to stop. This isn't life—this is hell."

"I know. But you have to trust me," Josh said. He stood and stuck out his hand. "Take care of her, Bob. It makes it easier for me. Do me one more favor, huh? Look in on Meg for me, and have one of the guys throw popcorn out for the sparrows now and then."

"And the hunt?"

"That's up to you. Just—"

"I know. Leave *him* for when you get back," Bob said, trying to smile.

Josh walked him back to the car where Grant was waiting. She looked into his eyes and said, "I don't like this, Josh. A few nights ago, I said you couldn't always stay in your little world, but I was wrong. Please don't leave. I don't want you to go."

Josh leaned over and kissed her on the cheek. "Thanks for bringing Bob. Go on. I'll see ya when it's over."

She didn't move. "Josh, please listen to me. It's gotten too political. There's no guarantee the promises Jennings gave you will be fulfilled. It's out of his hands now. It's not worth it anymore."

Josh said firmly, "It is to me." He broke into a jaded smile. "You're learning, Colonel. To them it's never as simple as right or wrong—it's what's *good* for the country. The problem is, none of us get to vote on what we think is *good*. The Burmese people know, and so do I." Josh gave her a last, lingering look, then turned and walked away into the darkness.

Josh walked past the guard into the bedroom, where Stephen was sitting on the bed staring vacantly at the far wall with tear-filled eyes. He spoke in a whisper. "As I watched the detective's wife being buried this afternoon, I thought of Mya. There was no funeral for her, Joshua. She deserved . . . she . . ."

Josh sat down and put his arm around Stephen's shoulder. "You have Jacob. Mya will always be with you through him like Jill is for me in Stefne."

"Joshua, please don't come with me. You might never see Stefne again. I couldn't bear that."

Josh closed his eyes and could hear the Shaduzup mission bell. *Clang! Clang! Clang!* He heard the people screaming as machine-gun bullets ripped through the air. The single gunshots and then the terrible silence, broken only by the last peal of the bell. No one was left to hear it—except him.

Josh's jaw muscles rippled as he squeezed Stephen's shoulder. "I'm not going because of you. I'm going for me."

PART III

CHAPTER 24

Northwest Airlines Flight 434 landed in Bangkok at 6:55 P.M. Minutes later Josh and Stephen walked past the baggage area and headed directly toward the Customs and passport-control booth. Both men had no checked luggage, only carry-on bags. After showing their Agency-made American passports, they were headed for the terminal when a man stepped up behind Josh and said with a grin, "About time you got your ass here."

Josh recognized the voice and turned around to face his previous operation commander, Buck McCoy. "You again, huh?" Josh said with a grin of his own.

"The director thought you'd like to see a familiar face." McCoy turned to Stephen. "Speaking of faces, how's yours, Mr. Kang?"

Stephen didn't speak but looked to Josh for an explanation.

Josh motioned to the Agency man. "Stephen, meet Buck McCoy, our contact."

"A pleasure, U McCoy. Thank you for helping us. Have you any recent news?" Stephen asked as he offered his hand.

"Yeah, but not here. We need to move it." McCoy turned and gave a short nod to two other Caucasians wearing sunglasses and flowered shirts. One raised a small radio to his mouth, and the other walked through the door used by employees and scanned the sidewalk for possible threats.

"Let's go," McCoy said. Josh and Stephen followed him outside to a new Mazda van parked by the curb. A mile from the airport McCoy finally turned around in the front passenger seat and looked at his passengers. "Sorry about the escort, but we're taking no chances. The

DDSI has people in town. I'm taking you to a safe house where you can rest until tomorrow afternoon. We're gonna fly you within forty miles of the border, then Jeep you into Xu Kang's camp."

"You said there were changes," Stephen said.

McCoy lowered his eyes, indicating it was bad news. "Stephen, your father collapsed from exhaustion two days ago. He'd been working day and night for weeks and finally just keeled over."

Stephen showed no emotion other than nodding his head once. Then he asked, "And my son?"

"He's fine. I saw him when I visited the camp four days ago. The old man has been taking good care of him. Look, Stephen, I know I'm just in a supporting role here, but I gotta tell you this. Your father has tried, but there's no way he can organize an army without our help. He just doesn't have enough trainers or the right equipment. You've got to talk him into letting us support him."

Stephen exchanged glances with Josh before looking back into McCoy's questioning eyes. He smiled and said, "You obviously don't know my father."

Still feeling the effects of the long flight, Stephen and Josh both went to their rooms right after dinner. Josh opened the door to his room and turned on the light.

"I thought you'd crash early."

Josh sighed and faced McCoy, who sat in a chair by a small table. The Agency man motioned to the chair across from him. "Sit. We have to talk."

Josh flopped down. "Can't this wait till tomorrow?"

"Look, Hawk, you've gotten involved in something that could get you killed. Some folks don't give a shit—they think you've got a death wish. I know better, and so does the director. Jennings is taking a big chance by keeping this from most of his people, but he says you get anything you want. We have an arrangement that I'll be the fall guy if it all turns to shit. I don't give a damn 'cause I'm only two years away from retirement, but between you and me, this op sucks. I've visited Xu Kang's camp, and as far as I can see they don't have a plan. True, they have people helping them in Rangoon and some high-level informants, but the old man is in over his head. Any kind of direct assault on Swei is suicide."

"What do you want me to do?" Josh asked, knowing McCoy was leading up to something.

"The only way to take care of the problem is to take Swei and his buddies out with small, direct-action teams. I gotta tell you, though, even that's very iffy. According to my sources, Swei is no dummy and he's taking no chances. The news conference he's got planned for the nineteenth is going to be inside the Ministry of Defense compound. The man knows he's a target, and he's keeping himself behind a wall. Hell, he's got tighter security than our president."

"You still haven't told me what you want me to do," Josh said.

"Fuck, Hawk. Old man Kang and Stephen respect you. Talk some sense into them. I'm on your side on this, but wasting hundreds of lives trying to assault the Ministry of Defense compound is not the way to do it. They'll just get themselves killed and Swei will be untouchable."

"You've got a plan, haven't you?" Josh said, seeing McCoy's impatient eyes twinkling.

"No, but I have an idea. I haven't told a soul 'cause it's out of right field and old man Kang would never buy it. All he cares about is his revenge. My idea might bring down the government without anybody pulling a trigger."

Josh leaned closer. "Why haven't you told anybody else about this idea of yours?"

McCoy's lips crawled back in a smile. " 'Cause the Company would definitely not approve. Shit, they'd can me if I even brought it up! It requires someone willing to expose a lot of shit that the intelligence community doesn't want aired to the public."

"And you don't care if the information comes out?"

"Hawk, I've got a mission straight from the director. He said to support you any way I can. I know the State Department and special-interest group assholes are pushing for us to recognize Swei's government. You and I know that's bullshit."

Josh leaned back and tilted his head to the side. "Alright, I'll bite. Let me hear this idea of yours."

McCoy looked up at the ceiling fan and began to speak. "What would happen if . . ."

Josh listened without so much as blinking—after McCoy's first sentence, he saw the idea had possibilities. McCoy finished by saying, "It's only an idea, but I could get you all the documentation and equipment you'd need to do it."

"Wait a minute. That's it?" Josh said incredulously. "You've told me how to get in and what to do once I get there, but you haven't told me how to get out."

McCoy lowered his eyes. "That's the part I haven't quite figured out yet."

Josh rolled his eyes. "Great. When you do, let me know, will ya? In the meantime I'll talk to Stephen and see what he thinks. I like it except for that last part."

McCoy got up and slapped Josh's back. "Sleep on it. Tomorrow the three of us can discuss it during the trip to the camp. Good night. Oh, just one more thing—tomorrow, it's *your* idea, so *you* bring it up. I'm just in a support role, remember?"

5 July, Thailand Border

Josh awoke to find his head resting on Stephen's shoulder. Stephen smiled and said, "You've been out for over two hours. I think we're almost there."

Josh looked out the muddy windows of the Jeep Cherokee and saw they were approaching a village nestled in a valley. No other vehicles were in sight, and it seemed to Josh that while he was asleep they had entered a time warp. Dark brown people were riding horses and mules toward the village. Each of them was carrying some kind of rifle.

The Jeep rolled slowly into town, and Josh's time-warp theory seemed like the best possible explanation. The street looked like something out of an old western. Horses and mules were tied to hitching posts in front of elevated plank walks and dilapidated storefronts with overhangs. Signs in Thai and English hung from the overhangs: HARDWARE, GUNS, MAMIE'S SALOON, HOTEL, and SADDLES AND TACK. The wooden sally ports were filled with people, young and old, all moving with a purpose. Some were in uniform, others in camouflage. Several young men and women were wearing T-shirts that read Rangoon University.

When the Jeep stopped, McCoy got out and let in the oppressive heat, plus the sound of music, laughter, an occasional scream, and distant gunshots. Josh stepped out of the vehicle and did a double take as three small reddish elephants plodded down the road, all carrying crates marked M-72 Antitank Rocket on their backs.

A burly Shan colonel approached with an old Horseman whom Stephen and Joshua recognized immediately. The Shan colonel began to speak, but the Horseman stepped forward and clamped his hands on both Joshua's and Stephen's shoulders. "Greetings and blessings, Saos. The gods have blessed us to have you return to our campfire."

Stephen's eyes misted. "Greetings and blessings, Horseman Lante. It has been many monsoons."

Joshua too was moved by the sight of the old soldier. Lante had aged and looked almost like their old Teacher. His moustache was snow-white and swept back like their old mentor's.

Joshua slapped his hand on the Horseman's shoulder. "To gaze upon you lifts my heart. I have thought of you often."

The colonel stepped forward to take control. He stiffly bowed his head to Stephen and Joshua, but his expression turned colder as he faced McCoy. "You must leave. We want no dealing with you."

McCoy nodded with a sigh of resignation and stuck his hand out toward Stephen. "Good luck. I'll be waiting for your radio message." He winked at Josh as he got back behind the wheel. "See you around."

The colonel turned and again bowed toward Joshua. "I am Colonel Banta, operations officer for the Chindit's army. Would you both please follow me."

Stephen bristled at the colonel's obvious attempt to ignore him. "I see you haven't changed, Banta. You still know nothing of manners."

Banta's face screwed up in a menacing scrowl, but he did not give voice to his feelings. "Come, your son is waiting at the headquarters."

"Where is the Chindit?" Joshua asked, falling in behind the colonel as they began to walk up the street.

"He is attending to several DDSI spies who were captured in the village last night. He will be back within the hour," Banta said, keeping a steady pace.

"Xu Kang is feeling better, then?" Josh asked.

Banta spun around to regard Josh with narrowed eyes. "How did you know the Sawbaw has been sick?"

Horseman Lante growled, "You are speaking to a Horseman. Speak with respect or I will give you a lesson in manners."

Banta sighed and nodded. "You are right, Horseman Lante. I apologize to you, Sao Hawkins, and to you, Stephen. I have not slept in three days. We have so little time and so much to accomplish. Please forgive my bad manners." Banta regarded Joshua. "You asked about the Chindit. I speak true when I say he is not well. He needs rest. He left our doctor's care this afternoon to deal with the spies who were trying to discover our plans. The Sawbaw wanted to question them before they were hung and didn't want Jacob or the students to see the questioning. The ants will make them talk."

Both Josh and Stephen shuddered. They knew the prisoners would be buried in ant dens up to their necks.

Banta stepped off again. "Come, we have much to discuss."

Josh and Stephen followed the colonel up an alley that ended at a huge stockade. They walked alongside the six-inch-thick bamboo wall until they came to a barbed-wire and wood gate.

Once they were inside, Josh's head spun as he tried to take it all in. The camp looked like a Southeast Asian version of Fort Apache, with the fence and guard towers made of yellow bamboo. Thatch-roofed huts and tents were laid out in regimental rows, and men and women marching in small formations kicked up clouds of red dust.

Banta pointed at a formation of small Karin tribesmen armed with antique rifles and swords. "Our army grows every day. All the minorities have joined us, as have many Burmans. The pye dogs will soon be with their ancestors." He continued walking up a gravel path under a large camouflage net toward a large sayo-wood cabin with an extended porch.

Stephen stopped suddenly when he saw an old woman wearing a blue turban sitting on the porch with a small boy.

Kaska saw Stephen and her eyes began to tear. Standing up, she bent over Jacob and pointed at his father. The small boy's eyes followed her extended finger and his face lit up. "Papa!" he yelled as he broke into a run. "Papa, you've come back!"

Stephen wiped his own watering eyes and ran to meet his son with open arms. He hugged the boy to his chest.

Josh continued up the steps and hugged the old woman. He said in Shan, "You're as beautiful as ever, housemother."

Her wrinkled face turned a shade darker and she slapped at his shoulder. "You lie, White Sao, but it is music to this ancient one. I missed gazing on you. Many monsoons have passed since you visited the house of Kang." Her eyes saddened. "My second daughter is with her ancestors. The pye dogs came."

Josh provided the customary reply. "She lived well. The gods are pleased with her presence."

"Ayee, they are very pleased."

Stephen came up the steps holding Jacob's hand. He faced the old woman and reached out to pat her right shoulder. "Greetings and blessings, second mother. I have missed your wisdom."

Kaska bowed her head. "Greetings and blessings, Sao. The gods are kind to return you safely. I . . . I tried, Sao. I fought the pye dogs but they took my second daughter. The gods are very pleased with her presence."

Stephen forced a smile. "Yes, very pleased." He squatted down to be level with his son and motioned toward Josh.

"This ugly, long-nosed American is your uncle Joshua."

Jacob stepped forward and extended his hand, Western-style. "I've read all your letters, Uncle."

Josh ignored his hand and shocked the round-faced boy by picking him up. "You can't be Jacob! The pictures I received were of a little ant. You are nearly big enough to be a Horseman. Who are you really?"

"Jacob! I am Jacob Kang, son of Sao Kang! You are supposed to shake hands," the boy exclaimed, confused by the strange greeting and the silly question.

Stephen shook his head with a smile. "Jacob, your uncle is to be excused, for he is crazy. He has no manners and is joking with you."

Josh laughed and hugged the boy to his chest. "Yes, I taught your father how to joke and I'll teach you, too."

Smiling, Colonel Banta stepped forward. "Come, Saos. I will show you to your quarters."

Josh put Jacob down and the boy again stuck out his hand. "I have practiced like Grandfather taught me for your arrival."

Josh stood erect, looked the boy in the eyes, and shook his hand. "Greetings and blessings, little Sao."

"Wall-come to 'ere, is a pla . . . plasure to you meet," Jacob said in halting English.

"The honor is mine," Josh replied in English as he formally bowed his head.

Beaming, Jacob kept pumping Josh's hand and switched back to Shan. "You understood me! My English was good, yes?"

"It was super."

"Supa?" Jacob repeated, releasing his grip and looking confused.

"It means 'very good,' " Josh explained in Shan.

Kaska intervened. "Come, third son. Horseman Lante and I need assistance in brewing tea for the Chindit and your father."

Jacob ran over to take Horseman Lante's hand but gave Josh a wink. "Supa!"

Stephen put his arm over Josh's shoulder as they followed the colonel. "If you corrupt my son, I'll bury *you* in ants."

Josh feigned a frown and began to bob his head. "Yes, Sawbaw. Anything else, Sawbaw?"

Stephen grinned and squeezed Josh tighter. "It is like the old days to see you joke and laugh. Jacob did not hear much laughter in Rangoon."

"Maybe we can change that," Josh said soberly.

Stephen looked his brother in the eyes. "Yes, maybe we can."

Banta led them into a large rattan-walled hut directly behind the headquarters. "The Chindit wishes you both to stay with him."

Stephen stiffened. "No, not here. A tent is fine. Have one of the servants move my son's things as well."

The colonel said angrily, "Your father wants you to—"

"He can go to a tent."

The three men turned to face the tall, silver-haired man who stood in the hut entrance. Xu Kang said, "Colonel, go tell the leaders it's almost time for our planning session. We will meet tomorrow night in the headquarters at seven."

Banta dipped his chin to his commander, gave Stephen one last warning glare, and strode out the door.

The old man smiled at Josh. "By the gods, I knew you would come!" He opened his arms and pulled Josh to his breast. "Greetings and blessings, old friend. Thank you for bringing me my son."

Josh could barely fake a smile to cover his shock. Xu Kang was only a shadow of the man he had been years before. His powerful body seemed to have shriveled and his face now had a pasty gray pallor. "Greetings and blessings, Sawbaw. I'm honored to be with you again."

The old man's faded smile dissolved as he faced his son. "I see nothing has changed between us, but at least you have come. We need you."

Stephen bowed his head. "Go back to bed, Father. You don't look well. I will talk to your colonel and see what I can do to help." Lifting his chin, Stephen marched out of the hut, staring straight ahead.

Kang looked at Josh, trying to conceal his broken heart. "Is his face wound painful?"

Josh saw that Xu Kang could barely stand, so he took his arm and steered him to his bed. He helped the old man down and took a seat beside him. "His face will heal, as will his heart from the loss of Mya. His presence here tells you he loves you."

Kang laid back on the reed mat and closed his tearing eyes. "He came only because of Jacob. It was an old man's foolish dream to believe that the passing of so many monsoons would teach him forgiveness. I'm weary, Joshua, but there is much to do."

"Sleep, Chindit. Stephen and I are here to help you, so sleep and regain your strength."

Kang's eyes fluttered open and he smiled faintly. "I knew you would come—I knew the gods would call you home."

Josh patted the old man's shoulder. "They've been calling me for a long, long time."

Colonel Banta showed Stephen around the camp and afterward led him into the headquarters. ". . . and as you saw there are Chin, Kachin, Meo, and Burmese workers. We have countless students, some doctors, and even monks. They have all come here and to other camps to get away from Swei and General Tan, who now runs the DDSI."

Banta sat down behind his desk and told Stephen, "Those you saw here and in the village are just the latest flood who have left our country. We send them back to join our silent army in Rangoon with orders to wait."

Stephen had not seen or heard anything that the CIA hadn't already told him, but now he looked at Banta hopefully. "Waiting for what?"

"Our attack, of course," the colonel said, as if it were obvious.

"Attack who and what? Please be more specific—I must know our plans."

Banta's eyes narrowed. "Sao, I have been with your father for twenty years. In that span, you and I have met perhaps three times. You have never shown your father respect and yet he has always spoken of you with love and pride. Today you showed him nothing but disdain. I had hoped you would come and help him, but instead you hurt him again. He needs no more wounds, especially from his son. Take Jacob and return to Bangkok. The Chindit needs only those who believe in him."

Stephen was about to respond when Josh walked into the office. He could see from the look on Stephen's face that something was wrong. "What's going on?" he asked.

Stephen motioned to Banta. "The colonel thinks I should return to Bangkok with Jacob."

Josh replied coldly, "I can understand why, after the way you treated your father. He didn't need that from you. He's down and you just pushed him down further."

Stephen glared first at Josh and then at the colonel. "I am staying. As son of the Chindit I will be recognized as second-in-command. Tell me the plans now!"

Banta kept his frown but smiled inwardly. He had just seen a fire in the younger Kang's eyes that he had seen in his Sawbaw's eyes many times. He shifted his gaze to Josh and motioned to the chairs. "Please sit, Horseman Hawkins. The Sao has commanded me to give him a briefing on our plans."

Banta stood. He dipped his head toward Stephen before turning and pointing at the map pinned on the wall. "The attack is planned for the eighteenth, a day before Martyrs' Day. We are planning to infiltrate small units across the border beginning tomorrow. Their mission will be . . ."

Stephen listened intently without asking questions until Banta began discussing the latter phase of the operation. ". . . and when the students have blocked the roads we will attack the compound with antitank rockets. Once the breach is made, we will move forward—"

"Too many will be killed," Stephen interrupted. He stood up and walked to the map. "There is a better way to get in."

Banta shook his massive head as if dealing with a recruit. "Sao, our people have made a complete reconnaissance of the Defense Ministry compound. There is no way in other than a head-on assault."

Stephen tapped the map. "Here is where we will get in."

The colonel looked at where Stephen was pointing and chuckled. "Sao, that is the Congress building. It is six hundred meters from the Ministry of Defense.

"Yes, you are right, six hundred meters. But that is where I entered the ministry every day for a year. There is a tunnel."

Banta's eyes widened. Stephen picked up a pencil from the desk and drew on the map. "The Congress Hall was built before the Japanese invaded. The British constructed an underground command post beneath it with connecting tunnels to other buildings and bombproof aboveground bunkers. Today just one tunnel remains. This tunnel runs from the Congress compound to the Defense Ministry, then four hundred meters beyond to the DDSI's underground command center. I know this because it was the only way the DDSI would allow me to enter their compound. They had me park my car at the Congress Hall. They would escort me to the tunnel entrance in the basement and lead me down the tunnel past the Ministry of Defense entrance to the underground command center."

Banta studied the newly drawn lines on the map. "I never heard of these tunnels before."

"They are a very well kept secret known only to the DDSI," Stephen said.

"How many guards did you see at the entrance of the tunnel at the Congress Hall?"

Stephen thought back and said slowly, "Two at the Congress compound gate entrance, two more at the Congress back and front doors, and two at the basement tunnel entrance. There were two guards at the Defense Ministry entrance as well." Stephen reached for his billfold and took out a yellow plastic card with his picture on it. "They know me, and I still have a pass to get in."

Josh shook his head and stood up. "Don't even think about it, Stephen. That card will just get you killed."

"Not if I have a concealed silenced pistol and a backup team to cover me."

Josh stared at his friend. "It's too dangerous."

Banta snarled at Josh, "He is right. Too many will die in a frontal assault. The tunnel is an excellent alternative." He quickly unpinned the map and laid it on the desk. "We need to change the plan and reorganize our assault force. What else do you know that will help?"

Stephen gestured toward Josh. "The date of the attack needs to be the nineteenth, during Swei's press conference. Joshua has an idea about how he can get into the Defense Ministry during the conference and expose Swei. It will also guarantee that that butcher will be in the compound when we attack."

Banta's eyes widened again. "By the gods! No wonder the Chindit wanted you two with him. You both have demon minds."

Josh stepped up to the map while searching Stephen's face for an explanation. Stephen had not mentioned the tunnel to him and Mc-Coy once during their discussions when traveling to the camp.

Stephen saw the questioning stare and set his shoulders with determination. "Little brother, it was best not to let your people know everything. Swei and his pye dogs must die. Your idea will help reach your country's goal—killing Swei will accomplish ours."

Banta clapped Josh's shoulder. "Tell me your plan."

Josh could see that Stephen was filled with too much hate to think with reason. He shifted his eyes to the colonel. "The idea is for me to . . ."

Ministry of Defense, Rangoon

Prime Minister Swei rapped his fingers nervously on the desk. "All of your white powder is gone?"

The Triad elder seated before him nodded. "Yes, it was a very bad miscalculation on our part. A group of men calling themselves 'cowboys' caused us much damage. Our San Chu was forced to leave, for these cowboys knew all about his business. We feel this group operates within the American government intelligence organization. It's very disturbing—we had no knowledge of such a group. Very disturbing, and very expensive for us. Also, an elder's son is missing. We believe he has turned traitor. This could substantially hurt our future plans in the United States. I see by your eyes that you are concerned about your funds. Have no fear, old friend. We will abide by our agreements, but we ask your assistance in helping us recover our losses. White powder is a very lucrative market. We need you to supply us with more of this profitable powder."

Swei's chest tightened. "With all respect, my friend, it will be impossible to do so once my country is opened to the West. I have already destroyed the production facilities, and—"

The gray-haired elder raised his hand and interrupted. "We are well aware of what you have done, and we agree that further direct involvement on your part would be unwise. We have a plan that we believe you will accept. Your northern country will be plagued by problems with rebels and bandits, so your army will have to seal off this troubled area. The rest of the country will indeed be open and prosper—in the north *we* will prosper. Give us two years of freedom to grow the flowers and produce the white powder near your northern border. Your government will of course receive 15 percent of the profits."

Swei felt his heart pounding through his chest. "People in the West will know."

"My friend, they *already* know about you. But they will accept you because of the profits you will bring them. Nations look out for their own wealth—we know this and have used it to our benefit for years. You will be giving your people jobs and rebuilding your country while you are making Western companies rich. No, the charade will be accepted as it is in South America. You just have to say and do the right things. Trust us on this. We know and will advise you."

Swei lowered his eyes in defeat. "I accept your wisdom."

General Tan paced in front of his superior's desk. "We should have known the fornicating Chinese would do this to us."

Swei sighed with resignation. "They ask for only two years. We will have to live with the arrangement. Stop pacing and tell me what has happened to Xu Kang."

Tan's hooded eyes smiled. "He is sick and weak. Our patrols have picked up students and others returning from his camp. They report the Sawbaw is very feeble and has told them to go home and wait."

"Wait? Wait for what?" Swei asked.

The thick-chested general grinned like a ferret. "For the gods to give them a sign."

Swei chuckled. "A sign? Well then, let's give Xu Kang one. I will announce during my press conference that I will grant him amnesty if he will stay in his beloved northern Shan state. We'll let the Triad deal with him."

Tan snorted through his nose in laughter.

Thailand Border

Colonel Banta pinned the map back on the wall. "I believe we have a good plan, Sao."

Stephen glanced at the notes he'd made. "Yes, it will work if all goes well and the students stick to the schedule." He shifted his eyes to Josh. "What do you think?"

Josh shook his head. "I still don't want you to lead the tunnel assault team. Let someone else do it."

Stephen leveled a stare at Josh. "And I don't like your going to the press conference. Can you think of substitutes who have our knowledge and can do what we can?"

Josh's eyes showed that he couldn't. He looked back at the map. "You still need information about the inside of the Defense Ministry, especially their command center."

Banta smiled. "No problem. We have a Burmese corporal who deserted to us a few weeks ago. He was a radio repairman for the Defense Ministry and worked in the command center. He did not know about the tunnel, but he has already made us sketches of everything else. He will tell us what we need to know."

Stephen patted Josh's shoulder. "Contact McCoy with the radio he gave us and start to make the arrangements for your plan. Have him pick you up in a few days to prepare. Colonel Banta and I will discuss our assault plan with my father and begin drilling the assault force." Stephen's eyes locked into Josh's. "I want you to take Kaska and Jacob with you and arrange for their safety in Bangkok."

Before Josh could respond, a captain ran into the hut. "Colonel Banta, we have found another spy!"

Banta slowly turned to Stephen. "What are your orders, Sawbaw?"

The title was not lost on Stephen. He took his father's pistol belt from a peg on the wall and put it on. Raising his chin, he said to the captain, "We'll make the pye dog talk—then hang him. Lead me to him."

Banta stepped up beside Josh as Stephen left with the young officer. "The gods have their wish. He is a Sawbaw now as was their will."

Josh took a breath for strength and walked out the door in silence.

CHAPTER 25

The next morning Josh was roused by a poke in his ribs. He opened his eyes and looked into the twinkling eyes of a small, mop-haired boy. "Uncle Joshua, my father said to wake you. Are you really my uncle?"

Josh sat up with a tired smile. "Yes, I am your uncle. And do you know what uncles do when they're poked in the ribs?"

"No," Jacob answered innocently.

Josh got up and peered down at him. "They poke back!" He grabbed the boy and began tickling his ribs.

Jacob laughed and fought back playfully. He finally broke away and dashed a few steps, then turned and yelled, "Come with me, Uncle! I'll show you where we eat and the rest of the camp. Grandfather has shown me everything. He is a great Sawbaw, and he has lots of horses in his other camp. He told me he would teach me to ride." He stepped closer with wide eyes and offered his hand.

Josh took it and allowed himself to be led down the hut steps. On the porch of the headquarters Stephen was sitting at a table with a group of men looking at a map. He glanced up when Josh passed and gave him a nod of thanks before looking back at the map.

Josh spent the entire morning with Jacob, who truly did know the camp inside and out. He was just as familiar with the seedy town that he was now escorting Josh through.

Jacob stopped and motioned to a shell-curtained door out of which music was blaring. "This is a soldier's rest place. The girls inside give them baths and make them forget their troubles. Grandfather says every soldier needs such a place to rest now and then. I hope I can be a soldier soon, since the girls inside are very pretty and smell wonderful. I like talking to them."

Josh nudged his guide along. "Yes, I'm sure. What's this up here?" he asked, pointing quickly at the next building.

Later that afternoon, Jacob led a weary American up the steps of the sleeping hut. Josh abruptly halted. Xu Kang sat in a chair on the porch with his feet propped up on a stool. His color had returned, as had his bright, infectious smile.

Jacob ran ahead and hugged the old man, and Xu Kang patted the boy's back. Then he gently pushed him back with accusing eyes. "Did you visit with the night hens again?"

Jacob lowered his eyes and motioned to Josh. "Uncle Joshua wouldn't let me."

The old man laughed and raised the boy's chin. "Good for him! Now go march with a formation of recruits and learn some discipline. There will be time for the night hens when you are older."

Xu Kang motioned to a chair beside him as Jacob ran down the porch steps. "Sit, Horseman. I hear my grandson took you on a tour of our host village. What did you think of it?"

Josh sat down and shrugged his shoulders. "It's interesting. I saw everything from raw opium to Coors beer, plus every type of rifle and pistol ever made. Why do the Thais let this place exist?"

Kang swept his hand toward the camp gate. "This is no-man's-land. It is where the traffickers, gunrunners, black marketeers, and political refugees come. The Thai border patrols leave this place alone, for it provides valuable information. Spies are everywhere, but I have known these people for years, so I know who the spies are."

Josh changed the subject. "Jacob's really something. I had fun with him today."

Kang leaned back with a nod. "He reminds me of you and Stephen when you were young. You two boys stole my heart then—now Jacob has stolen it again." The warlord turned and looked back at Jacob, who was marching at the end of a file. "I regret none of it and apologize to no man. I have lived life to the fullest and now gaze upon my grandson while his father takes my place as Sawbaw. I would change nothing, Joshua. The simple dream of an old man has come true. Is it possible for you to understand this?"

Josh patted the old man's back. "I understand, but I am very concerned about Stephen's leading the assault."

Kang shook his head and gazed into the distance. "He will not lead—I will. The gods have willed it. It is for me to enter the cave to face the cobras. I have seen the vision many times and must follow the gods' wisdom."

"Xu Kang, with all respect to the gods, you must let younger warriors lead. Your people need you."

"Ahh, spoken like an American. You worry about this old man and about our people. Joshua, every man has such a cave within him . . . but few face the darkness and enter. It is my *kan*. You, my son, understand *kan* . . . it has brought you home. I *have* to lead as you *had* to return . . . the gods . . . the gods have willed it."

Josh nodded in silent understanding, got up, and walked inside the hut. He lay down on his reed mat and closed his eyes to take a nap before the all-important meeting. He understood *kan* all too well.

Josh sat at the back of the crowded room. Four oil lamps hanging from sayo-wood beams cast a yellow-orange glow over the faces of the men and women who sat at the table. Sawbaw Xu Kang was notably absent from the group, making Stephen the oldest person at the table. To Stephen's right was Colonel Banta, who was completing a situation update by telling of Swei's planned news conference.

Josh scanned the young leaders' intense faces. They were students, businessmen, peasants, soldiers, and even a monk. They represented different races, sexes, beliefs, and religions, but they all had two obvious things in common—they considered themselves Burmese and they all desperately wanted change.

Josh shifted in his chair to watch Stephen and felt a chill. He had removed the bandage from his face to reveal an ugly, purplish-red gash across his cheek, and his burning eyes were locked in a distant, foreboding stare.

The colonel concluded his situation update, and every pair of eyes in the room looked at Stephen. He stood and smiled his father's confident smile as he looked into the expectant faces. "In seven days it will be over. We have one chance and it depends on perfect timing. The colonel has just told us General Swei will give a news conference in the Defense Ministry compound in seven days. During the conference, we will strike. We will begin the operation by . . ."

The evening grew longer but no one in the room moved; they all were held spellbound as Stephen spoke of his plan. Josh felt his heart pounding and the blood racing through his veins. Stephen Kang had become a true Sawbaw. He was giving his people hope.

Sitting below a window outside the cabin, Xu Kang leaned against the old sayo logs and listened to his son. A single tear trickled down the old man's face and dropped soundlessly into the dust.

12 July

The early-morning mist was rising from the damp earth as Jacob stood in front of his father. "Will I see you soon, Papa?"

Stephen reached down and picked the boy up. "Yes, in just a week we will be together, and I'll never have to leave you again." He gave his son a hug and set him down.

"Promise?" Jacob asked, searching his father's eyes.

Stephen smiled. "I promise. One week, son. Remember to take good care of Kaska—you are now her protector."

Jacob nodded and walked over to his grandfather, who kneeled down and hugged him. "No tears, little Sawbaw. Soon we will ride through the green mountain valleys and hunt the *gyi* and wild boar. What glorious days we will have, telling our hunting stories by the crackling fire."

Stephen found himself smiling as he watched his father lead Jacob to the Jeep. Josh walked up beside Stephen and offered his hand. "I'll see you in five days as per the plan. Until then, brother."

Stephen grabbed Josh's hand and pulled him close to his chest. "Take care of yourself, brother, and take care of Jacob for me. Promise me."

Josh patted Stephen's back and tried to step away, but Stephen held him in a vicelike grip. "Promise me, Joshua—you must promise me."

"I promise you, brother."

Stephen released him and nodded. "Five days."

"Five days," Josh said with finality, then turned and walked toward the Jeep.

Xu Kang buckled Jacob's and Kaska's seat belts and turned to Josh. "I will see you soon, so there will be no farewells between us. We will have such stories to tell at the campfires, eh?"

Josh forced a smile and clapped his hand on the old man's right shoulder. "You bring the zu, Chindit, and we will lie until the morning frogs croak."

The old man laughed and rolled back his shoulders. "The gods be with you!"

Xu Kang walked back to where Stephen stood watching the vehicle disappear down the rutted road. "Too many times I did what you are doing now—wishing things were different and that you had spent more time with your son."

Stephen reached out and clapped his father's right shoulder. "In five days it will be over. We will finish it together as father and son. The gods have willed it."

Kang's eyes teared. "Together it is, my son."

Ministry of Defense, Rangoon

Prime Minister Ren Swei stood in front of his office closet mirror as the tailor marked the cuff of his suit trousers. Swei looked at the reflection of his information minister, who stood behind him. "I've read the speech. I made only a few changes. However, I am not comfortable with the questioning period at the end of the conference. Cancel it."

The thin, bespectacled minister's shoulders sagged as he raised his hands in prayer fashion. "It is impossible, Prime Minister. The press releases and invitations have been out for weeks. It is expected in a democratic—"

"The prime minister said cancel it!" General Tan snapped from his seat near the door.

Swei raised his hand. "Wait, let him speak. Please, U Dau, tell me what is expected."

The little man nervously removed his glasses. "It would be expected of a leader who proposes a democratic government to answer questions from the press. It shows you have nothing to hide and are willing to communicate with the world. I will ensure that the press asks only questions you are prepared to answer and that no more than five questions are asked."

The tailor began pinning up the jacket material, and Swei straightened his back as he looked at himself in the mirror. "Yes, I agree. It will be a first in our country. Add that to the next press release."

Tan eyed the little minister with contempt. "How can you be so sure you can control the questions?"

"I will have a drawing, and those reporters who win will be given a list of questions the prime minister deems suitable. It is done all the time. They will understand."

"I don't like it," Tan said, shaking his head. "There will be television crews there."

Swei smiled. "I like it. I'll be seen as a struggling leader trying to save his country. I can always just say that I'm new to this but I am trying hard to become worthy of the position. Yes, I like it. Approved. Now, what is the latest count?"

The information minister put his glasses back on and took a small notepad from his pocket. "Fifty-two people representing twenty-one countries. The BBC will be filming for a documentary, and you already know about CNN and the Japanese television crews. Germany will also send a crew, as will Thailand."

The tailor nodded and Swei stepped down from the small stool. "I want nothing but the best for them when they arrive. Ensure the hotel staff knows to cater to all their needs and requests. That is all, U Dau. I will make out a list of questions for you this evening and send them over. Thank you."

Swei took off the suit jacket and handed it to the tailor. "Two black and one gray, as we discussed. Please leave us now." He waited until the tailor had shut the door before asking Tan, "Have the wage increases given us the needed rally supporters?"

"Beyond our dreams," Tan replied with a smile. "The government workers and even the students will be marching with banners to show their support. The army units we planned to bring in wearing civilian clothes are no longer necessary. Money talks. The people are ecstatic with the increases in pay; already the economy is beginning to rebound. The markets are flourishing. When you announce tomorrow that you will free all political prisoners on the nineteenth, any remaining opposition will vanish."

Swei nodded, then walked to his desk and looked out the window. "We have done it, my friend. Our dream is a reality. Nothing can stop us now."

Bangkok, Thailand

McCoy stopped once outside the chief of station's house and poked Josh in the chest. "If that old Shan woman spits betel juice in his house, the chief *and* his wife will kill you."

Josh shrugged. "Kaska carries a cup around with her. Relax, they'll love her."

McCoy's glare softened. "The missus liked Jacob well enough. Maybe she'll give the old woman a break. Come on, I've got to get you to the safe house and get you briefed. Your performance begins in five days—that's not much time to learn the lingo and memorize the names of the movers and shakers who will be there."

Josh turned and waved to Jacob, who stood by the window. "I really like that kid, Buck."

McCoy opened the back door of the sedan. "You'll see him again when the op is over. We've got work to do now."

CHAPTER 26

18 July, Mingaladon Airport, Rangoon

Josh stepped down from the Myanmar Airways Fokker F-28 onto the steaming pavement and followed the other twelve passengers toward the small terminal. His clothes were already soaked with sweat when he entered the stifling and crowded baggage area. After picking up his two large bags, he walked to the Customs gate, where he showed his U.S. passport, visa, and credentials. The Customs officer smiled when he saw the press identification. "Happy you here, Mis-tar Ness. Good things come now with new prime minis-ter. Walcome."

Josh nodded with a fake smile and took back his documents. Then he picked up his bags and strode toward the exit to find a cab. He had almost reached the door when a petite, attractive Burmese woman dressed in a traditional *longyi* approached him and bowed her head. "Mis-ta Nessa, yes?"

"Ness. Who are you?" Josh asked suspiciously.

"Sorry, Mis-ta Ness," the woman said with a happy smile. "I work at Ministry of Information and have come to escort you to hotel. All press receive very best treatment while in our country. Please, I take your bags?"

Feeling relieved, Josh returned her smile. "No, I can carry 'em. Just lead the way, and thanks for the lift."

The woman opened the glass doors for him and pointed to a Toyota van parked at the curb.

As soon as Josh sat down in the backseat with the pretty escort, the driver peeled away from the curb. The woman's smile was replaced by a somber, all-business look. "Colonel Banta want you to know all is ready. Last of the men infiltrate into city last night."

"You—you're with us?" Josh stammered.

"Many are with movement. Please listen, there is much more I must tell you. There will be a drawing this night, and . . ."

Josh walked into the Strand Hotel lobby and felt instantly at home. The British, pre–World War II relic was one of the oldest hotels in the city and had been his and Jill's home for weeks when he was assigned to Burma in '81. Nothing had changed. The antique ceiling fans still squeaked, and the late-nineteenth-century furniture in the lobby was in the same position. He scanned the people in the lobby before approaching the check-in desk. He noted two Burmese men who looked out of place among the small groups of chatting Western reporters. He knew the two men had to be DDSI keeping an eye on the guests. Putting on a weary smile, Josh approached the desk and spoke to the young man behind the counter.

"I'm Jeff Ness from the *Boston Globe.* You should have a reservation for me."

The desk clerk smiled as he looked up at the bearded man. "Ah yes, Mr. Ness, we've been expecting you. Your paper let us know a few days ago that Mr. Momery wouldn't be coming and that you were taking his place. Is Mr. Momery feeling better?"

"Yes, much better, thank you."

The clerk pulled a large brown envelope from a cardboard box and passed it across the counter. "You are nearly the last one to get here, Mr. Ness. All of the foreign media representatives are staying with us. This packet from our Information Ministry explains the schedule and includes your press pass. There is a meeting this evening in the lounge, and don't miss the buses tomorrow at 8 A.M. There will be no other way to enter the Defense Ministry compound. Here is your room key. I'll have a porter help with your bags."

Josh collected the packet and key with an inner smile.

Josh stood at the bar among a virtual who's who from the news and broadcasting world. Like the others, he was waiting for the scheduled meeting in the bar. Josh glanced around at the people, all of whom were wearing plastic-covered badges. At the top of each was a colored flag denoting their country, followed by the newspaper, magazine, radio or television organization they worked for, and finally their name. The crowd quieted when a small, well-dressed Burmese man stepped up to a microphone on the band stage. He tilted his head to the audience and stood erect with a big, plastic grin.

"On behalf of Prime Minister Ren Swei, I welcome you to Myanmar. I am aware most of you call our country 'Burma' but we prefer to use our language-pronunciation for our country. I am the prime minister's media and press relations officer, U Oo. I hope you have found your accommodations adequate, and I thank you for your attendance this evening. In your packets there is an advance copy of the prime minister's speech outlining his plan for our country's three-year rebuilding program and his plan for economic recovery. As your organizations requested, the prime minister will hold a question-and-answer period immediately after his televised speech. The general has allocated ten minutes for this session. In the interest of fairness, I have placed all of your names in this box. My assistant will now draw five names. These five reporters will be called on in the order selected to ask questions about the general's programs." Oo motioned to a small, dark-haired woman who walked up the steps holding a wooden box.

Josh coughed to hide his surprise. The names would be drawn by his pretty escort of that afternoon.

She shook the box and opened the top. Reaching in, she took out a folded piece of paper and handed it to the media officer. "The first question will come from a representative from the *Boston Globe*— Mr. Jeff Ness. The second will come . . ."

Josh headed for the bar and ordered a beer. Xu Kang's silent army had done its part—now it was his turn.

"It tastes like piss, don't it?"

Josh turned to face a big, blond man wearing a wrinkled khaki safari jacket. He read the name off the badge and put out his hand. "Yeah, Robert, but it's cold. I'm Jeff Ness."

The red-faced man shook Josh's hand. "Robert Fletcher, *L.A. Times*. You're a lucky sonofabitch. I'll give you five hundred for the spot."

Josh shook his head. "Sorry. My editor would kill me."

Fletcher frowned, bellied up to the bar, and called for a beer. He studied Josh's profile for a moment, then pursed his lips. "Haven't seen you before. You're a newbie, right? Newbies get all the fuckin' breaks. Well, you sure picked a helluva place to start. This fucking country is a dump."

Josh shrugged. "I haven't been here long enough to form an opinion."

Fletcher scowled. "I've been here for two days. Believe me, it's like stepping back into the 1950s. It's backward with a capital *B*. Aw, for cryin' out loud. Look who just came through the door. You're gonna love Freddie. He's a party animal. Hey, Freddie! Over here!"

Josh turned and froze. Shit! He'd been had.

Freddie, wearing a photographer's vest, approached with a confident strut. Grinning, he pounded the *Times* correspondent's back. "Well, I'll be damned. How the hell are ya, Robert? Haven't seen your ugly face since . . . Shit, I can't even remember!"

Fletcher elbowed Josh in the ribs. "Jeff Ness, meet Freddie Sloan, freelancer for anybody who will keep him in harm's way. Right, Freddie?"

Still grinning, Buck McCoy stuck his hand out toward Josh. "Right you are. Hi, Jeff. Any friend of Robert's is a friend of mine. What are you boys drinkin'?"

Josh shook McCoy's hand and tried very hard to break the agent's fingers. "Welcome to Burma, 'Freddie.' "

Stephen stood on Singuttara Hill's wooden platform and looked over the lights of Rangoon far below. Behind him was the city's most prominent landmark and one of Asia's greatest Buddhist shrines—the Shwe Dagon pagoda, a 2,500-year-old, 320-foot-tall, gilded Buddhist stupa.

The evening was still and quiet; the only sounds were the soft tinkling of the bells at the pagoda's pinnacle and the shuffling of the barefoot pilgrims who had made the long trek up the stone steps to pay homage. A light breeze carried the smell of incense to him from the hundreds of burning joss sticks by the idol. Stephen watched the silent people who had come to soothe their minds. He knew each would paste yet another thin gold leaf to the stupa in offering for prayers they hoped would be granted.

Seated on the step, Xu Kang looked up at his son. "They pray for what only mortal men can give them."

Stephen sat down by his father and said softly, "The radio relay team is in position behind the base of the pagoda platform. Our leaders report our mortal men are in position and ready for tomorrow."

The old man didn't seem to hear. He waved his hand toward the distant lake that lay glistening in the moonlight at the foot of the hill. "I still have that picture of you and Mya there on Royal Lake when you went sailing with Joshua and his wife."

Stephen looked up at the sky with a reflective gaze. "It seems like a lifetime ago. We believed things would get better. How were we to know it would turn out like this?"

Xu Kang patted his son's leg. "You will have your memories forever. There will be more with Jacob as you watch him grow."

Stephen broke his stare away from the countless stars and stood. Turning, he extended his hand to his father. "It's time for us to join our men. They are waiting."

Xu Kang took his son's hand and stood. Looking over his shoulder at the pilgrims, he smiled. "Tomorrow, you and I will answer their prayers."

Josh quickly grew tired of watching Fletcher and McCoy try to pick up a pair of long-legged blonde German reporters. He leaned over McCoy's shoulder and whispered, "Room forty-four—five minutes."

McCoy shrugged noncommittally and scooted his chair closer to the attractive reporter who had been giving him all the right signs.

Prime Minister Swei stepped into the empty press-conference room with his information minister and General Tan. The small information minister motioned to the flower-lined stage with pride. "The flower arrangements create an image of freshness and hope. We want the press and invited guests to see, hear, smell, and feel our new beginning. Your words, U Swei, will not be for the press. They will be for our people and the people of the world. They will see a gentle man, a phoenix, lifting himself and his people from the ashes of ruin. They will see a quiet, selfless man offering hope and a new future."

Swei's eyes sparkled as he straightened his back, lifted his chin, and strode up the steps to the podium. He looked out over the empty seats and could see his life's dream coming true. "My beloved countrymen, it is time for change. We have been living too long in the darkness bound by the chains of our past. Today, those chains are broken—forever. Together we will . . ."

"Yes, yes," the mesmerized information minister whispered.

Tan sat in a chair and smiled. Tomorrow would truly be a new beginning. The storm they had created was over.

When Josh heard the light tap at his door, he looked at his watch and cursed. McCoy was fifteen minutes late. He opened the door and was shocked to see McCoy, Fletcher, and the two German women, all loaded down with bottles of beer and yelling, "Surprise!"

"Party time!" Fletcher called out, brushing past Josh.

The women giggled as they entered with their arms around McCoy's waist.

Josh shut the door and turned around to grab McCoy. To his surprise, he saw that his visitors' festive smiles had disappeared, and they had begun inspecting the room for bugs.

McCoy motioned Josh closer, then whispered, "Cool it a sec while we check, then we'll talk." He inspected the radio, then tuned it to a local station playing Burmese music. He looked at the others, who shook their heads.

"Why are you in Rangoon?" Josh hissed.

McCoy motioned to the three people who were now sitting on the bed. "We came for the party. Hawk, meet the gang. Don't ask who they are—all that matters is that they're on our side. Now, tell us what's going on."

Josh shifted his eyes to the others before looking back at McCoy with a deadpan expression. "What are you talking about? I told you all about the plan."

Frowning, McCoy put his arm around Josh's shoulder. "Come on, Hawk. What's good for the good ole U S of A is what this is all about. We couldn't let you run this op on your own. You know it doesn't happen that way. Tomorrow we'll be there to make sure your end goes smoothly. Relax. The director is comfortable with your plan, so—"

"The director?" Josh snapped. "You told him?"

"Of course. His job is to make sure the president and the State Department aren't surprised. I didn't give him any specifics, but he knows it's going down. He has a few questions and concerns that I'm sure you'll be able to answer."

Josh's stomach turned to lead and dropped into his testicles; he knew what was coming.

"The first question is, What's Xu Kang's plan?" McCoy said. "And don't give me the same shit you fed me five days ago. We need to know exactly what the Sawbaw is going to do. Our ambassador is going to be at the press conference along with the ambassadors of some countries we happen to consider allies. Spill it, or you aren't going."

"You're threatening me?" Josh asked with a warning glare.

"Naw. Well, maybe a little. You see, we really don't need you anymore. Fletcher here could do your part. Talk to us, Hawk. We need to know."

Josh's jaw muscles twitched, and he put on a look of distress for show. He knew McCoy was bluffing, or the agent would have hit him with a needle or drugged him already. Josh forced his body to relax and nodded. "Okay. I'll tell you what I know. They're hitting the government's radio and television stations, all the army bases, and the military airfields simultaneously. Then they plan to hit the Defense Ministry and take out Swei."

"Bullshit. There's no way they can pull that off," McCoy exclaimed.

"Believe it. They're going to do it," Josh countered.

After exchanging glances with Fletcher, McCoy pinned Josh with his eyes. "When?"

"As soon as Swei finishes the conference. The assault on the Defense Ministry will come after a mortar attack, so if you want to protect the ambassador, make sure he stays in the conference room."

"Shit! Goddamn you, Hawkins. They're going to kill innocent people with a frontal assault."

Josh lifted an eyebrow. "They have people inside. The takedown will be very quick. There should be no civilian damage as long as they all stay inside that room."

Again McCoy looked at Fletcher, who sighed and shook his head. "The director is not gonna like this."

"He's not going to like it?" the taller of the German reporters said. "What about us? We're all going to be in there while a war goes on outside the doors. I say abort. This is out of hand."

"Greta, we don't have a choice on this," McCoy said harshly. He looked back at Josh. "What else?"

"That's it."

"You don't have a part in this, do you?"

"Nope. I just do my thing at the conference and let them do their thing outside."

McCoy's eyes narrowed. "You better be telling the truth. We're going to a lot of trouble to keep you covered on this. I've got an entire crew here, not just the people in this room. The dye job on your hair and a week-old beard is not going to keep you from being ID'ed. The director wants you to understand that if this is pulled off you don't go on the 'Tonight' show to talk about Company business. You are *not* talking after this thing, ya understand? And, watch my lips, you are *not* going to be involved in an armed rebellion. No tricks, no games, just do your part at the press conference. You got it?"

Josh nodded. McCoy raised his hand, extending a finger. "One more question. The director wants assurances this op is gonna stay nonpolitical, so the old man better not do anything stupid like try to take power himself, or appoint one of his buddies. He isn't that dumb, is he?"

Josh shrugged. "All I know is that he plans to take out Swei. The future was not discussed. That's an honest answer, so don't waste your time coming at me from another direction on it."

McCoy had watched Josh's eyes as he responded and had seen what he was looking for. "Okay," he said after a long pause. Then he nodded to his three assistants. "Go down to my room, and make it look good. I'll be there in a few."

Fletcher and the women picked up the beer and walked toward the door. At the door they began laughing, then walked out into the hall-way. Josh heard their raised voices even after his door had closed.

McCoy faced Josh. "Listen very carefully. We've got the equipment to knock out the TV cameras once the . . ."

Scowling, Tan stormed into the DDSI operations center. The waiting operations officer grimaced and spoke quickly. "General, I'm sorry I had to awaken you, but—"

"Tell me what they reported! And what you're doing about it!" Tan ordered.

The colonel held out a report form to his irate superior. "Our informers at the university reported a meeting tonight, and—"

Tan snatched the paper from the trembling man's hands. His face flushed as he read the words of the three informants. "A march? Who are the organizers? What is their intent?" he barked impatiently.

"No leaders took charge of the meeting. The informers reported that it seemed to be spontaneous—many students spoke in support of the march. I notified all of our on-duty teams to check with the informants to confirm their reports. So far they have learned nothing new. Should I call the prime minister?"

Tan reread the report and shook his head. "No, not yet. We don't have enough to justify waking him. It may be just what it looks like— a protest march. But I want all of the standby teams called in. Also, have some of these students brought in for questioning. Place the Strike battalion on alert and notify the Defense Ministry command center duty officer. Have him place the army units on alert. Tomorrow morning I want a complete summary of what our interrogators find out from the students. In the meantime, have the police establish barricades to block tomorrow's march."

The colonel bowed his head and strode over to a bank of phones and three waiting captains. Tan ran his eyes over the report once again, whispering, "What are you trying to do?"

CHAPTER 27

The lead bus turned onto Aungsan Street, the single artery leading to Burma's government complex. Sitting in the second bus, Josh looked out the window as his vehicle made its turn. Like a majestic king, the People's Congress Hall sat on a rise at the head of the street, looking down the mile-long avenue lined with Burma's government buildings. Set back a hundred yards from the road, the white, four-story, prewar Congress Hall stood alone and empty. Forty-five years before, the Hall had been the most powerful building in the nation. The stately office structure was surrounded by a lovely park and a six-foot brick wall. Ten acres of parks on both sides of the road separated the Congress Hall from the rows of other government compounds that served the new generation of politicians. Like fast-food restaurants on a busy strip, the other buildings were built closer together. Only by the signs could anyone distinguish them—the ministries of Trade, Finance, Resources, Information, and Commerce. Halfway down the street, Josh's bus stopped at the iron gate of the Ministry of Defense compound. Squat (only two stories) and made from brick, it looked like a prison, its high walls crowned with concertina wire. Josh glanced at a third compound, which was four hundred yards farther down the road—the Ministry of Security, home of the infamous DDSI. Unlike the other buildings, which needed paint and repair, the DDSI's concrete and glass structure glistened with newness, testimony to the priorities of the previous junta.

As the bus rolled into the Defense compound, Josh felt the first tremor of fear begin to build within him. The fear wasn't for himself but for the assault force that would soon be in a tunnel directly below him.

Sitting beside Josh, McCoy offered his hand. "Surprise me and don't do anything stupid." He sighed and smiled. "Good luck, Hawk."

Josh shook his hand without speaking and took his bag out of the overhead compartment. Seconds later he stepped down from the bus and, with the other media representatives, was escorted toward the main entrance. Glancing around the compound, he noticed that the security was very low profile. Except for the two guards at the gate, not a single soldier was visible. Instead, leisure-suited men wearing sunglasses and bad-news expressions stood around in pairs trying to imitate Secret Service agents. They weren't even close. They looked and dressed like what they were—hoods—with ducktails, tight-fitting pants, and white socks. Josh counted at least five pairs before he entered the building.

The interior of the building was like the sketch he had seen a hundred times, but bigger and in color. The huge, double-height lobby ran the entire length of the building to the rear entrance, which was identical to the front, all glass doors and a big portico. A white marble floor and teak-paneled walls made the hall look something like a church.

Josh followed the throng of reporters and television crews to tables covered with fresh fruit and pitchers of tea and coffee. The ever-smiling media officer stood behind the center table and raised his hands.

"Ladies and gentlemen, please enjoy our hospitality. The main conference room is behind me. Please get all your equipment set up now and take your seats by 9:45. Please refer to the seating charts available on the table. The prime minister's announcement will start at precisely ten. Thank you."

Josh slung his bag over his shoulder and poured himself a cup of coffee. He strolled toward the other end of the lobby. On the right a wide, white marble staircase led up to the second floor. On the left was an identical staircase that went toward the basement. Josh walked slowly, looking at the portraits of former military leaders hanging on the paneled walls until he reached the stairs leading to the basement. Taking another sip of coffee, he glanced down. At the bottom of the steps were double doors marked by a large sign reading Military Command Center.

He continued on to the rear entrance and noticed another security team just outside the glass doors, standing by some huge flowerpots. Turning around, he strolled back to get one more hit of caffeine. He was pouring himself a fresh cup when Fletcher and McCoy strolled up to him.

McCoy held up one of the seating charts and nodded toward the conference room. "Shall we take a look?"

The three men stepped inside. McCoy gestured to his left. "I'll be on the raised platform with the rest of the photographers and the TV crews."

Josh ignored him and walked down the aisle toward the flower-covered stage. He walked up the stage steps to a side door, opened it, and stepped into a hallway. A security team stood a few paces away and immediately waved him back inside.

"I'm looking for the men's room," Josh said as if desperate.

One of the guards stepped forward. "Please go back inside. Rest rooms are in main lobby."

Josh nodded thanks and retraced his steps to the conference room. He had learned what he needed. Behind the security men he had seen a landing with a staircase going down to the basement, plus another staircase leading up to the second floor. Josh felt a rush of confidence. His quick recon had confirmed everything the Burmese deserter had sketched out a week before. As far as Josh could tell, everything was exactly like he said it would be. If all went well, Swei would leave the conference room and go down into the basement, where Stephen and Xu Kang would be waiting.

McCoy strode up and asked angrily, "Where the hell did you go?"

Josh shrugged. "Tried to find a bathroom. Where do I sit?"

McCoy looked at Josh suspiciously for a moment, then nodded toward the front of the room. "The first row of chairs is for the prime minister's cabinet and military chiefs. The second and third rows are for the ambassadors and visiting dignitaries. The rest of the seating is for the press. I saved you an aisle seat so I could keep an eye on you. Fletcher will sit next to you."

"And the fräuleins?" Josh asked.

"They'll be right behind our ambassador to keep him covered. Anything I should know, Hawk—like what the fuck is going on?"

Josh glanced at his watch. He walked back toward the lobby and said over his shoulder, "Any of you guys want fruit?"

Outside, the two buses that had delivered the press were parked side by side in the parking lot. Behind the darkened windows of the buses, the drivers unlocked the doors of their rear bathroom compartments, which had been labeled "Out of order." Two Shan marksmen stepped out of each of the bathrooms holding sniper rifles with fat sound-suppressors attached to the barrels. The first driver opened his side window and nodded to the second driver, who raised a small radio to his lips and whispered, "Base, bus teams are in position. Over."

Colonel Banta, positioned in the park behind the Congress Hall, pushed the sidebar of his radio. "Roger, wait for the order. Out."

Stephen pulled up in a van to the gate of the Congress Hall compound. Smiling, he showed his pass to the guard. "Greetings, Sergeant. I see you too have to work on this holiday."

The sergeant recognized Stephen and shrugged his shoulders. "Yes, we are all on duty. I haven't seen you in some time, U Kang. What happened to your face?"

"A car accident. I am blessed to be living. Did you just come on duty?" Stephen asked casually.

"My shift just came on an hour ago. It will be a long eight hours, U Kang, but we are blessed. The others at the Defense Ministry will be on their feet for most of their shift. You may park in the back as usual. We're shorthanded due to all the other activity, so there are only two men at the rear security desk. One will escort you to the basement and unlock the tunnel entrance."

Stephen glanced in the rearview mirror and made sure there were no cars or people coming before lifting a silenced pistol from his lap. "If you move or speak, Sergeant, I will put a bullet in your forehead. Listen very carefully and you will live. Tell the other guard to come over and meet me. Now."

Shaking, the wide-eyed sergeant slowly moved his head while keeping his eyes on the pistol and called out toward the guard shack. "Corporal Naik, come and meet a friend of mine."

The corporal strolled out of the shack and approached the van. Stephen opened the door and leveled his pistol. "Move and you die."

The van's rear doors burst open and two men dressed in guard uniforms jumped out and pushed the two trembling men toward the guard shack. Stephen raised a hand-held radio to his lips. "Front gate secure. Out." He lowered the radio and spoke over his shoulder to the four men left in the back of the van while he drove up the banyan-tree-lined road toward the Congress building. "There are only two guards inside. Once I'm in, give me thirty seconds before sending in backup. Team two should open the rear gate and let the assault force in from the park."

The two team leaders acknowledged his orders with silent nods. Stephen parked in the back lot, put his pistol in his briefcase, and got out. He walked up the back steps to the huge teak doors and strolled inside to the security desk.

Both seated guards looked up as he entered. The senior of the two, a corporal, stood with a smile and offered a pen to the man he had seen many times. "It has been many weeks, U Kang. Bless Buddha, what happened to your face?"

Stephen set the briefcase down, opened it, and pulled out the pistol. "If either of you speaks, you will both die."

Sitting in his office in the DDSI underground command post, Tan lowered the phone handset. Shaking his head, he glanced across his desk at his operations colonel. "He's not taking calls or seeing anyone. He must be going over his speech a final time."

The colonel's facial muscles tightened. "The prime minister has to know."

Tan drummed his fingers on his desk for a moment before leaning back in his chair. "It's probably just as well. If we told him of the student problem, he would be distracted. We will handle the matter ourselves. What is the most recent update?"

"We have confirmed that the students are massing in the university park," the officer said. "Their numbers are growing by the minute."

"And what did we learn from those we picked up last night?" asked Tan.

Obviously uncomfortable, the colonel shifted in his seat. "They were very stubborn and required our most convincing methods. One died during the interrogation. The others did not tell us very much. The student meetings last night were rallies for the march this morning. Their intention is to march to the Defense Ministry while the media is there and demand that Prime Minister Swei step down and give control to a caretaker government. They want free elections within two months."

Tan clenched his fists. "Today . . . today of all days they come to pester us." He shook his head slowly, thinking. A moment passed before he asked, "And the police? Are they erecting barriers as I instructed?"

"Yes, General. I talked to the chief of police last night after our meeting. He has every available man and vehicle blocking the roads around the university. The students won't be able to leave the park."

Tan glanced at his watch. "Then they won't be able to ruin the press conference. Swei speaks in twenty-five minutes. Label them communist agitators for the benefit of the press who hear about their gathering."

The colonel was still concerned. "General, the barricade drains off

all of our police resources. No units will be available if other problems should arise."

Tan frowned, displeased with the lack of confidence his subordinate was showing. "What other problems? We have thought of every
contingency. You increased the security around the prime minister,
didn't you?"

"Yes, of course, just as you directed. Twenty two-man teams are
inside the Defense compound in civilian clothes, all with radios. I
also moved a Strike platoon of thirty men through the tunnel early
this morning—they are in the small conference room across from the
main press room."

Tan swiveled his chair around to look at a map of the city pinned
to the wall. "You also moved a Strike company here this morning, did
you not?"

"Yes. A hundred-man company with two helicopters is outside in
our parking lot on standby. Also, as you directed, I informed the army
to keep its units around Rangoon on standby alert if additional forces
are needed to stop the students."

Tan shrugged his massive shoulders. "Then why are you acting so
concerned? We have covered everything."

The colonel kept his brow furrowed. "The young woman who died
last night would not speak to us. I knew she was hiding something
and ordered the use of electrodes. She killed herself by swallowing her
tongue. One of the other students told us the dead woman had just returned from a camp on the border."

Tan's eyes widened. "Xu Kang's camp?"

"The student did not know, but I think we should assume so."

Lowering his head in thought, Tan made up his mind. "I will not
attend the conference. I'll remain here and watch it on television
while we monitor the student situation."

In the cavernous basement of the Congress Hall, the twenty-one-man
assault force fell silent as Xu Kang strode down the steps followed by
his eight remaining Horsemen. The old Sawbaw wore his Karen
sword in his beaded waistband. On his chest, pinned to his black tunic, were the medals presented to him by Chiang Kai-shek. His eyes
glowing and his shoulders back, he marched up to Stephen and said
confidently, "I just left our mortar units in the park. They are ready."

Stephen lifted his small, silenced submachine gun and pulled back
the charging handle to chamber a round. Facing the assault force, he
pointed to a small soldier who held a field phone and had a spool of
wire affixed to a pack on his back. "Corporal Chee will be trailing

wire so that I can keep in contact with the communications team and Colonel Banta on the Congress Hall roof. Colonel Banta has radio communications with the other units and will keep me informed of their progress. As I told you during the rehearsals, our radios will not work in the basement or tunnel. But we all know where to go and what must be done. Each one of you has lost a member of your family to Swei and his henchmen. In just minutes you will face the killers. Remember your family, remember how our people and villages were destroyed. Remember the Ri!"

Stephen nodded to his father, who stepped forward and took his submachine gun off his shoulder. "Fellow soldiers, our ancestors are with us and very proud. We fear no pye dogs, for our hearts are filled with revenge for what they have done to our people. We go into the cave for the future of our sons, our daughters, and our grandchildren. We go into the cave for Burma." He turned and nodded to his Horsemen, and they opened the tunnel door.

Together, father and son stepped into the darkness.

Seated in the fifth row on the aisle, Josh glanced at his watch, then looked over the crowded room that he would guess held just under a hundred people. He leaned over and whispered to Fletcher, "I'm going to open my bag in a few seconds and then push it over to you. Take out the stack of papers and hand them to me when I need them."

Fletcher dipped his head and whispered back, "The others are in place—good luck."

Josh leaned over, unzipped the bag at his feet, and took out a cassette recorder that he put in his lap. He scooted the bag toward Fletcher and settled back in his chair.

In his office directly above the conference room, General Swei slipped on his suit jacket with the help of an aide. The information minister tapped his watch and said, "It's time, Prime Minster. The cabinet and military chiefs have just taken their seats."

Swei collected his notes and shifted his gaze to his chief of security. "Any problems?"

The colonel came to attention. "No, General. My men are in place and have reported nothing unusual."

Swei nodded toward the four bodyguards waiting by the door. "Colonel, I want you and these security men to wait outside the side door of the conference room. I'll enter the room alone."

The chief's face screwed up as if he were in pain. "General, I don't recommend you—"

Swei raised one hand and cut him off. "It's about image, Colonel. Just do as I say."

When the information minister opened the office door, Swei adjusted his tie and strode confidently through the opened door.

The press room went quiet as the side door opened and the information minister walked onto the stage and approached the podium. He bowed his head and said, "Members of the government, ambassadors, guests, and members of the international press, it is a great pleasure to have you with us on this glorious Martyrs' Day. The prime minister has prerecorded his speech to the people in our language. It will be aired on television and radio as he speaks to you this morning in English. It is now my pleasure to introduce the savior of Myanmar, our esteemed prime minister, Ren Swei."

The cabinet officers and military chiefs of staff rose as the side door opened and Swei stepped out with a pleasant, practiced smile.

Raising his hands to stem the polite applause, he approached the podium and bowed his head to the audience. When he looked back up, his face radiated confidence. "My beloved countrymen, it is time for change. We have been living too long in darkness bound by the chains of our past. Today, those chains are broken forever. Together we will . . ."

In the basement below the conference room, two rooms down from the military command center, two guards stood at the heavy metal door to the tunnel. Hearing a buzzer, one of the guards opened a small, hinged metal flap to reveal a three-inch-square bulletproof window.

Stephen held his pass up to the glass and spoke into a mike box affixed to the door. "I have a report from General Tan for the on-duty operations officer."

The guard nodded and closed the flap, then began to unbolt the door. Stephen readied his machine-pistol, but two Horsemen suddenly pulled him back and Xu Kang stepped up to take his place. When the door opened, Xu Kang fired a short, muffled burst into the startled face of the young guard, shoved the door back with his shoulder, and killed the second guard with a three-round burst. Stephen and Horseman Lante rushed in and took up positions on opposite sides of the small room's door that led into the command center. Stephen waited until more men had come in and lined up behind him, then grasped the doorknob. He nodded to his father and swung the door open. The Chindit and the Horsemen went left in the hallway. Stephen and his men went right.

Upstairs, Swei paused and looked directly into the bright lights of the television cameras. "As of today, Myanmar is no longer a closed

country. I have ordered the borders opened, and travel visas will be issued to any Burmese citizens desiring to travel. And—" The cabinet
members and some dignitaries rose, clapping loudly. Swei glanced
down at his notes and smiled as he raised his hands. "—and with our
new loans the rebuilding programs will begin immediately. Irrigation
and well-drilling equipment are being shipped to our harbors as I
speak, and . . ."

Stephen peered around a corner of the hallway into the modern command center. Then he ducked back and nodded to three of his men.
Taking a breath to steel himself, he nodded a second time and they all
rushed in, shooting from the hip. The officers and enlisted men sitting at the consoles jerked and groaned as the burst of bullets stitched
their backs. The others in the room turned in shock at the muffled
pops and metallic clinks of weapon bolts slamming forward in rapid
succession. It was over in five seconds, leaving an eerie mist of gun
smoke. Hearing a voice, Stephen spun and faced a small television
screen within a console. He heard Swei speaking of giving amnesty to
the insurgents who had fought the government.

The assault team captain ran up and gestured behind him. "The
Chindit and his Horsemen have cleared the communications room
and offices."

Stephen pulled a map from his pocket, laid it on the console, and
pointed. "Have your men bolt these three doors that lead up to the
first floor. Leave only the lobby staircase open as per our plan."

The captain barked to his men to follow him and strode toward
the hallway. Seconds later, Xu Kang and his Horsemen entered the
hazy room filled with death and gray, wispy tendrils of pungent
cordite. Stepping over three bodies, the old man halted. Stephen was
standing in a pool of blood talking to Colonel Banta on the field
phone. "Yes, we have cleared the command center and have destroyed all their radios. We are moving to the stairway to wait for
Swei. Have the other units attack according to plan. Out." He handed
the field phone back to Corporal Chee and looked at his father. "It's
time," he said softly.

His eyes smiling, Xu Kang slapped a new magazine into his machine-pistol and patted Stephen's back. "Your grandchildren and their
grandchildren will speak of this day."

"People of Myanmar, on this Martyrs' Day, we are truly reborn. We
have a new future ahead of us, and together we can make our nation
great again. Thank you." Swei backed away from the podium and

bowed his head, accepting a standing ovation from his cabinet and dignitaries. After bowing his head several more times, he raised his hands and stepped back to the podium. "Now, I believe there are some questions from the press. Who is first?"

Josh stood and put the recorder on his seat. The hot camera lights shifted their beams and fixed on his back. The young woman who had escorted him from the airport stepped up and handed him a wireless microphone. Josh raised the device up and spoke in a friendly tone. "Mr. Prime Minister, I represent the United States. Sir, isn't it a fact that your loan guarantees are actually payments for tons of heroin that you shipped to the United States?"

Swei's eyes narrowed into slits and his facial scars turned deep purple. "That's ridiculous!" he blurted above the gasps of the audience.

Josh's voice grew louder and colder as he continued, "And isn't it a fact that you ordered the murders of hundreds of people who produced the heroin in facilities you had built? And isn't it a fact that your DDSI murdered hundreds of minorities and Burmese opposition leaders?"

Swei shook with rage. "All lies!" he yelled back.

Fletcher handed Josh a sheaf of papers, and Josh held them up. "Here is the proof!" Josh tossed the ream of paper toward the reporters. "The dates, names, locations, and amounts are all there! We know about White Storm!"

Swei's eyes widened in visible shock upon hearing his operation's name.

The information minister jumped to his feet shouting, "Turn off the television cameras! Turn them off!"

Fletcher stood on his chair seat and bellowed, "Tell us about White Storm, Prime Minister!"

One of the German women stood and yelled, "How many died of torture in Dinto prison?"

The other German reporter came to her feet and shouted, "How many women and children did you have murdered?"

Six hundred yards away on the roof of the Congress Hall, Colonel Banta watched the bedlam in the conference room on a small, battery-operated television. Seeing that it was time, he raised a radio handset to his lips. "Assault force two, stand by. All other units, execute now!"

In the park in back of the Congress Hall, mortar teams dropped high-explosive rounds into the wide mouths of their mortars. At the same time, one of the buses rolled out of its parking place into the driveway leading back to the front gate of the Ministry of Defense compound. The second bus stayed in place, but the two marksmen inside opened the dark windows just enough to rest their weapons and

aligned their scope hairs on the security men by the rear entrance. The driver softly called, "Now!"

The two rifles coughed. Fifty yards away, both guards' heads exploded and showered the bricks with blood and brain tissue.

The first bus rolled to a stop seconds later at the front gate and the driver swung open the bus door. The two uniformed guards strolled forward but were suddenly knocked backward, shot in the head by the snipers in the bus. The driver ran into the brick guard shack and pressed a large green button on the control panel to open the electric gate. The marksmen had already swiveled around and fired again. The two security men standing at the front entrance of the Defense Ministry building collapsed.

Seeing the gate opening through his binoculars, Colonel Banta yelled into a handset, "Assault force two, go now!"

In the Commerce Ministry's parking lot across the street from the Defense compound, twenty-four men jumped out of four vans and ran toward the open gate.

In the DDSI command post, General Tan's eyes were glued to the televised conference as he screamed into a radio handset at the security chief, "The press is making a fool of him! Get him out of—"

The operations colonel grabbed Tan's arm and yelled, "The army bases are under mortar attack!"

Tan's eyes widened. "What?"

"All the army bases around Rangoon are reporting being hit by mortar fire. The air base is being hit, too!" the flushed officer said before trying to take a normal breath.

Tan brought the radio handset back up. "Our bases are being hit by rebels! Get the prime minister to the tunnel now!" He dropped the handset and turned around. The control room was a madhouse. Excited voices were coming in over the radio speakers, and every phone seemed to be ringing.

A captain sitting in front of a bank of ringing phones and blinking lights hung up a handset and spun around to yell, "The radio station has been taken over!"

Another captain shouted, "The television station has rebels inside. They're Shan."

Tan turned and yelled to his operations colonel, "Call the Defense command center and make sure army units are responding!"

In the hallway of the Defense Ministry building, the chief of security exchanged glances with Prime Minister Swei's four bodyguards and the two security men posted by the staircase. All of them were

wearing radios and had heard Tan's report through their earphones. The chief spoke, trying to sound calm. "I'll get the prime minister, then we'll escort him through the tunnel to the DDSI compound." He opened the door, took a breath, and stepped into the conference room.

Less than twenty feet away, at the bottom of the staircase, Xu Kang and Stephen heard the entire conversation. They exchanged glances and smiled. Stephen backed up and whispered to the old Horsemen who filled the hallway behind him, "They will be coming very soon."

Inside the conference room, the press members were on their feet yelling questions at Swei, who stood on the stage like a statue. The security chief took his stunned leader's arm and steered him toward the door. The cabinet members and the military chiefs were pushing back reporters and photographers who had rushed toward the front of the stage.

Josh spun around and opened the back of his fake recorder. He took out a nine-millimeter Beretta and two black cylinders and was about to stick the pistol in his waistband when Fletcher grabbed his arm. "You're staying right here. The job is done."

Then, a loud crashing noise like a thunderclap caused everyone in the room to freeze. They all looked up toward the ceiling, hoping it had been a freak of nature and not a man-made sound. Then the second mortar shell exploded on the roof, sending a shudder through the building. One reporter screamed, but most were too scared to do anything but instinctively duck down.

Still holding Josh's arm, Fletcher was one of those who ducked. Seizing the opportunity, Josh kneed him in the groin, pulled free, and pushed his way through the photographers toward the stage. The third round hit, then the fourth, and plaster fell from the ceiling like huge snowflakes. McCoy locked the conference room's double doors and turned around, yelling, "Stay here and stay down!"

Some people ignored him and ran for the doors but abruptly halted upon hearing another sound, louder and more personal than mortar explosions. It was gunfire, just outside the big double doors.

"What?" Tan shouted, not believing what he'd just heard.

The operations colonel's face was pale. "The Defense Ministry command center is not responding to any of our phone or radio calls."

"Impossible!" Tan snapped. "They must be giving orders to the army units."

The colonel shook his head. "Sir, we have radios tuned to the military frequency. The military command center has not issued any orders or responded to the units that have been trying to call them."

Tan's eyes widened as he realized that the impossible had happened. "Call the security chief and tell him to check the basement before taking the prime minister down. Now!" He spun around to face the major who was posting the situation map. "Have our Strike company move into the tunnel and find out what's happening in the command center! Tell them there could be rebels in the tunnel!"

"... and rebels have attacked the army bases. General Tan ordered me to move you to safety!" the security chief shouted above the sound of exploding shells. Swei's pale face was twisted in shock and disbelief. The chief tightened his grip on his leader's arm as he led him to the basement stairs. He had just stepped down onto the first step when the frantic call from the DDSI operations officer came over his radio warning him of the possibility of rebels in the basement. The four bodyguards who had been walking down the steps heard the same call over their earphones and froze.

Holding Swei's arm tightly with one hand, the security chief pulled his Colt .45 semiautomatic pistol with the other and retreated to the landing. He whispered to the bodyguards, "You two check out the basement hallway. You other two follow five meters behind and cover them." He motioned to the two security men behind him. "The rest of us will cover from here."

Hiding behind a wall partition just inside the basement entrance, Stephen nervously looked across the hallway at his father, who was pressed against the wall beside the open door. They had both heard the footsteps start down the marble stairs, but they had inexplicably stopped. Stephen began to peer around the partition but heard a faint noise. It was different from before—whoever was coming down the steps now was trying to be quiet. Stephen made up his mind to rush out hoping he could get a good shot at Swei, but Xu Kang beat him to it. The old soldier stepped into the open doorway firing. Seeing their leader move, the Horsemen rushed forward to join him.

The lead bodyguard took Xu Kang's first burst in the chest, but the second man got off two shots before he was blown back onto the stairs. The two other bodyguards and the security chief fired their .45s into the charging mass of blue-turbaned Horsemen who ran through the door trying to get up the steps. The first two screaming Horsemen jerked and toppled over. Two more Horsemen fell, then another and another. Stephen had been blocked from seeing or joining the attack by the charging old men. The guns sounded like cannons in the enclosed stairway. He stepped out to join them but was grabbed from behind by Horseman Lante. Stephen fought against his grip, but the assault team captain helped Lante pull Stephen back and yelled to be heard over the furious shooting. "No! It's suicide, Sawbaw! Your father was wounded badly. We must wait for others from the assault force."

The captain released his grip and Stephen's glazed eyes focused. Lying in the doorway and blocking the exit were the bodies of six Horsemen stacked on top of one another. His father was being dragged back by Corporal Chee and another soldier. They laid Xu Kang on the floor at Stephen's feet and tore at his uniform to find the wound.

The old man tried to get up, but Stephen kneeled and gently pushed him back down. "Easy, Father. You've been hit in the stomach and—"

Xu Kang grabbed Stephen's shirt and pulled him down to within inches of his own face. "Get me to my feet—we must prepare a defense!"

Stephen tried to break his father's grip but it was like a steel vise. Xu Kang's eyes bored into his son as he commanded again, "Get me to my feet!"

Stephen reluctantly nodded to Chee, who had been trying to bandage the old soldier's wound. Horseman Lante and Chee gently held Xu Kang under the shoulders and pulled him to his feet. The Sawbaw staggered but regained his balance and straightened his back. Looking at Stephen, he tried not to show his pain and said, "Put a squad in the tunnel to defend the approach from the DDSI compound. Spread the rest of your men out to defend the staircases, and call Colonel Banta and inform him of our situation. Corporal Chee, you may now wrap my wound. Make it tight." As the corporal moved forward, the old soldier saw his beloved Horsemen lying dead a few feet away. He raised his eyes to the ceiling and said in a hoarse whisper, "Honor them, gods. Honor them."

Prone on the top landing, the security chief slapped another magazine into the butt of his pistol. Not receiving incoming fire, he slowly lifted his head and peered down the staircase. Four of his men lay dead on the steps, and below them in the open doorway was a pile of bodies. He ducked back and turned around. The two remaining security men were helping Swei to his feet. The chief pulled the radio from his belt and said rapidly, "There are rebels in the basement! All available teams move to stairways and block them from coming up. Strike platoon leader, send a squad to staircase number three to escort the prime minister."

An excited voice responded, "Colonel, this is Strike platoon leader. Rebels have come through the front gate and surrounded the headquarters! We are keeping them from entering the building, but we need reinforcements!"

The chief turned to Swei, who appeared to have regained control. "Prime Minister, rebels are inside the compound and have the headquarters surrounded! We're trapped!"

Swei's lips drew back in a cruel smile. "No, the rebels are the ones who are trapped. The army units will arrive and finish them."

A ten-man Strike squad came running down the hallway holding AK-47s. The chief waved the leader to him and ordered, "You and five men watch the staircase and ensure no rebels leave the basement. I'm taking the rest of your men with me. Where is your platoon leader?"

The squad leader pointed down the hall. "Sir, he's in the lobby with the rest of the platoon building a barricade to hold off the rebels."

The chief heard gunfire in the lobby and worriedly looked over his shoulder at Swei. "The reinforcements had better arrive soon, Prime Minister, or it will be over for us all."

"The army is coming," Swei said confidently. "We will finish these mongrels once and for all."

Inside the dark conference room, Josh was kneeling by the side door. Behind him, cabinet members, ambassadors, and reporters huddled together against the far wall behind a barricade of chairs. Josh opened the door just a crack and could see six soldiers in position facing the staircase.

"Satisfied, Hawkins?" McCoy said in a harsh whisper as he crawled up behind him. "Goddamn it! Your buddies are going to get innocent people killed."

Josh turned and snapped, "Just keep everybody down. We got problems—the op has turned bad."

In the DDSI command post, an officer tuned in the government radio station.

"*. . . Prime Minister Swei is a butcher who has killed hundreds of our people! Rise up, leave your homes, and march on the Defense Ministry! Soldiers, lay down your weapons and join us! Freedom is within us all. No more lies! No more DDSI! No more Swei! Join us! Join the free people of Burma!*"

"Turn that off!" Tan commanded. He looked at the situation map, which was covered with red stickers denoting rebel attacks. "You see what they have done, don't you? They focused our attention on the students, then hit us everywhere at once. It is a good plan, but they don't have enough soldiers to sustain such an operation for long. Once the army begins moving—"

The operations colonel stepped forward. "Sir, we have tried to convey your counterattack orders to the army, but we have failed. The rebels have cut all the phone lines and are jamming our military radios. We can communicate only with the police and our security chief at the Defense Ministry."

Tan could not conceal his shock. The colonel's assistant added to the bad news by holding out a report. "Sir, the police say their barricades have been breached. They report that the students are en route here and that people are streaming out of their homes to join them."

A captain ran over to Tan with a hand-held radio. "General, it's the prime minister. He demands to talk to you."

Tan closed his eyes for a moment before taking the radio and pressing the sidebar. "Prime Minister, where are you?"

Swei's voice boomed through the speaker. Tan heard gunfire in the background. "We are holding the first floor but need reinforcements. When will the tanks and infantry arrive?"

"A Strike company is coming through the tunnel now," Tan said. "We monitored the previous messages about rebels in the basement. The company will clear them out and bring you back here to safety."

Again Swei's voice filled the room. "Excellent! Helicopter in the rest of the Strike battalion and order in the tanks. We will finish these Shan bastards!"

Every officer in the command post stopped what he was doing and looked at Tan, knowing full well they could not communicate with the army to carry out the prime minister's orders.

Tan brought the small radio up to his lips and tried to sound confident. "Yes, General, they will be here very soon." He lowered the radio and looked into the accusing eyes of his staff.

The operations colonel lowered his head. "It's over. We must destroy our files and all proof of what we've done."

"Never!" snapped Tan. "Within an hour the rebels will have to fall back. They don't have enough forces to defeat us. We will crush them!"

The colonel's head snapped up. "The people know! Are we going to crush them, too?"

Tan's fierce eyes stabbed the officer. "We will do what is necessary!"

The colonel met Tan's glare and shouted, "The world knows what we've done! They know of White Storm! We must destroy our files."

Tan snarled, "No. We'll fight until the army comes. I'm going to join the Strike company in wiping out the rebels, then I'll bring General Swei back here." He brushed past the colonel and faced his staff. "Who will come with me?"

For an answer he got nothing but silent stares.

McCoy grabbed Josh's shoulder. "Don't do it. You'll never make it."

Josh could hear the mission bell ringing in his head as he shoved McCoy's hand away and stood. Lifting his pistol he racked in a round and flicked off the safety. Taking one of the flash bangs from his pocket, he twisted the cap, pushed open the door, and tossed the concussion grenade toward the six men standing in the corridor. He threw himself against the wall and waited three seconds before it detonated. Raising his pistol, he charged into the hallway.

McCoy cringed hearing Josh's pistol reports. "Goddamn you, Hawkins!" he mumbled as he crawled back toward the others.

Josh squeezed the trigger again and spun to face his fifth target. The stunned soldier was still seeing flashes before his eyes when Josh squeezed the trigger. The sixth soldier got his rifle up and fired a burst. Josh didn't flinch as bullets tore into the wall beside him—he was focused completely on his target, whose eyes were filled with horror. Josh squeezed the trigger and screamed, "Stephen!"

Stephen was issuing orders to his assault team leaders when the explosion and the pistol shots echoed through the hallway. When he heard the familiar voice shout his name, he ran for the stairway and yelled for his men to follow him.

In the tunnel Tan stepped over a dead Strike soldier and approached the company commander. The captain motioned down the tunnel, which was littered with bodies. "We lost twenty men, General."

"And the rebels?" Tan asked.

"Five of them were defending the entrance to the tunnel to the Defense Ministry—they're all dead. However, the door into the ministry is locked. My men are trying to open it now. If they can't, we'll blow it open."

Gunshots rang out. A sergeant yelled, "We shot through the lock! It's open!"

Swei stood in the middle of the lobby with his security chief and two bodyguards. Security men and Strike platoon soldiers were positioned behind barricades made of desks and tables in front of the shattered glass doors at both ends of the huge hall. Others were at windows in the first-floor offices. Mortar shells were still impacting on the roof causing plaster to fall from the ceiling. Everyone and everything were covered with a fine white dust.

The Strike platoon leader strode up with a worried frown. "Prime Minister, we've got the rebels outside pinned down, but the offices in the west wing are on fire. If the fire spreads, the smoke will force us out."

Swei motioned to the steps leading down to the basement. "The Strike company will be here any minute. They are clearing the tunnel and the command center. Once they get rid of the rebels down there, we'll fall back to the DDSI compound and let the army finish it."

Another explosion on the roof shook the wooden panels from the walls. The security chief took Swei's arm and guided him toward the small conference room. "It is safer inside here, Prime Minister."

As Swei and his security men stepped into the room, Stephen and Josh rushed into the lobby along with the seventeen surviving members of the Shan assault force. A Strike sergeant turned at the sound of boots on the marble floor. He screamed a warning then paid for it with a burst of bullets in his face. Stephen opened up on those at the front barricade while Josh fired at those positioned at the rear entrance. They stood back to back in the middle of the lobby. They and the other Shan screamed in defiance and riddled their hated enemy, who had been caught with their backs turned. The killing was easy.

Swei spun around when he heard the screaming and shooting in the lobby. The security chief pushed him back, unholstered his pistol, and ran toward the door with the two bodyguards.

Stephen saw them at the door. He whirled to fire but a bullet tore into his left arm and knocked him back.

Beside Stephen, Corporal Chee turned in a single motion and sprayed the men coming out of the doorway. His spray of bullets was low and hit two of them in the legs. They fell as if they had been tripped up by an unseen wire, but the third man kept shooting. Chee saw the attacking man's eye muscles twitch as he pulled the trigger and felt the burning pain of a blow to his chest. For an instant he thought he would be able remain on his feet, but his knees buckled and he sank to the floor.

Josh turned around feeling Stephen bump hard against his back. He saw Stephen had been hit and by reflex caught him before he fell. Holding his brother in his arms, he could do nothing to stop the oncoming attacker who was aiming a pistol at him. Then Josh saw the brilliant flash. The pistol fell to the floor, along with the soldier's hand. Xu Kang swung his sword again, burying the blade in the security chief's neck.

The shooting stopped, and cries of surrender echoed down the hallways from the few surviving Strike platoon soldiers and security men.

Helped by Josh, Stephen remained on his feet. He stepped toward his father but froze when Swei strode through the doorway.

Xu Kang and Horseman Lante raised their swords. Xu Kang snarled as he laid his blade against Swei's neck. "Get on your knees, pye dog, and beg for my mercy."

Swei's simmering eyes locked on the old man, and he replied with sneering contempt, "To a Shan? Never!"

Xu Kang smiled and lifted his sword. "So be it. You will never bark ag—"

An ear-shattering barrage of gunfire stopped him in midsentence. Xu Kang turned just in time to see the three Shan soldiers who were guarding the basement stairs topple over.

Swei started to grin—the Strike company had finally arrived!—but he shuddered as Xu Kang's bloodcurdling scream filled the hall.

"Ayeee!" the old man screamed as he and Horseman Lante ran toward the stairway with their swords raised. Stephen joined in the assault, as did Joshua and the remaining Shan soldiers. The men flung themselves down the steps to attack the oncoming human wave of brown-bereted Strike commandos.

The lead commandos coming up the steps did not see the screaming Shan until they leaped and were falling onto them. Then they saw only blurred steel as the swords slashed downward. It was too late to shoot—all they could do was scream in horror.

The Strike captain ducked Xu Kang's blade and it slashed into his lieutenant's shoulder. The captain tried to raise his rifle, but in the close quarters he couldn't free the barrel. He lunged instead, knocking the old man back. His weapon now clear he began to squeeze the trigger when Stephen shoved his pistol into the captain's face and fired. The officer dropped like a stone.

Upstairs, Swei stood transfixed in terror, then relief. The old Sawbaw and his men had temporarily stopped the momentum of the commando attack by the sheer ferocity of their charge, but now the numbers were telling as more and more Strike soldiers pushed up the steps. The few remaining Shan were like boulders in the middle of a stream, surrounded and trapped by the press of bodies eddying around them. Swei smiled and began to back up, knowing the boulders would soon be gone.

"Ayeee!"

The new war cry froze Swei in place. A screaming Shan soldier ran past him, then another and another, all sprinting toward the fight on the stairs. Swei turned and saw more Shan soldiers pouring through the shattered doors and over the barricade. He felt something tear at his cheek before he could take cover. Another bullet thumped into his chest and knocked him back against the wall. Writhing in agonizing pain, he slid down to the floor, leaving a bloody smear on the wall. He tried to breathe, but his bullet-torn jaw was attached by only a few strands of sinew. No air came, only a deep gurgling in his chest. As the last of the Shan soldiers passed by, he finally managed a tortured breath. Suddenly the burning pain became a distant throb and everything around him stopped spinning. He saw a new flood of attackers running through the shattered doors—students, men and women, screaming like animals. They ran into the lobby, picked up rifles from the dead and wounded, and joined the fighting on the stairs. Their determined faces sent a shudder of despair through Swei's weakening body. Too tired to fight any longer, he lowered his head and saw pink bubbles oozing out of a round hole in his chest. As he watched, the pink froth spread like a living thing. He tried to stop the oozing bubbles, but his hands were too heavy to move. As his heavy eyelids closed, Swei knew his dream was gone forever.

In the basement, Tan yelled for the Strike soldiers to keep pushing forward, but a cry went up from the top of the stairs: "Fall back! Fall back!"

The men in front turned and ran. Tan shouted and tried to shove them back up the stairs but it was like trying to hold back a flash flood. He raised his pistol and fired into the mob of rebels, then turned and fled with his terror-stricken men.

Ghostly pale and weakened, Xu Kang could not lift his blood-covered sword. Stephen held him around the waist and fought to keep them both on their feet as they were propelled forward by the screaming Shan and students. Finally, Stephen managed to step into the spacious command center, and pull his father out of the rampaging flow.

Xu Kang's sword clattered to the floor as he collapsed into Stephen's arms. His head rested on his son's shoulder, and the old soldier whispered, "Son, they are calling for me."

Stephen hugged him tightly to his breast, willing him not to give up. "No, Father, you can't leave me now. I love you. We have so much yet to do."

With the last of his strength, Xu Kang lifted his head and locked his fiery eyes on Stephen. "My . . . my sword."

Stephen lowered his father to the floor and placed the sword hilt in the old warrior's hand.

Xu Kang smiled and closed his eyes as he joined his Horsemen on an eternal ride through his beloved mountains.

Josh had broken out of the crowd chasing the Strike troops into the tunnel. He hurried into the nearly deserted command center and saw father and son clutching each other among the scattered bodies. He started to run, but Stephen's tear-filled eyes told him he was too late. Stephen slowly stood and smiled through his tears. "The ancestors are very pleased, Joshua. They have in their presence Sawbaw Xu Rei Kang, Chindit of the forest and Protector of the Ri. He will sit in the seat of honor at their side."

Feeling as if his heart were being torn apart, Josh tried to speak but couldn't bring himself to finish the ritual of words.

Stephen had taken one step toward his brother when he saw a man he recognized rise up from behind a computer console behind Josh. Stephen lunged as Tan fired his pistol.

Josh was knocked forward as the bullet hit him in the back of his shoulder. Tan began to fire at Josh again, but Stephen rushed past his friend. Tan locked on this new target and fired, and kept pulling the trigger again seeing Stephen wasn't going down. Jerking with each bullet's strike, Stephen finally fell to the floor, twitched, and lay still.

"No!" Josh screamed, spinning around with his Beretta raised.

Tan snapped off a hurried shot and saw the American stagger back, catch his balance, and raise his pistol again. Tan backed up and pulled the trigger, but the magazine was empty. The Caucasian kept walking toward him, rivulets of blood flowing down his forehead, nose, and cheeks.

Tan frantically threw the empty pistol and it struck the man in the left shoulder. He didn't flinch or blink, and his piercing eyes even seemed to smile. Tan screamed.

Joshua squeezed the trigger twice. He waited until he saw his target crumple to the ground before turning around. He couldn't seem to keep his head up. He saw Stephen crawling toward his father. Bending over to help him, Josh felt himself falling forward. He reached for his brother but a cloud of darkness enveloped him. He didn't hear his gun hit the concrete floor or his own voice cry out for his brother. He landed in a pool of warm blood and closed his eyes. He listened for the ringing mission bell, but there was only blissful silence.

Searching hurriedly through the bodies, Fletcher abruptly halted and yelled, "Christ! Buck, over here! I found him!"

McCoy strode over. "Goddamn it! Help me get his body out of here before the fire spreads to the basement. Holy shit! Did he just move?"

Fletcher quickly kneeled down to get a better look at the head wound, then felt for a pulse. He looked up at McCoy and said in disbelief, "He's alive."

McCoy shook his head in admiration. "The sonofabitch listened for a change."

"What are you doing here?"

Startled, McCoy spun around and saw Colonel Banta and ten armed men. "Relax, Colonel," McCoy said. "We were just looking for our man. We found him, so we'll be leaving."

Banta motioned to his soldiers, who leveled their rifles at the two men. He strode toward Josh but abruptly halted at the sight of his two leaders lying beside each other a few feet away. Tears welled in the corners of his eyes—he could tell from the trail of blood that Stephen had dragged himself to his father and laid his head on the old warrior's shoulder.

He continued over to Joshua and took his wrist. Feeling a strong pulse, he glared at McCoy and spat, "We will care for him. He is Shan, not *your* man."

"Hold it, Colonel," McCoy snapped. "Hawkins has to disappear—and fast. The Company can't be involved in this. We had a deal, dammit!"

Banta pinned McCoy with an icy stare. "It's not finished."

"Not finished? What the fuck is there left to finish?"

Banta picked Josh up in his arms and stood. "You would not understand. Do not worry, U McCoy. I will abide by our deal. No one will speak about the Sao being with us." He nodded his head and two of his men flicked off the safeties of their rifles.

McCoy raised his hands and backed up. "We have Stephen's son. Remember that, Banta, and remind Hawkins of it. If there's a leak, all of our work was for nothing."

The colonel regarded the CIA man for a moment with a pitying look before lowering his eyes to the bodies of the Kangs. "No, U McCoy," he said softly. "No matter what happens this day, it will not have been for nothing."

4 P.M., U.S. Embassy, Rangoon

"How bad was he when they took him?"

"He'll live," McCoy said into the secure phone. "He caught two. One went in the back of his shoulder and exited above his collarbone, nice and clean. The second one looked bad, but it was just a graze to his head. He's got a new part in his hair—he was lucky."

"You think he'll talk?"

"We have Stephen's son, Mr. Director. He won't be talking, at least not until we give him back. We've got the cover story in place. You should have enough time to come up with a plausible denial if something leaks. I think it's going to be okay. Hawkins is no dummy—he'll want to get on with his life and not have to worry about us—and Colonel Banta is sharp, so he'll play it our way. How 'bout your end?"

"When Hawkins stood up at the conference, all anybody saw on television was his back. The only problem will be the photos and TV tape from your end."

"My crew and I took care of all the TV cameras during the mortar attack so the tapes are okay. As far as the photos go, we did our best. I had the light crew beam him as soon as he stood. The pictures should be for shit, but no guarantees."

The director said, "Okay, we'll be monitoring the wire services and may have to pull strings if it's a problem. How about the bottom line? Does it look good for us?"

"Iffy, boss. The military is definitely out, but it's going down like we thought on the political side. No party or group has enough pull to take the lead, so it's gonna be a mess for a while. Swei and his crew have been dead for less than seven hours and the political party chiefs are already arguing over parking places. Nobody trusts anybody enough to form a coalition. It's gonna take a long time and a couple of changes of leadership before it smooths out. That's my best guess—the embassy and the State boys are burning both ends trying to make it work for us. The good news is that all the parties agree the country will remain open. That'll make the special interests happy."

"That is good news. Buck, what happened to us there can never happen again. Make sure. Let me know if you need more people. Just get it done, and stay within budget."

"Boss, we're workin' on it already. We've made plenty of contacts and should have a preliminary network established within days. The environment is right. I don't see a problem."

"Okay, Buck, I'm counting on you. Just one more thing. How did it go? Did the old Sawbaw do it right?"

"Boss, it was a good op. The old man and Stephen paid, but they had it wired right—they cleaned house with no spills. And boss? Our boy was right in the middle of it, and it was very heavy action. I wanna go on record on that. He did it right, and for all the right reasons."

"It figures. I'll get damage control to wrap this up. I'll cover him as long as he's quiet. Buck, this goes next door now. I'm out of it now, but I won't forget. Thanks."

"Just doin' my job. Out here, boss." McCoy hung up and walked into the next room, where Fletcher sat waiting. "Well?" McCoy asked.

"They took him up north after a doctor stitched up his head wound and cleaned out his shoulder. I understand he was too weak to walk but was conscious."

"You find out what Banta meant by unfinished business?"

Fletcher nodded but remained silent for a moment before looking into McCoy's eyes. "Hawkins has to preside over the funerals of the two Sawbaws. According to the Shan doctor I talked to, our boy is considered family and must be there. The burial is going to take place somewhere up in the mountains. It also seems Hawkins is going to be made a Sawbaw. And something about being given a title, 'the Protector.' "

McCoy's jaw tightened. "Hawkins can't be a Sawbaw. He's not Shan."

Fletcher shrugged. "They consider him one of their own. One more thing. While I was up there I was made by Banta's people. I thought it was going to be trouble, but Banta sent word to let me go and to have me pass a message on to you. We're not to tell the kid about his father and the old man. Sawbaw Hawkins, the Protector, will do it. What do you make of it? Will he stay on and lead those people?"

McCoy shook his head slowly as he walked to the window. "I don't know. For our sake let's hope not—he knows us too well."

"Buck, what did the Shan gain from all this? I don't see it."

McCoy gazed out the window reflectively and spoke as if in church. "Hope. They fought to try and hold on to their way of life. Time is running out for them, and they know it."

"You think they got it? Hope, I mean."

"Yeah. At least for a while. Hope for a better future is all any of us can ask for. For them it was worth dying for."

"Hey, Buck, it beats dying for money and power. Maybe it was worth it."

McCoy lowered his head. "Maybe it was."

CHAPTER 28

27 June, Bangkok, Thailand

The CIA chief of station stood at the gate watching the arriving passengers from Rangoon walk toward the airport terminal.

"That's him," he said, pointing Joshua out to his case officer.

The two men strode to meet the approaching passenger. The younger agent was about to speak when a wiry old man wearing a blue turban and a mean stare cut him off. His left arm was in a sling, but his other hand was reaching inside his dark tunic.

"It's alright, Lante," Josh said, patting the old Horseman's back.

The case officer eyed the old man nervously. "McCoy didn't say anything about you bringing a bodyguard, Hawkins. Tell him to keep his hand away from whatever he's carrying."

Josh kept walking.

The chief offered his hand and asked, "How's the head?"

"Where's Jacob?" Josh snapped.

"He's doing fine. I followed the instructions, so he doesn't know. And did you keep your end of the bargain?"

"It's over. I have nothing to say to anyone," Josh said coldly.

The chief saw in his eyes that he meant it. Relaxing his professional stare, he motioned to an approaching car. "The wife and I are going to miss Jacob. He's a good kid."

The car stopped and the case officer opened the door. Jacob got out with an expectant smile. The smile vanished at the sight of Josh's bandages and the sling the Horseman was wearing. His eyes swept

334

desperately past the two men toward the plane. "Where is Papa?" he asked, his voice cracking.

Kaska got out the other door. Seeing only Josh and the Horseman, she knew and turned away as Josh kneeled to take Jacob's hand. Without speaking, he placed Stephen's silver bracelet on the boy's wrist.

Jacob shook as tears began flowing down his cheeks. "He . . . he promised me."

Josh looked into the boy's eyes. "He and your grandfather are together in the mountains. They are riding with the other Horsemen and all their ancestors. The gods are . . ." Trembling, Joshua closed his tearing eyes, unable to finish the ritual. Seeing Jacob's anguish just added more pain to his own. For days the grief had been building within him like a festering wound—always there, throbbing, and trying to tear him apart. He wasn't ready to say the traditional words and release them. He wanted desperately to keep them with him.

Horseman Lante reached out and brought Jacob to his side. Leaning over, the old warrior tilted his head and said in a soft whisper, "Listen. Do you hear it, little Sao? It is the sound of the ponies' hoofbeats in the distant mountains. I hear the Sawbaws bellowing proudly as they return to the camp. The ancestors are rejoicing, for they have been waiting for them. What stories the Sawbaws will tell at their campfires! While we still feel the pain of their going, they are riding with the wind filled with happiness. Throughout our land everyone speaks of them and what they did together for our people. Years from now hunters will sit by their campfires and speak of the bravery of the Kangs. They are not gone, little Sao; they are in all of us. The story of the victory over the pye dogs will be told by fathers to their sons as long as the Shan live. The gods are truly fortunate to have them."

Jacob sniffed back his tears as he looked up at the old man. "My mother is in their camp, isn't she?"

The old man smiled. "Close your eyes, little Sao. Do you not see her smiling as the riders approach? She has been waiting for your father to join her. She is going to tell him of you and how joyful you were to hear the news. The news that Sawbaw Stephen Kang fought beside his father. 'Ayeee,' they bellowed, as together they charged the pye dogs. 'Ayeee, ayeee,' they cried out as the great Sawbaw's sword flashed, your father by his side shooting and fighting the filthy pye dogs. 'Ayeee, ayeee.' "

"Ayeee," Jacob whispered, seeing the battle.

Reaching out, Jacob took Josh's hand. "Can you hear them too, Uncle Joshua?"

Josh closed his tear-filled eyes and drew strength from the boy's touch as images flashed through his mind. A tingling sensation ran up his back and across his shoulders, and then he heard the faintest of voices in the wind. A single voice became louder and the image suddenly focused. They were standing together in a valley. Stephen was smiling and Xu Kang stood with his hands on his hips. "By the gods, this is a blessed day, Joshua Hawkins! In every village our people speak of us! We will live forever! Forever, Joshua Hawkins! Forever!"

Josh pulled Jacob to his breast and hugged him. "I hear them, little Sao. The gods are very honored with your father and grandfather's presence."

Jacob rolled his small shoulders back and lifted his eyes to the heavens. "Yes, they are very pleased."

Midnight, 29 June, National Airport, Washington, D.C.

The white Learjet rolled to a stop, and two cars drove out onto the ramp. The copilot opened the side door and extended the stairs. Josh took a step and turned around to take the other passenger's hand. "Welcome to the United States, Jacob. Look over there. That's the Washington Monument."

Jacob smiled. "Super."

" 'Bout damn time you got back."

Josh was blinded by the car headlights and could not see the speaker, but he knew the voice. Lifting his hand to block the glare, he stepped forward and opened his arms.

Kelly embraced him, then pushed him back to look him over. "Nice haircut, buddy. I won't ask who did your hair but it looks like they got a little too close. Well, looky here. You must be Jacob. I'm Terry Kelly."

Jacob didn't understand what Kelly had said, but he knew what to do when the stranger offered to shake hands. "Is a pleasure," he said.

Behind Kelly, a man cleared his throat and stepped forward. "Colonel Hawkins, I'm Deputy Director Thorn. The director regrets not being able to—"

Josh brushed past the man and opened the car door. "Shamrock, get us home."

"Colonel Hawkins, we need to come to an understanding right now," the deputy snapped at Josh's back.

Josh faced him with a glare. "Tell Jennings to back off. I'm not going to talk to anyone. Your people have debriefed me and warned me enough. It's over. I just want to go home."

"Look, Hawkins. We went to a lot of trouble to get the boy's paperwork taken care of, and we let the detective meet you as per your request. You can give me at least a minute to explain how things are."

Josh's glare softened and he walked with Thorn to the back of the car so Kelly couldn't hear their conversation. "I'm listening," said Josh.

"The press has been on a worldwide manhunt to find out who Jeff Ness was and who he worked for. They bought that he was killed in the headquarters by Swei's men because there were 'witnesses' to the murder. His body was subsequently burned beyond recognition in the fire that destroyed the ministry building. In his hotel room in Rangoon, the police found a Canadian passport saying he was Albert Werner, an investigative reporter from Vancouver. When they checked, the press found Werner fit Ness's description but that he had been missing for five years. The bottom line is, we have the press going nuts tracking down cold leads. A few have tried to link Ness and Werner to us, but without proof it's not getting any print. We want you to keep a low profile for a month or so. That means no working. Just take it easy. We figure it will blow over, but we'll be keeping an eye on you for a while. Am I making myself clear?"

"Perfectly clear," Josh said, and strode back to Kelly and slid into the backseat of the car with Jacob.

Thorn shut the door and leaned forward. Through the open window he said, "Hawkins, we'll be watching you."

Josh patted the driver's shoulder. "The Waterfront."

Kelly looked over his shoulder as the car pulled away. "Them spooks really know how to make a guy feel welcome, don't they? Besides the stitches in your head, how you doin'?"

Josh took Jacob's hand in his. "I'm doing better, now. Jacob and I have a lot of things planned. How's Stef?"

Kelly rolled his eyes. "I'm tellin' ya, Hawk, that girl is a pain. When you called and said you were coming in, I almost cried in relief—not 'cause of you, but 'cause of me. Stef has been drivin' me up the wall. She's been stayin' on your boat with Meg since the redhead got outta the hospital. I think they sit around thinkin' up shit just to pester me."

"You didn't tell them I was coming in, did you?"

"Are you kiddin'? I wouldn't have called 'em if you'd begged. They woulda made me bring 'em and I know they woulda killed that spook who just met ya. I did tell 'em about Jacob like you asked, but told 'em I didn't know when you'd be home. Oh, the lady colonel knows, though. I heard the spooks talkin' about it before you got in. I guess she's been workin' real close with them on this and done real good. She's been moved to the Company as their liaison with the military."

Josh looked at Jacob, who was staring at Kelly open-mouthed. "Did you understand some of his English?" Josh asked in Shan.

Jacob's eyes widened in disbelief. "He is speaking English?"

Josh smiled and translated for Kelly, who laughed and took Jacob's hand. "Wait until you meet my boys. They are your age. Tomorrow we are coming over to visit, and we . . ."

Josh smiled as he listened to Kelly, but he suddenly felt a strange tugging sensation. Then he heard her calling to him. Slowly he turned to look out the window at the distant, glistening waters of the Potomac. "I've missed you, too," he said in a silent whisper.

The car eased to the curb and came to a stop. Josh winced as he lifted his arm from around the sleeping boy.

Kelly whispered, "Let me carry him to the boat. Looks like your shoulder is still pretty sore."

The driver opened the door for Josh and then Kelly, who got out holding Jacob in his arms. "Been a long day for this little guy, Hawk."

Josh took a deep breath with his eyes closed. "Ya smell that, Kelly?"

"Yeah, it smell like fish."

"No, it smells like home," Josh whispered.

Kelly followed Josh into the dark boat cabin and laid Jacob on the couch. He turned to his friend and whispered, "Whatever ya do, don't tell Stef I picked you up. Tell her ya took a cab or somethin', okay? I don't want her bitchin' at me for a month of Sundays."

Josh embraced the detective with his right arm and pulled him to his chest. "It's a deal, buddy. And Kelly, thanks for being there tonight. I really needed to see a friendly face."

Kelly patted Josh's back. "Welcome home. Mary, the boys, and I will be over tomorrow. Get some sleep."

Stefne awoke when he kissed her on the forehead. Her eyes focused and widened, but before she could say anything Joshua put his finger to her lips. "Shhhh. Be very quiet. Jacob is asleep on the couch. How's my girl?"

Stefne rose up and hugged him, then pushed him back, whispering harshly, "Why didn't you call and tell me you were coming home? Are you alright?"

Josh took her hand, pulled her up from the bed, and led her through the cabin door and out to the cockpit.

Minutes later, after he had explained most of it, Stefne relaxed and sat back, resting her head on his chest. "Dad, promise me you won't leave again."

"I double promise, hon. How's Meg doing?"

Stefne cuddled closer. "She's still having a hard time walking with the cast, but it doesn't slow her down that much. She got you a couple of 8-track tapes at the flea market last week—Conway Twitty's greatest hits and a Roy Orbison tape." She sat up and looked into his eyes. "Dad, Glenn came by every night to check on me and Meg. She was worried sick about you. She loves you, Dad. You know that, don't you?"

Josh patted his daughter's shoulder and looked out at the shimmering waters of the channel. "She loves the army too, hon."

Stefne was about to speak when she heard the pier planks creaking. She saw who was walking down the lighted pier and got up. "I'd better check on Jacob. 'Night, Dad." She gave Josh a kiss on the cheek and disappeared into the dark cabin.

"Permission to come aboard, Skipper?" Glenn said softly.

Josh steeled himself and stepped closer, offering her a hand up. "I've been waiting for you."

Glenn felt a chill at his touch and the sight of his face in the moonlight. His eyes pinned her and kept her from embracing him. She tried to fight them but they held her in place.

"What did they tell you?" he asked as he led her to the cushioned seats.

"Everything. I'm so sorry about Stephen and Xu Kang. I know they—"

Josh shook his head and tried to smile. "Don't be sorry. They died fighting for what was right. Things are going to be okay. Jacob and I will be fine."

"What about us, Josh? It's changed, hasn't it?"

He turned and looked at the channel reflectively. "I almost stayed, Glenn—they wanted me to, but I couldn't. This is my home. To leave it would be to let it go forever, and I couldn't do that." He turned slowly and gazed into her liquid eyes. "This is the hardest thing I've ever had to do, but I won't ask you to give up what you have and start your life over with Jacob and me. You don't need my world. Stay in your world, Glenn; there's so much more to do, and you can make a difference because you care."

She held his gaze for a moment before lowering her head. "Josh, I have to tell you. I submitted my retirement papers this afternoon."

"You what?" he said, shocked.

"I put my papers in for retirement. They would have recognized

Swei's government, Josh. You and the others changed that, but they would have done it. I can't change anything, except my own life." Glenn lifted her chin and took a deep breath. "You've found another world, Josh, here on this river. Maybe I can find one somewhere, too."

She stepped forward and kissed his cheek tenderly. "Good-bye, Hawkins—take care of your world—I'm going to miss it." She turned around and strode for the pier, trying to hold back her tears.

Joshua took two big steps and grabbed her shoulder. "Hold it." He turned her around, lifted her arm, and reached for her wrist. "The first thing ya gotta do in Hawkins's world is forget this watch." He took it off and put it in her hand. "Glenn, I love you and want you with me. But it's just not me now. Jacob is my son until he grows old enough to go back and take his rightful place. It's your decision, but I love you and want you more than anything in the world."

Glenn smiled through her tears and drew back her arm. The watch arced upward and sailed through the darkness toward the shimmering water.

1 September

"And where do you think you're going, young man?"

"Aw, come on, Aunt Stef, today is the day," Jacob pleaded with his best puppy-dog look.

"No way, José! You're going with me and Bob to buy school clothes, remember?"

"I am not José. I am Jacob, and today *is* the day."

"Can it, Bud. You've been hunting every day for a month. Get your little butt outta the boat."

Jacob turned to look at Josh for support. "Uncle Joshuaaaa, do I have to?"

Josh shrugged. "Sorry, partner, you promised her and Aunt Glenn you'd go."

Jacob stood and switched to Shan as he placed his hands on his hips. "By the gods! Women will never understand the hunt!"

Josh laughed and leaned forward to pat his back. "And thank the gods for it. Go on. You'll be back in a couple of hours. Kelly and the boys are coming over to go fishing."

Jacob reluctantly took Stefne's offered hand and jumped up to the rail. As soon as his feet were firmly planted, she took his arm and marched him toward the stern.

Bob still stood on the bow looking forlorn. "Sorry, boss. I wish I could go with you, but—"

"Bob, it's a sale and we have to get there early!" Stefne barked. "Help Dad get the big trap out, and let's go!"

Josh shook his head. "And just think—in a month you're marrying her."

Bob winked. "Yeah . . . lucky me, huh?" He began to climb down to the bass boat but Josh waved him back.

"Naw, I don't want to go out alone. I'll just stay here and work on the boat. Give me a hand, will ya?"

Bob pulled Josh up and patted his back in condolence. "We'll get him next week."

Josh walked to the stern and sat down by Glenn, who handed him a beer. They watched in silence as Stefne and Bob marched Jacob up the pier.

Glenn finally broke her gaze from the small boy and put her arm around Josh's shoulders. "You all haven't had much luck catching the King, have you?"

Josh looked over his shoulder toward the river. "Don't tell anybody, but I fixed the trap so we'll never catch him."

"Why?" she asked, surprised.

Josh stared out over the water. "That's his Ri. He's the Protector—it just wouldn't be the same without him."

Glenn stood up and took his hand in both of hers. She ran her fingers over the silver band and said, "I love us, Josh. I love our family and our world. You couldn't make anybody any happier than I am."

Josh hugged her to his chest and looked up at the cloudless blue sky, knowing she was wrong. He knew Mya, Stephen and Xu Kang were up there smiling.

ABOUT THE AUTHOR

LEONARD B. SCOTT (Col. USA ret.) is also the author of the acclaimed novels *Charlie Mike, The Iron Men, The Hill, The Last Run,* and *The Expendables.*

Scott retired in 1994 as a full colonel after a twenty-seven-year career in the United States Army, with assignments throughout the world. A veteran of Vietnam, he earned the Silver Star and Purple Heart.

Colonel Scott now lives with his wife in his home state of Oklahoma and devotes all his time to researching and writing his novels.